FLUX

WORKS BY JEREMY ROBINSON

Standalone Novels
The Didymus Contingency
Raising The Past
Beneath
Antarktos Rising
Kronos
Xom-B
Refuge
Flood Rising
MirrorWorld
Apocalypse Machine
Unity
The Distance
Forbidden Island
The Divide
The Others
Alter
Flux

Nemesis Saga Novels
Island 731
Project Nemesis
Project Maigo
Project 731
Project Hyperion
Project Legion

Post-Apocalyptic Sci-Fi
Hunger
Feast
Viking Tomorrow

The Antarktos Saga
The Last Hunter – Descent
The Last Hunter – Pursuit
The Last Hunter – Ascent
The Last Hunter – Lament
The Last Hunter – Onslaught
The Last Hunter – Collected Edition
The Last Valkyrie

SecondWorld Novels
SecondWorld
Nazi Hunter: Atlantis

The Jack Sigler/Chess Team Thrillers
Prime
Pulse
Instinct
Threshold
Ragnarok
Omega
Savage
Cannibal
Empire

Cerberus Group Novels
Herculean
Helios

Jack Sigler Continuum Novels
Guardian
Patriot
Centurion

Chesspocalypse Novellas
Callsign: King
Callsign: Queen
Callsign: Rook
Callsign: King 2 – Underworld
Callsign: Bishop
Callsign: Knight
Callsign: Deep Blue
Callsign: King 3 – Blackout

Horror Novels (written as Jeremy Bishop)
Torment
The Sentinel
The Raven

Short Story Collection
Insomnia

FLUX

JEREMY ROBINSON

BREAKNECK MEDIA

For Cassie.
Now you can get a T-shirt.

1

"Ain't gonna ask again." The gun in his hand—a rusted piece of junk from a time before his birth—is more likely to explode in his face than put a bullet through mine. Even if it did work, his hand is so unsteady that the first bullet would likely miss, and anything fired after that would be thrown off by the weapon's recoil.

He digs a tan, plastic grocery bag from his pocket and thrashes it about until air slides inside and billows it open. "Where're your drugs at?"

I cut through the fried egg yoke on my breakfast plate, letting the yellow spill out. It's thick and viscous, like blood. The kid swallows. He doesn't have the nerve to shoot me, but he's working on it.

"How old are you?" I ask, smearing a chunk of egg through yolk and popping it in my mouth. When he doesn't answer, I add, "Secret to a good egg is simple seasoning. Salt, pepper, onion powder, and a pinch of chili powder. Can you smell it?"

I take a deep breath through my nose and watch the kid do the same. His ski mask hides his face, but his rising chest and pursing lips are obvious tells. As hungry as he might be for oxy, or some other pharmaceutical, his belly is growling, too.

When I carve into my syrup-drenched waffle, he all but licks his lips.

"Here's the deal," I tell him, taking a bite of waffle. "The half-stache framing your lips says you're pushing eighteen, maybe there already. You pull that trigger, you'll spend the rest of your life in a jail cell. If you're thinking no one will catch you, take a look at your hands. You're not wearing gloves. How many surfaces have you touched since letting yourself through my door? You haven't been keeping track. I have, and short of burning the place down, you're going to be easy to ID."

The kid's buying my bullshit, homegrown psy-ops, growing even more nervous as he starts to picture his life in a jail cell. But he's still got a finger wrapped around that trigger.

"Here's what I know. You're local, and like most people in Black Creek, your family has fallen on hard times. Father lost his job at the mine, maybe a few years back. Mom is overwhelmed by a few kids. You do your best to help out, but someone—not you, your skin, teeth, and eyes look good—is taking comfort in drugs. But the doctor won't prescribe more, money's tight, and people are desperate. What'd they offer you? Or did they threaten you?"

The kid's silence confirms my theory, but doesn't tell me whether or not he's here against his will. I give him a once over. He's skinny, but tall and strong. Built like an athlete. "Still in school," I guess. "So, you're getting at least one meal a day. What's your sport? Football?"

His eyes widen.

"You strike me as a quarterback. Means you're more than just a heavy hitter. Means you've got a head on your shoulders. Means you can make the tough calls under pressure. So I'm going to give you a way out, and the choice you make will affect your life from this point forward. You hearing me?"

His nod is subtle, but it gives me hope.

"You can pull that trigger, blow my brains across my kitchen cabinets, and rummage through my house for drugs that aren't here. After that, you'll spend a few days crying your eyes out, wondering when the police will come for you. When they do, you'll either eat a bullet or spend the rest of your days regretting the choice you made at this very moment."

I let that scenario sink in for a moment, then say, "Or you can get that food I fixed for you—" I motion to the plate on the counter behind him. It holds three fried eggs, two waffles, and three sausages. When he looks, I could tackle and disarm him in seconds, but if I make the choice for him, he'll be in someone else's kitchen before the week's end. "—join me, and talk this mess out like a couple of good neighbors."

When he hesitates, I add, "That's the way Jesus would want things done, wouldn't you say? Love your neighbor."

Southern Kentucky Appalachia is steeped in poverty, addiction, coal, and religion. The first two tend to suffocate lessons learned in church, but there isn't a young person in the region that can't rattle off the basic teachings of Jesus or sing a hymn. I'm guessing that the young man who broke into my house looking for an easy score bowed his head and begged for mercy before he went to bed last night. Probably before he let himself into my house, too.

Lucky for him, I know that compassion can stop a war before it begins. And while I haven't been to church since escaping Appalachia to join the military, I still remember enough to speak the language.

"You won't tell no one?" he asks. "Won't call the cops?"

"I don't make breakfast for people I want to send to jail. Far as I'm concerned, you haven't done anything wrong yet. Door was unlocked. Breakfast was waiting. And you brought an antique firearm to show me, on account of me being a collector."

"You ain't shitting me?"

"Food's still warm."

After a moment of hesitation, he lowers the weapon, picks up the plate and sits down. Gun on the table, he tears into the food with the ruthless efficiency of desperate hunger. Egg and syrup drips over the ski mask, which must be getting moist with sweat. It's ninety degrees out, and humid. He's dressed for the weather in shorts and a dirty gray tank top, but his head must be sweltering.

"You can take the mask off, Levi." I'm guessing at his identity, but everything I've observed about him, including the fact that he walked here, narrows the possibilities to a few families, only two of which have boys his age.

Yellow drips from his lip as he stares at me. "Shit."

"You got nothing to worry about."

He pulls off the mask, his appetite reined in by the shame of exposure.

"How'd you know?" he asks. "To fix a plate?"

"Took you three days to work up the nerve to walk through that door. First day, you left more tracks than a rutting hog. Second day, I watched you through the windows, skulking around in the woods. A lot of families in these parts claim to have some of Daniel Boone's blood running through their veins. I'm guessing yours isn't one of 'em."

He laughs at that, and stuffs a whole sausage into his mouth. After a half-dozen chews, he swallows the meat and says, "Pa used to take me hunting when I was a kid. When there was more game. Strip mine chased them off, and then... Well, I haven't been hunting in a good many years."

"Still know your way around the forest?"

"Walked here, didn't I?"

I grin. At heart, he strikes me as a good kid, under a lot of the wrong kind of pressure. "Who are you here for?"

"Grandma," he says.

"Parents aren't around?"

"Nope. I didn't want to, you know? I'm aiming for a scholarship. But she ain't long for this world and just wants to leave it without pain."

"She's not an addict?"

He shakes his head. "Curses the stuff mostly, but times are tough."

I don't have the guts to tell Levi that his Grandma probably wants the pills to end her life sooner than later. Despite breaking into my house, he strikes me as good people. That he'd risk prison to ease his grandmother's pain supports the theory. He doesn't flinch when I pull his revolver across the table, nor when I snap open the chamber. It's empty.

He huffs a laugh. "I ain't no criminal."

I can't help but laugh, partly with him, partly at him. Levi isn't stupid, but he's plenty naïve.

He leans back in the chair, belly full, looking satisfied.

"You good to go?" I ask.

"Go..."

"To work." I stand up, revealing the gun holstered to my hip. My uniform is basic—jeans and a white collared shirt. A jacket sporting the name of the company I work for, and the word 'Security,' rounds out my uniform, but I tend to not wear it unless there's frost on the ground. "Gets lonely in the woods, and I figure you owe me at least a day's work. Then we can talk about how to help your grandma."

He looks from the gun, to my eyes. Then he wipes his mouth and stands. "What's the job?"

When I hold up my ID badge, he reads my name aloud: "Owen McCoy," then his eyes shift to the company logo, and his smile falters. "Sonuva..."

2

"How can you work for *them?*" Levi asks, grasping the 'oh shit' handle in my pickup as we bounce down a water-worn, unmarked dirt road.

"Not sure you're in the best position to be judging folks," I say, steering over a rock that sends a shockwave through the passenger's seat.

"You did that on purpose," he complains.

"Just seeing if you're paying attention."

"I ain't stupid," he says, and I believe him, but his view of the world is narrow.

I avoid the next big rock and pothole. "You tell me. What's Synergy done that's so wrong?"

"Took jobs," he says without missing a beat. "Displaced homes. Stole land. Made the poor even poorer, while they all get fat off our land."

"You know how many locals applied for jobs at Synergy? They offered a bunch, you know?" I can tell by the look in his eyes that he didn't know, that he's just repeating the opinions of whoever spouted off about their own perceived injustices.

"Three locals applied for a few dozen positions," I say. "Know how many of them were hired? All three, including me."

"And what do they have you doing? Plunging their rich turds?"

"First of all, there's no shame in cleaning for a living. You know that as well as anyone in these parts. A good paying job, no matter what it is, is hard to come by. If you can afford a home, a vehicle, and food—not to mention health insurance on account of that job—you're doing better than most."

He doesn't outright agree with me, but he doesn't argue either.

"And what world do you live in," I say, "where a janitor carries a firearm?"

Again, his lack of answer is answer enough.

"As for your other complaints, Synergy didn't displace anyone. The people who moved away were paid well for their land. Well enough to afford something somewhere else, which as near as I can figure is just about what half the folks between Harlan and Pikeville dream about. The mine was already shut down and not about to re-open. No matter what people in Washington say, coal isn't coming back. Won't be any need for it soon enough. Synergy brought money and jobs and received contempt and distrust. It's not their fault people would rather wallow in drugs and alcohol than adapt to the modern world. As for the land, it was never yours. Your family might have worked in the mines, but they didn't own them. Corporations own mines, and when the coal runs out or doesn't get bought, they don't feel bad about leaving. And before them, all of this—" I motion to the thick Kentucky woods framing the dirt road that starts a half mile from my house and leads us up a steep, mountain grade. "—belonged to the Cherokee. If anyone has cause to split hairs about what's been done to this land, it's them."

The silence that follows my lecture is a good thing. Means he's thinking it over rather than just rattling off more preprogrammed propaganda. When it's clear his silence will have no end, I prod him with, "Nothing to say?"

"You got out," he says. "Military, right? Why'd you come back?"

"Aside from the good paying job?"

"Nothing good comes out of Black Creek." His head dips. Despite his talk of a scholarship, he doesn't believe he's got a future—here or anywhere else. His hopelessness has deep roots. "Can't think of a good reason to be here, money or not."

"I grew up in these woods, same as you, hunting with my father, same as you."

"Your father turn out to be a drunk asshole with a toothless mistress?"

"He didn't live long enough," I say. "Died in the mines when I was twelve. My mother passed giving birth to me. Dad raised me on his own. That house you broke into, and most everything in it, belonged to him. And since the mines only take care of you when you're digging, I spent the few years after his passing with my grandfather, who kicked off when I was in Basic."

"Still," he says, grinding anger between his teeth. "Your father didn't force you to live out of a car."

"You live in a car?" I ask, unable to hide my surprise. "Where's your mother?"

"Left with my sisters," he says. "Over in Big Stone Gap now, with her kin. They didn't want me, on account of how much I look like my devil father."

"And your grandmother?"

"Can't drive. Can barely walk. Basically trapped in the trailer with Pa and his lady."

"They fight a lot?"

"Every night."

"Your pa violent?"

"Not with Grandma."

No wonder she wants some narcotics. Who wouldn't? Before the conversation can continue, I slam on the brakes. As a plume of dust rolls past us, Levi leans back in his seat, eyes wide with surprise. "What the hell did you—"

I point two fingers at my eyes and then out the window. He looks, shaking his head. "I don't see nothing."

"Pretend you're young again," I tell him. "When your pa took you hunting, and wasn't yet an asshole. What do you see?"

He pops the door open, slides out, and scans the tree line, hands on hips. "Here," he says, pointing at the roadside brush, as I round the truck's front end. "Brush is disturbed. Something came through here."

"And?"

"And..." he says, scanning the area. His eyes land on the bright yellow No Trespassing sign. "Maybe they didn't see it?" he asks.

I point back down the road. The signs, posted every fifteen feet, are impossible to miss and are filled with the kind of language that leaves little doubt about anything good coming from leaving the road.

"Maybe it was a deer?" he says. "Last I heard, they didn't read too well."

"Last I heard, they didn't wear boots, either." I point to the dirt road beneath Levi. What looks like a single set of boot prints is actually several sets layered atop each other. Whoever came through here did their best to make the tracks look like a single person, rather than a group. But the last of them, likely a woman based on the shoe size, left her prints inside the others. It's subtle—Levi doesn't spot it—but the tactic rules out the kid's next theory.

"Maybe it's just a hunter who doesn't give a shit 'bout Synergy, or all the good they done for the community. Or were willing to do. Or whatever you all said."

"Let's see about that." I step off the road and into the forest's shade. The temperature drops a good ten degrees. By noon, the temp will be pushing ninety, even beneath the trees. By the day's end, if Levi lasts that long, we'll be soaked in sweat. So for now, I'll take what shade I can get, even though I suspect nothing good is going to come from what we find.

Levi creeps through the forest with me. His gentle steps on the layers of dried leaf litter reveal his father hadn't been a horrible teacher, at some point. Twenty feet in, we stop at a chain-link fence.

"Shee-it," he says, looking at the coils of razor wire topping the fence. "This electrified, too?"

I shake my head. "But it is patrolled."

"*All* of it? Synergy bought up half the land in town, and not just this mountain. That's more square miles than I, or anyone else, can walk in a day. Who got that shit job?"

I smile. He knows exactly who. "Mount Adel is all we need to worry about. And today, it's your job, too. But we don't need to walk all of it. Closer to the facility, security cameras do most of the work. But the perimeter? Today, that's me."

In truth, I don't need to walk the perimeter. As head of security, I could sit in a chair all day and task my subordinates with the grunt work. But I like the woods, and the exercise. Too much time in the office makes me stir crazy.

"But we're not going to be walking the fence today. We're going to track down whoever let themselves in." I motion to a portion of fence that looks normal from a distance, but up close, the severed links are easy to spot.

Levi seems pleased by the prospect of a hunt. He steps toward the gap. "Well then, let's get going."

My hand on his shoulder stops him. "You ever go on a hunt without provisions? Without being prepared? We'll get this taken care of, but there's a few things we need to take care of first, starting with you signing a few forms."

"I ain't signing shit."

"You are, if you want a job."

"Horseshit."

"You show me you can handle it, I'll put you on gate duty. Checking ID badges. Air conditioned. Decent pay. Synergy has a college program, too. Stick with it, part time, for the year, the company will help with your education, and a job will be waiting for you when you come back."

"And if I don't come back?"

I shrug. "Your choice, though they tend to make it worth your while."

"That's why you're back."

"Mostly."

"And you're doing all this 'cause I broke into your house?"

"Not because of it, despite it. What good is coming home, if I can't help the people here?"

His shoulders shrink. "What do I got to sign?"

"Standard stuff. Non-disclosure agreement. Liability agreement. W-2." I grin, knowing that none of that is standard to anyone in Harlan County.

"What's all that mean?"

"Non-disclosure means you won't tell anyone about what you may or may not see here. Liability means that if you trip and whack your head, you won't sue them for it. W-2 means you'll get paid."

The prospect of getting a paycheck melts his skepticism.

"You do good by me today, and we'll sign the W-2 before you head home." My heart sinks a bit when I remember that home for him is the inside of a vehicle. We'll have to do something about that, too, before long. "Now, let's get to—"

Before I can finish, Levi tackles me around the waist.

It takes all of my strength to fight my instincts. I could kill the kid before we hit the ground. But the attack is out of character, and the timing makes no sense. We fall behind a tree, landing in a painful tangle. When I open my mouth to demand an explanation, all the air in my lungs is shoved out by the concussive blast of my truck exploding.

3

Despite Levi protecting me from possible harm, I shove the kid away with a heavy hand. Not because I'm angry, but because I'm operating on instinct. Gun in hand, I scan the area for threats. A column of flame rises from the truck's front end, slowly working its way toward the back. The truck is a total loss. The brush on the dirt road's edge is on fire. Bits of metal and glass fragments pock the ground, some of it embedded in the thick-skinned oaks and maples making up the majority of the forest.

There's no doubt about it; Levi saved my life.

I turn back and forth, scrutinizing every shadow, every shift of light. The only thing I'm sure about when I lower my weapon, is that we're alone.

"You okay?" Levi asks.

I'm thrown by the question. Am *I* okay? Been a long time since anyone asked me that, and I can't say I appreciate it.

"You look a bit squirrelly is all," he adds, my irritation broadcasting at full power.

I force myself to calm down. To breathe. To *think*.

"What did you see?" I ask.

"Brick of C4," he says, dusting himself off. "Just sitting on the hood. I'm okay, too, by the way."

"Sorry," I say, collecting myself. Kid's right. I *am* squirrelly. Been a while since I've seen any kind of action. I like to believe I'm ready for anything, but my feathers are fucking ruffled like an ostrich in a tornado. "And thanks. You've got good reflexes—and instincts."

"Geez," the kids says with a grin, "I wasn't asking for a verbal blowjob."

I chuckle, despite the fact that *my* truck—not a company vehicle—is melting into slag, the heat of it emanating into the forest. "How do you know what C4 looks like?"

"Just cause I live in a car doesn't mean I've never watched a movie or played Call of Duty. Was a gray brick. Size of my hand. I wouldn't have noticed it if the red light hadn't started blinking."

"It was blinking?"

"That mean something?"

Explosives generally only have lights on them to reveal whether or not they're armed. A *blinking* red light serves no real purpose...unless... "They weren't trying to kill us."

"Sure about that?" Levi wipes his arm across his sweaty forehead. The heat from the blaze has raised the temperature.

I'm not, and he's right to be doubtful. Warning or not, the blast could have killed us both. That he spotted the explosive was luck. If he hadn't, we might both be dead. Whoever did this might not have wanted to kill us, but they were willing to take the risk.

"What now?" Levi asks.

I dig into my pocket, retrieving my cellphone. With a click, swipe, and a tap, I call Synergy's security office. It's manned around the clock. After the first two rings, generated by the phone to keep people from growing impatient with the connection time, I expect the call to be answered immediately. When it's not, I wonder if they've already detected the explosion. There aren't any cameras this far from the facility, but the boom was loud enough to hear for miles around—even with the trees deflecting the soundwaves. Either way, there should still be someone manning the security office. Of all the personnel under my command, only Kuzneski, Brown, and Harper are gun-toting former operators. The rest carry tasers and sit at desks.

Unless...what happened to me is happening up there. I look up the treelined slope of Adelvdiyi mountain, known as 'Adel' to locals. It means 'the mountain that shakes,' and while the area isn't known for its geological activity, I experienced the mountain's shaking once in my life. The day before...

I force my thoughts out of the past.

Far above, beyond my vision, Synergy's facility—most of which is underground—might be under siege. I don't know what they're working on. It's above my pay grade, and I'm pretty sure I wouldn't understand it, but the kind of security they have in place means it's valuable.

The ringing stops. It's followed by a moment of silence, during which I say, "Hello? Cassie?"

A shriek forces the phone away from my ear. For a moment I'm afraid the sound is coming from Cassie, the only member of the security team I address by her first name. That's mostly because we've been close friends for as long as I can remember. She was one of the three locals to land a job at Synergy. Like everyone else, she was dubious about the secretive mega-corporation moving into town, but she trusted me. And now she might be in danger.

My jangled nerves calm when the electric screech continues far longer than any person could manage.

"The hell is that?" Levi asks, looking at the phone.

"Some kind of interference," I guess, then I dial 911 and get the same results. "Looks like we're on our own."

"Would you say this is an average day on the job?" Levi asks, following me as I head back toward the road, giving the burning vehicle a wide berth. "Because I'm starting to think living in a car might be better."

Standing in the road, I follow the column of dark smoke rising high into the air. Black Creek is a small, struggling town, but the fire department is dedicated and professional. It won't be long before they spot the smoke and sound the alarm. But they won't really understand the situation unless someone tells them.

"Need you to stay with the truck until help arrives," I say. "Tell them about the bomb. Tell them I need help. The kind with guns."

"Like shit I will," Levi says. "I'm sticking with you."

I open my mouth to argue my point, but he beats me to it. "First of all, we don't know how long it'll take for someone to get here. Wind could shift and maybe no one will see it. I ain't waitin' out here all day. Secondly, whoever did this could be lurking around. Unless you're willing to give me that gun, I'm sticking with the man who's holding it. Pretty sure you know this already, but C-4 ain't exactly standard ordnance for anyone in Harlan County, and it sure as shit ain't for huntin'."

"Starting to get tired of you making good points and doing the right thing," I say. "But we're going to have to haul ass, two miles, mostly uphill, and you need to keep up. Think you can handle that?"

"I'm not a quarterback," he says. "Wide receiver. Try not to slow me down."

The rough, dry surface of the road is not easy on the legs. The terrain is uneven and hard, pocked with divots and rocks exposed by the previous spring's rain runoff. As uncomfortable as the road was to drive, it's harder to run. Fueled by pride, I keep my complaints to myself, as does Levi.

I'm still not entirely sure I've made the right choice, trusting a kid willing to break the law, even if it is for a good reason. But he's shown himself to be resourceful and resilient. Not many people could survive a bombing and then volunteer for an uphill run *toward* danger. His hands were shaking a bit, back by the truck, but he tamped down that nervous energy with a few firm squeezes.

When Levi slows to a stop, breathing hard, I wonder if he's misjudged his physical prowess. He's an athlete, but years of being underfed can reduce stamina, particularly when trying something new, like running up a mountainside.

"Need a break?" I ask, even though it's been just five minutes.

"You don't hear that?" he asks, lifting his shirt to wipe the sweat from his face.

"Hear wha—" A faint buzzing, like a swarm of angry bees, tickles my ears. I attempt to locate where it's coming from, turning my head side to side, but all I can really determine is that it's coming from above.

"Sounds electrical," Levi says.

As the noise grows louder, I can make out the crackle and snaps of arcing electricity. But there is nothing in these woods that could produce that kind of sound. No buildings. No generators. Synergy's electrical cables are underground. There's no reason for anything to be out here. What we're on isn't even a maintenance road. It's a rotting holdover from the old mine. I take this road, on occasion, to see how long it takes my staff to detect and stop me. That's what I tell them. The truth is, my father used to take this road to the mine every day. It's a straight shot from the house to the old parking lot, and we hunted these woods most weekends. Makes me feel close to him. Same with patrolling the forest. I left that off my application, but Cassie knows. Her father worked in the mine, too, though he escaped with his life. He passed, a few years back, from cancer, and now Cassie supports her mom.

Thinking of Cassie reminds me that she, and everyone else under my care, might be in danger. I take three more steps uphill, toward the sound, and then stop when it grows louder.

Commingling with the buzz is a deep resounding hum and a rumble, like the horns and percussion bits of an orchestra have decided to drown out the world.

Levi looks at me, genuine fear in his eyes, begging me to tell him I know what this is, that everything's going to be okay.

I can't do that for him. My heart pounds, surging adrenaline into my body, telling me to fight or flee, but there is no escape, and nothing to attack.

I glance uphill and nearly vomit as my vision distorts. The world becomes a kaleidoscope of color, like I'm seeing the mountain above through rippling water.

What's happening? I wonder, and then I mentally correct the question to: *What did they do?*

Levi and I fall to our knees, hands clasped to our ears. He might be screaming, I can't really hear over the sound, but I know I am. I can't hear my voice, either, but I can feel the scream's force scratching my throat.

The wall of sound passes like a freight train, the wail fading into the distance below us.

I push myself up and I'm struck by a wave of nausea. It rolls through me, starting at my head and running out my feet. Levi pitches forward and vomits. "Sweet fancy Moses on buttered toast. The fuck was that?"

Pretty sure he knows I'm as clueless as he is, so I don't bother answering. If that was from some kind of explosion, I can only imagine how much more powerful it was at the epicenter. At a mile and a half out, that shockwave was nearly enough to peel skin from bones. I can't imagine there's much left of Synergy.

"S'pose we'll be burying people more than rescuing them," Levi says, "don't you think?"

I push myself up, unable to answer. Though the distorted view of the mountaintop has faded, something seems off. The air is different. It's a good twenty degrees cooler. Smells off, too. Not bad, just different. Subtle in the way only hunters might notice.

"I reckon you're right about that," I finally say. "And it's gonna be more than we can handle."

I turn back, thinking about the fastest way to reach help. It's a three-mile hike behind us, but all downhill. Another half mile to my house. We can use the landline to call for help and be back at the facility inside an hour. I'm about to reveal my plan when I notice, once again, that the view is wrong.

Only this time, I know why. "The smoke is gone."

4

We stand there for a full minute, side by side in a kind of perplexed trance. We scan the sky for any hint of smoke, but it's just not there. The bright blue sky is unmarred.

"Smoke don't just disappear," Levi says. "Not like that. Even if someone put the fire out."

"The clouds," I say.

"Ain't no clouds, neither."

"That's the point," I say. "There *were* clouds. On our way up." I start noticing more aberrations. They're subtle at first, but once I see it, I can't *not* see it, and I can't keep myself from reacting. Unsteady on my feet, I lean forward, hands on knees, mind reeling.

"You gonna puke?" Levi asks.

"The leaves," I say, glancing toward him. From my lowered position, I can see his arm, the hair standing on end as goosebumps cover his skin. "The air."

I give him a moment to take it all in, and then I add another observation.

"The smell."

Levi takes a deep breath and whispers, "Snap my garters, it ain't summer no more."

Given that the trees around us have just started changing color, I'd place us around mid-October, which means we've leapt two months forward in time, or—

"Must have been that shit that passed by. Did something to the trees. To the air."

Or that. And while that's the most likely answer, it's also horrifying. Means the explosion's effect altered not just the trees, and the smoke, but also the clouds beyond. How far did the effect stretch? And if it changed the trees, what did it do to us?

"That'd be my guess," I say, trying to sound confident, leaving out the fact that the rough dirt road has been smoothed over, all signs of erosion mostly wiped away. I can almost wrap my mind around something affecting tree leaves, and a shockwave blowing away smoke and dispersing clouds, but how could it smooth out a worn path?

"Let's move," I say, starting back downhill. "Double time."

We jog in silence, gravity propelling us forward. And for a few minutes, I think our run for help is going to be uneventful. Then I realize we should have passed the truck, not to mention the scorched earth, and trees surrounding it. I slow to a stop and turn back.

"What now?" Levi says, skidding to a stop, fear in his voice. "You hear something?"

"You seen the truck?" I ask.

Levi stands beside me, hands on hips, catching his breath. "Ain't that the berries..."

I smile. When he's agitated, Levi is a treasure trove of Appalachian charm.

He offers a theory. "Maybe it was, I don't know, launched by the shockwave?"

It's not a bad idea, but the logic just doesn't add up. "If that were the case, we'd have both been airborne, too."

He folds his arms over his chest, the cooler air taking a toll on his exposed skin. "I reckon you can't tell me, and maybe this ain't the time to ask, but what is Synergy working on?"

"Right time." I say with a dip of my head. "And while I couldn't tell you if I knew, I actually *don't* know, and that I *can* tell you."

I start backpedaling down the road. "Just keep your eyes open for debris. If it was launched, it'll be somewhere downhill." We shift our attention forward again and follow the road. Instead of running, we maintain the cautious creep of a predator on the prowl...or that of nervous prey. I'm not yet sure which we are, but I can't shake the feeling that we are royally screwed.

I search the path for more strange changes, but everything else seems normal—as normal as fall in the middle of August can. I'm no scientist, but I can make peace with the idea of that pressure wave aging leaves and knocking shit around—even the clouds. But I cannot come to terms with the temperature drop, or the smell of decay in the air. Whatever that shrieking kaleidoscope was, it didn't just give the land the appearance of fall, it transported us smack dab into the middle of October.

"How far down does Synergy's land stretch?" Levi asks.

"All the way down," I answer, watching a bird flit through the sky. "And beyond. They own a good portion of the land in and around town. Bunch of the mountains. Not just Adel. But none of it is secured."

I point at a small bird, its wings green on top, yellow on the bottom, with a distinctive splash of black beneath its beak. I smile at the sight of it, transported through time to my childhood backyard, sitting in a lawn chair, sipping on Mello Yello, and watching birds at the feeder with my grandmother. "You know what that is?"

"A bird," he says. "That fence runs all the way down the mountain?"

"Yeah," I say, eyes still on the bird as it lands and starts singing a tune I haven't heard in thirty-plus years. "It's a Bachman's warbler."

"Something special about 'em?" he asks.

"They're extinct," I tell him, pausing to listen to the music, letting it retrieve fond memories of the gray-haired woman who made the finest beef stew and biscuits east of anywhere. "Since 1988."

"Well, they ain't extinct no more," Levi says. "You know, they get that wrong sometimes. Just last week, my biology teacher said that eastern mountain lions had been declared extinct, but I seen one just last year."

"Right about that," I say. "I've seen them twice over the past two years, but what are the odds that we spot a bird no one has seen in more than thirty years?"

"You a naturalist now? A bird watcher? How do you know they're still on the extinct list?"

"I don't," I say, a little begrudgingly. "But if this bird was anywhere in these woods before today, I'd have known."

"The all-seeing, all-knowing grandmaster of the deep woods, huh?" Levi is smiling despite the strangeness of our situation. "Must chap yer ass to be lost in your own backyard."

"Well, thank you, Billy Sunday, for stating the obvious."

Levi has a chuckle. "Billy Sunday. Military took you out of Appalachia, but something of these mountains stuck with you, huh? Kinda sad that part was ol' Billy."

Billy Sunday was an old-time baseball player back in the late 1800s when the sport was just starting to become a national pastime and players' images were immortalized on tobacco cards. At some point in his career, the Lord came callin' and he became an evangelist. Was a big deal in these parts, so much so that his name became part of the local lingo.

"As strange as your mystery chickadee might be...to no one with a life...I think y'all might want to have a look over this way." Levi heads to the roadside, hand over his forehead to block out the high sun. "Just a guess, but a missing fence is a might bit odder than the startling appearance of a bird."

"Missing fence?" I step past Levi, into the brush on the roadside. "It's just..."

I squint into the shaded forest. The fence runs along the roadside, somewhere between ten and twenty feet in from the tree line. Effective, but not an eye sore.

Not like the No Trespassing signs.

My eyes dart to the line of outermost trees lining the road. The signs are gone. All of them.

They could have been torn away by the pressure wave, I think, but I know it's not true, because as much as my mind is telling me it's impossible, Levi is right. The fence is missing. I step into the forest to confirm it for myself, to make sure the fence isn't farther in because of rough terrain or a free standing boulder, but that's not the case. The fence—miles of it, topped with razor wire—is missing.

"You don't need to act brave on my account," Levi says, standing behind me. "'Cause honestly, I'll feel better to know I'm not the only one shittin' my britches."

He steps past me, searching the forest. "It should be here, right? There's no way the whole thing got taken away while all the trees stayed rooted down. I mean, they anchor that shit with concrete. Down deep. A tornado'd lift these trees away before the fence posts. There ain't even holes in the ground."

"Don't need to tell me," I say, stepping back toward the road, feeling a little pale and numb.

"Just tell me what's going on!" Levi's fear is unvarnished and pure. All traces of masculine bravado have faded.

"Would if I could, kid. This is beyond me." The crunch of dirt and stone beneath my feet tells me I've reached the road. When I stop, the crunching continues, and it's joined by a low, monotonous rumble.

Heart beating hard, I turn uphill expecting to see another world-distorting wave racing toward us. But the mountainside is clear.

"A truck!" Levi says, stepping into the road.

An old Chevy pick-up bounces up the old road, the pace slow and steady, the man behind the wheel not in a rush. The brown truck looks familiar, and while my brain says it's old, maybe even a classic, it looks brand new.

We stand on the side of the road, waiting for the approaching truck to pull up. As it approaches, I'm struck with a sudden sense of deja-vu. The truck. The fall air. This road.

It can't be him...

When I see the driver's face, I understand, in part, what's happened.

"You gonna pass out?" Levi asks.

Breathing like I've just run a race, I manage to say, "Wave them past."

"But they can give us a—"

"Do it!" My clenched teeth and glare snap him into compliance. He waves the truck past as the driver begins to slow.

"Everything okay?" a familiar voice asks from the truck. A glance is all it takes to confirm the impossible, then I divert my eyes back to the ground, mind reeling. Takes every ounce of my strength to not fling the door open and tell him how much I miss him. But I can't. Because this isn't right. This isn't natural. And that's not *him.* Can't be.

"Fine and dandy," Levi says. He sounds a little strained, but still convincing. "Just out enjoying the October air."

"Good day for it," the driver says. I'm tempted to look up, to look him and his young passenger in the eyes, but I can't bring myself to do it.

"He okay?" the man asks about me.

"Out of breath is all," I manage to say, lifting my hand in a wave.

"Well, y'all take care," the driver says, "and if you hear rifle shots, just means me and the boy are having good luck."

After the truck accelerates up the mountainside, bathing us in a cloud of exhaust, Levi leans in close and asks, "What in tarnation was that about? We could have been in town inside'a ten minutes. Now we gotta—"

"That man was my father," I say.

Levi's mouth snaps shut. His brow furrows. And then he comes to the obvious conclusion. "Bull-sheeit. He couldn'a been much older than you. No way he's yer pa. And you said your father was—"

"Dead." I force myself to stand, sucking cool fall air into my lungs. "For more than thirty years."

"You lost me, chief," Levi says, looking both annoyed and afraid. Some part of him has gleaned the truth, but the rest of him isn't accepting it.

"That man was my father," I repeat, because I need to hear it as much as Levi does, "And that kid sitting next to him...that was me."

5

"Ain't no way," Levi says, waving his hands at me. "And I can't say I appreciate you screwing with me while some serious shit is going down."

I stumble off the road, clinging to a tall oak for support. "Wish this was a prank."

"Seriously, you're freaking me out, man." Levi is in my face, desperation fueling him more than anger. He doesn't want this to be real. But there's no denying the presence of my dead father and my younger self.

I remember today.

It's impossible to forget.

"We'll hear a rifle shot in a few minutes," I say. "I tag a buck straight off. My first. 'Bout a minute later, my father puts it down with a second shot, because I can't. I see it there, desperate for breath, shitting itself in fear, and I freeze up. A few hours later, I take another buck, bigger than the first. My father tells me, 'A man who can hunt these woods can feed his family, no matter the state of the world outside.' I put the second deer down myself."

"All your memories that vivid?" Levi asks, still doubting my ridiculous claims. "I barely remember last week."

"I don't remember all that because of today. I remember it because of tomorrow."

"What's tomorrow?"

"October 14, 1985." I push myself back from the tree, feeling a little more stable as I settle into this new unreality. "The day my father dies."

Levi leans back against a tree, mulling over my claims. "He didn't balk when I said it was October."

"I noticed."

"So, what? We traveled back in time? How's that even possible?"

"You're asking the wrong person," I say, head turning uphill, projecting my thoughts beyond my dead father and young Owen. Whatever is happening, it originated at Synergy. "But I don't think it was an explosion."

"Meaning what?"

"That we're headed in the wrong direction."

"If it's 1985, we're not going to find Synergy, we're going to find the Black Creek coal mine, fully operational and packed with workers."

"Not on a Sunday," I say. "My grandfather used to say, 'the mines control everything in Harlan county—everything but the Lord's day.' If the mine is there, it'll be empty. Running into workers is the least of our problems."

"How so?"

"If Synergy did this, and the facility is gone? I reckon we'll be stuck here." I step back into the road. The truck is long gone, out of sight.

Levi mutters and paces, kicking leaf litter, flexing his fingers. Then he shrugs. "Worst case scenario, we live in Black Creek when it was still a nice place, invest in Microsoft, and then move the hell away before it becomes a shithole. Hell, if you're feeling benevolent, you could invest your wealth in the community."

My first instinct is to argue against his spur-of-the-moment flight of fancy, but when I think about it—really think about it—I can't come up with a reason to say no.

Not being able to read my mind, Levi adds, "I mean, you live alone, right? No lady in your life, near as I can tell. Parents are dead. Hell, your pa bites it tomorrow. Maybe you could do something about that. My family is shit. I won't miss them, and they won't miss me. I got nothing to lose, and I don't think you do, either."

A concept reaches out from the depths of my mind, given birth by my long-since-diminished love of science fiction. "We'd create a paradox."

"A para-what?"

"If we change the past, we change the future."

"Ain't that the point?"

"Could be in ways we don't intend. Look, I'm already born. I don't need to worry about that, but you're not conceived for a while yet. What if something we do in the past keeps your parents from meeting? Then you'll never be born, and—"

"Ohh, wow." Levi seems more excited than horrified by the prospect of non-existence. "It's like that movie. With the guy. And the clock tower. And the truck of manure. The guy who almost boned his ma."

"Back to the Future."

Levi snaps his fingers. "That's the one. But it's a movie, right? Think any of that is possible?"

"If movies are our only source of information on the subject, I reckon that's about as good as knowing nothing."

"But the paradox thing makes some kind of sense."

It does, but I don't know what to say about it. We're so far in over our heads, it's mind-numbing. Nothing in my education or in my time as a U.S. Marine prepared me for anything like this. But this is still Black Creek, and if I can survive the 80s as a kid, I can do it again as an adult. "If we're stuck here...then we need to leave and let things play out. Short of killing ourselves, our presence will change the future, but maybe not for you."

"And your pa?" Levi asks. "You're just gonna let him die?"

"Who's to say I'd still be here if he didn't. I'm not worried about making it so I'm not born, but if my life..." I point up the dirt road. "...if *his* life...changes, then who's to say it's my house you break into? Maybe I'm married? Maybe I leave and never come back?"

"Maybe we'll *both* disappear," Levi says. "Then this will never have happened."

"Or maybe we'll both just cease to exist," I shake my head. This is why the sciences never interested me. I like problems that can be solved with a little equal parts brains and brawn. This situation calls for an inordinate amount of the first, and the only place we're likely to find that, is at Synergy—assuming they made the trip to 1985, too. "Too many maybes."

"Then what's the plan?"

"We're going to backtrack. Again."

"I'd rather go downhill," Levi complains.

"Black Creek might be a nice place to live in 1985, but it's still a small town smack dab in the middle of Appalachia. There's no one down there smart enough to figure this out. But, if we get to the top and only find a mine, we'll head to town, get a bite to eat—"

"If they take your fancy new bills."

Damnit. Kid makes a good point. "And we'll take it from there. One thing at a time, okay?"

Levi starts up the hill, his athletic stride reduced to the defeated, scuffing walk of a death-row inmate being led to the electric chair. "Sure you didn't slip some LSD in those eggs?"

"Wish that were the case, but—"

A rifle shot makes both of us flinch, despite the distance. We stand in silence, waiting for confirmation. It comes a minute later when a second shot tears through the forest. Young Owen McCoy has just learned how to take a life.

And it won't be the last.

For years, I hunted these woods, first to remember my father, and then to feed myself. Then I hunted people in the far reaches of the world, as a Marine Corps Raider. The unit name had been dropped following World War II, but resurrected unofficially during the nineties and officially recognized in 2015. We specialized in guerrilla warfare of the variety that won the United States's independence from Britain, and now frustrates the mighty U.S. military throughout the Middle East. Controlled chaos is the best way to describe what we did, disrupting supply routes, performing random strikes, generally making the enemy feel nervous 24/7.

Despite being good at my job, and the killing that came with it, the act of taking a life was always sour for me. I did it, today, for my father. Later, for my country. I hoped it would get easier. That I could watch a man's life fade and not be haunted by it. But I still remember the look in that deer's eyes—the one my younger self is staring at right now.

A shrink once told me it was because I came to associate all death with the passing of my father. That it increased my sense of empathy for the slain and for those that might miss them. She made it sound like a virtue. But when you're a Marine Raider, hesitation to take a life could mean death for the squad.

So I left.

Never thought I'd see any real kind of action again, and in a sense, I still haven't. But I can feel that old self waking up. My thoughts race with possibilities, with scenarios to explore, with courses of action to pursue. Adrenaline pumps through my veins, urging me to take action. But all of this is tempered by the unknown.

There is no enemy, I remind myself.

No one to kill.

No one to hunt.

No one to fear.

And then a gunshot tears through the woods.

Levi and I both flinch out of our thoughts.

"That you again?" Levi asks. "Tagging your second buck?"

I shake my head. "Too soon. And that was a handgun. Modern. Nine mil."

Three more shots ring out, and by the time the last round's echo has faded into the distance, I've broken into a sprint.

6

My thoughts race in time with my feet, starting with fear for my family, including my father—who's supposed to die tomorrow—and ending with my younger self, whose demise might erase me from history.

Why did I let them go? Whoever blew up my truck could still be in the woods. With the modern world missing, it never occurred to me that other people could have made the trip through time, too.

I slow when my father's truck, parked on the right side of the road, comes into view. It's parked at a sharp angle that looks haphazard. But I remember my father parking like that on hills, in case the gears slipped, or the brakes failed. Instead of careening down the hill, the angled vehicle would turn into the trees, or curve and come to a stop. He was always concerned about the safety of others. Had he been more concerned with his own safety, maybe he'd still be alive.

"Where'd you and your pa go?" Levi asks.

I point off to the right. "Tagged the buck about a half mile in. About now, we'd be carrying it back this way."

Saying it out aloud relaxes me some. The 9 millimeter shots came from the left. That doesn't mean there's no danger, but I don't think it involves my father.

Unless whoever fired those shots changed recent events. Maybe those rifle shots weren't directed at the buck. Maybe it wasn't my finger on the trigger.

I draw my sidearm, a Sig Sauer P220 Legion packed with 10mm rounds. It's a bit overkill for the job, but it feels right in my hand, and it's powerful enough that one bullet will solve most confrontations...if necessary. I haven't fired a weapon at a human being in many years, and I don't intend on doing it again any time soon. That's just not who I am anymore. I've evolved. Tried telling that to Cassie once, but any mention of evolution in these parts, even when biology isn't the subject at hand, closes ears and minds.

"Geez," Levi says looking at the weapon. "You fixin' to take down a bear?"

"Happens on occasion," I say, and he doesn't argue. While most black bears will run upon detecting the presence of a human being, chance encounters do happen. Catching a bear off guard, sleeping, or in the company of cubs, can quickly become a life-or-death situation. And while I'd feel horrible for killing a mother bear, I'd feel worse being mauled by one.

I step into the woods on the left side of the road, hoping whoever fired those 9 mil rounds hasn't crossed it. "C'mon."

"I'd feel better if I had a gun, too," Levi says, stepping into the woods behind me.

I'm sure he can shoot. Not many people in these parts who can't, whether they're a diehard gun owner or they just pop off a few rounds on the 4th of July. But he's still under my care, and on Synergy's land... albeit long before the company's existence. But I don't need to mention any of that, because, "I don't have a gun to offer you."

"What about that?"

He's pointing at my hip, where my non-lethals are clipped—a taser and a can of mace. "Why not?" I say, unclipping the taser. "You know how to use it?"

"Point and shoot?" he guesses.

I smile, turn the weapon around, and hand it to him. He feels the heft of it in his hands, seems satisfied, and then aims the weapon toward my face.

A series of options flash through my mind, none of them ending pleasantly for Levi. Then I notice that the weapon isn't pointed directly at my head, but just to the side, over my shoulder. Still, it's close enough to make me second-guess giving him any kind of weapon, even if it can't kill me.

I'm about to ask what the hell he's thinking when he raises a finger to his lips, shushing me. I don't need to ask him where to look. The raised taser is beacon enough. Moving slowly, I turn around and peer into the woods.

At first, I see nothing more than the maze of trees walling off everything beyond fifty feet. Then I see it, a subtle shift of shadow moving between tall trunks. It's a woman, hunched low, moving slowly and carefully, stalking like a predator. I catch just a short glimpse of her, moving in shadow. It's not nearly enough to identify her—if that's even possible—but she's not coming this way or even aware of our presence.

"Remember the boot prints?" Levi whispers. "The small ones."

I nod. Could this be the woman whose tracks were left inside her larger counterparts'? They exited the road on the same side as my father—*shit*—but they could have circled around. To plant that C4 on the truck, they would have had to.

The key to a successful hunt is stealth. As soon as the prey knows you're there, the advantage is lost—even when you're carrying a gun. Clear line of sight in the forest isn't easy to come by, especially if your target is running. So I don't hurry after the woman. I creep in her general direction, watching every step and keeping quiet.

Levi does an impressive job of matching my pace and volume. He's stepping where I do, breathing steadily, aware but not agitated. With a bit of training, and a good dose of discipline, he'll make a great addition to my team.

I'm not in the habit of hiring people on the verge of becoming criminals—for all I know, my house isn't the first he's broken into—but when I spotted him lurking in the woods outside my house, there was something about him that snuck past fight-or-flight and found its way to mercy. Maybe I saw potential in him. Maybe I just saw myself, under different circumstances. I don't know. But I'm glad I gave him the chance.

I'll be even happier with my choice if I can keep him alive and get him back to the present, where we belong, despite his fantasies of living the good life for the next thirty years.

When we close to within twenty feet of the woman, I hold up an open hand. Levi stops behind me, crouching as we peer around a tree. The woman has stopped, her back to us. She's squatted by a tree, looking at something on the ground. She's petite, maybe five feet tall, black hair pulled back in a tight pony-tail. She seems comfortable in the woods, and with the 9mm handgun she's holding. But the blue jeans, snug yellow T-shirt, and high-top Converse Chuck Taylors tell me she's not out here for a hike, or for any kind of criminal activity. The clothing also tells me that she's from our time, not because it doesn't look vintage—it does—but because like us, she's not dressed for the cold. Her dark skin is peppered with goosebumps.

Despite all the visual cues, I don't recognize her until she stands up. I've grown accustomed to seeing her in uniform rather than in her casual clothing, which in these parts is a style all her own, more suited to Southern California than Appalachia. "Cassie."

She flinches, spinning around, weapon raised.

I duck back behind the tree. As one of my oldest and most trusted friends, I don't think she's a threat, but she's spooked. Sometimes trigger fingers twitch.

"Who's there?" she asks without firing a round.

"You gonna shoot your only friend?" I ask.

"Owen?" Her voice is full of hope.

I step out from behind the tree to find her weapon already lowered. Nervous tension drains out of her when our eyes meet.

"The hell is happening out here?" She takes a moment to scan the trees around us, whose leaves were green not long ago and are now showing traces of yellow, orange, and red. She tucks the handgun into the back of her pants and rubs her arms.

She knows something changed. Probably experienced the same shockwave we did, but she doesn't know we're in the past. How could she?

"Not sure," I say, and I watch her tension return when Levi steps out behind me.

I raise both hands to calm her. "He's with me. New recruit."

She looks Levi up and down. "Uh-huh."

"What are you doing out here?" I ask, sounding a little bit more like her boss than I prefer.

"You triggered the motion sensors when you drove in," she says. "Harper clued me in when I arrived. Figured I'd chase you down early. Get some bonus points." To Levi. "He acts like your friend, but he's a hard-ass prick. No one likes him."

She gives me a wink, and then continues. "Hence the lack of uniform."

I don't need to ask about the gun. Like a lot of people in Harlan County, Cassie's seen her fair share of trouble. When she's inside the protective boundaries of Synergy, she doesn't carry a weapon, but on the outside, she's always armed.

"What made you think bringing a newbie on a breach drill was a good idea?" she asks.

"Wasn't a drill." I slip my weapon back in its holster. "And it wasn't me."

"Someone blew up his truck," Levi says.

Cassie's eyes widen. "I heard that. Not long before..." She motions to the colored leaves with her head. "...all this happened. Was headed to check it out when, well, I'm guessing you saw it...and felt it, too. You know what they're working on up there?"

"I'm fixin' to find out," I tell her, "but in the meantime, we have a few things to figure out, starting with what you were shooting at."

She rolls her eyes and deflates a bit. "If you tease me 'bout it or tell a soul, I swear to Jiminy Christmas, I will burn that shithole you call a house to the ground."

A slight grin is my only response.

She steps aside to reveal a corpse.

As Levi and I step in for a closer look, he starts chuckling.

"Hey," Cassie warns.

"I didn't promise shit," he says, "and if you think murdering a coon is gonna make me afraid of ya—"

I take hold of his arm and he falls silent. Honestly, he has nothing to fear from Cassie. She can put on a good show and look as fierce as anything else in the woods, but she's got a gentle heart. Still, it's not his place to tease her. That's my job, and I'll take care of that when we're safe—not trapped in the past.

"What happened?" I ask, crouching over the racoon. It's got three bullet holes in it, two in the side, one in the head. "Also, nice aim."

"Been practicing," she says. "Damn thing charged me. Out of its mind. Figured it had rabies, so I didn't want to take any chances. Put it down."

"Makes sense," I say, standing back up.

"Horse-shit," Cassie says. "*Nothing* makes sense." She motions to the dead racoon. "This little shit is about the *only* thing that makes a lick of sense."

She squints at me, stepping closer. She's a good foot shorter than me and maybe a hundred pounds lighter. But she still manages to intimidate like she's got rabies herself. "You know something." Pokes my chest. "What do you know, Owen? We've been friends for too long for you to think keeping secrets is a good idea."

"Right about that," I say.

"Then why haven't you told me?"

"Reckon you won't believe it until you see it for yourself."

"Look around you." She waves her hands around at the forest. "This is some freaky shit. I'm liable to believe just about anything."

"Suit yourself," I tell her, sharing a look with Levi.

"You definitely ain't gonna believe him," the kid says.

"It's October," I tell her.

She raises a single eyebrow. "Not August?"

"Not anymore," I say.

She sighs. "You're telling me we jumped two months forward in time?"

Her tone is hard to read. There's no way she believes me, but she's doing a good job hiding it. She's probably trying to suss out if I'm messing with her, or if I'm being honest and have lost my mind. "Backward."

Her stare loses some of its power. "What?"

"Cass, it's October 14, 1985." Before she can chew me out for screwing with her, I raise my hands. "You know what that date means to me.

You know what happens tomorrow. And you know I wouldn't dick around about that."

She grows somber. Confused. What she knows about the world and what she knows about me slam headlong into each other. As impossible as time-travel might seem, me making light of my father's death is even less likely.

I glance back toward the road. "I can prove it to you."

Before I can explain how, or take a step toward the road, a loud buzzing fills the air, high above us on the mountain.

Levi groans and does a good job verbalizing what I'm thinking. "Jumpin' Jahosafuck, not again..."

I run back to the road with Cassie and Levi on my six, reaching the dirt path just in time to see the roaring wall of distortion. I'm driven to my knees by the force of it, hands over my ears, scream drowned out once again. For a moment, I'm lost inside my own mind, unable to make sense of anything.

And then it ends, rolling downhill like a tidal wave. I take several long breaths, collecting myself. When I think I've braced myself for the worst, I look up and find myself unprepared. The woods are still present, but the road is missing.

7

Aside from a gentle breeze flowing through the once-again green-leafed trees, and the cheerful whistle of various birds, the world goes silent. Even Levi, who seems to have a colorful expression for just about any situation, is at a loss for words. The shift is dramatic.

"Owen," Cassie says, but her question is cut short when a flock of birds bursts from the trees around us and takes to the sky. There must be fifty of them, their plumes unmistakable.

Levi sees it, too, eyes tracking the flock. "Bachman's warblers."

"What the holy hell do birds have to do—"

"They're extinct," Levi explains, then motions to me. "According to him."

"Don't look very extinct." Cassie's in shock, coming to terms with the undisputable realization that we have, once again, been transported into the past.

"The mine opened in 1950, so we're sometime before that." I look at the trees again. They're lush with leaves. The temperature has risen by twenty degrees, and the air is thick. Summer has returned. "Let's call it summer, 1945."

While I'm sure about it being summer, the year is debatable without any landmarks to go by.

"You're saying we just traveled seventy something years into the past?" Cassie asks.

"I think 'traveled' is the wrong word," I say. "Were carried feels more accurate."

"Who gives a shit how we word it?" Cassie begins to pace, scanning the endless forest around us.

"And technically, we were *carried*—" Levi pauses to give me a smile. He's handling our second jump fairly well. "—just forty years, on account of us already being in 1985."

Cassie stops, levels her glare and her index finger at Levi. "Don't screw with me, kid. I don't know you, I'm not sure I like you, and I have a tendency to kick annoying men in the nuts."

Icebergs melt faster than Cassie warms up to someone under the best of circumstances. I don't see her getting chummy with Levi anytime soon, but that doesn't mean they have to be at odds. "Cass, I know this is messed up."

"On so many levels."

I nod, hands on her shoulders. "But I think our best way to handle it is as professionals."

"Professional what?" she asks. "Time travelers? I'm pretty sure even your training didn't cover temporal displacement."

"First, bonus points for the big words. That was like six syllables." She smiles. "Second, we know these woods, no matter what year it is. All of us do. We know how to survive. How to track. How to hunt, if it comes down to it. I think it's safe to assume that this...*effect* is originating from Synergy. And if it's still happening, then maybe the facility, the people who work in it, and the answers we all want, are inside. So until we know otherwise, we're going to do our jobs."

"Which means..." Levi says.

"Fall back to Synergy and do whatever it takes to make sure everyone there is safe."

"And twist some nipples until the asshats who did this get us home," Cassie adds.

Levi chuckles. Cassie might not ever be fond of the kid, but I can tell he's already taking a liking to her.

Even without the road to guide us, there's no question about which way to go. I start moving uphill, scanning the forest for any other changes, and the others fall in behind me.

I've led some of the world's most dangerous men through hostile terrain, filled with people who wanted to mount our heads on pikes, but as nerve-wracking as those missions were, this is worse. Not only am I in hostile territory—someone blew up my truck, and I don't think that was a coincidence—but the territory is changing in unpredictable ways. More than that, I'm responsible for the people with me. Cassie and Levi aren't Special Forces. They're not even soldiers. Levi is an amateur thief, and a really bad one at that. Cassie is capable with a handgun, but she's never had to fire her weapon at anything more dangerous than an irate racoon—and that was just a few minutes ago.

My thoughts drift to my father and my younger self, safe in 1985. But not safe. My stomach clenches, knowing what young Owen is going to live through tomorrow.

Not that it's tomorrow anymore. If my guess at the year is close, my father might not even be born yet.

Twenty minutes into our hike, the sound of trickling water ignites a desperate thirst. It's been hours since I had a drink, and most of that time has been spent hiking up and down this mountainside. I take a quick look at my surroundings, spot a familiar boulder, and put a mental pushpin in an imaginary map. "Big Stone Spring isn't far. It's a little out of the way, but I think we should—"

Cassie redirects her course. Knows where she is just as surely as I do. Big Stone got its name on account of the big stone that clued me in to our location, but when we were teenagers, most people called it Big *Stoned* Spring because people used it for a pot-smoking meeting place. Cassie and I both spent some time at the spring, playing cards, smoking doobies, and doing what most teenagers do in Appalachia—killing time.

We reach the spring five minutes later. It's little more than a gurgle of water rolling over a collection of loose stones. The fluid runs downhill in a series of small pools. Further on, it will be joined by other streams that feed a good-sized pond.

Cassie crouches by the spring, cups her hands beneath the water—chilled to the temperature of the Earth—and drinks. She does it right, avoiding the easily accessible pools of water where animals are more likely to drink, piss, and shit. Dehydration is a bitch, but giardia can be a killer if left untreated. And I don't think severe cramps, diarrhea, and vomiting will help us solve our current problems.

When Cassie's had her fill, I motion for Levi to drink next. While he crouches by the spring, Cassie takes in the scenery.

"More trees," she says before approaching one of the big maples that's still around during our time. She runs a hand over its bark. Decades from now, its pristine surface will be covered in initials, including both of ours. "It's like we don't exist."

"We don't," I say. "Not yet."

She shakes her head and leans in close. "Seriously, Owen." She's whispering, her distrust of Levi unabated. "Do you know *anything?*"

"You know I'd tell you if I did," I say. "I'm as clueless as you...which means I'm a barely functional adult."

She huffs a laugh. "Asshole."

"What are friends for?"

"You all gonna start making out or something?" Levi says, water dripping from his chin and soaking his tank top. He might be from the twenty-first century, but he drinks like a Neanderthal. "'Cause I can go wait behind a tree or sumptin'. Let you two get carnal or whatever."

Cassie grabs my shirt and pulls me closer. "What do you say, hoss? Up for a romp?"

We've known each other since first grade. By the time middle school came around, we were somewhat inseparable, but we haven't ever been anything more.

Then again, neither of us have really had anything close to a significant other in our lives...other than each other.

Cassie shoves me back. "I'm going to kick this kid's ass eventually. You know that, right?" With that, she strides away, heading uphill and forcing me to drink quickly.

While I cup water to my lips, Levi crouches down beside me. "Seriously, though, did you tap that? Because, man..." He shakes his head, and I know where he's going. "...I've always wondered what it would be like to be with a—"

I drop the water from my hands, grasp him by the shirt and say, "If you say anything about race, you're going to find yourself alone in the past."

"Whoa," Levi says, raising both hands and looking appropriately petrified. "I was gonna say a 'cougar.'"

"A coug—are you stupid?"

Levi looks clueless.

"Cougars are *old.*"

"Yeah?" Still clueless.

"How old do you think she is?" My forehead wrinkles. "How old do you think *I* am?"

"I dunno. Old. Like forty."

It's my turn to look stunned. "Cougars are forty?"

"Yeah, that's like the definition," he says. "Like I said, old."

"Forty isn't old," I say, releasing him. "And do yourself a favor; keep this to yourself."

"I ain't stupid," he says. "But that doesn't mean I'm not gonna—"

Cassie's sudden return draws a squeak of surprise from Levi. She lands in the stream beside me, grasping Levi and yanking him down over the incline. He falls onto his back, and for a moment, I think she's strangling him.

Then I see her hand, wrapped over his mouth instead of around his throat.

When Levi nods and taps her hands, showing he understands the situation, she draws back and turns to me. "Ten men. Some of them armed. Coming this way."

"Where?"

"North," she says. "Hundred feet out."

Geez, that's close, I think, and then I poke my head up over the stream's short ledge. It's just a quick peek, but I've been trained to spot and remember details with just a glance. There *are* ten men, all of them haggard and dirty. A few of them are limping. One looks close to death, and three of them have blood-soaked injuries. The strongest of them are armed, the man in front carrying a revolver. The rest carry rifles, one of which I recognize as a Winchester, not too dissimilar from the weapon I learned to shoot on. The rifle lacks the speed and firing capacity of modern weapons, but it's no less capable of taking a life.

On their current course, they'll pass by uphill of us and the stream. If we stay still and quiet, they might not ever see us.

Then all hope of avoiding confrontation evaporates, when one of them shouts, "Water ahead!" and starts hobbling toward us, eyes lit with the hot glow of desperation that leads men to make horrible choices.

8

"Weapons down," I whisper to Cassie, when she draws her pistol. "We're not a threat to them."

Cassie grimaces. "But—"

"For all we know, one of these men could be an ancestor of—"

"None of those white boys is my ancestor," Cassie says.

"Cass."

"Fine." She tucks the handgun back into her pants. "But if one of them looks at me funny..."

"I'll be the first to put up a fuss." I pat the holstered gun on my hip. This isn't the Wild West, but I'm still a quick draw and a better shot than most. I'd rather not shoot down men with whom I have no quarrel, but Cassie and Levi are under my care, and there isn't anyone or anything— now or in the past—that will stand in my way.

Cassie nods, and I stand up, acting surprised when the hobbling man nearly careens into me. But my act is not nearly as dramatic as the stranger's. He simultaneously reels back and pitches forward while shouting, "Good Lawd!"

Rather than allow the man to fall into the stream, potentially injuring himself and our chances of a peaceful encounter, I catch him in my arms. The man's bright blue eyes are offset by a beard full of crumbs, rotting teeth, and a stench that nearly forces me to drop him. The only thing about him that's familiar is the dry, black stain of coal on his clothes and beneath his nails.

"Arthur!" calls out the nearest of the men. The one with the revolver. Of the bunch, he's the best dressed, in a tattered suit coat which is free of coal. His face is covered in a thin layer of stubble, but he would have been clean shaven a few days ago.

They're on the run, I realize, *but from who? And why?*

"I'm all right," Arthur calls out, as I set him upright and ease him down onto the spring's embankment. He looks me in the eyes, his gaze penetrating. "Thank you kindly for the assistance."

"Weren't nothin'," I say, laying on my accent a little thick. It faded during my years in the military, but falling back into it is easy.

The rest of Arthur's men arrive a moment later. Those with weapons have them aimed, mostly toward me, but there is one rifle covering Levi, and one on Cassie. But these men don't look like fighters. Judging by the coal staining their clothing, they'd be more comfortable holding pick-axes than rifles. They're also exhausted and desperate, more interested in the water gurgling behind me than they are in the newcomers they've stumbled across.

"Don't let us slow you down," I say, arms raised, stepping away from the spring. "Have at it."

The well-dressed man motions Arthur to the spring. The man descends on the spring like a thirsty vampire, sucking blood from the Earth's neck. He gags and slurps as he drinks with abandon.

"Name's Charles Whalen," the well-dressed man says, his revolver leveled at my chest. "What're you all doing out here?"

"Hunting," I say.

He looks us over. "Don't see no rifle."

"Don't need one," I tell him, and motion to the gun on my hip. He'll recognize it for what it is, but it's different enough from anything he'd have seen that he might just believe the lie.

"Ain't nobody hunts with a pistol," he says.

"Ain't nobody can shoot like him," Levi says. "Once saw him take the—"

"Levi," I say, trying to prevent him from making claims I can't follow through on. Last thing we need is these men challenging me to shoot a fly off a leaf at fifty feet or some such thing. "Mind yourself, boy."

The last bit is to let Levi and Charles know that he's my subordinate. Cassie plays it smart, staying quiet, eyes on the ground. I'm not entirely sure of the year, but even though slavery is a thing of the past, this is still the South, pre-civil rights movement.

"I picked this up in Germany," I say, gambling with the year. "Took it from a dead Kraut. Packs a punch, and it's more accurate than any weapon has a right to be."

My claim seems to impress the lot of them. When several of the men glance toward Charles, I have no doubt that he actually fought in the war, which puts the year sometime after 1918.

"Who'd you serve under?" Charles asks.

Part of my education was a study of military history. When it comes to warfare, not repeating history isn't just about learning how to prevent wars, it's about avoiding the mistakes made on the battlefield. And both World Wars were full of mistakes. "Major Whittlesey."

When Charles's eyes widen, I know he understands what that means, and I hope he wasn't one of the other 194 men who survived the horrible events in the Argonne Forest. If he was, I'll really have to stretch the limits of my historical knowledge and my ability to bullshit.

"77ᵗʰ Division," I continue, as if he doesn't understand. "We—"

"He knows what ya did," Arthur says, standing up from the spring. His chest is soaked with water. "Not many men who served haven't heard of the Lost Battalion, surrounded by Germans, abandoned by the French, and shelled by your own forces. You walked out of that, means you're a survivor."

"Also means you have our respect," Charles says.

There aren't many things that offend soldiers more than stolen valor, but I'll deal with the guilt if and when we survive this mess. Also, I'd like to think my own service makes this a case of *borrowed* valor, rather than stolen. I offer my hand to Charles and give him my actual name and rank. "Captain Owen McCoy."

As the man shakes my hand, his face contorts again. "McCoy?"

I forgot that my last name carries a lot of weight in these parts. Some of these men would have been alive for the infamous Hatfield-McCoy feud that claimed dozens of lives and became an American legend. Since then, the McCoy name has been recognizable and respected in Kentucky...but who's to say these men are from Kentucky?

The shift in mood is subtle. Whatever respect being part of the Forgotten Battalion garnered me, my last name erased.

"Don't hold his name against 'im," Levi says. "He can be an overbearing prick, believe you me, but he ain't had no part in the events of past years."

"And you are?" Charles asks.

"Levi Hatfield."

I think he's laid it on a little thick. Running into a McCoy in the woods is one thing, but stumbling across a Hatfield and a McCoy together? They're not likely to believe his story. But then he goes and frosts his liar's cake with a surprising layer of history.

"I'm Sid's cousin, twice removed. Heard what happened. Was coming to help."

The lie is impressive. Not only does Levi know his local mining history—Sid Hatfield was gunned down by the law on the steps of the courthouse where he was surrendering. As the leader of a mining revolt, he'd become a regional hero and an enemy of the federal government. All of this took place in Virginia, home of the Hatfields. That these men are here in Kentucky means they were part of Sid's crew, now on the run from the law. Knowing that also gives me a year. 1921.

"With a McCoy?" Arthur asks.

"I saved his life," Levi says. "The man owes me."

Charles sags a little bit, the fight going out of him. "Well then, I'm sorry to tell you, you're too late to do any good. Sid's dead."

"What?" Levi's overreaction borders on the edge of believability. He might know his history, but acting is not his forte. "How?"

"They shot him and Ed Chambers dead in front of their wives," Charles says. "Right at the courthouse, if you can believe it. We put up a fine stink. Wounded a few of them. But they had the numbers and the guns. We've been on the run since." Charles purses his lips, thinking, and then adds, "You're more than welcome to join us." He motions to me. "Present company excluded." Back to Levi. "But the best thing you can do is go back where you came from. Live your life, best you can. I reckon we ain't long for this world. Best not throw in with us."

This is a test, I think. The Hatfield and McCoy feud went on so long and claimed so many lives because the families were fiercely loyal. Levi turning his back on Sid's men would prove that we've been lying up until now. While Charles can't prove any of this, he smells the stink of our horseshit. If Levi turns him down, he's likely to gun us all down.

The sound of horse hooves prevents Levi from answering, but it does nothing to improve our situation.

"The law!" one of the men shouts, adjusting his aim away from Cassie and toward the woods, where the sound is coming from. "They done found us!"

The ten men all but forget about us, taking up positions behind trees. Those with rifles prepare to fire. Those without wield knives and tree branches. Each and every one of them is prepared to go down fighting, and I'm pretty sure that's supposed to be their fate.

But it's not ours.

"Like it or not," Charles says. "You're with us now." He takes up position with his men, turning his back on us. We could shoot them in the backs, or flee, but when I hear the thunder of hooves approaching from behind, too, I realize he's right. The men gunning for Charles and his people are going to shoot on sight. Guilt by proximity.

When Charles hears the hooves coming from behind, he turns around and gives me a wink. "This feels familiar, right? Surrounded by the enemy. Outgunned. Outmanned."

"More than you'd ever believe," I say, drawing my sidearm. "You and your men handle the front, we'll deal with the men on this end." I give Cassie a nod and she draws her pistol from behind her back. The look on Charles's face is amusing, but I don't linger to enjoy it. A dozen armed men on horseback stampede toward us through the trees and time itself.

9

"Stay mobile," I tell Cassie. "Use the trees. And..." I don't want to say it, but this is life or death, even if there's nothing noble about taking a life. "...fight dirty."

"I don't think I'm going to get a chance to kick anyone in the jimmy," Cassie says, not understanding the depths to which a man or woman with a gun can stoop.

So I show her.

Though the onrushing men are still fifty feet out, I take aim at the man in the front. He's young and hungry for blood, trying to aim his pistol at me while riding a horse at full gallop. I take my time aiming, timing out the beats between each rise and fall of the horse's head.

I hesitate for a moment, knowing that if I pull this trigger I likely won't stop pulling it until either I'm dead, or a heap of men are. I'm reluctant to kill. I thought I had escaped a life of violence. But I'm more reluctant to die, and I'm sure as shit not going to let anything happen to Cass.

I fire. Just once.

The effect is immediate and catastrophic. The horse, now with a 10mm-sized hole in its forehead, collapses at twenty-five miles per hour. A thousand pounds of meat and hooves topples. The rider is thrown to the side, twisting in the air with a shout, before colliding with a tree. Ribs crack like fireworks.

As the dead—or dying—man falls to the forest floor, the two steeds directly behind the still toppling horse trip over its body. Two men are flung. One lands on his head, neck bending at a sick angle. The second man lands on his back, the air knocked out of him.

He'll be back in the fight inside thirty seconds. But there's no time to worry about him. The seven remaining horses and riders weave around the chaos, closing the distance.

I glance at Cassie and am met by pale astonishment. "Go!" I urge, and she springs into action, flanking left.

"Stay here," I tell Levi, stabbing a finger at the stream, "and stay down!"

I break right, heading uphill. Several shots ring out. Men scream behind me. Maybe they're Charles's men. Maybe the newcomers. It's hard to say, even when fighting an enemy that speaks another language. Screams are the same, no matter what part of the world you're in.

Bark splinters when I duck behind a tree. These men are capable fighters, but they're limited by 1920s technology. Reloading takes time, especially while on horseback. And their revolvers and rifles need to be reloaded far more often than my handgun, which carries ten rounds. The downside of this situation, aside from being outmanned, is that I've only got two spare magazines. Thirty rounds total. Well, twenty-nine. I'm not sure if Cassie has any spare magazines, and she already put three rounds into a racoon. She has at least ten rounds.

I lean out from behind the tree, fire a single shot into the chest of a man caught reloading his rifle. He drops from the side of his mount, revealing a man in a Stetson, leveling two revolvers at me.

The tree shakes from his assault. The man's heavy-hitting rounds eat up the bark. The man's aim and speed are impressive. If I were to poke my head out on either side, I'd likely lose it.

But he's not trying to kill me. He's pinning me down. Buying time.

When the pop of 9mm ammo fills the air, I duck down and lean out, four feet below where my head should be. Before the man can adjust his aim, I fire a round into his horse's ankle. The beast falls to the side, pinning the man's leg beneath it and providing a very easy shot for me. A single round through the top of his Stetson ends his fight.

I can't help but wonder how this battle turned out without us here. How many of these attackers lived? Given the shape of Charles's men, and their limited weaponry, I think most of the attackers would have escaped unscathed. Now...if I have my way, the only ones who survive will be those who turn tail and run. And I reckon not a one of them will do so.

I take a moment to catch a breath and compress my emotions. Killing these men is like killing generations of people. Everyone who would have descended from them will now never exist. I think. Time travel is pretty far out of my wheelhouse. But even if that's true, I'm not about to sacrifice myself or those under my care, including anyone still alive at Synergy, who, near as I can figure, are the only people who can stop what's happening.

A man on horseback rounds a stand of trees, shotgun leveled at my head. Knowing I can't dodge the full spread of a shotgun shell, I pull my trigger three times without aiming. The second round strikes the horse's flank. As it bucks in pain, the man squeezes his trigger.

I'm spun around by what feels like a punch on my left arm. The deep pain is followed by a cascade of bee stings. I've been hit, but it's not bad enough to slow me down.

Before the man can recover from the shotgun's recoil and his flailing horse, I put two rounds in his chest. With my tenth and final round already in the chamber, I eject the magazine and let it fall to the ground. My hand drops to my hip, snags a fresh magazine, and slaps it home. The entire process takes two seconds, and it's nearly half a second too long.

A rifle cracks. Bark and wood fragments spray into my face. A sniper's round has just missed my head. I slip to the tree's far side, pinned again and unable to follow my advice to Cassie. But she's doing a good job.

I watch her for a moment, slipping from one tree to another, firing shots when she moves. There are men on the ground and horses running free. I feel sorry that she's been forced to kill these men, but maybe she'll find comfort in the fact that, in the time we're from, they're long since dead. That is, if she doesn't also figure out that killing them might mean erasing their bloodlines from history.

Cassie makes another break for it, raising her gun to fire at a horse rising up on its hind legs, the rider intending to block himself while using the steed to bludgeon her. The *click, click, click* of an empty gun makes me wince. Whether or not Cassie has more ammo, she's never been in a gun fight, and counting bullets doesn't come naturally to most people. Not when men are screaming, bullets are flying, and death is a single mistake away.

She's clipped by the horse's hoof and sent sprawling to the forest floor. She attempts to stand, but she's tackled by the man who lost his horse.

I fire two rounds, both of them striking the man still on horseback. I can't do anything about the man on top of her—not at this range. A 10mm round could pass through her attacker and strike Cassie. Helping her means taking care of the sniper.

A quick peek to the left is followed by a bullet slamming into the side of the tree, nearly hitting my skull. I duck back and peek right before he can adjust. He's a hundred feet back, lying down behind a fallen tree, with a clear line of sight.

Not an ideal situation, but compared to the time travel conundrum, a gun fight is something I can solve.

Steeling myself to make a break for it, I glance across the stream to find most of Charles's men are dead. The crew who attacked them isn't fairing much better, though. There're just a few men left on each side. Charles and one of his boys are trading shots with three remaining posse members. Arthur and a stranger are locked in mortal combat, fighting for control of a knife.

When Charles puts a round in one of the posse members, resulting in a high-pitched scream, I run. Even trained soldiers can't help but glance away from the action when one of their own is gunned down. I extend my window of opportunity by firing three rounds toward the sniper, forcing him to duck.

Outside his zone of fire, I begin weaving my way in and out of the trees. He fires at me in rapid succession, but I'm never visible for more than a second, and never in the same place. He's not a bad shot, but he's not experienced in this kind of combat. If he was, he'd already be up and moving, rather than sitting still, trying to hit a moving target in the woods.

When I hear him curse, I holster my gun. It won't be necessary, and I've already used more rounds than I should have.

The man's eyes widen as I round the last tree dividing us. I've caught him reloading, but he's quicker than I expected. He chambers a round and swivels the weapon toward me as I close the distance. The rifle booms as I grasp the muzzle and angle it away and toward the ground.

Using my momentum, I shove the rifle hard, sending the butt into his face. Blood oozes from his nose, and then explodes, as I drive my foot into his gut, forcing the air from his lungs.

As he spills back, I spin the rifle around, chamber a bullet and fire it into his chest. The rifle is an M1917 Enfield, a common rifle of the period, with a mounted scope.

I drop to a knee, raise the rifle to my shoulder, and peer through the scope. The man atop Cassie raises a knife, prepared to stab her.

I have no choice.

If I don't fire, she'll die.

My index finger slips around the trigger and squeezes, but stops a moment before the hammer snaps forward.

Levi lunges into view, tackling the man off Cassie. The men separate, and I take aim again, ready to end the fight and keep Levi from harm. But I never get the chance. Levi sets on the man with a series of fast punches and kicks that lack skill, but are powered by raw ferocity. The man staggers back under the assault, but is reaching for a knife.

"Levi!" I shout, waiting for the opportunity to fire, but the kid is lost in the fight. Probably doesn't even hear me.

I flinch when the man swings the blade, but Levi reacts as though he was ready for the strike. He leans back just out of range, catches the man's arm, and shoves. With all his weight behind the attack, the knife stabs its owner. They fall to the ground in a heap. Levi rises, draws the blade from the man's side and then stabs him twice more, right in the heart.

I shake my head. This is going to scar him for life.

Cassie, too.

Whoever is responsible for this mess is going to have a lot to answer for...

"Hey," a gruff voice says from the stream. "Turn around, real slow like, or your friend loses his head."

...if we live long enough to find them.

10

The man speaking is dressed in a blood-soaked trench coat. He's groomed and tailored, but I don't think he's any stranger to violence and death. He seems fairly unshaken by the carnage surrounding us or by the fact that he's outnumbered four to one, if you count our 'friend.'

The man being threatened is Arthur, a knife held to his throat. Charles, brave as he was, lies dead at his feet.

I adjust my aim toward the man holding the knife. Looking down the pilfered rifle's scope, I could shoot him. It would be easy, and I'm not even that worried about what happens to Arthur. Pretty sure he was meant to die here today. "Who are you?"

The man scrunches up his face like I've just asked to have a look up his skirt. Then he says, "Sheriff Don Chafin."

I know that name. He played a major role in the infamous coal wars. To some he was a hero. To others, a devil. All depended on whether or not your lineage was steeped in coal or not. He was a figurehead of the outside world, meddling in coal culture, and in Appalachia. If not for him, the confrontation that led to Charles and his men fleeing west through the wilderness might have turned out differently.

I also know he didn't die today. Chafin survived well into his sixties.

"I have no quarrel with you," I say, lowering the rifle, much to Arthur's dismay.

"Afraid I have a quarrel with *you*," the sheriff says.

"We were just passing through," Cassie says, approaching with a slight limp.

"You okay?" I ask her.

She rubs her thigh. "Charley horse."

I glance up at Levi, knife in hand, standing a few feet behind Cassie. I give him a nod of thanks, which he returns in kind.

"If your men hadn't opened fire—"

"*You* don't get to speak to me," Chafin says, seething at Cassie and revealing himself to be a racist and an asshole. It's likely that Chafin's father, or grandfather fought in the Civil War. In our present, resentment toward the North and those freed by the war still burns hot in some areas of the South, never mind in the 1920s, when subjugation had only evolved into segregation. We shouldn't expect to come across anyone who's—what's the hip, new lingo? —woke.

"Can I kill him?" Levi says, stepping toward Chafin and catching all of us off guard. His dander is raised something fierce. The impact of taking a life has yet to settle on him. When it does...

Chafin presses the knife harder against Arthur's throat. The blade would have to cut through equal parts beard and skin to end the man's life, but it looks sharp enough to do the job.

I hold my hands out, one toward Chafin, one toward Levi. "You're missing the point, Sheriff. We don't know that man." I point to Arthur. "And we don't know any of the men you all gunned down. We were just passing through. Wrong place, wrong time. You don't need to kill him, and I don't need to kill you. Take your man. Go back the way you came. You'll never see any of us again."

I hope.

Chafin glares at me for a moment, no doubt weighing his options and whether or not I can be trusted. Then he reels back and clubs Arthur in the back of the head. He lets the man collapse at his feet and then waits with a tense face.

When I don't shoot him, he sighs with relief. "If you all really stumbled into this mess, you've got shit for luck."

"You have no idea," I say, looking over the field of death.

"But I've seen you fight." He's looking at me. "Could use more men like you. Especially on account of how you gunned down half my posse."

"I am sorry 'bout that," I say.

"Couldn't be helped," he says. "Wrong time. Wrong place. Right?"

I nod and hold the rifle up. "Mind if I hold on to this?"

"I ain't got no need for it," he says, looking at the dead and the collection of guns on the ground. "Got more than I can carry already."

"Take what you need," I say to Cassie and Levi. They set out among the dead, collecting gear.

I look about for a horse or two, but the steeds have all fled. All but one, lying on its side, struggling to breathe. Now that the fight is over, I regret having to shoot the animals, and I'm not about to let this one suffer. After crouching to pet its forehead and whispering an apology, I stand, take aim, and fire a single round into the horse's head.

When I look up, a stray tear in my eye, I note Chafin's attention.

"Seen war before," Chafin says. "Haven't yeh?"

A slow nod is my only reply.

"Likewise," he says, picking up a dropped revolver and holstering it. "We're square. I won't come looking for you."

"Appreciate that," I say, and I do. Having killed so many of his men, I fully expected Chafin to return with more. If we were still here, in this time, upon his return, the killing would have resumed, and I'd have been forced to take his life, too. But so close to the end of World War I, the respect for its veterans is powerful. I might not have fought in the war to end all wars, but I've killed and bled for the same country. Close enough.

After pillaging the dead for ammo, water canteens, supplies, and jackets—in case the temperature changes again—I lead Cassie and Levi away, leaving Chafin to regroup and try to figure out a way to transport his prisoner back to Virginia. Downhill, a horse whinnies. I think about going after it, but Chafin is going to need it more than us. His journey is long, and ours, if we're not interrupted again, is just over a mile uphill, though it's starting to feel a lot farther.

One step forward, two steps back...in time.

I smile at the thought, but don't say it aloud. Now's not the time for making jokes. Hell, on a good day Cassie would slug me for a joke that bad.

When we've put a few hundred feet between Chafin and us, and I'm confident he can no longer see us, I stop and sit atop a fallen tree. "Take a minute."

"We should keep moving," Levi says. He's doing his best to appear unshaken, but even a seasoned veteran can be left exhausted by combat. Not because of physical or emotional weakness, but because adrenaline wreaks havoc with the body, especially as the effects fade.

I hold up my hands so he can see them. Both are shaking. As are the muscles in my thighs and stomach. Feels like Rocky Balboa is using my insides for a punching bag. Adrenaline does a lot of good things in bad situations, increasing heart rate and blood pressure, expanding the lungs and throat, and allowing the blood to be more oxygen rich. All that fuel is pumped directly into the muscles and brain, letting people think faster, react faster, and on occasion, do the impossible, like lifting a car. But when the adrenaline wears off, blood sugar plummets, leaving muscles feeling weak and shaky. "If you don't let your body ease back to normalcy, when you try to climb this mountain, your muscles are going to cramp up. Won't make it far when that happens. We need a minute."

Cassie is accustomed to following my lead when it comes to the job. Not so much in any other aspect of life. But when it comes to combat and security, she knows the depth of my experience.

While Cassie stretches, Levi takes a seat, his back to me. Kid's got too much pride. Doesn't want me to see him going through the same shakes afflicting me.

"You did what you had to," I say to him, unbuttoning my shirt and trying not to wince from the pain in my left arm. I'm not sure how much damage the buckshot did. The arm is still fully functional, but the pain is ripe. "Ain't no shame in it."

"Didn't say there was." There's an edge to his voice. A few hours ago he was terrified to point an old gun in my face, and now he's stabbed a man to death. And by the looks of it, he's kept the knife, sheathing it on his hip using a belt he wasn't wearing earlier.

"I remember what it was like," I tell him. "First time I took a life."

He sits silent, but I can tell he's listening.

"Wasn't too different from this. An ambush. But not everyone I was with that day handled themselves as well as you." I look at Cassie. "As both of you." She gives me a weary grin. "While I wouldn't wish this shit on anyone, I'm glad the two of you are with me."

Cassie thumps her foot into Levi's thigh. "He don't give out compliments very often, so thank the man, or he's liable to start offering critique instead. You know what critique is, right?"

Levi huffs and smiles. Pushes Cassie's foot away. "Seems to me that you should be the one thanking me."

The good humor drains out of Cassie's face. She crouches down beside Levi and for a moment, I think she's going to ream him out. Then she says, "Thanks. Honestly. You saved my life."

She sits down beside him as a further peace treaty. I'm not sure she would have, if she'd known about the cougar comment. She digs into a satchel bag taken from one of the dead men. I focused mostly on ammunition for the rifle, but I took a coat that's now tied around my waist, and a full water canteen.

While they're distracted with the satchel, I remove my shirt. If the wound is bad, I'd rather not be doted on. Best case scenario, I'll be able to tend to it without either of them noticing. My triceps is bloodied, but the flow has stemmed.

I got lucky.

With a twist of skin and muscle, the wound is revealed. Three of them, actually. Two fine lines reveal where buckshot gouged divots in my skin, but failed to puncture. The third is a small, dark red hole surrounded by hot pink skin. I give it a pinch and wince when I feel the small pellet buried a half inch inside.

Cassie extracts a wad of ancient dollar bills from the satchel. She waggles them in the air. "Fat load'a good these'll do us."

Levi takes the money, thumbing through it. "Whataya reckon this is worth in our time?"

"Couldn't say," I tell him, and I don't really care. Money is the least of our concerns. Neither Cassie nor I complain when he pockets the cash. A pocket watch comes next. Cassie gives it a once-over and tosses it back to me without looking. I catch the watch in my right hand and turn it around.

The time reads 11:20. Given that the sun is still shining, I'm guessing that's AM. My forehead furrows a moment before a thought occurs to me. I lift my wrist and check the time. 11:20. We're being moved through years, but it appears the time of day is ticking on as usual. Weird, but not helpful, and not worth mentioning.

I pocket the watch and turn my attention back to the wound. While Cassie and Levi are still distracted, I grit my teeth, pinch the meat of my triceps between my finger and thumb, and squeeze toward the buckshot like I'm wringing out a tube of toothpaste. Pain swells as blood begins flowing from the small wound. I nearly shout when my fingers reach the buckshot. It resists for a moment, but then slips toward the entry wound. A moment later, the metal bead pops out of my arm and falls to the ground. I hold my sleeve over the small wound and apply pressure.

A block of paper wrapped in twine emerges from the satchel before Cassie discards the empty leather husk. She unties the knot, opens the paper and reveals several strips of dried meat.

"Well slap my ass and call me Nancy." Levi says before plucking up a piece of meat.

"I don't think that's a—"

Before I can finish my warning, he bites off a chunk of meat and all but melts in delight. "It ain't rancid," he says between bites. "Tastes fresh. Tender as shit, too."

When he notices Cassie and me watching him in cautious disgust, he stops midchew and says, "Ain't no bacteria around today that ain't a super version of itself in our time." Then he goes right on chewing.

"He's got a point," Cassie says.

My stomach growls, waging war against my mental defenses. Eating food from the 1920s that isn't wine or whiskey sounds like a bad idea—unless you're *in* 1920. I lift my sleeve away and watch for fresh blood. When none flows, I slip my shirt back on and reach my hand out. "Give me a piece."

Cassie takes one for herself and hands another to me. I give it a sniff and the war against hunger is all but lost. The meat smells of salt, pepper, garlic, and maple syrup. The protein and sugar will fuel our remaining hike and keep us from having to forage—assuming our uphill journey isn't interrupted again. I'm still not convinced it's the best idea, but I no longer think it's a *bad* idea.

After my first bite, all trepidation fades. Ten minutes later, the meat that was likely supposed to sustain the man carrying it for days, is all gone.

Belly full, I lean back in a long stretch, careful not to overextend my left arm, feeling ready to head out again.

"Thought your face looked familiar."

I open my eyes to find Chafin standing a few feet away, revolver leveled at my exposed core. "Any one of you even twitches, and your bossman gets a hole in his chest."

"Why are you back?" I ask. "Thought we had an agreement."

"Ol' Arthur started talking when he woke up," Chafin says. "Offered a trade. Information for his freedom. Man's as thick as a redwood. Believed me when I agreed to it. Then he reveals who you really are, *Mr. McCoy.* Wouldn't you know it, my ma was a Hatfield, and we know better than most how quick with the tongue you McCoys can be. So I've decided to *not* believe your story."

"And now you plan to bring us all in?" I ask.

"I'm fixin' to shoot you, actually." He raises his gun, and for a moment, I know I'm going to die. But then he hesitates, not because of Cassie or Levi, but because the air fills with the sound of angry bees, rushing down from the mountaintop.

11

"Don't throw up," Levi says, ducking his head down, preparing for the wave. He's more concerned about losing his meal than Chafin's threat, or the fact that we're about to be torn through time once more. "Don't throw up."

"What is that?" Chafin says, stumbling a few steps back, but keeping his weapon trained on me.

"Afraid this is where we part ways," I tell him. The sound of my voice is all but drowned out by electrical crackling filling the air.

The wave of distortion rolls toward us. It looks different this time—still impossible to see through, but where there was once a kaleidoscope of color, there is now a wall of shimmering white. The invisible orchestra rises up again, the deep resounding bass shaking inside my chest and distorting Chafin's scream.

I'm floored by the passing effect. I feel it roil through my insides, sending a chill to my core, before ripping out through my feet and plummeting downhill. But how far?

Eyes clenched, I feel the cold all around before opening my eyes and seeing the world made white. For a moment, I think the effect has somehow transported us to another dimension this time, a stark, lifeless place. Then I realize the truth: it's winter.

I stagger to my feet, untying the jacket and pulling it on. Cassie and Levi groan as they stand, shaky from the lingering aftereffects of time travel, and our recent battle. They're being worn down, but I'm impressed by their resolve. Once we're dressed in our stolen coats, I turn my gaze uphill.

"We're fighting time and the elements now. We need to hit this hill hard. Stopping could—"

"Eeeearrrggh!"

The scream makes me jump.

I spin toward the noise, drawing and aiming my handgun, the barrel snapping to a stop between Chafin's eyes. He's on his knees, undone by the time-wave and the jarring impact of being transported through time. Never mind the physical discomfort, the psychological impact of finding yourself *somewhen* else is enough to undo even a hardened man like Chafin.

I lower my weapon, crouch down, and pick up his revolver from where he dropped it. "Give it a minute. Catch your breath."

"Is this hell?" he asks.

"Winter in Appalachia," I tell him. "So, close."

"What's he doing here?" Levi asks, and it's the very question I'm asking myself.

"It's taking everyone," Cassie says.

"And not just from our own time." I glance at Chafin, whose feeble struggle to stand matches my effort to decipher the ramifications of what we've just learned. "Everything, from our time back, comes along for the ride." I tug on my coat. "Anything not part of the Earth. Trees come and go. The leaves change with the seasons. But anything...loose is carried through time."

"Not your truck," Levi points out. He's right. The truck throws a monkey wrench in my theory. "Maybe it's a question of mass and how close it is to Synergy?"

"Mass?" I squint at the kid. Didn't take him as the type to have paid attention in science.

"Yeah, like weight? Maybe the truck was too heavy. Or something?"

It's better than any theory I can come up with. "Maybe."

"So, then what?" Levi says. "We just need to make ourselves heavier? Root ourselves somehow?"

"We don't even know what year it is now," Cassie points out. "Even if that worked—and I don't think it would—living our lives in the past is not a solution. The further back we go, the worse things are gonna get for me."

"Far enough back," Levi says, "things aren't going to be pleasant for any of us."

I step away from the conversation. Something is nagging at me, nibbling at the fringe of my attention.

"Hey," Chafin says, standing on shaky legs. When no one responds, he growls a bit and says, "Hey! Someone tell me what in the name of the good Lord is going on? Where'd all this snow come from? How did we get here? It's summer, for Pete's sake!"

He's frantic. On the cusp of losing his mind. Can't say I blame him, but Chafin was a problem when he was balanced. If he can't pull himself together, we're going to have to leave him here, or... I shake my head. Killing an unarmed man, even if it would help our own survival, is not an option. Not in any time.

"You being here is as much a surprise to us as it is to you." Levi hugs his arms over his chest and blows steam from his mouth, up into the frigid air. While there's only a few inches of snow, it's covered with an icy sheen that cracks underfoot. The bare branches glisten with a layer of ice, giving the forest a magical feel. Despite the harsh conditions, I think we're lucky to have arrived after the storm of freezing rain. "Hell, us being here is a surprise. And for the record, we don't know what's going on, neither."

"What do you know?" Chafin asks, looking a little steadier.

The three of us are silent for a moment. Then Cassie asks, "You read?"

"A bit," Chafin says, eyeing his pistol, which I've tucked into my waist.

"How about H.G. Wells?"

The name is familiar to me, but I don't read many novels. If Cassie is asking about a writer, he must have been around before the 1920s. What's most confusing about her line of questioning is that I had no idea she was a reader. I haven't seen many books at her home, and she's never brought up reading anything longer than the Synergy Security Manual.

"Some," Chafin says, though he seems ashamed to admit it. Even in the future, admitting you're a bookworm in a land of rough coalminers is enough to make people not trust you.

"The Time Machine?"

Chafin opens his mouth to respond and then freezes in place. His eyes dart about the forest. Then his mouth slowly closes. He spins around, glancing in every direction. "Are you saying... No... It ain't—"

"Winter?" Levi asks. "'Cause it wasn't a minute ago. And now it is."

Chafin's bewilderment melts into despair. "It ain't possible," he whispers. Then louder. "How?"

"We don't know," I say. "We were carried through time, just like you."

"And likely anyone else on Adel," Levi says.

The nibbling becomes a frantic chew, and then realization draws a gasp from the depths of my chest. It's enough to make even Chafin flinch in fear.

"What is it?" he asks.

Cassie puts a hand on my shoulder. "Owen?"

"They're still here," I say, before looking her in the eyes, a new kind of fear burning in my chest.

"Wait," Levi says, "Who's still... Gal dang. Your pa. And *you!*"

We scan the woods around us like we might suddenly come upon them. But I know they're nowhere to be found. My father wasn't a foolish man. Anyone on Adel would have heard the gunfight with Chafin's men. With my younger self in tow, my father would have gone out of his way to avoid the confrontation.

But what else would he have done?

With the forest changed, and the road gone, he'd still know the mountain. Like us. And he'd have done what any reasonable person would do—head to town. Look for help. But there wasn't time to make it there. So now my father, who's supposed to die tomorrow, is stuck in the past, in the snow, without any way to get help.

On one hand, I'm afraid for them. For my father's life, but also for mine. If my younger self dies out here, will I, too? I was young and fragile back then, afraid of everything—unless my father was with me. Back then, he was larger than life. An unshakable behemoth who stormed through life's problems and projected confidence. He was my rock, until he wasn't.

I have no doubt that my father—a simple man with simple needs and desires—is as confused by what's happening as we are. But he'll be focused on me, and on surviving. They were dressed for fall, but my father could have a fire burning inside a few minutes. They might even be better off than we are right now.

Doesn't matter, I decide. They're family, and I won't leave them to go through this alone. "Change of plans," I say. Before I can explain, a nearby scream rises through the air, echoing in the leafless forest. I turn toward the sound, looking back in the direction from which Chafin came.

"What did you do with Arthur?" I ask.

"Left him tied to a tree," Chafin says, equal parts defensive and concerned.

A second scream is followed by a high-pitched. "Help!"

I scan the forest around us and then look uphill. My family, and the answers we need, are somewhere else on Adel. But I can't just leave a man to die—horribly, by the sound of it.

"Come with us or not," I say to Chafin. "That's up to you." Then I look to Levi and Cassie who both nod. They're on board with my plan, even if it does set us back once again. We strike out through the icy snow, our collection of footfalls sounding like crunchy cereal in a giant's mouth. Chafin hesitates for a moment and then follows.

As we approach the scene of the earlier battle, I slow down and do my best to walk silently, letting my weight push through the ice and compress the snow beneath. The others step inside my prints, allowing them to move without making a sound.

Ahead, I see bodies from the 1920s, half buried in the snow, like it fell everywhere but on top of them. I crouch behind a tree, leaning out to survey the scene. When I don't see Arthur, I glance back at Chafin. He points off to the left and I strike out again.

"Please, God! Someone!"

Arthur sounds close, just beyond a big oak. I creep up to it, as slow as I can. The only thing that can make a man scream like that usually has ears, and I'd prefer to not to be heard before understanding the situation.

Clutching the tree's bark, I lean out to the side and see Arthur, hands behind his back, bound to a birch tree.

Just a few feet away, licking a dead man's face, is the largest mountain lion I've ever seen—in person or in pictures. And while it's tasting the dead man, it definitely has eyes for Arthur, who makes himself the more interesting meal with each kick of his feet and each pitiful wail.

The big cat lets out a low growl, and for a moment, I think it's about to pounce. Then it turns and looks me dead in the eyes.

12

"What are you waiting for?" Arthur says, straining to be heard while not wanting to draw the cat's attention back to him. "Shoot the dang thing!"

"Cat's just doing what cats do," I tell him, without taking my eyes away from the feline. While I haven't ever stared down a mountain lion before, I know enough about them to not act rashly. First of all, the cat is far faster than me, and I'm not entirely sure I could draw and shoot it dead faster than it could charge and wrap its jaws around my face. Cassie might be able to gun it down while I'm assaulted, but not until after those inch-long canines have punctured my skull. I also don't want to kill it. Drawn by the scent of blood, it really is just fulfilling its natural role. The only reason Arthur was in any danger is because Chafin left him tied up, surrounded by the smell of death.

"Fan out to the sides," I tell the others.

"What in the hell for?" Levi asks.

"Intimidation," I say, hoping the cat is smart enough to know when it is outnumbered. I'm not sure what year it is now, but people have lived here long enough that I'm confident the cat knows we're dangerous. It might also know we're delicious, which could have something to do with its reluctance to back off.

The cat's eyes dart to the others as they step out on either side of me, their feet crunching loudly in the crusted snow.

"Bare your teeth," I say. "Growl."

Feeling a bit ridiculous, I follow my own advice.

Levi groans, "This is like gal-dang drama class."

Between growls, Cassie says. "You took a drama class?"

"There was a girl involved," Levi says before joining in.

The cat's ears fold flat as it takes a step backward. Our intimidation tactic is working, but it's also backing the cat straight toward Arthur, whose eyes are widening in abject terror.

"Shoot it!" he screams, regaining the cat's full attention.

I feel a sudden pressure on my hip and then a shift of weight, as my handgun is pulled up and away. The weapon rises, aimed toward the cat, which is standing in front of Arthur. I grasp the weapon as the trigger is pulled, angling it up. A single round blasts through the air, punching into the tree bark a foot above Arthur's head.

The sudden report makes the cat flinch, but it doesn't retreat. Then Levi steps forward, raises his arms in the air and shouts. "Rwar!"

The already spooked lion bolts, disappearing over a ridge in three long strides.

With a twist of my hand, I disarm Chafin, and in the same quick move I deliver a backhanded slap to the side of his face. The blow is hardly a punch, but solid enough to bowl the man over. He lands on the ground, stunned and rubbing his cheek.

"Thank Jesus," Arthur says, struggling against his bonds. "Y'all came back for me."

"And you sold us out," Levi says, crouching beside the man, knife in hand. It's the same knife he used to kill Chafin's man...and save Cassie's life.

Arthur eyes the blade. "About that..." He looks around the forest, at the dead men, and then at Cassie and me. He's trying to concoct a story, but he's coming up blank.

"You got nothin'," Levi says, leaning in with the knife.

"Now hold on a minute! I just—"

Levi slices, making Arthur jump with fright. When Levi stands up, sheathing the blade, the only thing cut is the rope binding the hairy outlaw to the tree. Arthur pulls his hands free, staring at them as a smile spreads.

"What're you doing?" Chafin says with a groan, pushing himself up. "Man's a criminal."

"Seeing as how you were about to murder me a few minutes back, I'd say you fellas have more in common than not." I holster my gun, buttoning it in place this time. I motion to Arthur. "At least this man was fighting for a cause that affects him and his own in the present day, and not a familial tiff that should have died out decades ago."

It occurs to me that it's entirely possible we've been transplanted to the years during which the Hatfield and McCoy fighting was at its fiercest.

"You got no love for your family?" Chafin says, climbing to his feet. "No respect for your name? For your history?"

"Only family that matters to me are the ones I can remember," I say, thinking of my father and my younger self, somewhere in these frozen woods, confused and afraid. I've always pictured my father the way I re-member him—strong, determined, confident—but now that I'm grown and projecting those qualities to those around me, I understand how, most of the time, it's an act.

The sound of crunching feet and cracking branches turns me around. I see a flash of Arthur sprinting downhill. Then he's out of sight.

Levi points in the direction Arthur fled. "So, yeah, think he remem-bers the mountain lion that dang near ate him?"

"Or noticed that it's not summer anymore?" Cassie asks with just a hint of a smile.

I'm actually sure he's keenly aware of both. "Means he's more afraid of something else." I look to Chafin, intending to level a Southern Baptist, condemnation-filled gaze at him. But I don't get the chance.

Chafin's head bursts in time with a rifle report. The red explosion is almost patriotic, flaring out like fireworks.

I dive behind a tree, unaware of who shot, how far away they are, or how many people we're dealing with this time.

Arthur wasn't running from us, or Chafin. He must have seen what was coming and decided to bolt rather than warn us, despite the fact that we saved his life...twice now, by my count.

"Don't know who in tarnation you bootlickers are, but you can get the blazes off my land, or I'll be forced to deal with you all in..." I draw my handgun slowly, glancing at Cassie. She's armed and ready to fight again, but she looks weary and disheartened.

I understand how she feels. Is everyone on this damn mountain going to try killing us?

"What the dickens..."

He's noticed the bodies.

While he's clearly not opposed to taking a life in brutal fashion, he wasn't prepared to come across the scene of a battle. And to be honest, I wasn't really prepared to fight one, or to return to the scene to fight a second.

"Look here." The man's voice has raised an octave higher, no doubt realizing that we've got the potential to be as dangerous, if not more so, than him. "You two Marys and your colored strumpet can vacate this here mountain, or I'll be forced to lay you down aside your friend there."

The threat lacks force and reveals his hand. *I'll be forced...* The man is alone, and judging by the slight slur in his voice, somewhat inebriated. That makes him dangerous, but also vulnerable. The drink doesn't seem to have affected his aim any, but it hasn't helped with his decision making.

"Firstly," I say, trying to emulate the man's accent, which is a strange mix of Southern, Scottish, and Irish. "The man you shot wasn't my friend. Truth is, he was a lawman. And I'm glad you put a bullet in 'im."

"Drat," the man says, no doubt thinking Chafin's death is going to bring him more trouble than he bargained for. I don't bother telling him Chafin's either a child in this time, or not yet born.

"Secondly, are you ol' Pete Boone by chance?"

The man's string of whispered curses are answer enough. Pete Boone was an infamous bootlegger, and I only know about him because my father used to tell me stories about him when we hunted these woods. Told me a fair share of other stories, too. About Indian burial grounds, buried treasure, and Civil War battles. Said the mountain hadn't known peace from the time of the dinosaurs until his father's generation. Seems my father's oral history was more accurate than I'd ever believed.

Tales of Pete Boone, said to be the great, great, great grandfather of Black Creek's most reclusive hermit, Bear Boone, were usually humorous and full of drunken antics. Murder had never been part of the lore, but clearly, the man has no qualms about taking a life.

Cassie catches my eyes, questioning what I'm doing with a stare.

"None of these people are our enemies," I whisper. "I don't want to kill anyone we don't have to."

She motions to Chafin's body. "He murdered him without warning. Without cause."

I offer a slow nod, and say, "Far as I know, there's only two people in these woods that haven't killed anyone."

She doesn't need to ask me who I'm talking about. I doubt the thought of my child-self and my father is too far from the forefront of her mind.

"I'm here on business," I say. "From North Carolina. Been sent looking for the best whiskey in the south. Something not yet on the market. People I work for are fixin' to bottle and market what I bring 'em. Along the way, I've heard tell that your corn whiskey is the finest."

There's a silent moment. Then he says, "Apple brandy ain't half bad, neither."

"Then can we talk business? Or are we gonna trade bullets?"

"You sound like a man with ballocks," Boone says. "Step on out. Let me have a gander at yah. Then I'll decide."

"Don't," Cassie says. Her concern is legitimate. Boone could gun me down the moment I step out, but I don't think he will. The man eventually made a small fortune from his bootlegging. Lost it all to gambling later in life—so my father says—but his ambitions were always grand. As long as he thinks my claims are legitimate, we shouldn't have anything to worry about.

I step out from behind the tree, handgun holstered, rifle aimed toward the ground. When I look up the mountain, the first thing I see is Boone's half-toothed grin. The second is the ten men flanking him on either side, all of them armed with revolvers.

"Well, shit," Boone says, and then he turns to the man beside him. "What are the odds we'd find another man wearing fancy clothes?" He squints at me. "You kinda look like him, too."

13

My backup plan, if my dealings with Boone went wrong, was to fire a few shots over his head and make a quick escape downhill. Despite this going very wrong, I stay rooted in place. Boone said he'd already captured a man whose clothing resembled my own, which I take to mean modern, and he looks like me. That can be only one person. But even if the man has my father, he made no mention of my younger self.

"Never mind what I'm wearing," I say, projecting my father's confidence. "You want to talk business or not?"

My stalwart focus on striking a deal and forced indifference to his revelation, not to mention the gaggle of armed men, broadens his smile.

"All right, all right." He waves me up. "But I can't promise things are gonna end well if I don't like what you have to offer."

"Owen," Cassie whispers. "These aren't good people."

"I'm sure people have said that about me a time or two," I say. "I can handle Boone, and I need to know if the man has my father."

A long sigh deflates her head into a slow nod.

Boone and his men let out a chuckle, and I don't have to ask why. From their perspective, I'm debating with the help.

"Well, you let us know when you're done consultin' with your wet nurse. We'll just wait right here. Ain't got nothing better to do."

Boone leans against a tree, chewing on a wad of tobacco. His good humor belies a growing impatience.

"Apologies," I say. "Our business isn't for the likes of these two. Just leaving them with instructions."

"To divulge the location of my operation should you not return, I suspect," Boone says.

I just smile and turn back to Cassie and Levi, who have stepped out from behind cover and approached me. "Wait as long as you can. If I'm not back inside thirty minutes, don't bother coming for me. If time changes again..." I take a moment to get my bearings. "...stay put. I'll find you."

"Stay put with the dead bodies attracting predators," Levi says. "Solid plan. How about we meet a few hundred feet away in the direction of your choice."

Makes sense. "Think you can get back to where the road should be?"

Cassie and Levi respond in unison. "Yes." Cassie shoots Levi a look to remind him who's next in the line of command and then replies again, this time on her own. "I can."

"You won't mind if some of my men wait with your people," Boone says, putting another monkey wrench in my evolving plan.

"Wouldn't want them divulging the location of your operation," I say, doing my best to sound indifferent to my friends' fate.

"No," he says, all trace of humor missing. "We wouldn't."

I hand my pilfered sniper rifle to Levi. I'm not sure how good a shot he is, but if he grew up hunting with his pa, he knows how to use it. "Only if it's necessary."

Levi gives a nod and backs off like I've dismissed him.

"Take care of the kid," I tell Cassie. "I'm kind of responsible for him."

"Good luck," she says. "With your father."

"Thanks." When she smiles at me, and I wonder if I'll ever see her again, it takes a lot of will power to not hug her goodbye.

She breaks the spell by saying, a bit too loudly, "Yes, massa. I will, massa."

I roll my eyes and tamp down my smile as I turn to face Boone and his men. I give a nod to the four gnarly looking bootleggers headed downhill to keep an eye on Cassie and Levi. They don't return the courtesy as I walk past them. They do eye me though, looking me over like I'm an enigma. Given their soiled state, along with the waft of earthy stank rolling off them, I suppose my cleanliness on its own is out of place. My jacket, taken from one of Chafin's men, isn't exactly spotless, but my face is clean and my beard is trimmed, matching the high and tight haircut I've kept since my days in the service.

Boone holds his ground as I approach. He spits a wad of tobacco on the ground between us to tell me I've gone far enough. He looks me up and down, souring at the sight of me. He twists his lips around, two slugs wrestling, then makes a popping sound with them. "Tell me 'bout this man you work for."

"James Sig Sauer," I say, when I notice him eyeing my weapon. "His father was a plantation owner, back when such things were profitable. When he inherited the business, Mr. Sauer started diversifying. First in fine weaponry. Now he's looking to expand."

"Into the liquor business."

"As previously discussed," I say. "Yes." I motion to the holstered handgun. "If your whiskey is as good as our firearms, I'm sure we can come to an agreement."

He motions to the gun. I've piqued his interest. "May I?"

I point at his men, letting my finger trace a slow line across each and every one of them. "You boys try not to blink."

I draw the weapon slowly, holding it up for them to see. In this time, the most advanced handgun they'd have seen was a six-shooter revolver. It's the weapon of gun slinging legends, but in a fight, it can't compete with the P220.

"Rounds are kept in a magazine," I say, ejecting it and holding it out for them to see the packed in bullets. "Ten rounds total."

I rack the slide, ejecting the chambered round and catching it. I pinch the round between two fingers, letting them see it for a moment before slapping it back in the gun. "Reloading is quick." I eject the magazine again, reach down to my belt where my last replacement waits to be used. I slap the magazine back in, chamber a round and aim it toward one of the men, who flinches back, stumbles, and falls over himself.

The rest of the men aim their weapons at me, but Boone waves at them to stand down when I lower my gun. He snaps twice and points to the pistol. I spin it around and hand it to him.

When he feels the weight of it in his hands, his eyes widen. "Damnation, that feels good." He looks down the sights. "How's the power?"

"It's what I like to call a 'one and done' gun." Inwardly, I cringe at the rhyme, but it sounds like the kind of thing a salesman might say.

"One what?" Boone asks.

"Bullet."

He smiles wide and I see more gaps than teeth. "I like that. One and done." He holds the gun up and chuckles. "And lookee there. Sig Sauer. He put his name on all his guns?"

"Most of the time," I say, "but customization is possible. For his business partners."

"Well, all right then." He turns the gun around and hands it back. "I think we should talk." Fingers to his lips, he lets out a shrill whistle, getting the attention of the men now standing near Cassie and Levi. "We good. Keep an eye on them, nothing more. Understood?"

The men nod, and Boone grins at me. "Your colored servant is a real cherry, but my men won't try nothing without my say so, no matter how pent up they might be."

"Appreciate that," I say, wrestling with the idea of slugging Boone and gunning the lot of them down. "Good help is hard to come by."

"Uh-huh," Boone says, and he strikes out through the snow, backtracking through the prints he and his men made before coming across us. Given the spacing between the prints, they were running, no doubt drawn to Arthur's screams.

"It ain't much farther," Boone says, after ten minutes of walking around the mountain.

"How big is your operation?" I ask.

"Big enough, but there is room for growth."

"How would you feel about relocating, should Mr. Sauer request it?"

"The land of milk and honey is filled with silk and money." He lets out a long hoot of a laugh and slaps the side of his leg. "You ain't the only one who can rhyme."

My laugh is phony, but convincing enough that Boone keeps his legs, and our conversation, moving along. "I'll go where the cash is, plain and simple."

"A man after Mr. Sauer's heart," I tell him.

The trees part and we enter a clearing full of small shacks, smoldering fires, and six homemade pot stills. At the center of it all is a large turnkey distillery, no doubt purchased with Boone's illicit earnings. A collection of women, as dirty and rough around the edges as the men, tends to the camp. They're working the stills, stoking the fires, preparing a meal, and chewing more tobacco than the men.

It's impressive, and I should be expressing my awe at the camp, and the strong scent of whiskey wafting in the air. But I don't. I can't. My full attention resides on the man bound and gagged on the far side of the camp. He's seated on a log, shivering in a T-shirt.

On the surface, he does look like me, if you ignore the tan skin. His pants are modern—black cargo instead of blue jeans. He sports the same kind of high and tight hair. The same deep forehead creases of someone who has seen action before. And he's fit—the kind of fit that only the self-absorbed and men of action are able to maintain.

What he's not, is my father.

"You know him?" Boone asks, noting my attention on the man.

I walk through the camp like I'm supposed to be there, stopping in front of the stranger from my time. "I don't know his name, but I know who he is, if that makes any sense."

"Not sure that it does." Boone crosses his arms, waiting for an explanation.

"I've been dogged during my journey from the south, by men of all sorts. Thieves. Lawmen. Guns for hire. Fended them all off. Like those dead fellas you saw in the woods. But the way they've been coming at me, trying to suppress my business—*our* business—has led me to believe that the federal government is working against my endeavors."

I look up to Boone. "He said a word yet?"

Boone shakes his head. "Not a lick."

I look the man in the eyes. "I reckon if he did, you'd hear a thick Yankee accent." Then to Boone. "How did you come by him?"

"One of my men found him passed out a bit farther uphill. Looks like he took a whack to the head."

He's right about that. The stranger has an egg on his forehead, stained red with blood, which someone was kind enough to wipe away.

"Why don't you just give us a demonstration," Boone says. "Show us what that gun of yours can really do."

"As much as I'd like to, I'd prefer to take this man alive and get what I can from him. I'm sure Mr. Sauer would like to meet the man sent to disrupt his business."

Boone has a good chuckle. "I'm sure he would."

"You understand what's happening right now?" I ask the bound man. "You understand the position you're in?"

He stares up at me, bright blue eyes unflinching. He knows the deal. Knows what I'm really asking him, one man from the future to another. Then he nods.

I shove a finger between his cheek and the gag, yanking it free.

"I'm not telling you nothing," he says, and I can't tell if his accent is supposed to be New York or Boston. Either way, it's shit, but I'm pretty sure that in the days before radio and TV, none of these men have heard an authentic accent from either place.

"You will," I tell him. Then I club him with the butt of my gun, knocking him unconscious. This man might not be my father, but I think he might have some answers. A group of people broke into Synergy and blew up my truck before everything went to hell, and I'm willing to bet this guy was one of them. One way or another, he's coming with me.

I stand up, holstering my weapon. "Now then," I say, rubbing my hands together. "I'll be needing a taste of your finest, and a full bottle for Mr. Sauer to taste for himself."

Boone's grin is as decayed as it is greedy. He waves for me to follow and then steps into a shack with three walls. Inside are several large barrels and an assortment of full bottles. He sorts through the bottles, clinking them about as he looks for the right one. "Ahh," he says. "Nothing can knock a man off his feet quicker than this batch."

When I step into the shack behind him, he turns around, bottle in hand. But he doesn't hand it to me. He swings it at my head, shattering the hard glass against my skull and dropping me to the ground. The last thing I hear is Boone and his men cackling with laughter.

14

I'm cold. My head hurts. I can smell blood—mine—mixed with the odors of burning wood and distilling alcohol. I fight against shivering, a sure sign of being conscious. The sharp sting on my backside reveals I'm seated in snow, hands bound behind my back, head lolled toward the ground. There are voices: men and women, but none close enough to hear clearly, and not nearly enough to suggest Boone and his men are still here.

"They've gone after your friends." The voice comes from my right, and I have little doubt it's the man I clubbed. The fake accent is gone, replaced by one that sounds more Southwestern, though it's hard to say. When I don't respond he says, "I know you're awake. We've both been taught the same tricks. You flinched when you came to."

Definitely ex-military. Probably special forces.

"Why are you here?" I ask without lifting my head or opening my eyes.

"You really want to do this now?"

"You have someplace else to be?"

"We both do," he says, revealing his concern for the people with whom he broke into Synergy, and as near as I can tell, with whom he kicked off this unholy mess. "And I nearly had my hands free before you decided to pistol whip me."

"I had someplace to be before you blew up my truck."

He says nothing, which is admission of guilt enough for me.

"You want the truth?" he asks.

"Why would I want anything else?"

He sighs. "You've gone through life thinking you're on the side of angels. You fight other people's wars. You kill who needs killing. You like to think you don't have a taste for it, but here you are, carrying a gun and wearing a uniform that gives you a license to kill in the right circumstances."

"Like when someone *blows up my truck.*"

"You're missing the point," he says. "You're a soldier. A *good* soldier. You don't question your orders, the mission, or the people in charge. You're loyal to a fault, and your loyalty is misplaced."

He's attempting to paint himself as the good guy, like corporate espionage can be justified. "Not sure how that's any different from being a soldier of fortune," I say, guessing that he's a mercenary.

"Only one of us is paid to be here," he says. "And it would take a lot more than 75k a year with benefits to compromise my integrity."

If the man knows my salary, he likely knows everything else there is to know about me. In that regard, he has me at a disadvantage. "Then what are you supposed to be?"

"To folks in the United States, the minutemen, who fended off Britain's armies using guerilla tactics, are legendary heroes. You were a Raider. You understand what they did and how they did it better than most. You respect it. Emulate it. Improve upon it. If we were a hundred years further back in time, you'd be fighting right alongside them. Without the minutemen, the freedom we enjoy wouldn't have been possible. I think we can both agree on that."

I say nothing. He knows enough about me that I don't need to.

"But to the British, they were something else. The minutemen fought without honor, without respect for the code of war. They struck at random. Caused chaos. Struck fear in all those loyal to the crown."

"So you're a terrorist."

"Only if you're a Redcoat. It's a matter of perspective. The people you work for—with big fucking blinders on—are not worth protecting."

I agree with his theory, but not necessarily with his conclusions. While it's true that I don't know the exact nature of Synergy's research, I know they've done right by me and my community, and they will continue to do so...

As long as we fill a need, I think.

In a painful flash, I realize I might have fallen into a modern version of the trap that ensnared so many people in coal country. But that doesn't make Synergy a target for corporate terrorism. They might be just another soulless corporation, but aside from the grumbling of locals still loyal to their previous master, I haven't heard any complaints about the company, any negative news reports, and have never had to fend off protesters. "What have they done that's so bad?"

"We're in the damn past," the man says through grinding teeth. He's losing his patience. "We're tearing through it. Shattering it. Have you even considered what the ramifications of all this might be? Outside of your own death, I mean? Try to forget, for a moment, that you're a grunt. Focus on the big picture. On the thousands of what-if scenarios. For all we know, this is happening all over the planet. Our world could be tearing itself apart. And you're worried about what? Cassie?"

"You know a lot about me," I say, taking some comfort in the fact that he doesn't seem to know my father and younger self are on this mountain, being whisked through time alongside us and a growing collection of violent, long-dead Appalachians. "But there are a few things you don't know."

"Try me," he says.

"I've been awake for fifteen minutes." I turn toward him for the first time. He's seated beside me, still wearing his black pants and T-shirt, his head stained with blood from where I struck him. He meets my gaze, unflinching. "And..." I draw my hands out from behind my back, shedding the rope used to tie me in place.

Then he surprises me by revealing his own hands. "These assholes have no idea how to tie a knot."

Tension swells between us. We both have reasons to attack the other, but that would only get us shot. The only way out of our predicament is to work together, and we both know it, no matter how much we don't like it.

As we both set to work covertly untying our feet, I ask, "You got a name?"

"You can call me Minuteman."

"Cute," I say.

"I'll just call you Owen."

He's goading me, knowing I can't react. "You're kind of a dick."

"I've been told." He slips the loosened ropes up and over his toes, and then leans back, sitting like he's still bound.

My efforts take a little longer because I'm doing my best to appear unconscious, which means moving very slowly. Minuteman is mostly hidden behind me, affording him a little more freedom of mobility.

"Despite what you think, I'm not your enemy." He sounds sincere, but he's no doubt been trained in the art of deception, just like me. Part of modern guerilla warfare is working your way into an existing community, gaining their trust, and recruiting them to fight alongside you. The more people you convert to the cause, the greater your chances of success. It's a technique I've used several times in the past without flaw...until Boone.

"And despite what you think," I say. "I'm not a killer. These people might be the ancestors of people I know from our time."

"Pretty sure a paradox is the least of our worries," Minuteman says. "If it will help you sleep better, I'll try not to kill them. But if they don't leave me a choice..."

I nod. I've made the same call several times already today. "I get it."

"Do you?" he asks. "Here's the real difference between us. The only value my life has over these people is that they can't stop what's happening."

"And you can?"

"I know to try."

"By killing a bunch of scientists at Synergy." I have zero doubt that was the original plan. Search and destroy. Equipment and personnel.

"First, I'm going to help them undo all this shit. Then...I suppose that depends on whether or not they've learned their lesson."

"And the people who try to stop you?" I ask, thinking of my crew still inside the facility. My friends.

He shrugs. "You know the deal. It's not personal. But I am giving *you* a chance to do the right thing. We could walk through the gate together. Instead of me blowing it up."

It's a tempting offer, but without a way to confirm anything he's said, it's possible he's just running a con-game on me. In his position, I'd do the same. Hell, we're about to run one together. But that's where our collusion comes to an end. His goal includes causing harm to the people I've promised to protect. That puts us at odds, even if we want the same outcome—to be returned to the present.

"You ready?" he asks.

In answer to his question, I flop onto my side and start spasming, making sure to keep my feet together and my hands behind my back. With all the movement, it's unlikely anyone will notice the ropes are missing.

"Hey!" Minuteman shouts. "Someone help him!"

Voices rise. A handful of men and women hobble over, their feet slurping through the mud created by burning fires and melting snow. But they don't lend a hand, or even get close enough to attack. They simply form a semi-circle around us and laugh at my misfortune.

"Look at him go!" a man shouts. "Like a fish with a hook in 'im!"

One laugh is louder than the rest. Closer than the rest. I open my eyes to find a beast of a woman standing just three feet away. She's dressed in a trench coat—my trench coat. Well, the coat I took from a dead man two hours ago, and thirty years from now. What I don't see on her, or anyone else, is my P220. But there is little doubt about who has the gun. Boone might not have been impressed by me or my story, but he had eyes for the pistol. Ultimately, that might have been my undoing. Immediate satisfaction of greed can sometimes outweigh the long-term benefits of patience.

Knowing my chances aren't going to get any better than they are right now, I shove my feet off the ground as hard as I can, spinning my body around. Laughter comingles with gasps. And then, before anyone can react, I kick out hard, connecting with the woman's knee.

The crack of bone, and the scream that follows, silences the laughter entirely. In the brief respite that follows, I hear the sound of distant gunfire. Then our fight starts.

15

I want to tell these people that violence isn't necessary. That they can avoid the pain and potential death by just letting us go, and getting the hell off this mountain before time slips again and they find themselves, like us, caught in the flux.

But I know it's not possible. I've seen enough killers to know these people won't think twice about taking our lives. We've seen their operation, and now I've attacked one of their own. I have no doubt Boone was planning to put bullets in our heads once he was done with us, so I don't feel horrible about what comes next. But I do regret it.

Taking a security job kept a gun on my hip, but I never believed I'd have to use it. The business of taking lives—for survival or for Uncle Sam—weighs heavy on the soul. I'd hoped to spend my life wandering Synergy's wooded fence line, accompanied by the memory of my father, letting my demons fade into the morning fog.

Alas...

I spring from the ground as the oversized woman collapses in a writhing mass, clutching her ruined knee. She'll survive the blow if she stays down, but she'll have a limp to remember me by. A rifle cracks as I kick it to the side. The man holding the weapon snarls in frustration, but the sound is cut short when I chop his throat.

The rifle comes free as the shooter crumples to the ground. I wield the weapon like a baseball bat, clutching the hot barrel and swinging hard at a woman charging with a rusted butcher knife. As the blade comes down, I connect with her clutched hand. She shouts in agony as her fingers break. The blade twinkles like a disco ball as it spins away, forcing several of the bootleggers to duck.

In the brief respite, I glance at Minuteman, watching him work through a gaggle of men and women with the same speed, skill, and ruthless attention to subduing his enemy without killing them.

He's an impressive fighter, and if I'm honest, a bit more in his prime than I am . His attacks are fluid, lacking any trace of hesitation. He's ten steps ahead of the bootleggers, who are half drunk on their own product, and likely haven't been in a fight with anyone who wasn't also inebriated.

No matter how impressive a fighter is, there's not much he can do about a shotgun shell, though. When I spot a man with an early pump-action shotgun, raising the weapon toward Minuteman's back, I abandon my fighting stance and dive over the woman with the broken hand. A quick roll and I'm back on my feet. The man doesn't see me coming until I've already got a hand on the fore-end. I pump the weapon in rapid succession like I'm working out with a shake-weight, ejecting four shells and rendering it useless just as the man pulls the trigger with a *click.*

"On your six," Minuteman says. It's not a thank you, but there's no doubt now. We're in this together. For the moment, we're brothers in arms.

I kick hard without looking and feel the soft impact of a man's gut. A loud, "Oof!" is followed by the sound of a crumpling man desperate to suck in a breath. Like the other people we've incapacitated, he's out of the fight for now, but will live.

When I turn to look at the man, I'm caught off guard by the sight of two women, barreling over him, empty hands outstretched, dirty fingers hooked to rake and claw. There's no avoiding or deflecting them. The pair collides with me, and the three of us spill to the ground.

They lay into me like beasts, screaming and scratching. But there's no skill behind the attack, and even less thought. They're lost in rage, probably because I've injured someone important to them. Instead of kneeing me in the nuts, or gouging at my eyes, they tear at my chest, doing a number to my shirt and scratching my skin, but little else.

As a man with a ridiculously large mustache closes in with a hammer in his hand and murder in his eyes, I clutch the womens' hair in my hands. With a yank, the pair comes apart, and with a shove, their heads collide. It's not enough to knock either unconscious, but it knocks the fight out of them.

The mustache-man swings hard with the hammer, letting out a bellow. I roll backward, narrowly avoiding the strike. Instead of hitting me, the hammer slaps into the muddy earth. The man gives it a yank, but the tool-turned-weapon is stuck. He pulls hard with a grunt, giving me time to get to my feet and plot a counter-attack.

But it's not necessary. Minuteman soars through the air, driving his foot into the side of the man's head. The man topples like a felled tree, landing in a cushion of slush.

I spin around, fists clenched, ready to continue the fight. But it's over. A dozen men and women are on the ground in various states of consciousness and injury. But none are dead.

Minuteman doesn't strike me as the merciful type, and his business on this land, in any time, is illegal. He's a killer, of that there is no doubt, but he's also a professional. Though they were armed, it was clear none of these people were a significant threat, not like Chafin and his men, and not like Boone and his.

I'm about to ask him why he went easy on our attackers when the distant pop of a 9mm handgun reminds me that the bootlegger hit-squad has gone after Cassie and Levi.

When Minuteman turns toward the sound of gunfire, I say, "I could use your help."

He turns away from the gunfire, looking uphill. I'm not sure if he's looking toward the carved-flat summit where the Synergy facility was built, or if he's thinking about his own people. Either way, it's clear his attention is someplace else. "I could ask the same of you."

I back away, stepping downhill, resisting the urge to sprint. I'm not comfortable letting this man out of my sight, but subduing him in time to help my friends isn't possible. Hell, I might not even be *able* to take him. And if I could, what am I going to do, run down the mountain with him slung over my shoulders?

I decide to put a pin in our confrontation. "Whatever you were planning—"

"It's too late to finish," he says, crouching down to recover the pump shotgun and its ejected shells. "We're clearly too late."

As he sets about reloading the weapon, I ask. "You were trying to prevent this?"

"This is just one of a dozen theoretical outcomes for what they were doing."

When I say nothing, he says, "You really have no idea, do you? What they were doing? The forces they were playing with?"

My blank stare is answer enough. He shakes his head, not quite in disgust. It's more like disappointment.

"You're not exactly the bad guy I was told you'd be." he says and then he grins. "Would have made killing you easier."

I'm the bad guy?

My face must betray my twisted up emotions, because Minuteman chuckles at me, shaking his head. He pumps the shotgun, chambering the first of four shells. When the mustached man reaches up for the weapon, Minuteman slugs him back down to the ground.

I stop in my tracks as his last words filter past my confusion. *Would have made killing you easier.*

Instead of putting a handful of metal pellets in my chest, Minuteman catches me off guard by throwing the loaded weapon to me. I catch it by the barrel as the sound of more gunfire rolls up the mountainside. The sharp crack of a rifle tears across the landscape, no longer being answered by the 9mm's report.

"Better get moving, soldier," he says. When I turn around and sprint downhill, I hear his voice chasing me. "Good luck."

I race through the camp, leaping from the clearing into the woods, and I charge downhill without returning the sentiment.

What Minuteman and his people had planned to do at Synergy is a mystery, but a man like him could be capable of anything from corporate espionage to wholesale destruction. Based on the state of my truck before I was swept into the past, I'm thinking it was the latter.

My thoughts focus on the truck. Why did he wait to detonate the bomb? Minuteman isn't the kind of person that makes mistakes like that. Despite his parting joke, killing me had never been the plan. It's conceivable he hadn't intended to kill anyone, which begs the question: *What was he planning? And why?*

Having to ask that question at all irks me. Now, anyway. Before today, I was happy to live a simple life, collect a paycheck, and do my job. But my ignorance to Synergy's work has put me, and those I've brought to the company, at risk.

And that seriously pisses me off.

The cold air burns my lungs as I sprint. My body groans from the effort, not so much from the run—gravity helps me along—but from the cold. I forgot to reclaim my coat, and my backside is still wet from sitting in half-frozen mud. If I don't warm up soon, I might have to add frostbite to my growing list of problems and physical ailments. The small hole in my arm and the wound on my head are bad enough. Missing a few fingers might make firing a weapon or even throwing an effective punch a challenge.

The sound of gunfire stops. I try not to consider the mind-numbing scenario in which I'm too late and my friends have been gunned down. But it's impossible not to think about, and if that's the case, Boone and his men will not receive the same merciful treatment as the men and women sprawled out in the slush behind me.

A body on the ground slows my run to a jog. With snow underfoot, a quiet approach is impossible, but slowing down prevents me from missing details. Like the spent bullet casings covering the ground like pepper over mashed potatoes. They look homemade, the kind you'd expect to find in this era. I slow even more at the body, taking a moment to look at the fallen man's face. I wince at the two, small bullet holes in his forehead. They're dead center and just an inch apart—the spread of a marksman...or woman.

Farther on, I pass two more bodies and then a scattering of 9mm shell casings. There are enough of them that I'm positive Cassie ran out of ammunition, which is probably why I haven't heard shots in a while. Scanning the collection of tracks, I piece together the scene. The initial point of conflict is marked by a line of deep footprints facing off against two more sets, just ten feet away. There's a lot of movement through the area as Cassie and Levi moved to several fallback positions behind large trees. Then I find Cassie's and Levi's path of retreat, which has been followed by more than a dozen men, all of them headed downhill.

Away from Synergy and the answers held within its walls.

Shotgun in hand and ready to even the odds in favor of my friends, if they're still alive, I charge downhill. I make it only ten steps before a branch slides out from behind a tree and between my legs. There's a stab of pain in my shin as I stumble. When I look back to face my attacker, I fail to notice the large fist approaching my face until it's too late.

Aww, shi—

16

"You need to get up."

The warm comfort of darkness surrounds me, beckoning me back to unconsciousness. "I'm staying here."

"No choice in the matter." It's my father's voice, calm, but with a hint of irritation. He's not one to easily lose his temper, but this is an old fight, and one I never win.

With a click, my bedroom light flares to life, squeezing my eyes shut. I reel back from the glow, like a vampire from the sun, pulling blankets over my head. "Can't we just skip one week?"

My father's weight on the bedside rolls me against his back. I'd never tell him, but I take comfort in his strength, in his indomitable will, and his strident sense of right and wrong. He brings order to the world.

"You know why we go."

I do, but I'm not going to say it.

"The last thing your mother asked me to do was raise you in the church, and come hell or high water, I aim to fulfill her dyin' wish."

"But why?" I ask. "She's not here to know." I instantly regret the words, but I stand by the question. Fighting against the urge to apologize, I wait for an answer.

"Son..." His heavy hand rests on my back. "I struggle with my faith. Ain't no secret in that, but I'll be damned before I give up the possibility of seeing your Ma again. So I go to church, every week, and try to scrounge up enough belief that I might someday find myself in the same place as your mother. Had you known her... Had you had the chance to love her... I reckon you'd want to do the same."

The heartbreak in his voice brings tears to my eyes. I hide them, and my face, under the blanket. My biggest regret about my mother's death is that my birth was the cause. The conviction of my father's words makes me miss the possibility of a mother, but my father has always been enough for me. If not for his pain, I'm not sure I'd ever know I was missing something.

"Can I wear my jeans?" I ask. He typically makes me get gussied up for church, and each year he spends money he shouldn't on a new suit for me. I have a collection of them in my closet, from toddler size to my now eleven-year-old size. I've sat through hundreds of services wearing those suits and have recently come to the conclusion that God would prefer us naked. Not because he's a perv, but because that's how he intended us to be. Getting dressed up in a way *people* think is nice isn't going to help with the problem of sin. Pastor says that's grace, but he dresses nice, too.

Sometimes I feel like I'm the only one really paying attention to the words, 'cause I don't see them playing out in the congregation. When the preaching is done, the hymns have been sung, the benediction given, and the pot luck food is warming up, the women gossip. The men brag and boast. The kids fight, steal, and bully. And yet, if you walk into that white-steepled building in anything less than a suit no one in these parts can really afford, you're destined for the fiery pits of hell.

I shake my head under the blanket, rolling my eyes. I fail to see how the people in that place, who seem to have no understanding of what Jesus taught, will help me or my father work up the courage to believe in God and see my mother again.

"You're old enough to make that decision for yourself," he says. "I'm not going to force clothes on to you, but as long as you live under this roof, you'll be joining me every Sunday. Understood?"

I nod under the blanket, relieved that I don't have to wear the suit, but horrified by the prospect of being condemned by our friends and neighbors for it.

His weight lifts off the bed. "Pancakes are on. Be ready in ten. When church lets out, we'll hit Adel early and see if we can't bag a deer."

"What do you mean, early?" I ask. "Church doesn't get out until nearly noon."

"Forgot to tell you," my father says. I peel the blanket back to watch him maneuver his way past my toys, toward the window. He gives the shade a yank and lets it spin up, revealing just a hint of orange light in the East. "We're going to the early service. Now..." He stands above me, a slight grin on his rugged face that's framed in a graying beard. "Get up!" He yanks the blankets off me and the whole house begins to shake.

I spasm into sudden and full alertness.

"Get up," my father says, yanking me to my feet. "They're coming back."

"Dad," I say, confused by the sudden transition from my bedroom— the same room I sleep in now—to the woods. "What are you—"

"Ain't your pa, fella," he says, clearing the fog of confusion. He leans me against a tree, holding me in place. "And I'm sorry for knocking you for a loop. Never was good at pulling my punches. But I thought you might have been one'a them. Judging by your clothes, I reckon you're one of us."

I look him over, dressed in camouflage, looking as powerful as I remember. I can smell his Old Spice, and it nearly brings tears to my eyes. My father is real. And alive. And damn near to hugging me. But something about him is not like I remember.

He's afraid.

Not for me, or for himself. A small hand clutches his pant leg. I'm standing behind him. The younger me. I didn't live through this. I have no memory of it. I can't say for sure how I'm feeling, but I have a pretty good idea.

If Dad's afraid, I'm terrified.

"I'm good," I say, pushing myself up. In truth, I'm still a bit dazed, but I've pushed through worse. Survival sometimes demands discomfort. "Who's coming?"

"I don't know what to call them," my father says. "A bunch of hill-billies wearing rags and carrying antique weapons."

"Were they chasing a woman and a young man?" I ask.

"Friends of yours?" He doesn't wait for any answer. "They were in a bad sort. Outgunned. Normally, I would'a helped them, but..." He glances back at younger me, who's just starting to poke his head out to look at me.

When I say, "Family comes first," he looks relieved. Then his eyes widen a bit. "You're the fella from the road. Out for a walk. The younger fella, he was with the woman."

I nod. "That's them."

Downhill, a tree branch cracks.

"We should hide," he says.

That shouldn't be difficult for the two of them. Both are dressed for the hunt, wearing camo from head to toe. I remember the clothes being sweltering in the summer heat. They're probably not quite enough in the current frigid conditions, but neither of them are shivering.

"Up there," I point to a fallen tree, its branches still intact and full of dead leaves, forming a mesh of broken lines. Like my father's camouflage, it will conceal us from sight, but allow us to keep an eye on anyone searching for us.

"They'll track our prints," he says, and curses under his breath. He's just realized that approaching the battle scene was a mistake that's left him and his son exposed to men prone to violence.

"Walk backward," I say, "Owen first. Then you. I'll follow." I look the pair over. "Where's the rifle?"

My father's face screws up with suspicion. *Shit. I used my name.* Before he can point that out, I address it. "I heard you talking, before I opened my eyes. You said his name."

I can tell he's not sure whether or not he did.

"And I know you have a rifle because you were out hunting. Heard the shots earlier."

Another cracking branch, this one closer, forces him to let go of his doubt. He reaches behind the tree I'm leaning against and plucks out the old Winchester 1895. It's a powerful weapon best known for being the rifle of choice for President Roosevelt while on African safari. I'm not sure how many animals he killed with the weapon, but it's damn near powerful enough to take down most anything he encountered. My father will have it loaded with four rounds of 7.62x54mmR, which are rimmed and still used in some of the world's armies, most famously in the Russian Dragunov sniper rifle. I haven't seen the rifle since I was a child. Unlike the house, which I inherited, the rifle was one of the many heirlooms sold off by my grandfather, who'd acquired it during World War II. It's like seeing an old friend again.

"What makes you think you're a better shot?" he asks, holding the weapon back.

"I had a good teacher...and I'm a Marine." I give my haircut a rub, like the high and tight style is all the proof he needs. "Trust me. You take care of your son, and let me take care of the both of you. I'll die before letting anything happen to you."

The conviction in my voice seems to surprise my father, dissolving his apprehension. "And this?" He reaches behind the tree again, recovering the pump shotgun. "I reckon it's not yours."

"No, sir," I say. "But you should hang on to it. I can do more with the rifle."

He mulls that over for a moment and then offers his hand, taking time for a proper introduction despite the fact that Boone and his men might be coming our way. "William McCoy."

I shake his hand. He's got a firm, almost painful grip. The moment is surreal. I'd only ever experienced the gentle side of him. He could lose his temper, and was a firm disciplinarian, but never violent. Never scary. Now, as an adult, I can see in his eyes the potential for both. "Kevin," I say and then throw in the first last name that comes to mind—Cassie's. "Dearborn."

There's a flicker of excitement in Owen's eyes as he leans out around our father and looks me in the eyes for the first time. I've looked at my own eyes in the mirror countless times, but seeing them in a head that is not my own...but *is* my own...is almost disorienting. When he sees me, Owen looks a bit disappointed, but then collects himself and then offers his hand.

I hesitate to shake it. I've seen time travel movies where touching yourself in the past can blow up the universe. But since neither of us are in the right time, and movie science is questionable to say the least, I take his small hand and give it a shake. Then I point to our hiding spot and tell him, "Hurry. Backward the whole way."

My younger self gives a nod and sets to the task, walking backward uphill, leaving a trail that gives the appearance of someone approaching, not leaving. With all the other tracks around, I reckon Boone and his men won't give them a second glance, but if they do, they won't have a reason to follow them.

My father hands me the rifle and keeps the shotgun. I take it in my left hand and run my right over the barrel. Then I look down the sights, give it a heft, and pat the weapon's side with the same affection you might show a pet dog. I run through the routine each time I hold a new weapon, or in this case, an old one. I've done it since...

Crap...

I glance up at my father, whose expression has turned suspicious again. He's looking at my eyes, *really* looking. I can see the question on the tip of his tongue, but he's interrupted by the sound of voices, agitated and close.

"Go!" I whisper, and I turn to guard his retreat.

17

There's no time to follow in my father's reverse footsteps, so I duck behind a broad tree and watch his progress. Steam puffs from his living lungs as he walks backward up the hill, following Owen's small prints, step for step, leaving only one set and obscuring the child-size depressions which would stand out in these woods, in this harsh time.

He gives me a concerned look, but the sound of voices, nearly on my position, chases him into the tangle of dead branches and leaves. As soon as he's on the ground, the camouflage he's wearing makes him invisible.

I, on the other hand, am very visible. The moment someone walks past this tree, the pale white skin of my bare arms and face will stand out.

The tree's rough bark feels good on my back as I lean against it. I roll back and forth, letting the trunk scratch and massage some tension away. Then I stand still and close my eyes. My breathing slows and grows shallow, preventing the fog of exhalation from giving away my position.

"I still don't know what she was shootin'," a man says. "Ain't never seen a gun can fire that many bullets, that fast. And tarnation, could she shoot."

"This is why they should'a never been freed," Boone says. "Didn't I tell ya, Buck? Trouble. All of them. Woman like that belongs stooped over in a field, not shooting up my mountain."

The racism might be genuine, but I'm pretty sure it has more to do with bolstering their bruised egos. Sounds like Cassie gave them a fight they won't forget. The question is, did she survive it?

I turn my attention away from the sound of their voices and to the crunch of feet in snow. There's just two of them, heading back uphill.

Questions compound and mix with anger.

Knowing my father and younger self are watching, I point two fingers at the fallen tree and then my eyes, pulling my fingers down and closing my eyes. I hope he understands my meaning. Owen might be me, but he's still a kid, and I don't want him, or myself, having the emotional scars of seeing what comes next. I have no intention of killing either man, but if I'm left without a choice, I won't hesitate.

And if it turns out Cassie or Levi have been killed...

"At least I got this. Pretty and deadly. Mmmhmm. Sure wish I knew what kind of bullets it takes." Boone walks past the tree's right side, holding my handgun up, admiring its futuristic shape. The slide is locked back, the ammunition spent, no doubt fired at Cassie and Levi.

He doesn't notice me until I'm in motion. He spins, wide-eyed and blood-spattered. The rifle's butt catches him in the forehead, toppling him back. He lands on the snow-covered slope and slides several feet before coming to a limp stop.

His compatriot, Buck, a mountain of a man carrying a shotgun, is quicker than he looks, but not very smart. I dive behind the tree as the man wages a one-man war against its bark, like the pellets might some-how penetrate the wood and strike me. All he manages to do is create several bald spots on the tree's surface, and empty his shotgun.

When I hear the first useless trigger pull, I round the tree and raise the rifle. My instinct is to put a bullet in the man's head, but my intention is to capture him and Boone alive. But Buck has adjusted to the situation, swinging the shotgun like a bat, connecting with the rifle hard enough to knock it from my hands.

I have a moment of concern for the rifle's welfare, afraid I've taken the heirloom from my father only to see it destroyed a few minutes later. Worry shifts from the rifle to my life when Buck swings a second time, nearly taking off my head.

The shotgun slams into the tree when I duck, splintering more wood from the old oak and shattering the weapon. Had that hit my head, I'd have a shotgun-shaped indentation in my brain.

The impact forces a shout of pain from Buck, but he's undeterred. While the people Boone left behind at the camp weren't fighters, this man is no stranger to action. He's shit with a shotgun, but given the thickness of his knuckles, I'm guessing Buck's weapons of choice are his fists. He takes the pain in stride, never losing focus, closing the distance again.

I've fought men like this before. Powerful. Indomitable. The secret to defeating them isn't matching them punch for punch, seeing who can deliver the most pain in the shortest amount of time. It's the technique perfected by Muhammad Ali—the rope-a-dope. All that muscle needs oxygen and the more he swings and misses, the more exhausted he'll become. Sometimes it takes minutes, sometimes just thirty seconds, but the big man will eventually lack the strength to lift his own arms. That's why the best fighters find a balance between power and endurance. It's what separates the—

"Oof!" The second punch in a surprise combo strikes my arm. I stumble back, gripping the numbed limb. The man is faster than he looks.

I take another step back, rethinking my strategy. Buck smiles at me, mistaking my movement for fear, or perhaps retreat. He's certainly humbled me, but I don't back down that easily.

Buck peels his jacket away. It's lined with thick fur that gave him a bulked up look. With the coat missing, I can now see that he's got the body of a fighter, not to mention a good foot on me, and several extra inches of reach.

What he doesn't have, is training. But I'm not going to underestimate him again. Assuming he can fight as well as, if not better, than me, I need to come up with a way to end this sooner than later.

When in doubt, fight dirty. I don't think it will make my father proud, but we'll be alive at the end.

I glance to the rifle. There's a chance I could reach it before Buck could land a punch, but then again, he might crack my skull before I could lift it out of the snow. When he steps closer, cracking his knuckles, the possibility is eradicated. The only way to reach the weapon is to go through him.

Matching his pace, I back away, inflating his sense of superiority while simultaneously frustrating him. When he raises his hands and waves me toward him, shouting, "C'mon!" I grant his wish.

I charge.

He throws a punch that would likely have killed me if I hadn't slid onto my back. Snow and the steep grade carry me under his swing and toward the exposed soft spot between his legs. One good shot and the fight will be over.

I kick hard, planting the sole of my foot between his legs. But the soft squish of compressing testicles is missing. All I feel through my boot is the firm resistance of barren taint.

Stunned, I look up into Buck's eyes and see shame-fueled rage. I don't want to know how or why, but the man whose name suggests animal masculinity and has the body to match, has been castrated.

"Fuck," I mutter as his big foot rises above me and crashes down toward my face. My hands and arms scream in pain as I catch his boot. There's a moment of equilibrium, but his strength and weight over-power me. Before he can compress my face, I twist his foot hard, and kick out his planted leg.

He topples back, falling downhill, but he has no trouble rolling back onto his feet.

I scramble up and decide to press the attack. I leap into the air, sailing toward his head thanks to my elevated position. My airborne foot will deliver the same kind of knock-out kinetic energy that his punches contain...if it connects.

It doesn't.

Buck swats my foot aside, sending me into a chaotic tumble. If that wasn't bad enough, he grasps hold of my belt and propels me downhill. I fly out over the descending ground and careen toward a painful landing.

The only things that save me from certain doom and death, are the cushion of the snow and the angled terrain. Instead of coming to a sudden, bone-breaking stop, I hit the ground and slide. A sapling gives me a good whack in the back of the head, but I escape the embarrassing failed attack without significant injury.

Buck sets upon me as I stand, forcing me into a discombobulated defense. I do my best to duck and weave his series of quick punches, but he connects three in a row, stunning me and leaving me wide open for a haymaker that will end the fight.

I can't match his strength, so I decide to fight smart.

As his arm comes around toward my head, I snap a quick strike into the inside of his arm, just a few inches above his elbow. He shouts in pain, as I crush a knuckle into the pressure point. The strike numbs his arm, diffusing the muscles behind his punch, but since an object in motion tends to stay in motion, his fist continues forward into my face.

I'm sprawled to the ground, but spared the knockout force of Buck's punch thanks to the pressure point and rolling with the impact rather than trying to resist it.

"Wha'd you do to my arm?" Buck shouts, clutching the limp arm.

The pain and tingling consuming his limb will fade in seconds. I scramble to my feet, mentally preparing a series of strikes I think will end the fight. But the moment I stand, the world starts to spin, and I drop back to my knees.

Buck grins at my delirium and takes a step toward me, cocking back his still fully functional left fist.

Then he flinches to a stop. His eyes roll back as he snaps rigid and then falls facedown into the snow.

My father stands behind him, clutching the shotgun he used to club Buck. "No offense," he says, "but you were getting your ass kicked."

I laugh. I've never heard my father say anything remotely unsavory, but like many parents, the guarded language used around children fades when they're out of earshot.

He reaches down a hand and yanks me to my feet. While he binds Buck's hands behind him, I trudge over to Boone, who's just coming to. Before he can push himself up, I put a knee into his back and let my weight rest on it. "I'm going to ask you some questions, and if I don't like your answers..."

Motion draws my attention uphill.

Young Owen is out of hiding and watching me closely.

Behind him, the mountain is lost in a cascade of shimmering light.

18

"Owen!" my father shouts, his arms outstretched toward his son.

I'm faster than I remember being, sprinting down the mountainside, eyes wide. "It's happening again!"

The sound of his voice is drowned out by the growing buzz and rumble.

"It will pass," I say, attempting to reassure my father. "We'll be okay."

He says nothing, but gives me a serious stare after collecting Owen in his arms. As a father, his sole mission right now is to keep my younger self safe. The look in his eyes says he has no idea how to do that, and that he doesn't share my faux confidence, though he attempts to hide that from Owen.

"Just close your eyes and hold on," he says. "It will pass. Just let it pass. Stay relaxed, just like before."

I find myself taking his advice. While keeping my weight on Boone's back, I let myself relax, welcoming the flux, rather than resisting it.

Boone, on the other hand, loses his shit. He hasn't lived through this yet. Hasn't been torn from his own time and deposited in another. Hasn't seen the distorted wave rolling down the mountain, or experienced the thunderous roar of its passing. His scream blends in with the cacophony of sound.

I close my eyes to avoid feeling sickened by the sight of the world shattering and bending around me. My insides twist as the effect passes through us, but it's not nearly as bad this time. When the sound of it races downhill, I open my eyes again.

Steam rises from my wet arms. Goosebumps rise up as the temperature shift hits my skin. It's at least eighty degrees. For a moment, I think it's summer again, but then I look up and find the trees covered in buds, ready to sprout leaves. A warm spring, the air perfumed with the smell of new growth. This is my favorite season in Appalachia. It feels hopeful, even if nothing has changed for most of the people living in these mountains.

Beneath me, Boone heaves. I stand before he can puke, watching as he retches into the damp, leafy forest floor. "What..." he manages to say, but that's all he gets out. He doesn't need to finish the question.

"I'll wait 'till you're done giving your lunch back to the Earth," I say, "then I'll attempt to explain what I know—" I meet my father's eyes, and then my own. "—to all of you."

It takes Boone's body another thirty seconds to stop revolting against the sudden shift through time. He pushes himself against a tree trunk, staring up at the blue sky above, now easily visible through the collection of ruby buds. "Where is the snow?"

All the fight and bravado have fled Boone. He's now just a confused and weary man. His friend, Buck, has been spared the negative effects of being carried through time on account of his being unconscious. He'll be thrown for a loop when he wakes up, both from the shift in time, and the concussion he'll no doubt be sporting.

Speaking of concussions... While some of my nausea fades, a good portion remains. I'm not a hundred percent steady on my feet, either. All thanks to Buck's giant fists. If I don't get some rest soon, reaching Synergy and finding Cassie and Levi will be the least of my problems.

I collect my father's rifle from the ground, where it's partially embedded in soil. Has the terrain changed? It looks largely the same, but it's possible the ground has shifted. I glance uphill and note that fallen tree behind which my father and Owen hid is now standing tall.

My eyes widen as I consider the horrifying question: what happens if time shifts and you're standing where a tree once was? Or even worse, another person?

"Ain't you gonna answer me!" Boone looks close to losing his mind. A man of his education during this time period is more likely to chalk up the change in season to witchcraft. Appalachian people have always been a superstitious lot, believing in supernatural hoodoo as surely as they do Jesus Christ.

I sit down across from him, rifle cradled in my lap. I massage my temples and try to think of a way to explain what's happening.

"Hey," my father says. He's standing above me holding out a hand. "For your pain."

I hold my hand out and accept three acetaminophen pills. Then he unclips a water bottle from his hip and offers it. I take the pills and the water, grateful for my father's preparedness. I nod my thanks, swallow the pills, and turn to Boone. "I'm going to ask you a question, and I want a straight answer."

When he says nothing, I ask, "What year is it?"

His face screws up. "Now why would—"

"Answer the question," I growl, my patience for long-dead assholes at an end.

"1887," he says. "Now what—"

I hold out a hand, silencing him. I look my father in the eyes. "And what about you two? What's the year?"

"1985," Owen answers.

"That ain't..." Boone shakes his head. "You've lost your minds."

"And for you?" my father asks, already catching on.

"2019."

I see a flicker of surprise in my father's eyes, then resignation to the fact that we're being tossed through time.

Owen, on the other hand, is thrilled. "You're from *the future?*"

"Horseshit," Boone mumbles.

"Are there flying cars?" Owen asks. "A colony on Mars? Teleporters?"

I forgot how much I used to love science fiction. "None of those things. But we do have the Internet."

He's hardly impressed.

"And robots that look like people."

His eyes widen. "Like the Terminator?"

"Arnold Schwarzenegger was the governor of California," I say, remembering that I had a poster of him in full Conan regalia, posing with Red Sonja, on my bedroom wall.

"Whoa," my young self says, now impressed with the future, despite the lack of flying cars and interplanetary colonies.

"Fail to see how he'd make a worthwhile governor," my father says. "More muscle than brains."

"You don't even want to know who our president is." I chuckle, picturing my father's response to the news. He's a staunch Republican, but in the 80s politics still had a measure of sanity. Then again, it was Reagan who ushered in the age of celebrities becoming politicians.

"I'm sorry," Boone says, and then shouts, "But I don't know what in tarnation you all are going on about! Where is the damned snow? Where the hell are we?"

"We haven't gone anywhere," I tell him. "We're still on the same mountainside. Still in the same woods. We're just in a different time period."

"What'a you mean, 'time period?'"

"I mean it's no longer 1887."

"And what year are you proposing it is?"

I shrug. "No way to know unless we meet someone. Since the first wave in 2019, I've experienced four jumps back in time. The first was 1985." I look at my father. "That's when I ran into you in the truck. We were still trying to figure it out."

"But you knew something was off," my father observes. "I saw the way you were avoiding looking at me. Even now, it's making you uncomfortable."

I see where the conversation is going, and I know where it ends, but I'm not sure I'm ready for that, and I have no idea what the consequences might be. When it comes to Boone, and Chafin, and Arthur, and all the men associated with them, I can't think of a solid connection to my future. But my father and my younger self... Everything said and done in their presence could affect my future.

"Best guess," I say, hoping to shift the conversation away from that questionable subject, "we're sometime in the 1800s. Longest jump back so far was sixty-four years."

"But you don't know. They could be longer."

I shake my head. "I don't know much of anything, aside from the fact that the people responsible for all this are at the top of this mountain."

"At the mine?" my father asks.

"Ain't nothing up there but stone and wind," Boone says.

"In my time, the mine is closed." I note the disappointed look on my father's face. He invested his life—literally—in that mine, and he believed in its long-term potential to transform our community. "A company named Synergy bought Adel and a lot of the land in and around town. I'm not really certain about what they were doing, but I know there was a lot of cutting edge science involved."

"You're saying we've been caught up in some kind of physics experiment gone wrong?" my father asks.

"That's pretty much the gist, yeah."

"And you know this because..."

"I work for them."

My father tenses.

"In security," I add. "I didn't know what they were doing, and I honestly still don't. But I aim to find out, and if I can, set things right."

"Then we'll be joining you," my father says.

"I ain't going nowhere with any of you all," Boone says. "Might as well shoot me now. Get it over with."

I push myself to my feet, doing my best to hide my continuing state of wooziness. I brandish the rifle, letting it make up for my lack of physical prowess. "You're going to go back to your people and see that they're okay. Then you're going to *not* attack, kill, or capture anyone you might come across, from *any* time. If you find someone, tell 'em what you know and try to keep them with you. Whatever enemies you had, they've likely not yet been born. You understand?"

"Can't say I understand." Boone pushes himself up. "But I'll do what you ask until I find out you're lying or this is some kind'a hex."

I motion to Buck, who's just beginning to stir. "And take him with you." The rifle is heavy in my hands, but I manage to raise it toward Boone's head. "Now then, before all that, what about my friends? Are they alive?"

Boone nods. "Last I saw 'em."

"And that was?"

"Downhill. About a quarter mile. Farther, by now, if they haven't been caught."

"How many men did you send after them?"

"Ten."

"Anything I can say to make them believe you sent me to stop them?"

"Shoot enough of 'em and they'll start listening," he says with a lop-sided grin. When I don't smile with him, he clears his throat. "Apologies. That wasn't actually a joke. Just struck me funny, is all."

I sigh at the idea of taking more lives, but I'm not fond of my only other option. When Buck grunts and rolls himself over, stunned and disoriented by the change in scenery, I motion to him and say, "Explain the situation as best you can to your man, here. Send him back to your people."

"What about me?" Boone asks.

"You're coming with us." I look to my father, and without saying a word ask if he's alright with that arrangement. I probably should have asked him first, but I'm not about to abandon Cassie and Levi, and there's no way I'm letting my father and Owen out of my sight.

A subtle nod from my father confirms our plan moving forward and that all the admiration and affection I've had for my father's memory wasn't tainted by the many years without him. He's as brave and strong-willed as I remember...only I don't remember this. If I did, at least I'd have some inkling of what we might run into on this time-fractured mountain-side. Based upon my experiences so far, I'm pretty sure it will be nothing good.

19

The next thirty minutes is a rather boring hike leading downhill, away from my ultimate goal, but toward the people I've sworn to protect, a promise that now extends to my father and young Owen. At least, I *think* we're headed toward Cassie and Levi. Tracking them is all but impossible thanks to the missing snow and the new set of trees. Any tracks they had left—footprints, bent branches, gouges in bark—have been erased by time, in reverse.

All that remains of Cassie's and Levi's flight are mostly concealed bullet casings, and the occasional dead body. Each time we come across a corpse, I'm terrified it will be one of them, but one after another, we uncover Boone's men. He reacts with a kind of detached disappointment, muttering about each man's failings.

But then we run out of bullets and bodies to follow.

And honestly, I'm relieved. Cassie and Levi left a long trail of corpses in their wake. I don't blame them for it. Boone's men would have done the same to them. But this morning, Cassie set out for another boring day on the job, and Levi to break into my house to steal drugs for his grandmother. Neither of them would have guessed they'd be forced to gun down a variety of men, though I suppose that's normal compared to being shunted back in time.

I'm reluctant to shout for them. I don't know who or what is hunting these woods, but experience has taught me to err on the side of caution. So I'll have to track them with logic.

I've counted six bodies. That means four of Boone's men are still alive. It's been a while since I saw a 9mm casing, so it's likely Cassie and Levi are just on the run now. To put the most distance between themselves and the men chasing them, they'd follow the path of least resistance. In this case, that's downhill.

I glance toward Adel's peak, cloaked in forest, impossible to see from here. I'm separated from my ultimate goal by a long hike. Moving farther from Synergy isn't going to solve our long-term problems, but I'm bound by loyalty.

For now.

There will come a time when I put the mission first. 'No man left behind' is a nice sentiment, but it's always coupled with the unsaid 'but not at the risk of mission failure.' That's the cruel nature of combat. If Cassie and Levi were soldiers, I'd have already abandoned the search and struck out for Synergy. I'm sure Minuteman is following that course of action, which is why I need to seriously start thinking about doing the same.

He struck me as a decent man, but also very well trained, and seeming decent is easy for a disciplined sociopath. I have no idea what his plan is, or how many people are on his team, but I can't imagine him breaching the facility without confronting my people.

Fifteen more minutes, I tell myself, *then we're turning back.*

"Worried about your friends?" my father asks, Owen's hand clasped in his. My child self has been chomping at the bit, wanting to run ahead despite the danger. I remember running up and down Adel while my father trudged behind, not because he was out of shape, but because he carried all our gear. I think it made him happy, to see me enjoying the forest that meant so much to him, but now...

He's got a vice grip on Owen's hand.

"They're tough and smart," I say, the words sounding hollow. When he raises a skeptical eyebrow, I smile. "How can you tell?"

"You purse your lips," he says. "Like someone else I know." He glances down at Owen, who's oblivious to the conversation, as his eyes dart from tree to tree, squeezing his lips together.

"Huh..."

"So what's it like, in the future?" he asks.

He's trying to take my mind off my worry, parenting without knowing that's actually his role in my life. "In some ways, it's the same. You'd recognize most of it. Everything is a little shinier and sleeker, but not completely unrecognizable."

"So no USS Enterprise?"

"There's an international space station," I say, which catches Owen's attention. "Some people have lived in space for more than a year."

"They can do that?"

"Well, they stretch out a bit, and they lose a lot of muscle mass on account of the zero gravity, but light speed travel is still a ways off. I suppose a space station is kind of Star Trek. Oh..." I dig into my pocket and feel the slender shape of my phone, which Boone's men failed to take. "And we do have these."

I hand the device to my father, but it fully captivates both Owen and Boone, who has slowed his pace to take part in the conversation. "That thing made of obsidian?"

"Hardly," I say, and I push the power button. When the screen glows to life Boone reacts as though he's been struck by lightning. "Tarnation!"

"Whoa," Owen says, reaching out for the device.

When I look down at the screen, I have a moment of panic. My lock screen wallpaper is a photo of my grandfather and me, taken two years after my father had passed. I hold my thumb over the sensor, quickly unlocking the phone and switching the screen to a collection of app icons over an image of the Appalachian mountains at sunset.

"What is it?" Owen asks, as I let him take it from my hand.

"It's like a tricorder and a tablet computer in one," I say, knowing he and my father will both understand the references. Boone is out of luck, but I really don't give a shit. "Technically it's a telephone, but it can do a lot more. They're called smartphones."

"Like the Apple IIc?" Owen asks.

"More like a few thousand of them." I turn the phone around in his hand so he can see the logo on the back. "Same company, though."

"Can you call someone on it?" my father asks.

"If there was still someone we could call. And it won't work without a series of cell towers. They're like antennas, broadcasting the signal. So I can't call Synergy, either. It's mostly useless, unless you need a calculator or Pac-Man."

Owen gasps, retaining his childlike fascination despite our circumstances. "This has Pac-Man?"

I was a resilient kid. I suppose that's how I survived my entire family's passing and still turned out okay.

Boone on the other hand, is about as resilient as a bag of feathers in a tornado. His face slowly morphs into a kind of outraged horror, eyes locked onto the glowing screen. "It's the Devil's work!"

I have a good chuckle at his expense while looking for signs that anyone has come through these woods. "There was a time when gunpowder was magic."

"In our time," my father says, "people have been to the moon."

"*On* the moon?"

My father is blowing his mind, even more than the phone.

"One small step for man, one giant leap for mankind." He smiles. "I saw it on television."

"What's a television?" Boone asks, looking torn between the urge to flee, screaming madly, and fascination. Having seen the iPhone, he can't deny I'm from when I said. I doubt he can make any sense of it. I barely can. But he's coming around to the basic concept.

"Like this," my father says, motioning to the phone in Owen's small hands. "But bigger. When I was a child, they were black and white. Most folks in these parts didn't have 'em, but we had family friends who—"

"Whoa, it has a camera," Owen says, working his way through the intuitive icons, menus, and options like a true child, unafraid to experiment with technology. His first venture onto the Internet is still several years away, when he and ten other boys manage to download a pixelated photo of Christie Brinkley in a bikini. The image came from one of the boy's home computers, but we felt like we'd jumped into the *Wargames* movie and were paranoid the government would come looking for us.

Young Owen holds the phone out, "Look! There I am!" I crouch down beside him, feeling a strange kind of affection. He's separate from me, but also me. It's been a long time since I heard this iteration of my voice, but it's triggering all sorts of memories, old emotions, and a sense of wonder I've long since lost.

When my head is next to his, I realize the similarities between our faces is noticeable, even with my aging and facial hair. Before I can move, he snaps a photo and then starts laughing. In the background is Boone's ridiculous-looking wide eyes and gaping mouth.

"Tarnation," he says in a hush, leaning forward to look at his own image. He rubs his cheeks. "I need a bath."

"Need a lot more than that," I tell him.

"Which one of you is his father?" Boone asks. "Cause I thought it was this feller," he gives my father a backhanded whack on his shoulder. "But I'll be damned if he isn't your spitting image."

"You know what they say about the Appalachians," I say. "Not a very big gene pool."

Boone's face screws up. "A what-pool?"

"You married to your cousin?" I ask.

"Ayuh."

"That's what it means."

Owen's chuckling puts a smile on my father's face, but his scrutinizing gaze turns me away. I pluck the phone from Owen's hands. "Gotta save the battery. Just in case."

"Aww, for what?" Owen asks.

I tap on the flashlight. "In case night comes around."

My father's firm grip on my shoulder stops me in my tracks. I'm sure he's about to confront me about who I really am, but he motions for silence, and then for everyone to get down.

Distracted by the younger me, I missed the shift in terrain, from sloped to level, and the glow of a clearing ahead. Beyond the whoosh of wind slipping between budded tree limbs, there's something else.

A growl.

Two growls.

Staying low to the ground, we work our way forward, moving from tree to tree until we're gathered behind a fallen oak, gazing into a clearing that is still present in my time.

Owen and I whisper at the same time, "The Indian graveyard."

Except the Indian in this graveyard is very much alive. As is the mountain lion she's staring down.

20

"What in tarnation is an Injun doing on *my* mountain?" Boone asks.

His indignation annoys me, in part because Adel isn't *his* mountain in any time, and if anyone has a right to be here, it's the Cherokee nation, who lived in Appalachia for thousands of years before being forced to follow the Trail of Tears westward.At the same time, I understand his confusion. There hasn't been an official Cherokee tribe in Kentucky since the early 1800s.

We've jumped back another sixty years. Maybe more.The question of when we are needs to wait, and honestly, I'm not sure it's really important. The mystery isn't *when* we are, but how the hell we're getting here, and how we can undo it.

The Indian woman is dressed in a wraparound deer-skin skirt and a poncho-style blouse. Her straight, black hair hangs to her shoulders, decorated by a single braid hanging over her forehead, interlaced with feathers. Moccasins cover her feet.

In some ways, she's what I imagined a Cherokee woman to look like, but she's more real and less stereotype. Her brown eyes burn with fearless defiance of the cat's superiority, despite the fact that she is armed only with a hatchet.

"We need to help her," my father says, his hand on my shoulder.

Owen stands beside him, wide-eyed at the scene playing out in the location we both remember as the Indian graveyard.

"Intend to," I say, raising the Winchester, feeling right at home looking down its sights.

I line up the cat, slip my finger around the trigger and...the cat bolts toward the woman. Hitting a moving target isn't easy. I can do it, but it takes time to lead the target and account for vertical motion. With only twenty feet between the pair, I don't have time to adjust and fire without the risk of putting a bullet in the woman.

But it's not necessary. The cat leaps, paws spread wide, claws extended. The woman dives to the side, swiping her hatchet out. She strikes the cat, drawing blood.

It's hardly enough to kill the beast, but the wound makes it think twice. The dance between predator and prey is always a matter of life and death, but it's not always the prey who dies. A good kick from a zebra can crush a lion's skull. A buck can put an antler through the eye of a grizzly. Even a bite from a frenzied rabbit could get infected and lead to death. That's part of why predators focus on the sick and the weak. They're not only easier prey, they're also safer.

The cat holds its ground, hissing at the woman while testing its weight on the now bleeding forelimb. Weight tested, the cat decides it's hungry enough—because I kept it from eating the dead bodies, and apparently, it never ran into Arthur. I track it with the rifle, but the woman is between us.

The Cherokee woman is clearly a skilled fighter. This might not even be her first time squaring off with a big cat. But that doesn't mean she's going to win this fight, and I haven't seen a mountain lion bigger than this one, though I suppose they're probably quite common in this time period. At least in the Appalachians. Maybe. We could be in the 1700s or the 500s. Life for the American Indians was largely unchanged for thousands of years before European colonizers—my ancestors— wreaked havoc on the land and its people. I'd like to think I'd make different choices than they did, that I wouldn't be party to genocide in the name of God, but being from the twenty-first century has allowed me to see the world with different eyes.

I raise the rifle skyward and squeeze the trigger. Once again, the cat flinches, snaps its eyes toward me, and glares. Then it bolts, tail snapping as it vaults out of sight.

"Stay here," I tell the others, but I'm mostly concerned with the first impression Boone might make. I step into the clearing as the woman spins around to see who fired the shot. She's immediately suspicious of me, maintaining her defensive stance and wielding the hatchet.

I hold the rifle out to the side and raise my other hand, open palm in a universal, 'I mean you no harm,' gesture. She doesn't react, so I step closer. "Are you hurt?"

She squints at me, but I can't tell if she's sizing up my character or my physical prowess.

"You're safe. I won't harm you." I stop ten feet away, standing in the center of the clearing, surrounded by foot-tall grass that must have sprung up the moment the winter fled. The air fills with the sound of birds and the scent of some fresh-blooming spring flowers.

My guard drops, and it's the moment the woman has been waiting for. She lunges forward, swinging hard with the hatchet, aiming for the center of my forehead.

I swing the rifle up, gripping it in both hands just in time to block the hatchet from splitting my head in two. The impact is harder than I was ready for, but my defense does the trick.

"Stop," I tell her, but I've left myself exposed, and she takes advantage of it.

Her kick to my gut is solid and well executed, spilling me back. While she caught me off guard, I do the same by yanking my hands up as I fall. The combined force of my fall and pull is enough to wrench the hatchet from her hands and fling it behind me.

I drop to one knee, sucking in a deep breath. The woman takes an aggressive step toward me, but she stops when I turn the rifle on her.

She knows what it is, which narrows down the time period to sometime between the late 1600s to early 1800s.

"Please," I say. "I don't want to hurt you."

"All you know is hurt," she says, her command of English perfect, her accent all Cherokee.

By 'you,' I understand she means Europeans. Her disdain makes me think we're closer to the early 1800s, when the natives were forced from their lands. But that's probably a few years off, or she wouldn't be here.

"I saved you," I tell her, motioning to where the lion fled.

"I did not need saving."

She's as obstinate as she is powerful. She reaches behind her back and draws a three-inch blade.

"Seriously?" I say, but I regret my tone. I don't know what this woman has endured at the hands of men who look like me. It's possible she's the last of her people. She might be here to mourn the passing of some relative slain by white men.

Her reply is a snarl, then a lunge. When I don't shoot her, a confident grin spreads across her face.

She thinks I'm out of ammunition.

"I got 'er!" I turn toward the sound of Boone's voice, knowing it leaves me open to attack, but that the woman will have to push past the rifle to put her knife in my side. It won't be much warning, but it should be enough.

When I see Boone cock back the woman's hatchet and heave it toward her, I forget all about her. "No!" I shout, swinging the Winchester out and knocking the small ax to the ground.

I don't have three inches of metal sticking into me, so I assume saving her life—again—made an impression. When I turn around, she's holding her ground, but looks more confused than angry.

"I don't want to hurt you," I say, and I drop the rifle at my feet. Then I hitch a thumb toward Boone who looks even more confused than the woman—because why wouldn't you just kill a stranger on sight?—and I say, "Him, I want to hurt."

A slight grin says I'm making progress. She says, "Tell your friends to come out."

"So we're straight," I say, once again motioning to Boone. "*He* is not my friend."

"Why is he with you?"

"It's complicated." When I see that's not nearly answer enough, I add. "His men, of which there are many—" She scans the forest behind me. "They're not with us. Some of them are hunting down my actual friends, who, *like me,* don't want to hurt anyone."

"Even though you are capable of it?"

I'm not sure if she is referring to my skill as a fighter, or the fact that I have a rifle. Either way, anything other than honesty isn't going to fly with this woman, who I'm darn sure is a good judge of character. "Very capable."

Her smile spreads a little further. "I have known men like you." She waits for me to react with a smile of my own, then she adds, "All died violently."

I don't ask why. I suspect it's a wound not worth picking at. Not right now, anyway. Instead, I agree with her, but include her. She's as much a fighter as anyone I've known. "That's often how things end for people like us."

She nods at the strange compliment, and I motion for my father and Owen to join us. "Come on out."

The pair slip out of the woods. My father glares at Boone, aiming the shotgun toward him and motioning for the man to join us. Boone is far from our ally, but since experiencing the time shift, and learning when we're from, I haven't sensed any hostility from him. That doesn't mean I wouldn't like to kick his ass and send him on his way, but for now, I need him to diffuse the situation with his men...if we can ever find them.

I offer my hand, wondering if people in this time period shake hands in greeting. "I'm..." Shit...what name did I give my father? I can't remember the first name, so I just use the last name. "Dearborn."

She takes my hand in hers, giving it a curt shake. "Inola," she says and then she translates. "Black Fox."

"You are all dressed strange. Are you hunters?" she asks.

"Not exactly," I tell her. "I was a soldier, long ago. Now...honestly, now I'm just lost."

She looks from me to my father and then to Owen. Her eyes flash with recognition. "You are family?" She motions between my father and me. "Brothers?"

I shake my head and attempt to redirect the conversation. I'm sure it will come up. My father already suspects. I can see it in the way he looks at me. But there are enough problems to deal with and enough mysteries to solve right now. "This is Owen," I say, pointing to my young self, and then to my father. "And this is William, his father." Then to Inola. "Are *you* a hunter?"

"Trader." She closes her eyes and gives her head a shake. "Used to be. Now, like most of my people, I am saying goodbye before leaving our ancestral lands."

A little bit closer to the Trail of Tears than I thought.

"Payin' respects to who?" Boone asks. "This really an Injun grave-yard?"

Owen tugs on my father's arm. "Did you know this was a real Indian graveyard?"

My father just looks stunned by everything, slowly shaking his head.

Inola points to a mound of earth at the center of the clearing that is not there in my time, or in my father's time. It's fourteen feet long, four feet tall, and five across. A little large for a burial mound...unless it's a whole family, which I suppose could be the case given the time period.

"Tsul'Kalu," she says.

"Is that a relative?" my father asks.

Inola's face screws up like even we should recognize Tsul'Kalu's name. When none of us shows any hint of understanding, she grunts in frustration, or maybe disgust, muttering something in her native language before explaining. "Tsul'Kalu. God of the hunt."

"A god is buried on my mountain?" Boone says, sounding amused and intrigued.

"Adelvdiyi belongs to no man," Inola says.

"Then who does it belong to?" Boone asks, expecting his question to somehow stump her.

In answer, she turns her head toward the burial mound.

21

I step closer to the massive burial mound, which probably contains a tall man who convinced the locals he was a god—which still happens in the modern world. My father told me stories about the Indian burial ground, about how the spirits of long-since-dead natives walked the forest at night. I'm pretty sure the stories were intended to keep me from wandering off in the woods alone. Maybe I'll ask him. It wouldn't be a stretch to think that Inola's parents and grandparents conjured similar tales to keep their children out of the endless forest.

But Inola is no child. Best guess, she's over thirty. While her tan face is free of wrinkles, there are a few strands of gray on her head, betraying her age. That she thinks a god's remains lies in the dirt means the Cherokee nation as a whole believes the legend of this site.

If you ask me, it's just a mound of dirt covered in grass. That it's missing in my time is a bit odd, but its presence here is just another story. Over the years, Adel has seen its fair share of tall tales, though I am coming to realize that most of them are true, and few of them were exaggerations. The mountain really has seen its fair share of historical drama, a good portion of which we've managed to whisk away into the past.

Layers of history co-exist on this mountain now, and eventually, I fear it's going to get a little overcrowded. I hadn't noticed before, but the forest is absolutely brimming with bird songs. Some I don't recognize. They must be from species that went extinct before the 1980s. Where there was an occasional call in my time, there is now a chorus of chirps, as generations of birds gather together and enjoy the sudden spring. How many other populations are growing with each jump? How many predators? How many people? We've come across a lot of people already. Could there be more? Will they be dangerous like Chafin and Boone, or kind like my father and, I think, Inola?

When I peel my eyes away from the burial mound and turn to Inola, I notice her arm is covered in streaks of blood. Seems the cat managed to cut her as well. "You're hurt."

She looks at the scratch and shrugs.

"That needs to be cleaned and dressed," my father says, reaching out for her arm. She yanks her arm out of reach, tensing. My father raises his open hands. "I only mean to help. It could get infected." He turns to Owen. "The first aid kit."

I still remember where we kept the kit, in my right-hand cargo pants pocket. We carried it with us every time we ventured into the woods, but never had a reason to use it, until now. Owen produces the kit and hands it to my father, who pops open the plastic container, revealing sterile bandages, band-aids, antibiotic ointment and a few other tidbits, none of which make a lick of sense to Inola.

She looks from the kit, to my father, and then to Owen and me. "Where are you from?" She motions to Boone, who is wandering the field, maybe looking for tracks, but who shows no sign of running. "Him, I understand. You three... Even your clothing is strange."

"That's hard to explain," my father says, and I think he's actually going to try explaining the concept of time travel to an ancient Cherokee woman. "We are from a faraway place. A more...advanced place, technologically speaking. Look..." He cracks open the package and pulls out a roll of gauze. "It's a bandage."

She doesn't look convinced.

"I only want to help," my father says, and something about the way he says it—the earnest look of his eyes, I think—puts her at ease and brings a smile to her face.

"And in return?" she asks, still suspicious. It's the question of a woman whose life hinges on bartering. Or, at least, it did. Now she'll be forced to move westward on a journey she might not survive.

"How about your friendship?" my father says. Inola almost winces at the suggestion, perhaps because we're strangers in the woods, or because we're all white men, or simply because it's a strange request in any time. But she once again finds comfort in my father's eyes, which makes my father happy in a way I've never seen. When I see Owen's confused expression, I know it's not something he's ever seen, either.

I have no idea if my father dated or even fancied a woman after my mother's death. I was a kid, so the subject never really crossed my mind. But he never brought anyone home to meet me, and never seemed to pay any particular attention to women at church—the one place we mutually socialized. But there is no doubt about it, my father is attracted to Inola...and I'm not sure how I feel about that.

There's a part of me that's always pictured him as a hopeless romantic, married to the memory of my mother, who at this point in his life has been dead for eleven years. I don't feel any real loyalty to my mother. I never knew her. I just hadn't considered that my father might be lonely. Then again, I'm his age and single, too. So, there's that. Maybe what I'm feeling is jealousy.

Inola lifts her arm toward my father, agreeing to his offer of medical treatment.

My father takes a small bottle of alcohol from the kit and unscrews the cap. "This will clean the wound, but it will hurt a little."

"If it hurts a lot, you will share the pain."

My father's smile is wry.

"Wouldn't have it any other way."

And now he's flirting. I'm out. And so is Owen. We step away together, hands in our pockets. After a few steps we stop in front of the burial mound and look at each other.

He raises an eyebrow, and I match the expression.

He wiggles both of his ears, and I do the same.

I remember practicing these things in the mirror.

Flaring nostrils come next.

"Easy," I say, and flex my nose.

"You're not like most adults," he says.

I'm not sure that's true, but I say, "Okay."

"I mean, you're old. Like really old. But you're nice."

"How do you mean?" I ask. He's seen my violent side on full display.

"Like Pa."

Like Pa.

"*Your* Pa."

He rolls his eyes.

Hold on a second...

"What?"

"You know what."

I've never pictured having a conversation with myself, but I'm not really surprised with how it's going. We might not be thinking the same thing, but we're on a similar wavelength, like twins separated by thirty-four years. He's missing a lot of what I've gained over the years, and I've forgotten most of what's still fresh for him, but somewhere in the middle, we're the same person.

"When did you figure it out?" I ask.

"Well, it wasn't your good looks," he says and chuckles. "What happened to us?"

I don't remember being a witty kid. I do remember trying to make people laugh and failing. Conservative church goers in Appalachia aren't well known for their senses of humor. I suppose we have the same sense of humor, though.

"You still kind of look like me," he says, more seriously. "And there's this..." He points to the scar beside his eye, received when he—when I—tripped into the corner of a table. "And this..." He points to a scar above his eyebrow, delivered by a German shepherd who decided to eat my cheeseburger at a church BBQ, and then my face. It's a unique set of scars.

"Wasn't until I saw the photo of you and Grampa that I was sure, though."

"Think Dad knows?"

Owen shrugs. "Didn't say anything about it, but why would he? Even *you've* been trying to hide it. Not sure why."

"Back to the Future," I say.

He nods. "Paradox. Right. Well, too late for that. I mean, you and your friends killed some people that weren't supposed to die today, right? We saw the bodies."

When I say nothing, he asks, "Where did you learn that anyway?"

"I was...*you* become...a Marine Raider. Special Forces."

His eyebrows rise. "Like *MegaForce*?"

"'The good guys always win,'" I say, quoting the movie.

"'Even in the 80s,'" he finishes, and we have a good laugh.

It's official, I like me. "But we didn't have flying motorcycles or gold spandex suits."

"Too bad," he says, and we stand there, side by side for a moment, looking at the massive grave site. I think he's probably picturing himself as a futuristic soldier, but he catches me off guard by asking, "Why wasn't Dad in the photo?"

I'm frozen for a second. How can I tell myself that my father is supposed to die tomorrow? I can't, is the answer. "He took the photo."

"Huh," is his noncommittal response. I'm not sure if he believes me or not, but I get the sense he also doesn't want to hear the truth. I'm glad when he moves on. "So your fake name... That wasn't very smart, using Cass's last name."

"Suppose not."

"So, what about her? Does that mean you're still, we're still...?"

"Friends? Yeah."

"Just friends?"

My young self catches me off guard again.

"Yeah."

"Too bad."

Did I have crush on Cassie? I've had so much history with her that it all just kind of blends together. What he doesn't know and what I can't explain is that after Dad died, I had trouble getting close to anyone. The pain of death changed me. This time tomorrow, he'll be just like me. Maybe. "Things just didn't work out that way."

"I like you a little less," he says with a grin. "I suppose she's married to some fella we don't like, and has kids of her own?"

"Actually, no. She's here, with me."

"She came *back in time* with you? And you don't... You haven't..." He rolls his eyes and shakes his head. "Didn't work out. Wait, she's the one we're looking for? Who's in danger?"

The kid's feathers are ruffled. All traces of apprehension are swept away. However strong my feelings are for Cassie, eleven-year-old me wore them a lot closer to his sleeve.

We spend the next ten minutes waiting for Dad to finish, and talking about Owen's life and mine. I avoid the details of how things happen, just in case, and he tells me about things I had forgotten. Each story chips away at old memories and feelings, long since walled away. I nearly cry a few times but hold it in because he'd no doubt sense I'm holding out on some painful information.

"Hey," Boone says, crouching by the clearing's edge. "Whataya make a this?"

He waits for Owen and me to approach, then he raps his knuckles on the ground. Instead of a dull thud, there is a hollow, metallic gong. I crouch and slide my hand across the smooth surface of a metal pipe that should not exist in this ground, let alone in this time. Given the subtly of its arc and the resounding nature of the sound, I'd guess it's close to eight feet in diameter.

"This is from the future," Boone says, eyes a little wild, "ain't it?"

"Reckon it is," I say, "But I didn't know it was here."

"Me neither," Owen says. Our house is less than a mile south from here.

I gauge the pipe's direction and turn my head toward Adel, laying down an imaginary track. If it continues straight, it would work its way up, straight toward Synergy.

"What'd you find?" my father asks, walking over with a patched-up Inola by his side. She looks as confounded by our discovery as I am.

I give the pipe a knock and know my father will understand it. "Runs toward the peak."

"Toward the mine," he says.

"If it's from my time," I say, and it looks like it is—the metal is free of rust or corrosion, "then it's not the mine it leads to."

"Your time?" Inola says. "What are you—"

Before she can finish the question, the answer comes rolling down the hill.

Owen manages to ask, "Already?" before the flux hits.

Now that I'm ready for it, the nausea caused by the wave of sound and distortion transplanting me through time is less severe. My father and Owen handle it fairly well, too. Boone is laid out again, writhing and cursing. Inola falls to her knees, eyes closed, body trembling. She's feeling every bit as horrible as Boone, but is managing it far better.

My father crouches beside her, a gentle hand on her back. "It will pass."

And then it does. The flux rushes beyond our sight, leaving a lush green summertime downpour in its wake. Lightning cuts through the sky above. The boom of thunder makes Boone squeal in fright.

Before I can fully take stock of our situation, Owen tugs on my arm the same way he does to my father. When I look down at him, he motions his head toward the far side of the field, where the burial mound is.

Where the burial mound *was...*

22

"That can't be good," Owen says.

"Just means that whoever was buried there isn't dead yet," I tell the younger version of myself.

He nods. "Kind of what I was sayin'."

"And maybe wasn't born yet," I add. "Either way, he wasn't a god."

"Tsul' Ka... Tsul' Kabuki?"

I have a good chuckle at my expense. "Tsul'Kalu. If there's a twelve-foot-tall hunter-god wearing a kabuki mask in these woods, I'm liable to shit a brick."

Owen's eyes spring open. "You said—!"

"You will, too."

"But Dad will—"

"Dad uses the same language," I tell him. "Just not around you. But, I wouldn't give it a whirl any time soon."

My father steps between us. "What are you two yammering abou—" He sees the now empty field. "Oh."

"What has happened?" Inola asks. She's looking at her hands, watching the rain run over her skin. She turns her eyes to the sky full of twisting gray clouds, angry at our arrival. The air is thick with ozone and humidity. Had I been at home, I'd have sat on the front porch and enjoyed the spectacle, at my age, and Owen's. Out here, without cover, trapped in the past, it's not exactly a good time.

"We haven't gone anywhere," my father tells her, motioning to the clearing, which is familiar in every way except for one. "It's time that has changed. We've traveled into the past."

Instead of reverence or awe at the burial mound's absence, Inola looks mortified. I thought she'd be happy about the apparent resurrection of a god. "Tsul'Kalu wasn't a nice god of the hunt?"

"He wasn't like your Jesus Christ," she says. "Mercy, grace, and forgiveness are not his virtues."

"What *were* his virtues?" my father asks.

Inola's frown deepens. "Hunting. Everything."

"Everything?" Owen asks. "Including every...*one*? Like people?"

"He was a monster. The slayer of man and beast. My ancestors' reverence for him was not adoration, but fear." Inola looks ready to bolt, but manages to hold her ground.

"Then why were you paying your respects?" my father asks.

Inola is disgusted by the suggestion. "I came to spit on his grave, on behalf of all Cherokee, before we left our lands for good."

"Well, then it's a good thing he was dead when you spat on him," I say with a smile. I nearly say something about how a real god couldn't die, and certainly wouldn't be buried on a mountainside in Appalachia, but her sour reaction to my comment clamps my mouth shut.

"How is this possible?" she asks.

My father starts to explain the situation as best he can, and Owen and I step closer to where the mound had been. There's not even a hint that something is missing. The ground is flat and covered in tall green grass, bending under the weight of heavy rain.

"What do you think?" I ask my younger self.

"It's horse..." His voice drops to a whisper. "...shit."

"What is?"

"The god stuff."

"Yep. Anything else?" I'm really just trying to distract him from the horror of our situation, not that he's struggling. Maybe it's me who's struggling. At age eleven, I haven't experienced the mind-numbing pain of loss, or seen men under my command gunned down. He's seen a lot already, but he's still been spared the worst life has to offer.

He looks around the clearing, eyes locking on where we'd been standing. "Look at the grass. It's missing where our legs were." He's right, and it's an observation I failed to make.

We crouch by the leg-sized holes. There are beds of neatly cut grass blades where our toes had been. Where our legs stood, there's nothing. "Objects from the future displace what's in the past."

"That's probably a good thing." Owen says and then he scans the field. "Where's that kooky guy?"

Shit.

Boone.

I stand up, worried that he'd finally decided to cut his losses and strike out on his own. But he's right where we left him, by the field's edge. He's on his hands and knees pulling up grass.

When Owen and I approach, Boone looks up. "It ain't here no more."

I don't need to ask what he's talking about. The massive pipework in the ground is more of a mystery than the burial mound, and it's much more pertinent to our situation. I'm intrigued by Inola and her stories—this is my backyard—but it's not going to keep us alive, find my friends, or get us back to our own times.

I kneel down beside him and start yanking up grass. Owen joins us and we quickly clear the growth and then several inches of mud. When my fingers scrape against something solid, I stop digging and give it a knock. The metallic echo is the same as before. Apparently, there's just more soil atop the pipe in this era...whenever that is.

Hands covered in muck, I hold them out and let the rain rinse them clean. My whole body is saturated. If not for the summer heat, I'd probably be shivering. If we jump back into winter right now, we're screwed.

Lightning flashes and thunder booms, as a stiff wind blows through the trees, pulling green leaves free and twisting them through the air.

Boone ducks from the sound and shouts over the rolling roar, as it fades into the distance. "We need to find shelter!"

"Our house isn't far," Owen says, and then he thinks better of it. "Oh. Our house isn't there yet."

Honestly, I'm not sure if it would be there or not. These pipes are from the present, but so was my truck.

Unlike Boone, shelter is not at the top of my priority list. And right now, neither is finding Cassie and Levi. The shift from winter to spring made finding them a near impossible feat. With the rain obscuring our visibility and the thunder and wind drowning out our voices, we could pass within fifty feet of them and never know it.

The best way to help them, and my family, is to get to Synergy, find out what's going on, and put a stop to all this before Minuteman and his people turn the place into a shooting gallery. If that's his intention. Circumstances put us at odds, but do the laws of the United States apply when the country hasn't been founded yet? Whatever is happening here, it's bigger than Synergy. Bigger than my present. And the potential ramifications grow with each jump back in time. I'm not sure how far back we are now, but it won't be long until we're the only people of European descent on the entire continent.

My father leads Inola over. She looks confused, but not quite outraged by what he's told her. Then again, she believes in a giant human-hunting god, so maybe the concept of moving through time won't be a stretch.

"You see?" my father says, motioning to the exposed pipe. "This is from the future."

"What is it?" she asks.

"A pipe," I tell her. "A tunnel. Made of metal. Big enough to..." It's big enough to walk through, that's for sure. That there is any part of the facility I don't know about is problematic. It's my job to protect it. The existence of this conduit means I haven't been told the truth about the facility's size. How far-reaching is it? Where does this tunnel lead?

I turn left, imagining the pipe's progress. It would cut past my house, maybe a hundred yards to the side, where some road work was done a few years back. Beyond that, it would eventually reach town. From there, it's anyone's guess. There's no way to know where it ends, but I know where it begins.

"We need to reach the peak," I declare.

"What 'bout yer friends?" Boone asks.

"They'll have to wait," I tell him. "Along with your men. Not that you're concerned about them."

He gives a noncommittal shrug.

"What is on the peak?" Inola asks.

"The people who did this." I motion all around, at the sky, the rain, the summertime trees. "And no, they're not gods. They're just men and women who didn't know what they were mucking with."

Or maybe they did. Either way, I'm going to get answers.

I stand and say, "I'm going to move fast, and straight." I'm about to suggest anyone not up for it can wait here, but who's to say the next jump won't turn the clearing into a killing field. The best place for these people to be, loved ones or not, is with me. "So try to keep up."

"We could use your help," my father says to Inola. He might be right, but I think his invitation has more to do with his concern for her well-being.

She watches a purple streak of lightning carve its way across the sky, and then turns her head toward Black Creek, several miles toward the south.

Was Black Creek built atop her tribe's location? I wonder, and then I shake my head at the moral inadequacies of my ancestors. *Of course it is. What better way to erase the past than to build on top of it?*

Inola is the first to strike out, heading uphill. When we follow, she looks back at me. "Can I go back home?"

"I don't know," I tell her, deciding that honesty is the best course of action.

"Can you stop it?"

"I'm not sure." I break into a jog. My body aches, but I push beyond the pain, focusing on the weight of the old rifle in my hands, and the deadly potential it possesses. "But I'm going to try."

Determination carries me for another twenty minutes, straight up the mountainside. And then exhaustion slows me to a walk. No one complains when I slow. Our clothing is saturated. All of us are carrying more pounds than we're used to. I peel off my T-shirt and wring it out.

I wipe my face with it, pressing it on my eyes for a moment. When I pull it away, I flinch to a stop and nearly spill backward down the incline.

My father catches me with one hand while clasping a hand over Owen's eyes.

"What is it?" Boone asks, trudging up behind us.

The grizzled beard and weathered face are hard to mistake. "It's Arthur," I say, even though I'm the only one of us to have ever met him.

Then Inola fills in the detail I left out for Owen's sake.

"It's *half* of Arthur."

23

"Dear Lord Almighty!" Boone shouts as he stumbles back, nearly catapulting himself down the mountainside. My father would normally chide someone for using the Lord's name in vain, but Boone's words sound more like he's honestly beseeching God for help. That alone says a lot. Boone's a hard man. He shot Chafin in the head without so much as a, 'How do ya do.' But this...this has him rattled.

And he's not alone. I've seen my fair share of horrors and taken more than a few lives in my time, but I've never encountered something like this.

Arthur hasn't just been killed, or even simply dismembered.

He's been put on display.

The top half of his body is impaled on a sturdy tree branch that's been cleaned of twigs and leaves. I step around his body, which is dangling ten feet over the ground, trying to figure out how he was placed there. Behind him, I see that the branch forks, both prongs punched into his back, keeping him upright, even as the branch bounces in the wind. His arms flop loose. His jaw hangs open. The skin around his eyes sags.

"What are you thinking?" my father asks. I'm surprised that he's brought Owen back to the scene, but when I look for the boy, I find him twenty feet downhill, his back turned. Seated beside him is Inola, her hands clasped behind her, slowly shaking her head.

"His body is still in a state of primary flaccidity," I tell him, and when I see his confusion, I add, "Everything is loose. Means he died sometime in the last two hours. Probably in the last hour." I point to the stretched and torn skin hanging from his mid-section. Pink droplets of rain-thinned blood drip from his body. Beneath him, the ground is stained dark red. I point to the blood-soaked earth. "They put him up there pretty quickly after killing him. And they did it recently."

The more I whittle down the time-table, the more tense I become. I've got the rifle ready to go, but still aimed at the ground, my finger resting beside the trigger.

"How can you be sure?"

"The rain," I say, putting my hand out to watch the torrential downpour splash off my skin. "In a few minutes, the blood will be washed away. Means he only recently stopped bleeding out. Means this happened in the past few minutes."

My father snugs the shotgun against his shoulder, eyeing the forest, our home-turned-nightmare. "And it just happened to be in our path. Maybe it's a coincidence?"

"You don't believe in coincidence," I tell him.

"No," he says, looking into my eyes. "I don't. And we can talk about that later."

He's figured out who I am, of that I have no doubt. But unlike Owen, he's not ready to completely accept me as his grown son. And I don't blame him.

I'm not sure what kind of man he wanted me to become. We never got a chance to have that conversation. There's a chance I've fallen short of his hopes and expectations. He's seen the violence of which I'm capable. Seen the boy by his side grown up, bringing pain into the world. He wants better for Owen, I realize, and now that I've met my younger self, so do I.

But for that to happen, my father must live. Screw history and the potential paradoxes. Owen needs a father. *I* needed a father, and now we both have a chance to get that back.

"Boone," I say, waving the man over. He creeps up the hill, ducking away from the half-corpse. "Would your men do this?"

"Heavens, no." He wrings his hands together. "We ain't opposed to taking a life here or there on occasion, but this man wasn't just killed." He glances up at Arthur and shirks away. "He was mutilated. Desecrated."

I find it odd that Boone feels that desecrating a dead body after the soul has left it is somehow worse than the act of killing, but he's also right. To a point. Being impaled on the branch, displayed for all to see, is a desecration. Being torn in half... I'm pretty sure that's just how he was killed. I don't see any stab wounds or cuts of any kind. He was just yanked in half.

"The horses," I say, speaking to myself, but loud enough for my father and Boone to hear.

"What horses?" Boone asks.

"The man you shot. He and his men rode in on horses. A good number of them are loose on the mountain. If someone rounded two of them up, they could have done this." It's a primitive way to kill people—using horses to tear someone in half—but it sends a clear 'stay the fuck away' kind of message.

"But why?" Boone asks.

"Wouldn't we all like to know," I say.

"I'd really rather not," my father adds, "given the choice." He looks a little ill, keeping his eyes turned away from Arthur's body. What does it say about me that I can both look at him and take my time examining his wounds? It's revolting, but whatever part of me that should want to run from this has been dulled. Just another way I'm not the man my father probably hoped I'd become.

"It's a scare tactic," I say, forcing confidence. "Arthur was alone, exhausted, and unarmed. This wasn't done out of strength. It's an act of weakness. Two or three men with horses, probably terrified by what's happening."

I run through a mental list of possible suspects, but don't come up with anything that makes sense. Minuteman didn't strike me as the sadistic type, and I doubt he'd hire people prone to atrocities. Boone's men are the most likely culprits, but if he's the hardest of that lot, I doubt any of them would have the stomach for something like this. That means there's someone else on this mountain, but from which time?

"We need to press on," I tell them. "The answers we need are at the peak, and the longer we wait, the harder it's going to get."

Inola, who's been strangely silent, helps Owen to his feet, and stands between him and the body as she leads him uphill, past the grisly scene.

The rain doesn't let up as we continue our course uphill. I take the lead with the rifle, Owen behind me and my father behind him. Boone follows in the rear, muttering to himself, occasionally asking for a weapon that he's not going to get from me. I don't trust him. He might be 'with us' now, but the moment a better situation comes along, he'll throw us to the wolves.

Speaking of wolves, we're far enough back in time now that they're back on the list of predators we need to watch for. There are big cats, bears, wolves, and the worst of them—people.

For a while Inola stays close to my father, but then she strikes out to the side, weaving back and forth in front of us. Hatchet in hand, low to the ground, she stalks up the mountainside, looking for signs of danger.

She's done this before, I realize.

She's moved through these woods, wary of the danger her fellow man presents. If there is any sign of danger on our way up the mountain, she's not going to miss it. Her zig-zag path requires her to hike further and faster, but she doesn't seem fazed by the workout. In her time, there're no such things as couch potatoes, microwave dinners, or automobiles. She's accustomed to being on her feet, and her stamina reflects that lifestyle. Even I couldn't keep up with her.

Our progress is slow, but steady. Synergy is just an hour's hike. I try to decide what to do first—check in with my crew, get my family someplace safe, or kick down the laboratory doors and demand answers—but I decide to play it by ear. I have no idea what I'll find. The facility could be in ruins. The scientists could be dead. Minuteman and his people might have already taken control. I doubt there is a plan I could come up with that I won't have to abort the moment we arrive.

So I focus on the here and now. Staying alive and reaching the peak are my current mission objectives.

I'd like to say the forest is quiet, but the hissing rain drowns out everything, even the squelch of my wet footsteps. Visibility is crap. The only way I know we're headed in the right direction is the constant upward slope. And it only gets worse when a thick fog settles in, as it's prone to do in the Appalachians.

Inola slips in and out of existence, a silent ghost moving through the fog and rain. Her presence is both comforting and surreal. When I see her, part of my brain sees a woman in costume, acting silly, but the rest of me knows that she is real. That all of this is real. I'm back in time with my father, myself, a bootlegger, and an American Indian, trudging up Adel, through lands guarded by the mutilated corpse of a man from the 1920s.

It's almost enough to make me laugh.

Then I hear a bird call.

While there are plenty of birds on the mountain, they've fallen mostly silent in the rain and thunder. What I heard was the call of something large. Something different. I tense for a moment, aiming my rifle toward the sound, until my father places his hand on the barrel and eases it down.

Then he raises his hands to his mouth and performs his own bird call.

The reply comes immediately, and this time with a sense of urgency. It's Inola. She's found something.

"Hang back a bit," I tell my father and Boone, creeping toward the sound. They keep a twenty-foot distance between us as we move toward Inola. Any further and we might lose each other in the fog.

"Inola," I whisper.

"Here," comes the reply. She's just ahead, on the far side of a broad tree. When I see blood on the bark, I raise an open hand to the others, motioning for them to stop. Then I ease myself around the tree.

Inola is crouched, her back to me. She glances over her shoulder. "I think I found the rest of Arthur. What's left of him."

Steeling myself for the worst, I step around her and find myself totally unprepared. My stomach sours, and I turn away. After taking a moment to collect myself, managing to not retch, I return to the scene, better prepared, but sure I will have nightmares of this moment.

Arthur's lower half is here. His organs are strewn about, tangled in the mess of entrails. But that's not the worst of it. His legs have been separated, the pants torn away, and the flesh...eaten. Down to the bone. Raw.

Again, I nearly vomit, but I manage to switch off my emotions and turn on my analytical mind, as I did when we encountered Arthur's upper half. There is still meat on one thigh, and on one calf. Preserved within that flesh are long gouges. Teeth marks. Large teeth marks.

Arthur was eaten by an animal, and given the bite radius, I'd guess it wasn't the mountain lion, a pack of wolves, or even a bear. Whatever it was, I don't want to stick around to find out. "Let's go," I say to Inola, "and do not tell the boy."

She nods, eyes wide with fear that she is doing a decent job of hiding, and we return to the others. "What was it?" my father asks, squeezing Owen to his side.

"I think..." *How can I put this?* "I think we jumped a bit further back in time."

"How far back?" Owen asks.

To when predators were big enough to tear a man in two and peel the meat from his legs in a few bites, I think, but I say, "A lot further."

24

"My legs hurt," Owen says, after we've maintained a rapid pace for fifteen minutes. The moment the words have left his mouth, my father scoops him up and carries him without slowing. I forgot how strong he was. That anything could kill him seemed impossible to me then. Because of that, Owen is the least afraid of our group. Boone has sensed our fear, maintaining the pace while wheezing for air.

My father holds the shotgun out to Inola. It's too awkward to carry both the weapon and Owen. "Know how to use this?"

She takes the weapon. Looks it over. "Is it a rifle?"

"Shotgun," he says. "Same idea, but for close range. Pull the trigger to shoot..." He points at the fore-stock. "...and yank that back to chamber a new round. You've got four shots."

"I know how to handle a shotgun," Boone says between gasps.

"Not a chance," my father and I say in unison.

The things sons pick up from their fathers...

The rain has faded into a drizzle, but the fog remains, the moisture slowly drifting back into the sky from where it came. I wring out my shirt and slip it back on. The fabric is clinging, but cool.

"How much further?" Owen asks.

"Twenty minutes," I say, thinking it's probably closer to thirty. We're close to where the dirt road leading to Synergy's rear gate will be in a few hundred years, but the terrain is unfamiliar. The trees are different. Landmarks are missing. In many ways, it's a new mountain. But up is still up, so we'll get there eventually.

When we reach a point where, in my time, the trees had been cut away by the mining operation, I slow my ascent. Not just because the terrain is even more unfamiliar, but because I sense something off. It's a smell, subtle, flowing downhill. Traces of gun metal and sweat. There are people ahead, and they're afraid. But they're also armed.

I duck down behind a tree and don't have to motion for the others to do the same. When I turn around, they've all taken cover. Inola is by my side, shotgun in hand. She scrunches and taps her nose. She smells it, too.

And then cutting through the forest, is a voice, booming, masculine, and electronic. "Lay down your weapons and surrender. You will not be harmed."

When Inola's eyes go wide, I whisper, "He's not talking to us."

Distant branches crack, grinding under something heavy. I try to get a look, but the forest is thick with trees, which no longer exist in my time, and a lingering curtain of mist. I can't see more than forty feet, and we're a good four hundred feet from the action. The voice is amplified, making its distance hard to peg. That we can smell the people to whom he's talking means they're not too far ahead.

If they fall back, we might find ourselves in the middle of a firefight. I turn to the others. "If this comes our way, run east, along the side of the mountain." Downhill is the most obvious choice for those running away from a fight. If the people above us turn tail, we'd quickly find ourselves in their midst.

If I had to guess, I'd say the people in question are Minuteman and his men. I can't think of a good reason for Boone's people to head toward the peak. But the electronic voice is a mystery. There's a megaphone in the security office, but that would sound like a man's voice amplified. This, while masculine, sounds computer generated. Robotic. The inflections are off.

"This is your final warning. Lay down your weapons and—"

"Now!" A woman's voice. Something about it is familiar, but before I can process it, gunfire erupts. I press myself into the Earth and motion for the others to do the same. The gunfire is directed uphill, but it won't be long before the return fire begins, and when it does, every shot that doesn't find a target, or a tree, will come blazing downhill.

Explosions shake the mountainside. Grenades. They're waging an all out war, and I worry for a moment that the people they're attacking are my security team. My instincts are telling me to charge up the hill, identify the enemy and help the good guys, but there are two problems with that scenario. First, I'm not sure who the good guys are. Minuteman and his people might very well be doing the right thing. That doesn't make my security team evil. They're just doing their job. Second, I'm not about to abandon my family.

When the return fire begins, my internal struggle is the first casualty. A rapid-fire stream of bullets tears through the air, buzzing even more loudly than the time flux. *It's a mini-gun,* I think, before a cascade of stray bullets nearly tears my hiding-place tree in two.

I check on the others to find all but Boone face down in the dirt. "Get down!" I hiss at Boone, but he doesn't listen to me. The sound of futuristic combat, coupled with the fact that he's something of a coward, spurs him into frantic retreat.

Ignoring my advice, he runs straight downhill, standing tall in the line of fire and heading straight back toward Arthur's dismembered body.

Trees crack and splinter under a continuing fusillade of hot metal spewed by a weapon with a seemingly endless supply of bullets. Definitely not part of Synergy's security profile. Clouds of bullets filter through the gaps between trees, some of them punching into our cover, the rest zipping further downhill. Three of them find Boone's back.

He's launched into the air, sailing through his own blood as the high velocity rounds exit his body. He sprawls to the ground, a tumble of loose limbs, and slides to a stop. I hear a wet, whispered, "I hate this cussed mountain." Then he falls still. I don't need to check him to see if he's dead. Even if he's still clinging to life, there's nothing to be done for him.

The bullets stop spraying after a solid thirty seconds of hell. The whine of a spinning-down mini-gun follows.

And then, aside from the distant rumble of thunder, silence. No screams. No return fire. No running footsteps. Whoever was fighting on the hill above, they're all dead.

The sound of grinding gears and breaking branches keeps us in hiding. Hushed voices follow, not amplified and not afraid. There's ten minutes of subdued activity and then it fades, heading uphill. The battle has been won and the victors are returning from where they came—Synergy.

After five minutes of silence, I lift my head and look uphill. Trees have been decimated by the firepower, several cut in half. But I see nothing else. That doesn't mean we're alone. The fog is still thick. I'd prefer to wait a while longer, but a howl from below makes the hair on my arms flare to life. The deep bellowing sound is like no creature I've ever heard. I'm not sure if it sounds angry or hungry. Either way, I don't think we want to be here when it arrives, and I have no doubt it will. Drawn by the sound of battle and the smell of blood carried downhill by the wind, most apex predators will come to inspect, especially if we're in a time when men with guns aren't the dominant hunters.

"Stay close," I tell my father and Owen as I stand. "But not too close. If things go bad, just run."

My father wants to argue. He's no coward. But with Owen by his side, he knows where his responsibility lies.

Owen, on the other hand, says, "We won't leave you."

"Owen," my father says.

"We can't!" My younger self yanks free from my father. The idea of watching himself die is no doubt incomprehensible. While we're the same person, we're also different people, but that hasn't stopped us from finding an instant rapport and connection, like brothers whose first eleven years of their lives were identical.

I crouch in front of myself and hold his shoulders. "I know none of this makes sense. I know it's confusing, and scary, but you need to listen to Dad. If I know you're doing that, then I can do what I do without worrying about you. Make sense?"

"You're gonna kick some..." He glances at our father and then says, with a bit of defiance. "...ass?"

"Only if I have to." I stand and turn uphill. "And I really hope I don't."

Because I'm pretty sure we wouldn't stand a chance.

Despite the howl from below, we make slow progress as we creep toward the peak. While my imagination conjures monsters behind us, I know the real world ahead contains a modern kind of monster. The higher we climb, the greater the destruction, all of it leading to a swath of earth that's been chewed up by bullets, framed by a collection of fallen trees. When I spot the first body, I motion for the others to wait and enter the killing field on my own.

There are four bodies lying in pools of their own blood.

All of them are wearing black masks and high-tech body armor, the likes of which I've never seen. However strong their armor was, they didn't stand a chance against the mini-gun rounds. Two of the four have missing limbs. The other two have softball-sized holes in their torsos.

I flinch at the sound of footsteps behind me, but it's just Inola, hatchet in hand, ready for a fight. She's an impressive woman, but like me, she's unprepared for the carnage. She winces and asks, "What could do this to men?"

"Other men," I say, and I crouch by the nearest body. "Keep watch?"

She nods and sneaks past the corpses, entering the still pristine forest above. I check the bodies for ID and weapons, finding nothing. Whoever killed these people, who I'm now sure are Minuteman's people, picked the bodies clean.

I pull back the mask and stare into the eyes of a man I do not know. In life, I imagine he was intelligent and powerful. A former soldier. I move on to the next two bodies, expecting to find Minuteman's face, but I'm greeted by the blank stares of two more strangers.

I pause before withdrawing the last mask. My father is leading Owen past the killing field, covering the boy's eyes as he moves uphill. He frowns when he sees the dead, but then catches my eye, taps on his

ear, and points downhill. He's decided to move upward because someone, or something, is coming up the mountain.

Driven by curiosity, I peel back the final mask and am flung backward by shock and horror. I manage to squelch an anguished sob, telling
myself it's not real. It's not her. Fighting back tears, I collect myself and
crawl back to the body, feeling my professional demeanor slipping away
into abject sorrow as I look down into Cassie's dead eyes.

25

How did she get here?

Why is she dressed like this?

Did Minuteman somehow manage to recruit her, or has she secretly been with them from the beginning?

She wasn't too far from the truck explosion. Could that have been her? It would explain why it wasn't detonated until we'd stepped away.

But would she really do that to me? I can't believe it's possible. She wouldn't betray me. This whole time, lost in the past, the only thing I've been sure of is Cassie's friendship, that she'd have my back, no matter what.

I should have kept looking.

I should have found her first.

"I'm sorry," I whisper, tears dripping onto her blood-soaked cheek.

"You knew her?" Inola asks, crouching beside me. Her voice isn't exactly compassion, but I get the sense she understands my grief. She's lost people, too. Given the era she's from, probably a lot.

When I can't manage a reply, she says, "You loved her."

The words hurt. My chest constricts.

Desperate for air, I crawl away from the body while Inola replaces the mask.

"Who is it?" Owen's small voice makes me flinch from sorrow's grasp.

I wipe an arm across my face, smearing tears, but doing little else to hide my anguish. When I ignore him, he asks again, a little louder. "Who *is* it?"

I can't do it.

I can't tell him. The pain I'm feeling now is familiar. An old friend come to pay me a visit. I've regained my father at the cost of my best friend, who should have been more.

I'm caught off guard when I'm shoved from the side. "Who is it!" Owen shouts, tears already in his eyes.

"You don't know her," I say. "Not yet."

I push myself up, trying to shove down my emotions, not just for Owen, but for all of us. This is the second worst moment of my life, but every second we linger puts me in greater danger of having to relive the first.

When I look at my father, I see wet eyes and intense compassion that catches me off guard. In that moment, there is no doubt.

He knows.

Who is under that mask.

Who I am.

And that in my time, he's no longer around.

My feeling of loss compounds, and when my father reaches his arms out to me, I'm undone. I all but fall into his embrace. He rubs my back as I weep into his shoulder, all the military training in the world unable to cope with my emotional cauldron.

"I got you," he says.

I'm not sure how long we stand like that. Probably not long enough.

When I lean back, Owen sniffles and wipes his nose. He must sense the same thing my father does—seeing him is hard. It's amazing, but it's left me vulnerable, for the first time in a long time. I've spent my whole life walled up and cut off. Hell, it took Cassie's death for me to admit I loved her. No wonder nothing ever worked out between us.

With my father back, and the chance to save his life within reach, the mortar holding my emotional walls together is crumbling.

"I think he knows," Owen says.

My father smiles. "I've known for a while." He lifts my chin. Looks me in the eyes. "There isn't a father who loves his son that wouldn't recognize him at any age. I'll admit, the beard threw me off, but you've got my father's eyes." He looks at Owen. "Always have."

"You can't go to work tomorrow," I blurt out.

"Can't say I was planning on it," he says, looking around to remind me we're stuck in the past. Then he grows serious. "Why?"

I struggle to say it. Owen is right here. But this time, the news won't be devastating, it will be hopeful. Tragedy avoided.

He beats me to it. "Something happens, doesn't it? At the mine. Because of the earthquake this morning."

"Earthquake?" I ask, but then I remember. The day before my father passed, there was an uncommon earthquake, the likes of which have been recorded throughout Black Creek's history, mysterious because they never seemed to have a cause.

The date and time of my arrival in 1985 coinciding with the earthquake couldn't be a coincidence. And all those past quakes...they must be periods in which this time-bending effect briefly touched down, like a skipping rock over a pond.

"What happens?" my father asks, somber now. He's not sad about his own death, but he can see how profoundly it affected me.

"Cave in," I say, feeling no need to retell the story in detail.

"Who else was caught in it?" he asks, more worried about the safety of others, no doubt already planning to upend time to save them, too.

"You're the only one who didn't make it..."

"Dad dies tomorrow?" Owen asks. He looks petrified.

"It's not going to happen now," my father says, rubbing Owen's head. "Even if I could go to work, I wouldn't, and I'd make damn sure no one else did until it was safe."

Owen gives a little nod, but keeps his eyes locked on mine.

"You'll be okay," I tell him.

"But you weren't," he says.

"No," I say, and before I can elaborate Inola emerges from behind a distant tree and shushes us. I didn't even notice her leave.

Instinct chases my emotions away. I hold my breath and listen. The faint whine of small spinning motors fills the air.

"Sounds like an RC plane," Owen says.

"Close," I say, scanning the sky above the thick layer of trees. I've heard the sound before. It's a drone. Not the missile-firing kind, but given the destruction wrought on these people, I doubt its use is recreational.

Owen spots the two-foot-wide, eight prop drone at the same time I do, whispering, "What is that?"

"Recon drone," I say.

"Someone is watching us through that?" my father asks.

Owen tenses, ready to bolt. "Should we run?"

I don't know the answer to that question. Right now, running and staying have the same odds of getting us killed. I look to Inola, as the other person with some kind of combat experience, hoping for an opinion, but she's vanished again.

They never saw her, I realize.

Despite being from a time long before drones, and Marine Raiders, she's doing a much better job at stealth and evasion. Then again, she doesn't know that this drone is likely controlled by the very people we need to confront. I've never seen the drone before, but it is clearly a product of my time, a fact that is confirmed when the masculine, electronic voice fills the forest once more.

"Who are you?" It hovers close enough for me to see the camera on its underside swivel toward my father. And then to Owen. "State your names, and—"

The camera locks on to me, and the voice goes silent for a moment. Then, "Owen McCoy?"

"Who am I speaking to?" I ask.

"Dr. Langdon."

Dr. Elias Langdon is my boss. Actually, he's my boss's boss. He not only owns Synergy, he's also the lead scientist. What is he doing monitoring the feed of a security drone I didn't know we had?

"Can I ask...what year are you from?"

"2019," I say, and then I motion to my father and Owen. "Same as them. They got caught up in whatever's happening." I'm not sure why, but I'm not about to fully trust my employer. Too much bad shit has gone down, including the brutal killing of these people. I look straight at the camera, and hopefully at Langdon. "Do *you* know what's happening?"

"We're still teasing that out," Langdon says. "But we're hopeful the effects can be resolved and everyone restored to their rightful times."

"And what about them?" I motion to the dead bodies and watch the camera swivel toward them. "Will they be restored to their rightful times?"

"Not alive," Langdon says.

Was that a joke? Was that supposed to be funny? I've only met Langdon a few times, but he didn't strike me as someone who'd be flippant about the deaths of four people.

"But yes," Langdon clears his throat. "Their...demise is unfortunate, but necessary, I'm afraid. They were heavily armed, and their actions could have severely undermined our ability to rectify the situation. Their group of radicals was not unknown to us."

"That's why you have attack drones I wasn't aware of?" I ask.

"I hoped they'd never be needed," he says, "and I think you'll agree that sending a robot into battle is far more humane than putting the lives of your security team at risk."

I'm not sure Minuteman would agree, but I don't argue the point. It's the same justification the U.S. Military uses to send its own drones in pursuit of terrorists. And it won't be long before robot battalions are rooting out the enemy, rather than men who can bleed and die. It's not even the distant future. It's the near future. Or, if you're a high-tech research company with far reaching resources, the present.

Emotion sneaks up on me. "You did put a member of your security team at risk. Did you even bother to identify the bodies?"

"I assure you, all members of your security detail are alive and well."

"Cassie." I say, glaring into the camera. "Cassie Dearborn."

"What?" Owen says, his voice rising. "Cassie?"

Damnit.

"As I said, all members of your security detail are alive and well, including Ms. Dearborn."

"Bullshit."

"We picked her up along with a few men from the early nineteen hundreds...or was it the late eighteen hundreds? I'm having trouble keeping track. This is a busy mountain. She was with a young man. I believe his name was Levi."

Then who...?

I glance at the masked body of the woman I was certain was Cassie.

"Mr. McCoy," Langdon says. "Would you like to come in out of the cold? Well, it's not cold anymore, but you understand. I'm sure your people would like to see you, and I think your friends would enjoy having walls around them. The mountain is not safe."

"I've noticed," I tell him, and then I consider our options, which are to either destroy the drone and try to sneak in, or simply follow the drone. It's an easy call, and I make it for all of us. "Lead the way."

The drone spins around and sets out on a slow upward course, setting an easy-to-follow pace. A flicker of movement in the corner of my eye catches my attention. I glance without turning my head and see Inola, matching our pace up the mountain, a hundred feet to the side. I give her a subtle nod. She's made the right call by staying hidden. I hope Synergy is a safe haven for my family, but there's something off about Langdon, about Synergy's drone usage, and the fact that Cassie is, without a doubt, lying dead behind me.

26

"Been a long time since I saw the mountain like this," my father says, motioning to the thinning forest surrounding the peak. Like him, his father was a miner who worked at several other sites near Black Creek. My father hiked these woods before Adel's summit was cleared, strip-mined, and had holes dug in her sides.

He points uphill to where a line of clear blue sky can be seen beyond the trees. "Top is just ahead."

"Think you might have this confused with another mountain," I say, doing my best to hide all traces of fear. The buzzing drone is just ten feet ahead, and I have no doubt that the people on the other end can hear our every word. What they can't seem to hear is the occasional shift of leaves behind us, revealing Inola's mostly silent pursuit.

"This is Grayson, right?" my father asks.

"Adel," I say.

"Ahh."

It's a tenuous ruse. While Grayson is a nearby mountain, it has never been home to a mine. And Adel's stripped and striated peak is hard to confuse for another mountain. While her base is intact and pristine, the upper quarter, in my time, is home to layers of barren stone.

Now that I see the mountain's true, untouched beauty, I regret ever having felt fondly for the mines. Money and the promise of creature comforts is enough for people to turn on nature, no matter how impressive it might be.

When the drone reaches the clearing ahead of us, it turns around and hovers in place.

"I'm afraid this is where I must ask you to leave any weapons you might have," Langdon says.

"Synergy requires me to carry a firearm," I point out.

"Not any longer. Our new security measures are more than adequate."

"New since when?" I ask.

"Well, today."

While it's odd that they wouldn't have filled me in on such drastic security changes, if they had any idea that their experiments might lead to this... "Why wasn't I informed about the changes?"

"Corporate secrecy, I'm afraid," Langdon says. "You never know who you can trust."

"You once called me the most trusted man on Synergy's payroll." It was during our second meeting, after I had created a series of new security protocols designed to keep everyone safe. His approval led to the hiring of extra security staff, including Cassie.

"I did?" The drone is motionless, but I get the sense that Langdon is searching his memory. "Oh, yes. In regard to your security refinement. I'm afraid much has changed since then."

"I've noticed." I think back to the bodies. While lethal force is authorized inside the facility, people who have breached the perimeter fence are supposed to be met with non-lethal force. Had Minuteman's people engaged first, that would be different, but the only bullet casings littering the ground around those bodies were 7.62 rounds—the bullet of choice for mini-guns, not the kinds of weapons a serious operator like Minuteman, or research facilities, would use.

I've got serious apprehensions about following this drone, but I suspect retreat might put us at odds with Synergy's new security, and I can't take that risk with Owen and my father. The devil I know and all that.

A distant roar sifts through the trees. Speaking of the devil I *don't* know.

The drone tilts at an angle, then zips closer to us, the camera pointed downhill. For a moment, I'm worried it will spot Inola, but she's nowhere in sight. When the sound doesn't repeat, the drone makes a slow spin toward me. "Forgive my ignorance, but do you know what made that sound?"

"Best guess," I say, "Some kind of large predator."

"Can you be more specific?"

"Something from the ice age?"

"Unlikely," Langdon says. "While it is impossible to determine the precise year without seeing the stars, based on the size of the gravitational wave, and previous observations, we believe the current year is 800 B.C., give or take a handful of decades."

When the roar repeats, a little louder and closer, I say, "Whatever it is, I'd rather figure it out from behind Synergy's walls than standing out here, exposed."

"Right," Langdon says, "Of course."

I lean the Winchester against a nearby tree. The weapon will be easy for Inola to find, which is good, because whatever is stalking the woods sounds big and unfriendly. She already has the shotgun, but it holds only four rounds and there is still a good number of unsavory people about, and the mountain lion, and who knows what else we've picked up along the way.

"Lead the way," I say.

We resume our upward hike. The trees thin and then, sunshine. For a moment, bathed in yellow, surrounded by damp air and smell of fresh growth, I feel a sense of peace. We're above the fog here, and when I look into the distance, I can see the familiar Appalachian range, mostly swallowed by a soupy layer of gray mist.

It's when I focus on what's in front of me that things become unfamiliar. There are some things I recognize. The main science building and its futuristic shape, like Disney's Omni Center squished into the shape of a peanut. But there are several other buildings rising up behind the wall. Buildings that weren't here two days ago...along with the wall itself.

Synergy's first line of defense is the outer perimeter barrier. The chain link fence combined with the signs threatening legal action, not to mention the razor wire, are enough to deter even the most foolish vandal. The second line of defense is—was—a taller fence, also topped with razor wire, and patrolled by three armed guards—Kuzneski, Brown, and Harper.

This...this is different. And impressive.

Instead of chain link, there is a line of five-inch-wide metal posts separated by two-inch slits. Not only does the top come to a razor-sharp point, but the sides look like serrated knife-blades. Climbing the ten-foot-tall fence would be all but impossible. The simple act of grasping it might result in the loss of several fingers.

Instead of one guard shack by a chain-link rolling gate, there are now two metal towers. Long windowless slits on the tower walls would allow those inside an easy-to-fire-from, hard-to-hit position from which to fend off intruders. I can't see what's hidden within, but I have no doubt that there are hidden weapons pointing outward, maybe even tracking us right now.

"No comment?" Langdon asks as we approach. "This is all new to you, yes?"

"Most of it."

"And?"

"I'm impressed. You could fend off an army."

"And we have," he says. "As you've already seen."

"I'm not sure I'd call four people an army, but I see your point." Keeping my tone more interested than threatening is tough. I want some answers, and right fucking now, but that's not going to happen if I'm combative, or if he senses any judgement on my part. I remember Minuteman's impression of me, based on his research, and decide to stick to the script. "Far as I'm concerned, if you keep cutting my checks, I'll keep doing my job. Though I would appreciate knowing exactly what I'm up against."

"Also a fair point," Langdon says, "but explanations will have to wait. As for your job, I'm afraid your services are no longer required."

Three more drones rise up over the wall and take up positions around us. None of them are armed, but they're still intimidating. Owen clings to my father's leg.

"You have nothing to fear, as long as you cooperate," Langdon says. "And I do apologize for the circumstances and sudden termination, but our situation is extremely fluid, and I'm afraid we must take precautions."

"I can help," I tell him, trying to sound confident, and loyal.

"Perhaps," Langdon says. "But for now, the best place for all of you to be is out of the way."

And with that, the massive spike-topped gates open inward, revealing what once was a parking lot and is now closer to a military forward operating base. But instead of soldiers, there are drones. Dozens of the flying machines are lined up under three large open structures, allowing them to come and go. I watch one buzz down from the sky, slip into one of the buildings, and dock with a charging bay. It was all done so fluidly that I suspect it was on autopilot, controlled by AI rather than by a human operator. Several warehouses that weren't here before contain who knows what, but they're being patrolled by what looks like an armored dune buggy with tank treads.

I remember the sound of grinding treads in the woods. The vehicle doesn't appear to be armed, but it's large enough to sport a concealed mini-gun. I confirm my suspicions by looking down at the dirt beneath my feet, where a collection of human footprints has been run over by several pairs of treads. This is the path taken by Cassie's killers.

I pause at the threshold, taking everything in.

My father stands next to me, holding Owen in his arms now. "This is where you work?" he whispers. Like me, he's equal parts impressed and terrified. Rightfully so. People don't prepare for war unless they're expecting one.

"No," I say. "This is different. This is...new."

And then it all makes sense.

From the very beginning, I have assumed that it was *my* Synergy that caused the flux, that they had accidentally triggered our jaunt through time. But this isn't where I work, and while Dr. Langdon might still be running the show, he's not the man I've met.

He's the man he will eventually become.

"This isn't from my present," I tell my father. "It's from the future."

27

"You are correct, of course," Langdon says from the drone, as it leads us toward an unfamiliar building. The square, brick and steel building is built like a fortress, with tall walls, high windows, and two staggered levels. The second floor is a bit smaller than the first. Outer stairs lead to both roofs, which are walled in and perfect for fending off an attack. If I were to design a fortified security building, it would look like this. "This facility is from your future, Mr. McCoy. In fact, you inspired much of what you see here."

Maybe I *did* design the fortified building?

"How far in the future?" I ask.

"Seven years."

"All this is seven years?" It doesn't seem possible that the almost quaint Synergy facility I work at could become this shining beacon of militarization in seven years. But nations have been destroyed and reborn in less time, so I suppose it's possible. I just can't fathom what would transform a company, whose outward appearance favored the local economy, people, and environment, into...this.

Four drones zip past in formation, flying up and out of the facility before diving down the mountainside. All around, the sounds of machines at work fill the air, buzzing, grinding, and churning. Just below the din is a constant but pulsating hum, like muffled energy. I can feel it in my legs with each step, subtle but ever-present.

Even stranger than all of this is that I haven't seen a single person. Synergy is both full of, and completely devoid of, life.

"A lot can change in seven years," Langdon says, and I sense a bit of remorse in his voice. "The world is a different place than you know. Science, once revered for its contributions to society, became the scapegoat for all the world's perceived problems. Facts no longer mattered. Truth was shunned. Violence won most arguments. The world became petty, ruled by squabbling children. The town that once embraced this company turned against us in the name of Jesus himself. Several employees were slain, including members of your own team."

"Not Cassie," I guess, trying to sound hopeful.

"She survived," Langdon says. There's a hint of something in his voice. Anger, I think. It's hard to tell without being able to see his face.

"While there were still some countries open to the reality of scientific knowledge, advancement, and achievement, much of the world had resorted to a kind of suburban tribalism. Sensing a civil war brewing, I took steps to ensure the safety of my staff, and our research.

"But it wasn't enough. Attacks on the facility became more organized. More deadly. I thought I had prepared for the war to come, but in the end the only way I could save my work was to retreat."

"Into the past?" I guess. Some of what he's saying gels with the existence of Minuteman and his people, but I find it hard to believe that Cassie would get caught up in the kind of religious fervor he's describing. It's been a long time since I set foot in a church, but even *I* know that Jesus would turn the other cheek before raising a hand in violence. Then again, history is full of people using God—all gods—as justification for unspeakable violence against people of other races, religions, and regions. The Spanish Inquisition. The conquistadors. The Nazis. Modern white supremacists. The very founding of the United States. All that blood in the name of a God who so clearly opposed violence. I wish I could say Langdon's story is completely unbelievable, but it's not. The rumblings of such a future already exists in my time. The only real stumbling block is Cassie.

I just can't imagine a future where she is a militarized religious zealot.

"Why not just leave?" Owen asks.

The drone continues toward the building, but the camera swivels toward the boy. "Everything you see and cannot see around you is unique and irreplaceable. Nothing like it exists anywhere else in the world."

"I feel like that's obvious," my father says with a slight grin. "Seeing as how we're a thousand years plus in the past."

The comment manages to get a chuckle out of Langdon, which is good. I'm having a hard time not sounding combative, and the moment Langdon figures out I'm not with him, I'll be against him. That's not going to go well for us. My father's lighter touch is welcome.

"But there must be something else," my father says. "Something that ties you to this mountain. It's a special place for anyone who stays here long enough. We all have our reasons for calling it home, and coming back to it. I grew up here. I'm raising my son here. My wife is buried—"

The drone stops, the camera locked on to my father's face.

Something he said hit a nerve.

And then, I know.

"Jacqueline."

While Langdon was the scientific and entrepreneurial genius behind the company, his wife was the heart and soul. She made time to connect with everyone, bringing a touch of homestyle affection to every meeting. I only met her a few times, but every encounter was positive, and the one time I saw her with Langdon, I knew he adored her. The coldness I sense in him now, even through this machine, only makes sense if she is no longer here. "How did it happen?"

The drone continues forward, hovering at half pace. Langdon is silent for a good ten seconds, and then says, "She died in that first attack. Killed by the people of Black Creek, whom I had hoped to help. Whom she had convinced me to help. I would have been happy to buy all the land and send everyone away, but she insisted we do the right thing. And what did we get for it? A revolt. Violence. Blood. All of which you did little to stop. As dedicated as you were to this company, you wouldn't kill the people of Black Creek in defense of my wife."

The contempt in his electronic voice is potent. While he might not blame me for his wife's death, he is no friend of my future self. But would I really not defend Synergy from any threat, even one that I know? "That doesn't sound like me."

"Like I said, a lot can change." The drone pauses by a metal door on the side of the brick building. It turns to my father once more. "My wife is buried on this mountain as well, and now, I'm afraid, all I'm married to is my research."

The door opens on its own, providing entry into a long, sterile, white hallway with no markings, no décor, and no guards. "Mr. McCoy... all *three* Mr. McCoys, please step inside."

The threat isn't overt, but it sets my insides twisting. He knows who my father and Owen are. Knows what they mean to me. Knows I will do anything to keep them safe, including unconditional surrender. He hasn't pointed a weapon at me, but there's no need. We're surrounded by a robotic army from the near future and have already seen the damage they can inflict.

"I realize this must be disconcerting for you," Langdon says. "You've had your world turned inside out. But there have been some positive benefits, wouldn't you say? Reunited father and son...and son. A life spared, a young life free from grief. Let's say we keep it that way."

I allow my father and Owen to enter first, taking one last look around, searching for weaknesses and finding none. I step into the hall and follow my father toward the ominous unknown via a featureless corridor. Our footsteps echo as we walk, but the ever-present droning buzz lingers behind. I turn to face Langdon's drone. This is, apparently, where we part ways.

"Take your first right. The rest will be self-explanatory. Should our quest come to a successful conclusion, you will be allowed to leave, and with luck, live out the rest of your natural lives."

With that, the drone's camera retracts into its body before it turns and zips away. A moment later, the door closes on its own, leaving us alone in the barren hallway.

"Sorry I brought you here," I say.

My father shakes his head. "No way to know what we'd find. And near as I can tell, this is still the only place you're going to find answers.

And if I'm honest, I'd rather be in here, where the guns are pointed out, instead of at us."

He's got a point. The mountainside is far from safe. But I'm not convinced Langdon will honor his offer to let us live if his mission, whatever that is, is successful.

"I think it's cool," Owen says. "Did you see all the robots? It's like *Blade Runner* out there, but for real, and without Harrison Ford."

"You've seen *Blade Runner*?" my father asks.

"At Scott Flanagan's house," both Owen and I say.

"Keep moving," says an impatient voice, broadcast from a hidden intercom. Aside from Langdon, it's the only other trace of humanity we've encountered. "And I don't want any shit, so don't give it to me."

I recognize the voice. It's different, angrier, but the inflections are the same. I take the lead, heading for the T junction ahead. When I turn the corner, I'm faced with a gateway and a glassed-in security booth. Behind the glass, I look into a pair of eyes that are familiar, but changed. Where there used to be good humor, there is now only disdain and scars. Still, I'm relieved to see him. "Kuzneski, what are you—"

"Shut the fuck up," he snaps. Of all the men on my team, he was the closest to being a friend. But whatever goodwill there once was between us has clearly been lost.

"I don't know what I did to you," I say, "or how things played out, but that's not who I am."

His glare softens for a moment, but then flares back to life. "It's who you will be, and that's enough." He points his chin at my father and Owen. "Is this little asshole your kid self?" Though we've just recently been picked up, he's been briefed on who we are and when we're from. He's surrounded by four screens I can only see the back of, but I'd guess three show security feeds and one allows him to communicate with Langdon, or whoever else is in charge around here.

"*You're* an asshole," Owen says. My father holds him tight, but doesn't scold him for the language.

"Yeah, that's you," Kuzneski says, and pushes a button. The door beside his station unlocks with a *thunk* while a buzz fills the air. "Enjoy your stay at hotel fuck you. If you need anything, feel free to eat a dick."

I smile despite myself. He genuinely doesn't like me, but I can't help but be amused by his foul-mouthed sense of humor, no matter how dark or foreboding it has become.

"Don't smile at me," he grumbles. "Just...don't."

My father opens the door, revealing what might have once been a dormitory for security forces, now used as a jail, and it is overflowing with prisoners.

"It's not too late," I tell Kuzneski. "Whatever reason you're still working for him, we can work it out."

"Funny," he says. "You said the same thing before doing this—" He traces his finger along a scar on his cheek. "—and this." He tugs the collar of his shirt down, revealing an old bullet wound. "There are more, too, but I'm not a fuckin' stripper. Now..." He flips me the bird and then uses the extended finger to point toward the open door.

My father and Owen wait just inside, frozen by dozens of people who have stopped what they were doing to stare at the newcomers. I'm about to try getting through to Kuzneski one more time when I hear my small voice say, "Cassie?"

28

Cassie's face transforms from confusion to recognition to unfettered delight upon seeing Owen. Here is her old friend, just as she remembers him, before he was lost to sorrow and hardened by the military. She shoves her way past the strangers between them and crouches down to place her hands on his face.

The moment must be strange for Owen. This Cassie is thirty years older than the one he is friends with, but he had no trouble recognizing her.

"There you are," she says, looking in his eyes, seeing something in him that's been missing in me. She kisses his forehead and pulls him into a hug.

Then she looks up and sees my father. As tears fill her eyes, she all but leaps into his arms, "Mr. McCoy!" Despite them being nearly the same age now, she still refers to him the way she did when we were children.

"You've grown up," my father observes. To him, the reunion is different. He saw eleven-year-old Cassie just yesterday. I think he's a little thrown by her affectionate response, but eventually he wraps his arms around her.

For him the reunion is a leap through time, for Cassie, and for me, it is a kind of resurrection.

When she finally sees me standing there, eyes wet, she slips away from my father and gives me a slow, gentle hug. I attempt to blink away tears as she cries into my chest. This isn't just about my younger self's appearance or my father's return. She's as relieved to see me alive as I am her.

This is my Cassie, I tell myself. The woman in the woods is her future. Was her future. Whatever brought her to that point, I'm going to stop it.

When we separate, it's by inches, just enough to look each other in the eyes. Before she can speak or move any further, I lean down and place my lips against hers. It's the most gentle and loving physical contact I've had with another person in all my life. We're locked there for what feels like hours and we separate only when the silence around us hints that we are being watched—by everyone.

"What was that for?" Cassie whispers.

"Making up for lost time."

"Yyyes!" Owen says with a pump of his fist.

After a good laugh, I say, "Apparently I've been waiting a long time to do that."

"Too long," she says.

And then the romantic moment comes to a sudden end. "I was wondering when you two would finally bone."

Kuzneski. He's left the security booth and entered the barracks full of people he's holding prisoner? Then I realize that while his voice is the same, the tone is different. His smiling face is free of the scars I gave him, and his eyes are devoid of loathing. This is my Kuzneski, still dressed in his Synergy security uniform.

Despite the sour circumstances, he greets me with a smile and a firm handshake. "Holy turdballs, is it good to see you. Have you seen the shit going on around here? I mean, time travel? Shit. And my future self? What an asshat."

Seeing him gives me hope that the rest of my people are alive and well. "Where are the others? Brown? Harper?"

His smile fades. "Dude..." A slow shake of his head tells me everything I need to know, but I can see there's something more weighing on him.

"What is it? What happened?"

"It was like a cull, man." Kuzneski steps closer, lowering his voice but not nearly enough to conceal his words from anyone around us, which is a lot of people. "Those robots. Fucking robots. They appeared out of nowhere. Like an army of them. And they just tore into people. But not everyone. It was like they had a kill list. They'd lock on to a target, pause for a second and then either blast them to bits or let them go. Far as I can tell, those of us who were spared have our future selves to thank."

Like me, even Langdon must not know what would happen if your past self died. Would it create a paradox? Would you cease to exist? The safe bet, in their situation, was to gather up their past selves and lock them away for safe keeping. But that would mean...

"What about Langdon?"

Kuzneski hitches a thumb over his shoulder. "In the back room, talking to some guy dressed like he's from the 1920s, but I'm telling you right now, he's ex-military or something. Has the same kind of 'I could rip your throat out with my pinkie toe' look that you sometimes do."

"You can do that?" Owen asks, eyes wide.

"No," I tell him.

Kuzneski seems to notice my younger self for the first time. Gives him a double take.

"It's me," I say. "He's me."

"I'm him," Owen says. "But younger, and still good looking."

Kuzneski's eyes widen. "Holy shit." He looks at my dad. Sees the familiarity. Knows what it means. "Holy shit!" He's smiling again. "Dude, you must be psyched. I mean, ho-ly-shit. Right?"

"Holy shit," Owen says with a smile, and this time my father places a hand on his shoulder, prompting a quick apology. "Sorry."

"I'm a bad influence," Kuzneski says as an apology to my father. "It's why I don't have kids."

"Or a girlfriend," Cassie adds.

"Hey, until like ten seconds ago both of you were part of the solo master debating team, so—"

"What's a master debater?" Owen asks. "Like someone who's good at debating?" He looks at me. "I thought you were a soldier."

"Oh, he likes to play with his gun—oww!" Cassie slugs Kuzneski in the shoulder. "Okay, okay, I'm just glad to see you guys."

"Likewise," I say. As much as he might be introducing my younger self to a bevy of new foul language, I appreciate the levity.

"You want to see the man in charge?" Kuzneski adds. "Not that he's in charge. But you know what I mean. He's the only one with any kind of sense about what's happening."

I scan the throng of people, looking for anyone who might be trouble or pose a threat. Most of them have been plucked out of various time periods, from the 1980s on back. They're sitting on the hard linoleum floor of the twenty-foot-wide, thirty-foot-long space that has three dorm rooms, complete with three sets of bunk beds, on each side. Like the rest of the building, it's a sterile and depressing place, reflected in the eyes of the folks watching me back.

Some of the people are Boone's, all the fight taken out of them. The few people from the present I recognize are Synergy employees, though I don't know their names or positions. But if they're alive, it means their future selves are here, and allied with the sinister version of Langdon.

A group of Cherokee Indians are gathered in the corner, keeping to themselves, eyeing everyone else with suspicion, which makes sense. In their time, they're being hunted and chased from their lands. And now they're prisoners. What must be confusing for them is that they're sharing this prison with mostly white people. Likewise, most of the people from various futures are keeping a watchful eye on the Indians, who have been stripped of their weapons like everyone else, but look far more capable of kicking some ass.

And it's probably true.

But they're no less afraid.

I decide to address them first. The best thing all these people can do to help our current situation, if there is any way to help it at all, is to work together.

"Give me a minute," I say to my father and Cassie, and I head for the group of Cherokee.

They tense at my approach, but take no action. There are four men and three women, all in their late twenties and thirties I'd guess.

Not quite elders of the tribe, but responsible adults, probably with children of their own to worry about. I squat down beside them and ask, "English?"

"Only the elders cannot speak your language," a young man says. He's full of spitfire despite his obvious fear.

"Do you know Inola?" I ask.

The man's face lights up. "Where is she?" He looks around the room, desperate.

"Not here," I tell him, "But she was safe the last time I saw her. She's outside of this place, but—"

The man grips my arm. "Outside is *not* safe."

"Because of the..." I can't think of how to describe the robots. "Because of this place?"

He looks offended by the suggestion that it is Synergy he fears. He leans closer and whispers. "Tsul'Kalu."

I nearly say, 'Are you serious?' but I manage to hold back. Who am I to throw water on their crazy beliefs while we're several hundred years in the past. The world is full of unbelievable things. Instead, I nod and say, "I met Inola by his grave."

He gives his head an exasperated shake. "I told her not to. And now he hunts again."

"Because the grave is missing?"

The man seems to melt in fear. I've just confirmed his worries.

I take hold of his wrist, getting his full attention. "Who is Inola to you?"

"My sister," he says.

"And your name is?"

"Waya."

"Listen, Waya, I am your sister's friend. We fought side by side. And I will do everything I can to reunite you with her. But for now, can you do something for me?"

He waits for my request in silence. I motion to my father and Owen. "That is my brother and his son, both of whom are also Inola's friends." *Especially my father,* I think. "Watch over them when I am not present. If you can do that for me, I will do everything in my power to protect your people, including Inola."

He ponders the offer for a moment and then gives a half nod. It's not the most enthusiastic agreement, but I'll take it. I offer my hand and he takes it. After a firm shake, I say, "Thank you," and I return to my group.

"Those are Inola's people," I tell my father. "The man I was talking to is her brother, Waya. He's not the most personable guy, but stay with them and they'll keep you both safe." I tousle Owen's hair with my hand.

"You know we hate that, right?" Owen says.

I smile down at him. "That's why I did it."

Then I turn to Cassie and Kuzneski. "Far as I'm concerned, all of these people are under our care. Doesn't matter if dickhead versions of ourselves have hijacked our present, keeping these people safe is our job."

Both nod in agreement.

I'm about to have Kuzneski lead us to my Langdon, when I'm struck by the realization that someone is missing. "Where's Levi?"

Cassie frowns, and for a moment I fear the worst.

"We got separated when Boone's people came for us. Last I saw him, he was headed downhill."

From what I've seen, the farther he gets from the mountain, the safer he'll be, but I still don't know how far the time flux effect reaches. I'd hate for him to wander beyond its range and be stuck alone in the past.

"Not your fault," I say before she can apologize. "The only way we can help him is to put a stop to all this." I turn to Kuzneski. "Where is he?"

He motions to the rear-most bunkroom with his head and then leads the way. Most everyone in the room watches us go. Some, like people from the present, and Boone's people, recognize me to some degree. Some of them might even fear me. The rest just seem to understand that I'm taking charge, though I can't yet say if they resent or welcome my addition to Synergy's temporal internment camp.

I open the door and step into the room unannounced. Despite the cramped conditions in the main hall and the adjoining dorm rooms, there are only two people here: Dr. Langdon...and Minuteman.

29

My emotional gut says to start throwing punches and wait until Minuteman regains consciousness to ask questions. But my logical mind keeps me rooted in the doorway. Minuteman's presence irks me for a number of reasons, but at some point in the future, Cassie decided to trust him. To fight alongside him. At the very least, I'm going to find out why before slugging him.

When the room's two occupants see me standing there, I'm surprised to see relief in their eyes, including Minuteman's. There's a flash of recognition, followed by disappointment. I'm not who they were hoping for.

"We don't have time for your bullshit," Minuteman says, his mood souring as I step further into the room.

I pull a chair out from under a desk, spin it around and take a seat. "Afraid I must insist."

When Cassie enters behind me, Minuteman's eyes light up again. Langdon stands to greet her. While my interactions with the boss have been positive, they've been few and far between. To hear Cassie tell it, she and Langdon have had a few long conversations about a mutual hobby—crocheting, of all things.

"Hey," I whisper to Minuteman while Cassie greets Langdon. "That's not her."

"You saw her? The others?"

"Four of them," I say, glancing at Cassie to make sure she's still engaged. "They didn't make it."

"How?" The question comes out as an emotion-fueled grunt. He's barely holding himself together at the news, which means he cares about his people.

"Mini-gun. Didn't stand a chance."

"You were there?"

"Nearby."

"You see what we're up against now?" he asks.

I give a nod. "You should have told me you were from the future. That my time wasn't the first jump."

"Didn't know if I could trust you," he says. "You're a good company man, remember."

I angle my head toward Langdon. "Hasn't stopped you all from becoming pals."

"He was part of the plan. You're a wildcard." He leans closer, speaking in low tones. "How would you have reacted if we'd just approached you after that first jump back in time?"

"Before or after my truck exploded?"

"That was for your own good."

"You were trying to protect me?" I nearly laugh at the idea.

"Look..." He takes a moment to gather himself. "We need to stop measuring dicks, okay? You're here, you look like you're ready to do something stupid, and I'd rather we operate on the same team. So full disclosure." He leans back and raises his voice. "Cards on the table time. For both of you."

Cassie is a little thrown by her inclusion in the statement.

"How about all three of us," Kuzneski says, closing the door.

Minuteman looks ready to argue, but gives in without a fight. He's weary, and dressed in 1920s clothing not much better than rags, looking more than a little bedraggled.

"I'll tell her," I say, holding out a hand.

"Tell me what?" Cassie asks.

"What's your real name?" I ask Minuteman.

I can tell he's not accustomed to answering questions while being held prisoner. Like me, his training is to resist questioning, but he's not being interrogated. I'm simply asking for his trust, as I'm sure he will soon do of me.

"David," he says. "Sergeant David Flores, U.S. Army Ranger. Retired."

He holds my gaze for a moment. Knows what that means to me. We're both Special Forces, and while we never served together, there is an unspoken bond of having fought and bled for the same team. I don't have to like him, but I will respect him for his service.

I turn back to Cassie. "Flores is from the future, which is where all this started. Our time was the second flux. It was his people who blew up my truck, to keep me out of the way—"

"And keep you alive," Flores says.

His statement trips up my flow for a moment, but I press on, focusing on explaining to Cassie—and Kuzneski, who's now leaning against the door, arms crossed. "He's part of a team that came here to stop what's happening, he says."

"Screwed the pooch on that one," Kuzneski mutters.

"I found the other four members of his team on the mountainside. All of them dead."

The news deflates Langdon.

"I'm sorry about that," Cassie says to Flores, and then to me, "But what does that have to do with—"

"You were one of them," I tell her. "Your future self was here. Was part of his team." When I look into Cassie's stunned eyes, I see a flash of her dead-eyed stare, face covered in blood. "I thought..." I shake my head and sigh. "I thought it was you."

"But it *will* be me?" Cassie asks. "How long from now?"

"Seven years," I say. I turn to Minuteman for confirmation, and he nods.

"The odds against your fate repeating are astronomical," Langdon says, taking hold of Cassie's hand.

How can the instrument of all this pain and suffering be the kind man comforting my friend?

Death transforms the living.

I know that first hand. Perhaps he is even more unprepared for it than I was at eleven?

"If the timeline continued on course, your future self would know to avoid the situation that led to your death. But...I do not think that will be an issue. With each leap back we're tearing away layers of space-time, taking people and places, like lint on a piece of tape. Every stop picks up a little bit more...though not everything. But we're not just lifting the lint away, we're lifting a *copy* of it. Creating new time-lines. New dimensions of reality."

"Then what—" Kuzneski asks. "We're not real?"

"As real as any dimension. We're simply experiencing the moment of dimensional split in a way our senses can perceive. According to the many-worlds interpretation, every decision we make creates a myriad of alternate dimensions where we make different choices. The result is an infinite number of dimensions where anything is possible. For us, it's more visceral, as we're not just peeling away from our former lives, but also back in time, picking up more and more lint as we go. That is, if Mr. Flores's description of what's happening beyond these walls is accurate."

"It is," I say.

"So, we're living in a big Schrodinger's Synergy," Kuzneski says. "Dead and alive at the same time. Except some of us are alive twice and some of us are dead once." He looks at Cassie. "Sorry."

"First," Flores says. "I'm impressed you know that. Didn't think you were that smart."

Kuzneski offers a fake smile and middle finger. "Don't be a dick. I'm not that guy out there."

"Second, some of us are alive *three* times." Flores looks at Langdon to explain.

"We believe the effects are far reaching."

"*Beyond* Synergy?" I ask.

"The facility stretches far beyond the mountain," Langdon says.

I grip the back of the chair, taking out my frustration on the hard wood. "Why didn't I know that?"

"Your job was to protect our people from harm, and everything within our perimeter. The rest of the facility is underground."

I remember the large pipe running through the Indian graveyard, and the roadwork completed near my house. "The tunnels leading down the mountainside."

He nods, but I can tell there's more.

"What *is* this place?"

"A particle collider," he says. "The largest in the world. Built under the mountain."

"And under Black Creek," I guess, and I don't wait for confirmation. "Which means there are layers of town, and all the people in it from multiple time periods. That could be thousands of people, many of them armed, and all of them terrified."

I can't help but picture a bloodbath. Then I fixate on one possibility. One person, cast through time, who means everything to me and to Owen. I turn to Cassie. "Three lives. You were in town the day before my father died. We had planned to meet after church, but my father took me hunting."

Her eyes widen. "I was shoe shopping with my mother."

I try to figure out a way to reach town and save Young Cassie, as much for myself as for Owen and my Cassie. But saving them won't be possible as long as we're being catapulted through time. And that's not going to stop until all of my questions have been answered, starting with...

"Three lives," I say to Flores. "You weren't talking about Cassie."

He shakes his head. "I was talking about the man who brought us here. About the man who inspired us to risk everything, to fight against a lunatic whose actions could destroy the universe—" He looks at our Langdon. "Sorry." Then back to me. "The man who knew this mountain better than anyone, who loved this town and the people in it. Who Cassie would do anything for, including die." He leans forward, eyes intense. "I was talking about you."

30

"Am I dead?" I ask, and then I mentally adjust for the fact that I am one of three people. "Is *he* dead?"

"I'm not sure," Flores says. "We were separated on the mountain. He gave himself up to save me. That was before Boone's people found me. You ever catch up with him?"

"Stray fire from a drone dropped him."

"Huh." He's unmoved by the news.

"He wasn't all bad in the end," I say, surprised by my defense of the man.

Flores gives a nod like he already knew that. "When you're up against the kind of people we're facing, most bad men look good in comparison."

Langdon rubs his head. It must be hard to hear that in seven years, you'll be a monster of a man responsible for the deaths of hundreds of people, not to mention an entire town being ripped through time. But if he's right, the man before us will never become that monster. They are separate and disconnected by time and space. In theory. The only real way to test that would be to kill someone from the past and observe what happens to his future self. Someone expendable.

Someone like me. If the future me—the rebel leader waging war against his former employer—is still alive. "How does that happen? How did we get to...this?"

"We meet, a year from now. You hire me a few months before this place becomes a shit show."

"When my wife dies of cancer," Langdon says, cloaked in a shroud of dismay. What killed her in the future will still kill her now, but in a year's time. He might not become a madman, but the sting of death will leave its mark. It's already got its talons in him. I can see it in his eyes.

"Cancer..." I say.

"You were expecting something else?"

"Your older self claimed the people of Black Creek killed her. Said the country was on the brink of civil war."

"Never happened," Flores says. "And our country was a mess for a while, but was actually on the mend. He was fishing for sympathy. Trying to improve his image. Which means he's probably not done with you."

"Peachy keen," Kuzneski says. "He's done with me, though, right?"

Flores looks at Kuzneski for a moment, but says nothing. Then he turns to me. "I've been with you...with *him*, ever since. Wrecking your truck. That was you. And it wasn't just to protect you. It was to keep you out of the way. Not that it helped."

"He could have told me the truth."

"He didn't think so."

I'm having a hard time believing I wouldn't trust my future-self just seven years from now. Am I really that blindly loyal? Would I have defended Synergy even from myself? From Cassie? Without the experiences of the past day, without seeing everything for myself, maybe I would have. At the very least, I would have slowed them down. Not that it helped, like Flores said.

My future self might have inspired Flores and Cassie, and those other folks now dead in the woods, to fight the good fight, but he wasn't prepared for this. And now his people are dead. Knowing exactly how hard that will be for him, I determine to not repeat his mistakes.

Problem is, I'm even less prepared for this dangerous new Synergy, not to mention everything we've encountered along the way.

What *do* I have?

Flores, if he'll follow a younger version of his friend. Kuzneski and Cassie. My father and Owen are a no-go, but Inola, who is—as far as I know—still stalking the mountainside, will fight for her people. Five people against a futuristic army, who our more prepared, more heavily armed counterparts couldn't handle.

Step one is getting the hell out of this prison, which shouldn't be hard. With evil Kuzneski the only guard, all we really need to do is either trick him, or wait for someone new to open that door. If he's facing his younger self, he won't pull the trigger. Won't risk killing him. But once we're outside, where endless drone eyes are watching, it won't be long before we're discovered. And when that happens, we're mini-gun paste.

We'll need to get to the trees. If we can find Inola and—

"You're doing it," Flores says.

I snap out of my machinations. "Doing what?"

"Planning," he says. "You make a face."

"You do," Cassie says.

"It's kind of like..." Kuzneski stares off at nothing while moving his eyebrows up and down. "Like a golden retriever in deep thought. Only not as smart."

Kuzneski manages to get smiles out of Cassie and Flores, and I can see how they'd be friends, united by my future self. Who is not here.

"And if I am?" I ask.

"I'd rather fight and die," Flores says, "then give up and live."

Kuzneski raises his hand. "Is there a 'fight and live' option? Because, you know, that's probably better. I mean, you sound super badass. Like John McClane badass. But I'm partial to not getting shot. Or eaten. Or whatever the hell else has been going on out there."

"That's the plan," I say. "Fight and live."

"Is it?" Kuzneski asks. "Because really, what *would* be the plan? I mean, how do we stop all this?"

"That's what *he's* going to tell us." I point to Langdon, who shrinks in on himself a bit. As much as he doesn't like who his future self has become, he's a scientist, not a fighter. And he's not crazy. Not yet.

"Even if we stop the time...the..."

When I can tell he's struggling to come up with the right word, I offer, "Flux. That's what I've been calling it."

"Time flux," he says it like the words taste bad, but he moves past the issue. "Even if we stop it, we still have to deal with all this." He motions to the room's four walls, but his imaginary reach envelops all of Synergy and the monstrous creations standing sentinel over it.

"One problem at a time," I tell him, "but the quick version is this: if we can cut the power, it will interrupt his ability to control the drones."

"They can operate autonomously," Flores says.

"But they need to recharge," I point out. "I saw the docking bays. No power, no recharge. He'll have a window to reverse what we've done, but—"

"So we make it irreversible," Cassie says.

"Leaving all of us without power," Langdon says. "In the past. With no way to return."

"Huh? With no what?" Kuzneski says.

Langdon rubs his forehead, looking a bit peaked. "We're in a new dimension, and with every flux, we move on to another. There is no future for us to return to, because here, the future has not yet happened. The year in which we stop will be our home, forever."

That takes a moment to sink in. If I wasn't sitting already, I'd have plopped down into the chair. Kuzneski leans against the door and slides down to the floor. He doesn't have a wife or children, but he was close to his brother and his parents. Now he knows he'll never see them again, no matter the outcome.

Cassie steps closer to me, putting a hand on my shoulder. I take her hand and hold it tight. Whatever happens, at least we're in this together. With my father. And Owen. And maybe even Cassie's younger self.

At least I have my family, I think, and then I realize that, for the first time since I was a day older than Owen, I've got a lot to lose.

"And now you're caught up to me," Flores says. "That's about as far as I got with him before you arrived. He was about to tell me how all of this is possible."

"I don't know," Langdon insists.

"But you have an idea," I say.

"A hypothesis." He squeezes his hands like he's holding two invisible stress balls. "Synergy was built for the express purpose of detecting sub-atomic particles, like the Higgs Boson."

"Higgs bosom?" Kuzneski asks.

Langdon grunts his disapproval and continues. "The Higgs *Boson* is also known as the God Particle, simply because of its importance to the standard model of particle physics. We're looking for its antithesis."

"So..." I say, "the Devil Particle?"

While I'm not exactly a churchgoer, the analogy doesn't put me at ease.

"I prefer to call it the 'Langdon Particle,' but for those who prefer quirky nicknames, yes. It is the anti-particle to the Higgs Boson. Together, they create a kind of supersymmetry that keeps the entire universe stable. Where the God Particle contributes to universal mass, binding things together, the Devil Particle is the force pushing the multiverse ever farther apart. Theoretically. I have yet to discover the particle. But if it is real, and the hypothesis correct, it is possible that my future self found a way to disrupt the two particles' symmetry, releasing gravity waves capable of bending time and space."

"How could two little particles bend time and space?" Kuzneski asks.

"If you believe that all of creation came from a subatomic particle a million billion *billion* times smaller than an atom, then this is really just par for the course. When it comes to the subatomic and theoretical physics, size often doesn't matter."

"And if all that is accurate?" I ask. "How would we stop it?"

He looks confused for a moment. "I thought that was already established." When no one speaks he says, "Cut the power."

"*That's it?*" Kuzneski says.

"Well, it would stop the reaction. Free the particles from whatever effect is controlling them." Langdon says. "The collider has been running this whole time."

"How do you know that?" Cassie asks.

"Listen," Langdon says, and everyone goes still. In the silence that follows, I don't hear much, other than voices on the door's far side, but I feel a gently pulsing vibration beneath my feet. I felt the same outside, when standing on Synergy's concrete foundation.

I'm about to ask how to cut the power when I notice the vibration growing more intense. And I'm not alone.

"Umm," Kuzneski says.

Langdon grips the bed cushion. "It's happening again." When none of us reacts with more than a groan he says, "Hold on to something! The reaction is quite powerful at the epicenter!"

The roaring buzz explodes around us, along with a mind-bending warping of everything I can see—time and space bending before my eyes. Then I'm lifted off the floor and sent flying into the ceiling.

31

I don't remember feeling gravity's return or hitting the floor. I barely remember colliding with the ceiling, but I don't think that's what knocked me unconscious. My head hurts, but not concussion bad, which is good. I'm not sure how many whacks to the head I can handle in one day without becoming a useless lump.

I'm lying on my side, head on my arm. Sore, but alive.

I open my eyes and find Cassie lying beside me, eyes closed. For a moment, I imagine this is a lazy Saturday morning. That we're waking up together. That we're more than friends, and I think we are now. Maybe. The moment is broken when groans from the hallway beyond the closed door reach my ears.

I stretch out and place my fingers against the side of her neck. I don't immediately find her pulse, but I don't need to. My touch makes her eyes flutter and open.

"Okay?" I ask.

She grunts, pushing herself up. "Think so."

"How in the name of Captain Crunch's testes did I wind up on the floor?" Kuzneski asks. His back is on the floor, but his legs jut straight up against the bed. He leans to the side and flops over. "Wait, now I remember. I was fucking flying. *Again.*"

"Again?" Flores says, sitting up on the top bunk opposite Langdon, who is exactly where I last saw him, still clinging to the bed.

When Kuzneski sees Flores has been spared the pain of being dropped down onto the hard floor, he says, "Seriously? How lucky is this asshole?"

Not very, I think, but I keep the observation to myself. If his story is true, he came to Synergy to stop Langdon from unleashing hell on Earth. Instead, he got swept up in it, and lost all his friends—including future me and Cassie—in the process.

"The effect was far more powerful this time," Langdon says. "Before, it lifted us a few feet off the ground, but nothing like this. If not for the ceiling..." He looks up, no doubt imagining the sky above.

"Will it be like that for everyone?" I ask, concerned for Inola, not to mention the layers of people in Black Creek.

Langdon shakes his head. "We're at the epicenter. Whatever is happening in the collider, it's directly below Synergy. Here, we experience it as an eruption of space-time. On the mountainside, it would be more like a pyroclastic flow of bending space-time as it races outward."

"Sounds about right," Cassie says.

"But I can't imagine what we just felt would react gently with the world beyond Synergy." Langdon says.

"Any ideas why that one was more intense?" Flores asks.

Langdon pales a bit. "A more powerful flux."

Kuzneski pushes himself up. "Meaning?"

"A *larger* flux."

I look to the walls, expecting to see windows, but find none. I don't remember any in the outer hall, either. Whenever we are, it's beyond the dawn of civilization in the Americas. At this point, I'm not sure it matters how far back we go. It's possible there are still Cherokee tribes about, but if the jumps continue to grow, we'll eventually predate the human migration that brought people out of Africa, across Asia, and down to the Americas via Russia and Alaska...if that's how it actually happened. In this universe, our band of time travelers might become the very first Americans.

The question is why?

Why go back at all?

Why take all these people?

Why risk playing with science as powerful as the God and Devil particles?

Part of the answer comes in a moment of realization. My Dr. Langdon is here, but Jacqueline is nowhere to be seen. Future Langdon has reclaimed his wife a year before her death. But why would he do that...

Unless...

He has a cure, I think. Something from the future that would have saved her now. That *will* save her now. But even if he manages to save her, his mind won't be restored. You don't create a robotic army, slay dozens of people, and tear an entire community through space-time if there is a shred of sanity left in you.

But I understand his motivation. I already decided to save my father from his fate in the mine, to change time for my own selfish gain. I wouldn't have sacrificed an entire town, but I was willing to risk the unknown consequences of altering the past. Now that I know we're in a new dimension of time-space, I can protect my father, free of guilt. But that doesn't absolve me of being willing to take the risk. And it doesn't absolve Future Langdon for what he's done.

Thinking of my father, I yank open the door and find myself facing a room full of people in various states of recovery. Some are still unconscious, being tended to by those who have already woken up. The segregation I found when I first entered has evaporated. People are helping who they can, whether or not they come from the same nationality, tribe, or time.

My father is being tended to by one of the older Cherokee women. He's got a good gash on his head, either from hitting the ceiling, or the floor on the way back down. Owen looks no worse for the wear, crouching beside Dad.

"That was a big one," he says when he spots me approaching.

"Dad okay?" I ask him.

"Fine," my father says. "You learn anything interesting?"

"Nothing that will put you at ease," I tell him. "But a plan is coming together."

The Cherokee woman removes her hand from the bandage on his head and lifts his hand up to hold it. "Thank you," he says to her, receiving a nod in return before she moves on to help others. Then he turns back to me. "Something dangerous, I reckon?"

"Just sitting around is dangerous," Owen says.

"Hopefully not for much longer," I tell him. It's wishful thinking. Our plan is really just a bullet-point list of goals, completely devoid of how to make them happen. But it's a start.

The problem is that offering everyone unrealistic hope doesn't seem honest enough. Not for my formerly deceased father and my younger self. "You should know...this is permanent."

"Living in this place?" Owen asks, looking around the cramped quarters.

"Living in the past," I say. "We might be able to stop our backward progress, but we can't undo it."

Both of them take the news a bit better than I was expecting. My father takes my hand. "Near as I can tell, we have just about everything we had back home."

"Even more," Owen says, smiling up at me.

If all of us survive.

"Listen, we need to—"

"Upsee-daisy, asshole," Kuzneski says. His tone throws me for a moment, until I realize it's coming from the main door rather than from the bedroom.

I nearly rush him. This is the moment we've been waiting for. But he's armed with an assault rifle, as are the men flanking him. Between them there is enough firepower to cut down every man, woman, and child behind me.

"What do you want?" I ask, standing my ground.

"It's not what *I* want, it's what the big man wants." Future Kuzneski points a finger at me. "And right now, that is you."

When I don't move or respond, he adds, "Don't make me 'or else' you, man."

I glance back to the bedroom door, where Cassie and younger Kuzneski are watching. The two Kuzneskis flip each other off. Same gesture. Same timing. Their synchronicity seems to annoy both of them.

"Now," Future Kuzneski says, but I still don't budge until Cassie gives me a nod. There's no choice. We both know it. I turn to Owen, say, "Take care of your old man," and then I give our father a smile.

And with that, I head for the door, arms raised. I'm fully expecting to be bound, but Future Kuzneski just turns and heads for the door, allowing me to follow him, flanked by the two guards. Again, I could attack. Disarming the men and shooting Kuzneski in the back would take seconds.

But then what?

I'm not being roughed up or mistreated. If Future Langdon saw me as a threat, I'd certainly be in chains. He's not a fool. Despite my future self being at odds with the man, I have yet to tip my hand. If his impression of my current self is different to that of my future self, well, maybe he thinks I'll toe the line. And I reckon I'll let him go right on thinking that until I decide to pop him in the face and stop this crazy train through time in its tracks.

I'm led down the hall toward the door through which I entered the building. Kuzneski stops by a door and opens it to reveal a closet. He slips into a winter jacket before tossing one to each of the men behind me. "Colder than a Yeti's taint out there." Rather than offering me a coat, he closes the closet door and exits the building.

Arctic air rolls through the open door, flooding the hallway. It's cold enough to take my breath away, burning my exposed skin. Just a few minutes in this frigid air will do permanent damage. Part of me wants to be the tough guy and step out into the cold. Put on a show of strength by resisting its effects. But I'm not fighting for my pride here. I'm fighting for the people in this building, and at Adel's base. I need to play it smart, and that means not losing my fingers.

I yank open the closet and pull out a jacket for myself.

"Hey," one of the guards grumbles.

He flinches back when I give him a death-glare and say, "Try to stop me."

Kuzneski has a good laugh at the guard's expense, but it's short-lived. His teeth are already chattering. "Fuck, it's cold. Let's go already."

Blinding white light stuns me for a moment. The late afternoon sun blazes down through a deep blue sky, reflecting off a five-foot-tall wall of snow surrounding Synergy's perimeter. The amount of snow on its own is strange, even for an Appalachian mountaintop in the middle of winter. But it's made more dramatic by the lack of trees. The forest is missing.

Kuzneski notes my attention on our surroundings and says, "Welcome to the Ice Age, asshole."

32

"I know the way," I say, when Kuzneski course-corrects me with a shove.

"Maybe I just enjoy pushing you," he says.

"What happened between us?" I ask, doing my best to not glare at the man. It's not too difficult as he still has the face of my friend...with a few scars courtesy of my future self. The obvious answer is that we chose different sides of a fight, like brothers in the Civil War. I have trouble believing this is just about money for him. He doesn't seem surprised about being thrown back in time, where money is useless.

"You did." He shoves me again.

"How?"

"You already forget the scars on my face and chest?"

"It's more than that."

"Fine," he says, yanking me to a stop. "You want to know? You really want to fucking know?" He grips my coat and yanks me close. His words come out as a grinding growl, partially drowned out by the frigid howling winds. "I'm your inside man, and if you don't stop asking me questions, you're going to blow my freaking cover. I'm here because it's where you, where *future you*, wanted me." He gives me a violent shake for the two men watching. "Do you know how hard it is to act like an asshole all the time?"

We look each other in the eyes.

"Okay," he says, trying hard not to smile. "It's not that hard. But just sitting on my hands while Dr. Doom shoots us back in time ain't easy."

I'm not sure what to say, or if I should even respond. I want to believe him. I'm desperate to believe him. Not only because it means I didn't get all my future friends killed, but it means that we have a real hope of escaping this prison and putting a plan into motion. But he's been playing the part of future, evil Kuzneski a little too well, and I'm not about to give up any incriminating information about myself, my plans, or the people with whom I'm conspiring.

"You have no idea how relieved I am to hear you say that," I tell him.

"You have a plan?" he asks.

"Honestly, I was thinking I'd hear Dr. Doom out," I say, "and go from there."

He looks displeased by that but says nothing. The two guards step closer, emanating an aura of Arctic impatience.

Kuzneski gives me another good shake and shouts, "Harper and Brown are dead because of you! Look at me sideways even once more, and I will shoot your ass dead."

I'm stunned. "Is that true?"

"Mostly," he says, lowering his voice again. "But they had it coming." With that, he shoves me to the ground, laughing as I sprawl backward. Then he gives me a kick and says, "Move!"

The foyer of the research facility is exactly how I remember it, with a few modifications. The two-story space no longer has a reception desk. The front wall is all glass, looking out at the perimeter wall, and the mountainous view beyond.

After passing through the second set of double doors, I pause to look at the view. I've stood atop this peak more times in my life than most people. The view is familiar to me, but the mountains stretching into the distance are not... Well, not exactly. The topography is changing—shrinking really—but Adel is just as tall as ever, the local landscape no doubt preserved by Langdon's experiment.

The rest of the foyer, as I saw it just yesterday, was corporate and sterile, neither pleasing nor offensive to the eye. It moved people in the direction they needed to go and served that singular purpose with the bare minimum of décor and furnishings. Now...it looks like the living room of a big game hunter, minus the mounted heads, though I suspect that might be something added later. A wall of exotic species from across time. How long before that mountain lion ends up on this wall, its fangs bared at the bald man sitting on the brown leather couch, facing the stone-encased, real, wood fireplace.

The fire fills the large room with intense warmth that sends a shiver through my body, as the temperature change burns my cheeks. The air is rich with the aroma of wood smoke. Birch, by the smell of it. Great for setting a mood, but the soft wood burns fast. Not the most efficient choice.

"I know what you're thinking," the bald man says. I can only see the back of his head, a dull orange glow atop his polished dome, reflecting from the warm, colored, recessed lighting above. But I recognize Langdon's voice. "That a clean facility like this shouldn't have a wood fireplace. That it will promote dust. That our experiments might be corrupted."

I didn't think any of that, but I say, "It crossed my mind."

"Then you'll be relieved to know that the days of experimentation have come to an end."

Is he going to pull the plug on the collider? Park us in some predetermined time? I step around the faux country living room, complete with several comfy chairs, a braided rug, and an afghan over the back of the couch. Gas pops from the burning logs, making me flinch.

I'm on edge, expecting the worst.

What I find, as I round the couch, is...normal.

Future Langdon sits on the couch, cradling a cup of what I think is hot cocoa, a pair of plaid slippers on his feet. He's dressed in flannel, smiling at the now sizzling fire. Aside from the lack of hair, he looks the same. Actually, he looks happy.

When I see the person seated in the tall chair beside the couch, I realize why. Jacqueline gives me a forced smile and turns her eyes down, ashamed to hold my gaze too long. She's not being held prisoner. There are no chains binding her. But where could she go? How could she hope to change anything? And Langdon *is* her husband. He might not be the man she remembers, but she undoubtedly feels some responsibility for him.

Seeing the warm setting and Future Langdon's comfort in it, I worry that this frigid wasteland might be our final destination.

"When *are* we going?" I ask, trying to sound more interested than revolted.

He cracks a wide smile. "How does the saying go? That's for me to know, and you to find out. When we get there, of course. But it will be worth the risk and the sacrifice. The ultimate journey. The pinnacle destination."

I glance back at Future Kuzneski, who shrugs and shakes his head. He doesn't know either. *Does anyone know?*

Jacqueline does. The way she's shrinking into her chair shows her hand. And it's not good. But we're already in a new dimension. Already lost in a time before our nation was born, perhaps before mankind reached North America. What difference will another hundred thousand or hundred million years make? The flora and fauna might change, but the fact that we are lost in time forever—that's a done deal.

I don't think he'll give me an answer, so I drop the subject. My immediate concern is the protection of the people under my care, including generations of people occupying my home town. "Why am I here?"

"You work here," he says, cracking a smile that no one else shares. He rolls his eyes. "So serious. Here's the situation. You're in a pickle. On the one hand, you're a loyal company man who has proven himself competent. I have relied on you in the past, and hope to do so again. On the other, you're a soldier looking for a cause, which I'll admit I might have supplied for you. Part of you wants to throttle me right now..." He glances back at Kuzneski and the two guards, who have remained by the doorway. "I have no doubt you could break my neck before anyone could raise a hand against you."

He's right about that.

"But you won't. Because doing so would jeopardize the lives of people for whom you care a great deal." He takes a sip of hot cocoa, stands, and approaches the fireplace. "Heat is a glorious power. It gives life, and it takes it away. From it, all things were created, and by it, all things will be undone."

"You're losing me," I tell him, thinking he sounds a bit more like a televangelist than a physicist.

"Pardon my philosophy," he says. "How are your father and younger self settling in?" When I don't answer, he says. "I also know of your affection for Cassie Dearborn, not to mention his—" He tilts his head toward Future Kuzneski. "—younger self. And let's not forget about your beloved cesspool of a backward town. I wonder how many people are alive down there. I wager there's a full-scale war between peoples, races, and generations. That is humanity's way, after all. Stick to your own, kill what you don't understand."

He makes a popping sound with his lips and places his mug on the mantle. "There I go again. You asked a good question to which I provided an unsatisfactory answer. I must admit, I am so accustomed to being at odds with you that having a normal conversation is something of a challenge."

He's not hiding the fact that my future self is his enemy, which is interesting, but it also means he knows that I know. It occurs to me that there might be hidden cameras in the bunk rooms. That he heard everything we talked about. Or maybe Future Kuzneski—being the inside man he claims to be—watched the feed and briefed him, leaving out incriminating details?

I reckon I'll never know, unless I allow this conversation to flow in the direction of Future Langdon's choosing. I stay quiet and let him get to the point.

He steps up close to me, within reach. I could kill him... He'd barely have time to register my hands on his head before his neck snapped.

He stares into my eyes, daring me.

With each second he allows to pass, I relax a little bit more. Killing him right now would solve nothing. I know this. He knows this.

"We have an understanding, then?" he asks.

"We do."

"Very good. I need your help with two problems." I wait for him to continue, playing the good soldier. "The first is rather abstract. A mystery, in fact. The second, well, it's one you are uniquely qualified to handle."

"And that is?" I ask.

"You," he says.

33

The cozy feeling of the foyer fades, the farther away I'm led. I recognize our path through the facility for the first few turns, but then I realize the floor plan has changed. The offices have been replaced by large, windowless rooms with solid steel doors. In fact, the place is almost built like a submarine. While drywall covers most surfaces, I'm pretty sure the underlying walls are solid steel, rather than wood.

Has it always been like this?

I'm not one to pay attention to construction techniques, but the solid steel element and giant bolts stand out. The building has been adapted, but for what?

Time travel?

Future Langdon stops in front of an unmarked steel door with a thick latch holding it closed. "He's in here."

"I'm in there?"

"If you were the same man, we wouldn't be standing here talking, would we?" He smiles, and I force myself to return it.

Don't make it too easy, I tell myself.

"And if I do this for you?" I ask. "If I get you the answers you want? What do I get in return?"

He scoffs. "Well, your family to start."

"And the other people being held?" I ask. "And anyone still alive in town?"

He squints at me. "What are you really asking?"

"They're going to need someone to lead them. Someone to keep them alive whenever you end up taking us."

His smile grows and makes me uncomfortable. The Langdon I knew was a positive guy. He smiled a lot, but not like this. Future Langdon's toothy grin is almost predatory. He's closing in on his quarry, whatever it might be, and he's willing to do anything to catch it.

Part of me wishes that he'd brought Jacqueline along. Whether he's lost his mind or not, she'd temper his mania. Without her here, I have no idea what he's going to ask me to do. But I'm pretty sure it's going to be horrible for me.

For both of me.

"You want to what? Be president of Black Creek? Give birth to a new humanity in a world before mankind?"

His questions hint at how far back he intends to go, and it's disconcerting to say the least. "Something like that," I say. "You can stay here. Do whatever it is you're doing. But let me help them survive. We're in the past, but that doesn't mean we can't have a future."

"Ever the public servant."

"Keeping people alive is my job."

"Including me?"

"As long as you don't kill people who pose no threat...yes."

"I'm glad you said that." He yanks the door's latch, unlocking it. "Because the version of you behind this door *is* a threat. To me. To you. To everyone you just asked me to protect."

"What do you want from him?"

"Answers," Future Langdon says. "About his people. How many he came with, and which one of them is...enhanced."

Enhanced? I have no idea what that could mean, but he clearly thinks my older self will.

He shakes his head and sighs. "Just get me details about his team."

He pulls the door open and I barely notice the room.

All I can see is myself.

I step inside and for a moment, my mind says I'm looking in a mirror. But there are a few differences. Gray hair on the sides of his head, and his chin. There are a few scars on his shirtless body that I don't yet have. And then there are the fresh wounds. The two that have been bandaged, on his shoulder and in his side, have the round blood stains of bullet holes. But the long straight cuts across his chest, the freshest of them still trickling blood down his stomach, are new.

They're torturing him, I realize, and then I see the room for the first time. It's not large, a ten-foot cube. The back wall is taken up by my older self, hands and feet bound to the wall, arms spread wide like some kind of Jesus figure. Countertops on either side of us are littered with the tools of torture. Spikes, blades, heat sources, construction tools, saws, electrical clamps. There's even a small cabinet filled with vials of drugs. This is not a hastily assembled torture chamber. This was planned by someone who knows what they're doing.

I run through a mental list of past Synergy employees and the few current that I've met. None of them struck me as men capable of something like this. Not even Langdon. He approves of all this, but he is not the architect.

When the door closes behind me, I ask, "Are you okay?"

My older self glares at me. He's putting on a good show of strength, but he doesn't have a lot left in him, which probably has something to do with the blood staining the grated floor beneath him. "I should have known you'd play the good company boy. I used to be so weak." His eyes flick up to the left.

"I'm trying to keep people safe," I tell him. "That's something you used to care about, too." I turn to inspect some of the tools lining the counter, casually glancing at the ceiling in the corner of the room where a security camera watches and listens.

He let me know to guard my language. While there might be some grains of truth in his feelings toward me, he knows I would never turn on myself, that I would never support what Synergy has become.

His strength wavers, the weight of his body pulling hard on his wrists.

They're killing him. Horribly.

"What do you want to know?" he asks, his voice a gravelly whisper.

"Just give me a *minute*, man." I feign exasperation, picking up a long, serrated knife, shaking my head and putting it back down. When I turn back to face him, the look in his eyes confirms he understood my clumsy message: *Minuteman is alive.*

"How many people did you come here with?"

"Four," he says, wisely leaving Minuteman out of the count. "But you already knew that, didn't you?"

Shit. My message about Minuteman has clued him in to the possibility that the rest of his team didn't make it. That *Cassie* didn't make it.

"There's no one else?" I ask. "Someone...enhanced?"

The screwed up expression on his face is the same one I make when I hear something ridiculous. He coughs hard, blood staining his lips.

I scan his body for bruising and find it on his side. He's bleeding internally. The right doctors would be able to help him, and Future Langdon might have them on staff, but this future iteration of myself would never go for it.

"I just need to hear it," he says. "Tell me the truth. Is she gone?"

My closing eyes weigh down my head.

"Was it Langdon?"

My head dips a bit lower. When I look back up, meeting his tear-filled gaze, I mouth the words, "I'll kill him."

"But she's still here," I tell him aloud. "From my time. And earlier."

"Then you still have something to live for," he says. "Something to fight for."

"We're here, too."

That catches him off guard, and for a moment he fights against the unconsciousness threatening to whisk him away.

"Age eleven," I tell him. "A day before Dad... He's here, too."

He coughs in surprise, and then in pain. "Dad? *Alive?*"

I nod.

Tears leave clean streaks behind on his cheeks.

"Then you have more to fight for than I ever did." He's got more to say. Things that would fuel my fight, but speaking the words would put

Future Langdon's trust in me in peril. His body sags again. "Do you remember Marjah?"

Marjah is a small town in the Helmand province of Afghanistan,
one of the most dangerous and deadly in the region. While men
from the 3rd Battalion, 6th Marine Regiment held the perimeter, my
job was to recruit local villagers. No one knew that the Taliban had
arrived before us. We found ourselves pinned down by enemy com-
batants, taking fire for two straight days. I lost three men, but in the
end my squad was saved by an Army Ranger Sniper. It wasn't our
proudest moment, a bunch of Marines being rescued by an Army
boy. I never met the man who saved us from nearly a mile away, but
I'll never forget him.

I'm expecting more, but he lets the story hang there, like I'm
supposed to understand what he's getting at. So I prod. "Well?"

"Just give me a minute," he says, taking a deep, raspy breath, *"Man..."*

I try not to react, but it's hard. The man who saved me all those years
ago is in the next building over. No wonder I trust him so much in the
future.

I give the slightest nod of understanding while he holds my gaze.

Then his jaw pops to the side a little, and I hear a muffled crack.

"Save them," he says.

Then his eyes roll back.

His body twitches.

Foam gurgles from his mouth.

"No!" I shout.

Behind me, the door is flung open. A pair of doctors rush in. They
had no intention of letting him die, but he's just made saving him
impossible.

As I stagger back into the rear wall, Future Langdon rushes in,
face red with anger. "What happened?"

"Cyanide," I say. "Hidden in a false tooth. It's an old spy trick. You
should have looked for it."

"He's right," one of the doctors says, and something about his voice
sets me on edge. I don't recognize the man, he just sounds heartless. The
kind of sociopath it takes to run a torture chamber. "He can't be saved."

"Then you failed," Future Langdon hisses at me, and I suspect that I will soon replace my now dead older self.

I stammer for a moment, choked up after watching myself die, but I manage to say, "H-he told the truth. You heard him. He had four people with him. And they're all dead. The moment he pieced that together, he didn't have a reason to live."

"Suicide risk is not part of your profile," Future Langdon says.

"I'm not him." I point to my dead self, as the doctors unclasp his wrists and let the body fall to the floor.

"You're sure?" he asks.

"Reading him wasn't hard. Whatever problem you're dealing with, it's not him, or his people." I turn away from the sight of my body. "And it never will be."

"That is...unfortunate," Langdon says. "Dr. Robles."

I take note of the man who looks up—the architect of my future self's torture—committing his pock-scarred face, round glasses, and wispy balding hair to memory.

"Incinerate the body."

"But—"

Future Langdon holds up a hand, silencing the man before he can say exactly how he'd like to desecrate my body.

"Out of respect for the living," Future Langdon tips his head toward me. Robles lowers his head in submission.

"Thank you," I say to Future Langdon, as he leads me out of the torture chamber. They're the two hardest words I've ever spoken.

"Perhaps you should save your thanks until after you've seen what we're...what *you're* up against."

I don't like the sound of that, but until I've gathered all the intel I can and have gained his trust, I need to play along. Then I'll think about wrapping my hands around his throat.

34

Future Kuzneski meets us at the security control center, which is four times the size of what I'm used to. Where there were once three screens displaying a total of twenty-seven camera feeds, there is now a wall of large flat-screens surrounding one massive screen. There are at least fifty camera feeds from inside the facility, various points around the mountain, and what looks like a misshapen 3D-puzzle of Black Creek.

"Wait here," Langdon says, stepping inside the room. I can't hear what he's telling the two men monitoring the feeds, but large chunks of the wall go black. He's either hiding something from me, or trying to keep me focused on his problems, and not those of the people I care about. When he's done, all videos from Synergy and Black Creek have disappeared, replaced by a large number of feeds from the facility's perimeter and the mountainside.

"You okay, dude?" Kuzneski whispers. "You didn't look great before, but now... What happened?"

"I killed myself."

"You look pretty alive to m..." Realization settles atop him like a lead blanket. "Oh. Shit."

He looks ready to lose control, but reels himself back in with a sniff and a stretch of his face. "Did you learn anything from him?"

"Only that all his people are dead," I say. "Except for you."

"Damn..." He leans his back against the wall.

"What about you? What do you know?" I motion toward Future Langdon. "About him? About *when* he's taking us?"

"Wish I had answers, but..." Kuzneski shrugs.

"What did he offer? Couldn't have been money."

"Why not?"

Does he not know? Did I not know?

"This is a one-way trip."

He squints at me. "Bullshit."

"According to Langdon's younger self, we're creating new dimensions of reality with each new jump. Our future won't be there, even if we could reverse direction and go back."

He doesn't look dismayed, shocked, or even frightened.

He looks pissed.

Like he's just found out the Rolex watch on his wrist is a Casio in disguise.

Like he's been conned.

Because he has been.

Future Kuzneski is *not* my inside man.

"Come in," the elder Langdon says. I step inside the command center to find all the screens now displaying external feeds. The large screen holds a paused video of the forest, taken before our arrival in the Ice Age. I'm caught off guard when I see the rest of the large space. There are twelve terminals, all manned by men wearing VR headsets. The displays in front of them show aerial views of Synergy and the surrounding mountain.

This is where they control the drones from. Given the large number of drones, both flying and grounded, I reckon that the machines can operate autonomously, or under direct control. They're searching the surrounding mountainside, but for what?

From above, I can see that the forest still exists, encased in thick snow, but still present. The tree line is just a bit further down the mountain, about where it began in my time, thanks to the strip mining.

"We've been losing drones," Langdon says, pulling my attention back to the big screen. "This is how it began."

The video feed plays, showing a smooth recording of the forest. The image suddenly goes shaky and drops straight down. Then static.

"Looks like your pilot ran into a branch," I say.

"That's what we thought at first, but the drone was self-piloting at the time, and they have a perfect track record with avoiding even the smallest obstacles. We sent a recovery team and found this."

An image fills the screen. The drone is lying on the ground, crushed and torn apart.

"Then, someone shot it out of the sky. I don't know if you've noticed, but there are a lot of armed and frightened people on the mountain."

"There was no evidence of gunfire, and that doesn't explain the wreckage. It would take a very strong man with a sledgehammer to do that."

"Also, not out of the realm of possibility." My doubt is frustrating him, but I can tell there's more. "Show me the rest."

A second drone feed plays, ending in nearly the same way, except this one is smashed against a tree twice before the video ends.

"It was plucked from the air and manhandled," Langdon says, stating the obvious. But then he adds, "It was twenty feet up when that happened. It wasn't long after this that we started finding bodies."

I nearly point out that there are a lot of bodies on the mountainside, too, which is ultimately his fault, but I can't deny playing a part in some of their deaths.

A third video plays, and this time the footage is uninterrupted as the drone slides up to a corpse lying in a tree's branches. It's stretched out and bent, like all the joints have been popped out, or worse. Given the amount of blood soaking the man's body, it's possible his 1920s-style clothing is the only thing holding him together.

The video feed switches again. This time it's a woman. She's lying on top of a tree, impaled by several branches, as though she'd fallen out of the sky.

Another feed shows what's left of a Cherokee Indian, his arms and legs removed and piled beside his torso, most of the meat missing.

"You thought this was me?" I ask. "Future me? I can't imagine any timeline where I'd be a part of this."

"You were...are...a resourceful man. When faced with overwhelming odds, you generally find a way to even them. Given your history with psy-ops, I thought you might be trying to put the fear of God into me."

"By killing innocent people?"

He shrugs. "Fire with fire."

I decide a moral argument is not in my best interest, and that full disclosure in this case, will benefit all of us. "I came across a body like this. The flesh was eaten by a large predator. Probably a bear. If it's an extinct species—something with the power of a grizzly—that could explain the killings. I've also seen a large cougar stalking the mountain. Many predators are known to hide their kills in trees, so maybe—"

"It's not a bear," Kuzneski says.

I glower at the man operating the displays. "Show me."

"This was our first view of direct contact," the operator says, playing aerial footage of a drone flying fifty feet above the forest canopy. "Center of the screen. Close to the horizon."

When I see it, I'm not sure what I'm looking at. It looks like a fly buzzing straight up past the camera. But what appears to be close at first, looks far away as it grows larger. And closer. I identify the projectile as a basketball-sized rock just before it careens into the drone.

"Have you heard of anyone in the history of Black Creek that built a catapult?" Langdon asks. I don't bother replying. He already knows the answer. And I'm pretty sure that no one in the history of catapult building ever had enough skill to shoot a small moving drone out of the sky.

"You have another theory?" I ask.

"One that I am loathe to subscribe to on the fact that it is both improbable and impossible." He looks me in the eyes. "Someone threw it."

I couldn't throw that stone more than a few feet. I doubt the strongest man on Earth could get it much further. "Then this is something we agree on."

"What *don't* we agree on?" he asks, suddenly suspicious.

"I just watched myself take a cyanide pill to avoid being tortured by your very own Dr. Mengele. I reckon a generous helping of revulsion is appropriate. I understand that you were defending what you've built. That Synergy was under attack from him. And that he took his own life. But there is no time where I will abide by torture."

Standing my ground puts our faux relationship at risk, but letting all that be swept to the side like it was nothing...

He'd see through it eventually.

"Well..." Langdon grins. "If he was telling the truth, as you believe, there will be no need for such tactics in the future, or rather, in the past." He gives the operator a backhanded tap on the shoulder. "Play the last video."

Unlike all the other video feeds, this one is at ground level, bumbling up and down as a tank-treaded drone rolls over uneven terrain. Its mini-gun is pointing straight out in the feed, like it's a first-person-shooter video game.

Then it stops.

The camera whips from side to side, tracking a shadow of movement. The blur is so fast that making it out is impossible. I get a sense that I'm looking at a man, but the scale seems to be off, or the trees in this part of the forest are small.

It disappears in a thick copse of trees. Is that it? I actually jump when a hand snaps into frame, grasping the mini-gun, wrapping meaty, thick, and pale fingers around the coffee can-thick barrel. Then the whole vehicle is wrenched off the ground and flung skyward. The video records a spiral of forest and sky until it drops back down and goes dark.

An image of the massive hand returns to the screen. It's human, but is far too large. Too strong.

"What do you make of this?" Langdon asks.

I step closer, trying to take in the details. Aside from the very pale skin, it looks human, except...not. Something is off. I place my finger on the massive index finger and then slide it over the knuckles, one by one.

"My screen," the operator complains when my finger leaves a smudge. He falls silent when I continue counting aloud.

"Four...five..." I look at Langdon. "Six."

35

"It would appear that I am not the only monster whisking through time," Langdon says. The words are loud enough for all to hear, but I think his inner monologue has just escaped the confines of his mind. Perhaps there is a part of him that knows what he is doing here is wrong?

"The fuck is that?" Kuzneski asks, leaning closer to the screen, recounting the fingers on the massive hand.

I surprise everyone, including myself, by providing an answer. "Tsul'Kalu."

Langdon turns to me, waiting for more.

"A Cherokee god of the hunt. It was buried at the bottom of the mountain, in a clearing not far from my home."

"Since when are gods buried in Appalachia?" Kuzneski asks, his distaste for the region shining through.

"The stigma around Appalachia has nothing to do with the landscape or the people who called it home before coal mining's slow demise left people jobless, hungry, homeless, and desperate. And if you spent more than a few minutes in Black Creek, you'd realize that stigma is based on a very small portion of the population. Most—"

Langdon silences me with a raised hand. "While I appreciate your loyalty to your home...and to this company, I'm afraid off-topic tangents at this crucial time will just not do. Tsul'Kalu. Tell me more."

"After one of the last jumps back, the burial mound was gone." I point to the screen. "Which I reckon means the man on whom the legend was based could have been alive and taken along with us."

"That's not a man, dude," Kuzneski says. "Those fingers are like bananas. Like big fuckin' bananas."

"Well, yeah," I say. "He was a giant."

Langdon's eyes widen. "The burial mound. Was it present in your time?"

"Stories about the clearing being an Indian burial ground were passed down by my family, but the mound was never there. Not in my lifetime, or my father's. Why?"

"There are legends, not just in Appalachia, but throughout North American Indian tribes, of a race of giant men with six fingers and six toes. Double rows of teeth. Dark red hair. Slanted eyes."

I nod. "But they've never been more than rumors. Legends."

"Because there is no evidence," he says. "Not because it doesn't exist, but because it was gathered up and sequestered by people who feared what it meant for humanity."

"Who would gather up giant skeletons?" Kuzneski asks.

"The Smithsonian Institute," Future Langdon says. "It sounds like a conspiracy theory, but most conspiracy theories are born out of a nugget of truth. In my experience, even an atom-sized bit of truth leads to amazing discoveries."

I'm about to unleash a little sarcasm, but I'm distracted by a surfacing memory—not of an event, but of a passage from the Bible. I spent my childhood ignoring sermons, but keeping an open Bible on my lap. I would read what I considered the interesting bits. The fall of Jericho. David and Goliath. Pretty much all of Revelation, and a certain passage in Genesis that always sparked my imagination. "Nephilim."

Langdon nods. "That is one theory, yes. Demon-fathered demigods living among us." He turns to the screen. "And dying among us. Nephilim or not, at least you know it can be killed."

Damnit. This is why I'm here. Why he's taking a risk with me. He needs someone with my skill-set to kill the one thing left he perceives as a threat to his personal mission.

I'm about to pre-empt his request for aid with a 'Hell, no,' when one of the drone pilots says, "Sir!"

At first, I can't tell which of the men has spoken, until he adds, "I might have something here."

"What is it?" Langdon asks, as we crowd around the man, looking at the footage from his aerial drone. "Hold on, there's a fire, too, I think."

The column of smoke is easy to see. "It's a campfire," I guess. "Someone is trying to stay alive in this frozen hell."

The drone maintains its altitude, some two hundred feet above the mountain's slope, flying closer to the smoke column. The camera angles down, revealing three people huddled around what is closer to a bonfire than a campfire. Remembering how cold it was out there, I'm not surprised. It would take a significant heat source to combat the Ice Age chill. Whoever built it knew what they were doing, digging a large pit first, big enough for the blaze and several people to escape the wind. But it's a stop-gap measure. The snow will melt out from under the fire, extinguishing the flames.

"How long until the next flux?" I ask.

"What makes you think this isn't our final destination?" Langdon asks, showing a complete lack of concern for the people trying to fend off frostbite.

I consider it for a moment. The cozy foyer seems to fit the theme, but not even a madman would want to live atop a frozen mountain. "How long?"

"I'm not sure," he says. "It's not an exact science. But I know the duration between the gravity waves is growing longer, carrying us further back with each...what did you call them? Flux? I rather like that."

Seven years does change a lot, I think, remembering the younger Langdon's sour face when he adopted the term.

"I'm sorry," he says. "I'm talking over you without explaining."

"Don't bother," I say. Not only do I have a pretty good idea how all this is happening, I also know how to stop it. I just need the chance. To him, I just sound uninterested, because I am. Big picture or not, the lives of the people below the drone concern me, in part because of my humanitarian instincts, but also because I recognize one of them.

Inola sits by the fire, hands raised toward the flames. She's got the shotgun and the Winchester with her. I'm not sure who the other two people are, but their clothing suggests they're some of Boone's crew.

"Just let me get out there," I say. "Those people—"

"Which one?" Langdon asks, leaning closer to the display. "Which one of them do you know?"

I don't see any point in lying. Inola's association with me was short-lived. He has no reason to fear her. The problem is, he has no reason to risk resources to bring her in from the cold, either.

I tap my finger on the screen, pointing out Inola. Behind me, the screen-Nazi groans when my finger leaves another smudge. "It's not even your screen," I grumble, and then I say, "Her name is Inola. She's a Cherokee Indian. She told me about Tsul'Kalu."

With that, I've solidified her value as an intel source. The giant stalking Adel is a bump in the temporal road that he had not accounted for. His drone army can deal with any human threat they encounter, but Tsul'Kalu—if that's who's really out there—has proven to be too much for his machines. If she had information about the giant, especially how to kill him, then that's intel worth retrieving.

"Do you have any transports?" I ask.

"For this terrain?" Langdon asks, shaking his head. "She will need to be rescued...on foot."

"I'll need a team," I say without hesitation.

"Hell to the no," Kuzneski says. I can't tell if he's still playing his part, or if that was a genuine reaction. The threat is real. Reaching Inola and those people is going to hurt. But it's a risk I'm willing to take, and I know a few other brave souls who will take the risk with me.

"People I trust," I say. "Just a handful. To watch my back. If that thing is out there, I'm going to need—"

Langdon waggles a hand at me, already nodding. He levels his gaze at his Kuzneski. "Get him who and what he needs. Then...how does the saying go? Grow a dick and go with him."

"I'm not sure that's actually a saying," Kuzneski says, and when Langdon glowers at him, he adds, "But, yes, sir."

"Umm," the drone operator says.

When I look back to the screen, Inola and the two people are frantically dumping snow on the fire, extinguishing it. Without the heat, they won't last long. So what could... "Do you have audio?"

The operator yanks his headset cord out and the audio feed switches over to a pair of speakers. A haunting howl fills the command center.

Tsul'Kalu.

I grip the pilot's shoulder. "Take the drone down!"

"Do it," Langdon orders, willing to take the risk for what Inola knows.

The drone drops down through the leafless trees, maneuvering its way through the web of branches. Twenty feet from the ground, sliding through the steam cast off by the now soggy firepit, the drone comes to a stop. Framed in the center of its lens is Inola, shotgun raised up. She holds her fire, knowing the drone might not be a threat, but that firing will further attract the attention of a very real threat.

"How do I talk to her?" I ask.

The drone operator reaches out and toggles a mic. Despite being in VR, muscle memory guides his hand.

I lean closer to the mic. "Inola."

"William?" She sounds hopeful, and in doing so has given away her closeness to my father.

"Owen," I say. "Listen. I'm coming for you. Just try to stay hidden. Try to stay alive."

A howl replies. Louder than the first. Inhuman.

"We can't stay here," Inola says to her companions. "Go!"

While the two strangers make a break for it, leaving easy to follow tracks in the deep snow, she turns back to the drone. "Hurry." She glances toward the sound of cracking wood, eyes flaring wide. Then she bolts.

The drone tracks their flight for a moment, and then spins toward the sound of yet another roar.

The pilot shouts in surprise as what looks like a stone-tipped spear impales the flying machine. Gears grind as the drone drops from the sky, landing upside down, the camera still sending its live feed. The sound of large feet, crunching through the snow, booms from the speakers. We watch in silence, transfixed as a massive foot, with six toes, steps in front of the camera.

"Holy shitlesticks," Kuzneski whispers.

The drone is lifted off the ground, passing by the mostly naked form of a massive man, covered in thick tufts of red hair. *Sasquatch,* I think, trying to make sense of the monstrous form by identifying it as a modern myth, rather than an ancient one. A moment later, when the thing opens its mouth, I know I'm wrong. Its two rows of large teeth, the canines as large as my thumbs, crunch down on the drone, killing the feed—and my hopes of finding Inola alive.

But I'm still going to try.

I clutch Langdon's shirt and pull him close. "Is there any way to get there faster?"

He glances at my hands.

I release him.

Then he turns to Kuzneski. "See to his needs. Show him the tunnels." Then to me. "If you find yourself in dire circumstances, there will be no help coming."

"Wouldn't expect it," I say, and I head for the door, Kuzneski at my back, and what seems like a fairly good chance of a horribly painful death ahead of me.

36

"Tunnels?" the younger Langdon whispers, when I explain what's happening. "There are conduits running under the ground, stretching to various parts of the collider, and the power station on the far side of town, but tunnels? No. They must be future additions."

I look over my shoulder to confirm that Future Kuzneski is waiting by the door. Inside man or not, the people kept in this small prison don't like him, and he isn't keen to stand among them. Gives me a chance to have one last private conversation, assuming the microphones hidden around us aren't sensitive enough to pick up our hushed words.

"Where is the power station?" I ask. It feels like a ridiculous question. As Synergy's head of security, I should have been made aware of such things, but even present-day Langdon kept some secrets.

"Far side of town, to the south. Oak Tree Lane. It's fed by the solar array, but...it was never designed to handle the load this facility must require, nor the particle collider's continuous function."

It's easy to read between the lines. Whatever was there before has likely been upgraded. "And to shut it down?"

He shrugs. "I'd assume there is a main breaker, but there should be people monitoring the power station. They'll know how to shut it down."

And will probably be heavily armed.

"You're sure about this?" Flores asks, looking over my shoulder toward my father and my younger self. His concern is touching in that it is neither for himself nor me, but for my family. When I explained about the tunnels connecting the facility to various parts of the mountain, the collider, the town, and the power station, the response was mild surprise. When I told them we were going after Inola and might have to face the actual Tsul'Kalu, I saw a mixture of trepidation and disbelief. And when I said that both my father and Owen would be accompanying us, utter shock was the response.

"Aren't they safer here?" Cassie asks.

Common sense says yes. They're protected by buildings designed to withstand the rigors of time travel and the various environments encountered along the way, and to repel a paramilitary force led by my now-dead older self. Beyond these walls is an unforgiving, ever-changing ancient world full of threats known and unknown, but in here, they're bargaining chips.

Future Langdon knows that. With them here, my hands will be tied. I'm sure he wouldn't approve of them leaving, but he told Future Kuzneski to get me what I wanted and never explicitly said to hold them. If Kuzneski is the man he claims to be—or wants me to believe he is—he's not going to defy me.

"Okay, so, quick recap," my Kuzneski says. "Step one, take the tunnels out. Two, rescue this Inola chick from some big, dead god-dude named Tuna Casserole or some shit. Three, instead of coming back where things are safe and warm, we push on to the power station and...flip the switch?"

"Then we come back," Flores says, "And put an end to this for good."

We all know that he intends to kill Future Langdon. I'm not sure I'm on board with that—execution removes any chance at redemption, and if there is any chance of undoing this mess, it will happen only with his cooperation. While the younger Langdon doesn't believe it's possible, I haven't lost all hope of returning to the present.

But now is not the time to have that discussion.

"You don't have to come," I tell them.

Younger Langdon raises his hand. "I—I'm not."

Not only is the scientist not built for the challenges ahead, I suspect he'd never leave without taking his wife. And right now, she's even further away from him than the future is from us.

Since there is no question about Cassie's and Flores's choices, all three of us turn to my Kuzneski.

"Oh, like I'm the only one who might be a chickenshit, is that it?" His offense is partly genuine, but mostly good humored. He knows as well as we do that the allegiance of his future self is questionable at best. Speaking of which...

I turn to Flores. "The other Kuzneski claims to be my inside man, that he was planted here in the future. Any truth to that?"

He looks unimpressed. "If he did, he kept it a secret from me. But you were a bit...paranoid. Played your cards close to the vest. Only Cassie had your full trust."

"And I'm not her," Cassie says.

"We can't trust that motherfucker," the younger Kuzneski says, and his opinion tips the scales. No matter what he says, or how he acts, Future Kuzneski is still the enemy.

"Until we're away," I say to Flores, "you need to keep playing the part." I motion to his old clothes.

"I reckon that won't be too tricky, y'all."

Cassie and I share a wide-eyed glance. Flores's Southern accent is one of the worst I've heard.

"Are you supposed to be Australian?" Kuzneski asks.

"Just...don't talk." I stand and head for the door. "We're leaving in one minute."

I haven't told my father all this yet. He's still in the main room, seated with the Cherokee people he and Owen have befriended. But I don't think it will take long to get him on board.

Upon hearing the plan, my father pauses for a moment, looking down at Owen. I know how seriously he takes the job of being a father, how it would crush him if anything ever happened to his son. I've been on the other side of that situation. I think if anyone else had approached him with such a dangerous plan, he'd have shot them down.

But *I* am his son, too, and if anyone cares about Owen as much as my father, it's me. "If I thought it would be safer here—"

"We're coming," Owen says to me, and then to our father, "We're going. Inola needs us. Black Creek needs us. We can't just sit here and do nothin'."

My father huffs a smile. "Like son, like son."

"And father," I say, knowing he's warming up to the idea.

"What did you see out there?" he asks.

"Nothing good," I say, and I catch Cassie's eye as she steps out of the bedroom. I tilt my head toward Owen and she understands.

"Owen." She motions him over and crouches down to speak with him.

Afforded a moment's privacy with my father, I come clean, in part to help him understand, but also because he might be the only person that can help me process what I've experienced.

"What is it?" my father asks.

"I found...me," I say. "Another me. Older than you. He was leading an attack on Synergy to stop all this, but he failed. He'd been tortured... cut open. God knows what else."

Tears form in my father's eyes. Despite the age of my future self, he was still my father's son. "And you agreed to work with these people?"

"His—*my*—dying wish was for me to stop all this, and protect my family. I can't do that if you're here. I can't—"

"Your dying wish?"

"I—he...killed himself."

My father sags a bit, shaking his head.

"I'm not sure he would have survived if he hadn't, but—"

"He died on his terms," my father says, collecting himself.

"He did."

"And so will we." He puts a strong hand on my shoulder. "Now, let's go. And this time there isn't a single Hatfield to slow the McCoy boys down."

I smile and say, "Just a nutjob with a drone army and an ancient, Cherokee, giant god-thing who enjoys hunting people for sport."

"You assclowns ready to roll?" Future Kuzneski asks from the entrance. He's dressed in winter gear and armed with an AA12 Assault Shotgun. It's a beast of a weapon, with so little recoil it can be fired one-handed—if you're strong enough to hold it—and the drum magazine contains thirty-two cartridges.

"Someone's got their panties in a twist," the younger Kuzneski replies, heading for the door. "Shit, you're grumpy."

"Fuck you," Future Kuzneski says.

"Fuck *you*," the younger replies.

"Let's go." I lead our ragtag group toward the door.

"Whoa, whoa," Future Kuzneski says when he sees Owen among us. "You want to take a kid out there?"

I'm not sure if he's concerned or trying to keep Owen here without being blunt about it. Neither makes a difference. "He's coming." When I move past him with Owen in tow, he says nothing else.

I'm happy to find warm clothing and weapons have been provided, but they're not for everyone. Future Kuzneski hands out three pistols. One to me, one to Cassie and one to the younger Kuzneski. The handguns lack the decimating stopping power of his shotgun, but I'm comfortable with the P220, and it packs a punch. Giant or not, a few 10mm rounds will take care of our demi-god problem.

"Don't I get a gun?" Flores asks, his accent still hideous, but who knows, maybe that's how hillbillies talked in the past?

"Why is the country bumpkin coming with us again?" Future Kuzneski asks.

"He knows the mountain," I say.

"Better than you?" the older Kuzneski doesn't sound convinced.

"Nobody know this mountain better than a bootlegger," my father says. "Living here, hunting here..." He nudges me. "Even working here ain't nothing compared to running, hiding, and fighting with the law. I reckon he knows these hills better than the lot of us combined."

Flores just nods in agreement, and Future Kuzneski rolls his eyes.

We're led outside and to what looks like an open manhole cover. Two guards stand on either side of the hole, shifting back and forth, trying to look tough despite the cold.

"Everyone in," Future Kuzneski says.

I go down first without questioning him. The tunnel is dimly lit by recessed yellow bulbs. Thick cables run along both side walls. The floor is flat and textured, providing traction for the small vehicles parked nearby.

Younger Kuzneski drops down from the ladder behind me, takes one look at the vehicles, and says, "You're kidding me. They've got freaking mini-tanks and flying drones, and we're taking golf carts?"

Owen arrives next. "Cool!" He claims a front seat, and I sit beside him, behind the steering wheel of the second vehicle. My father and Cassie join us, while both Kuzneskis and Flores take the lead cart.

"Try to keep up!" Future Kuzneski says, and then he guns the electric vehicle. The tunnel leads down a gentle slope, which becomes steadily steeper, following the mountain's grade. Branching tunnels cut off to the sides, some leading straight out, some angled down, some reversing back uphill. It's like an army of mole men have been busy creating an underground minotaur maze.

Future Kuzneski seems to know the tunnels well enough, taking several turns without missing a beat. He's either faking it, or he knows exactly where he's going. After just ten minutes, we screech to a halt beside a ladder leading up to a closed hatch.

Without waiting for permission, I start up the ladder, unlock the hatch, and shove. There's a moment of resistance before I get my whole body under it and heave. A thin seal of ice cracks, and snow tumbles in and across my face. I lift the heavy metal disk, and more than a foot of snow, up and away. Pushing snow aside, I climb out of the hole, draw my weapon, and scan the mountainside. Several sets of footprints descending the mountain from above are just ten feet away. Mixed among them is a trail of massive, bare footprints.

I follow the trail downhill and nearly stagger back into the hole, numbed by what I've discovered. Had Flores not braced me with his hands, I would have. "Watch where you're—" His rebuke catches in his throat. He's seen it, too. "Oh...God..."

37

"Dad," I say, leaning over the hole. "Stay down there. Cass, stay with them." The argument on the tip of her tongue is cut short when I say "Please," and my voice actually cracks.

"What the hell did you find?" the elder Kuzneski asks, showing no sign of following us to the surface.

"I'm going to either need you and your shotgun up here, or just the shotgun," I say to him. "Take your pick."

The debate takes longer than I'd prefer, but he steps toward the ladder, shotgun over his shoulder.

"Chris," I say, using his first name to help distinguish which of the two I'm talking to.

Doesn't work.

They both look up and say, "Yeah?"

I point my finger at the younger of the two. "Stay put, but I'll be needing that." I shift my finger to the handgun he's holding. Without any resistance, he tosses the weapon up into my hands. As the older Kuzneski climbs, I address my father. "Only reason you should come up here is if I call you. Sit tight until we get back."

"What if you don't get back?" Owen asks.

It's a great question to which I don't have an answer.

"We'll jump that hurdle when we get to it," my father says, then looks me in the eyes. "But come back."

"I reckon I'll do my best," I say.

"Do better than that," Cassie says.

I smile at her, lingering over the hatch, not because I'm lost in the melodrama of what could be our last goodbye, but because I really don't want to face the carnage behind me.

"You looking for a smooch?" Future Kuzneski says. He's reached the top of the ladder. I'm blocking his ascent.

I lean back and let him pass. He climbs up through the thick snow, then stands and dusts the white away. "Now, what in the hell has your panties in a—"

He turns and sees it.

"Fuuuuck."

"That's one way to put it," Flores says, his phony accent gone, his military demeanor showing through. He's out among the mess, crouched down, inspecting the remains of horrific violence.

"Hey," I say, catching his eye. I toss him the handgun.

"Thanks," he says. "This used to be two people."

I look over the scene, trying to control my puke response, and I do my best to unpack the details. While the rest of the forest is coated in a smooth layer of thick snow, the patch of white just downhill is a wavy mess. Warm lumps of flesh and coagulated blood have melted through the snow before freezing in place. Body parts are scattered over the forty-foot wide area, strewn about at random.

"Were they eaten?" Future Kuzneski asks. He's pitched forward, hands on knees, a little bit of drool dangling from his lip.

"Hey," I say to him, and nod my head at his shotgun. "Stay on guard or give it to me."

He slips the AA12 around his shoulders and into his hands, but looks no more ready to do battle.

"Doesn't look like it," Flores says. "Everything is here. Well, almost."

"What's missing?" Future Kuzneski asks.

I notice a moment before Flores reveals the horrible detail. "There's no skin."

And with that, the elder Kuzneski retches into the snow, adding one more pocket melted by human fluids.

Chased by the scent of bile, I trudge into the field of death. Visually, the carnage is mind numbing. I see bits and pieces of bodies that I can't even identify. Unexpected colors jump out at me—white and yellow. I've seen death before, but not like this. The only thing keeping me together is that the scene has been frozen solid and made odorless.

The trees around us, many of them pines, where there will one day be oaks, sway and groan in the wind, keeping me on edge.

Tsul'Kalu could still be nearby.

"Why take the skins?" Flores asks, standing. He ejects the pistol's magazine, inspects the rounds, and slaps it back in.

"I don't even want to guess." I wade through one of a few clean paths to the death field's far side, stopping when I see a large set of bloody footprints leading away, following a much smaller set of prints.

For all I know, Inola is one of the two people torn apart and scattered behind me, but I don't think so. Or maybe I just hope not. Inola is resourceful. I didn't get a good look at her two friends, but if they were part of Boone's bedraggled clan, I wouldn't expect much for them. If not for Inola, I'm sure they would have died before Tsul'Kalu found them.

"Let's move," I say, following the oversized footprints that are twice the size of mine. If foot size is relational to height, that would put the giant at a little over twelve feet tall. Flores follows without complaint, but Future Kuzneski lingers by the open hatch.

"Close that," I point my gun at the open hatch, "and move your ass, before I put a round in it."

He hesitates a moment and then closes the hatch. Tsul'Kalu could never fit through the small hole, and I doubt he could force his way down, but I don't see the point in taking chances.

The tracks take us downhill, weaving a chaotic path through the shrunken pine forest. I can't tell if Inola was trying to leave a confusing trail, or was just running in a panic. If she saw what happened to the others, panic would be understandable. Muscles in my gut twitch with tension at the idea of confronting a giant from the past capable of skinning people alive. It's not just brutal, it's malicious, which I suppose could be explained by the Nephilim theory. But demons fathering children with human women? I shake my head at the idea. It's more likely that this is a man with a genetic aberration, or a human growth hormone disorder—like Andre the Giant, though I doubt he could have torn a person apart with his bare hands.

When I pause to inspect the trail ahead, Flores and Future Kuzneski stop beside me. After a moment, Kuzneski says, "So are you going to tell me who this wolf in a hobo's clothing really is?"

Flores gives him the same answer he gave me. "Sergeant David Flores, U.S. Army Ranger. Retired."

"So you were with *future* him?" Kuzneski asks, and then looks at me. "And you *knew*."

Tension builds.

Kuzneski's grip on the AA12 tightens.

A howl tears through the air. Downhill. Not far. It sounds angry. Primal.

I hold a finger to my lips and then creep forward. Flores follows on my six, while Kuzneski pauses for a moment before joining us. I'm sure he'd like to complain about our situation, or the fact that I lied about Flores and my now-dead older self, but he shows uncommon restraint by keeping his mouth shut.

When the trail takes us into open terrain, I leave it and head for the cover of thick trees. I move between the tall trunks in a crouch, creeping closer to the sound of a deep resonating huff. The giant is irritated.

Then I see it. Just the back of its head at first. The size of it and the deep red color of its hair make me feel like I'm in a sci-fi movie, like what I'm seeing is being controlled by a gaggle of people wielding remote controls. But it also has a very alive quality to it—the way the hair blows in the wind, the fog rising with each throaty breath—that tells my brain two things: this is real. And: get the fuck out.

Ignoring my brain's second order, I stalk closer, placing each foot into the snow as slowly as possible. The giant's skin is pale, but covered in tufts of hair, thicker than what's on its head, but just as dark red—almost maroon.

Like blood.

We're just twenty feet behind the beast when I hold up a closed fist. Flores and Kuzneski both hold their positions behind two trees.

When the giant stands, I reel back. I thought it was already standing. Its thirteen-foot height eradicates my genetic aberration theory. No human being has ever been this tall. The tallest person I've ever heard of was in the Guinness World Book of Records, and he was just shy of nine feet. That's impressive, too, but overly tall people are lanky. They look awkward. Unable to grow into their height. They're stretched out. This giant looks more like an oversized extra from the *300* movie. His sculpted muscles twitch just beneath the skin, exuding power.

With a flick of its arm, the thing flings a beige colored cloak around its back. For a flash, I see its waist, wrapped in tan fur.

It's the mountain lion, I realize. The giant had been nude, and is now making new clothing. My eyes flick back to the cloak, and I nearly retch. Two human skins have been tied together in a bloody tapestry, still slick with gore on the inside.

He's not a man, I think. *He's a monster.*

The demon story is more and more likely.

I force my eyes away from the skins and focus on the rest of him. Despite his reputation as a hunter, I don't see a single scar on Tsul'Kalu, at least not from behind. With a grunt, he slams his huge hands into the ground, throwing snow and dirt behind him.

He's digging. Rooting something out. Or some*one.*

I catch Flores's and Kuzneski's eyes, hold up my gun, and mouth the words, "On three."

Both nod.

I lift my hand, raising one finger.

With a quick glance around the tree, I pick my target—the giant's head.

I raise a second finger, imagining my next steps. I'll slide out from behind the tree and fire three rounds. My instinct will be to put a few rounds in its core, too, but I'll leave that to Kuzneski. The short version is that when I raise my next finger, Tsul'Kalu isn't going to look much better than the carnage he left in his wake.

My fingers lock at two when I hear a loud crunch of snow behind me. Did Flores or Kuzneski move? How could they be so careless?

Tsul'Kalu grunts and whips his big head around. For a moment, his eyes lock on me, peeking out from around the tree. He squints at me with intrigue and then...amusement?

This is wrong, my inner voice shouts. *Get away. Get away now!*

Then another crunch of snow pulls the giant's gaze away from me, past Flores and Kuzneski. I follow the sound uphill and see the source for myself: a saber-toothed cat, low to the ground, ears folded back, teeth bared, and ready to pounce.

38

I'm not sure where to aim. Tsul'Kalu knows we're here, and he needs to be put down. He's as close to pure evil as I've ever seen. But he's also got the cat's full attention. I have little doubt it was stalking the three of us, but now it has eyes for the giant.

The cat's spotted gray fur slides over its muscles as it creeps nearer. While it's closer to the ground than the giant, pound for pound I'd put them in the same class. The giant has human intelligence—I'm assuming—and impressive strength on his side, but the saber-tooth has massive paws hiding long retractable claws and a pair of eleven-inch-long canines. Of the two, the cat would appear to have the advantage. It's built for hunting in the cold. But Tsul'Kalu, god of the hunt, has proven himself to be more than savage.

So I don't point my gun at either of them. The only way we all survive this battle is to not be here when it ends. I raise an open palm to Flores and Kuzneski, ordering them to do the same.

Tsul'Kalu catches my eye, gives me a wry smile, like he's in on a joke at my expense, and then turns his full attention to the cat. His confidence unnerves me.

The cat stops its approach, lowering itself into the snow, muscles coiled. Its back-end twitches back and forth. Eyes narrowing, its focus is unflinching—until the giant leans forward and bellows. The sound shakes through me, using my ear drums as punching bags.

The cat flinches back, its ears folding down tighter. Its massive jaws open, letting out a much quieter, but no less threatening hiss. As intimidating as Tsul'Kalu might be, the saber-tooth isn't backing down. It doesn't see the giant as a potential meal, it sees him as competition infringing on its territory. Like all predators, it will fight to the death—even when the odds are against it—to protect its hunting grounds...and the prey within them, which right now includes us.

With surprising speed, the cat launches from the snow.

Tsul'Kalu raises his forearm to block the attack and quickly learns it was the wrong move. The cat's massive canines pierce the forearm, punching through one side and slipping out the other.

Instead of a flash of pain in the giant's eyes, I see...pleasure.

Then they fall back into the snow, the cat's rapid-fire claws raking at the giant's sides.

And he doesn't scream.

Not once.

With the battle fully engaged, I shout, "Inola!"

I take a step closer to where the giant had been digging, but I don't have to get any closer, or repeat her name. She crawls from a subterranean den, likely maintained by some Ice Age creature that's made itself scarce. Her face twists in revolt when she sees the giant and the cat locked in mortal combat, but then she run-trudges through the snow. She's shivering hard, her meager clothing not up to the task of fending off the frigid endless winter, but she's still clutching the Winchester.

Why didn't she shoot it? I wonder, but I decide now is not the time to ask. I shed my jacket and wrap it around her. "Let's move!"

Kuzneski doesn't need to be told twice, but Flores wavers. "We could kill it now. Both of them."

He's right. Between the four of us, we could probably make sure neither beast walks away from this. But I suspect neither of them will already, and Inola is hypothermic and in danger of losing some fingers and toes if we don't get her warmed up. "The people we can save are more important than the ones we can kill."

Flores smiles. "That was the first time you sounded like him. Like you."

"And what would he have said if one of his people wasn't immediately obeying an order?" I ask, helping Inola uphill, past Flores.

"Move your—"

"—fucking ass, soldier," I finish for him.

"That's the line." Flores falls in behind Inola and me, watching our six, or maybe just watching the battle unfold. I don't turn back to look, but I can hear enough. Tearing flesh. Breaking bones. The savage cat's roar. The most unnerving thing about the audio-savagery is that through it all, Tsul'Kalu never makes a sound. No scream of pain. No roar of anger. Just silence.

Part of me wants to believe it's because he's dead, that the cat's initial attack did him in and now it's just venting on his body. But I don't think that's the case. The giant's confident eyes burn in my mind. He knew he would survive, and that smiling stare was a promise that we'd meet again.

The uphill climb through knee-deep snow feels like a dream, arms and legs pumping hard, getting nowhere, the monster creeping up behind us. But every time I look back, the forest is clear, and we're making actual progress. I lose sight of Kuzneski, but find him again, waiting by the open hatch. He's got the AA12 pressed against his shoulder and aimed straight at me when we round a tree.

For a moment, I think he's betrayed us, but then he sighs and lowers the weapon.

"Hurry up," he says, shivering more from fright than the cold.

Inola stumbles in the snow, falling to her knees. I can't imagine how tired she must be. As I wrap my arm around her waist and hoist her back up, Flores arrives and supports her on the other side. Together, we hustle the remaining ten feet to the open hatch.

"Go in first," I say to Flores. "Support her weight while I lower her down."

"I can do it," Inola says, her defiant strength showing even while her eyes start to close.

As Flores lowers himself into the hatch, a howl rolls through the forest, and it's definitely not the saber-toothed cat. Tsul'Kalu has won the brawl of giants, but he must be injured. Those teeth through his arm should be enough to slow him down, never mind the lacerations on his sides. If he doesn't bleed out and die right now, infection will get him.

He wouldn't be the first god to die in battle with a great beast. Of course, we're early enough in human history that he might now be one of the first.

Flores climbs halfway down the ladder and then reaches up. I brace myself on either side of the hatch and lower Inola down. My muscles twitch from the effort, but not because she's heavy. The cold is seeping through my jacketless clothing, constricting my muscles and skin. The promise of warmth rises up from the tunnel below. The subterranean air isn't exactly warm, but the ground's natural insulation keeps the tunnels at a relatively balmy 55 degrees.

"I have her," Flores says. I slowly release Inola and watch her slide down, guided by Flores and received by my father.

"We heard howling," Owen says from below.

"Nothing to worry about," I say, feeling just a little bad for lying to myself.

Owen looks relieved, but Cassie is unconvinced. Her jaw is clenched tight, and she's doing a tension-filled, impatient jig. If not for her serious eyes and the gun in her hand, I'd think she had to pee.

I step back and nod my head to Future Kuzneski. "After you, princess."

He manages a smile. "Only way I'm going to gain everyone's trust is to not be a dick, right?"

He's right, but the question remains: *why is he trying to gain our trust? Is he one of the good guys, or will he betray us?*

"Besides," he says, "if I don't let you go first, I'm pretty sure Cassie will nut punch—look out!"

He shoves me into the snow. I don't see what happens next, but I hear it. A wet smack is followed by a wheezy groan.

One of the saber-toothed cat's teeth, root and all, protrudes from his chest. It's a kill shot, right over his heart. He's still standing. Still conscious, but with his heart no longer pumping blood, he's got just seconds left to live.

And he uses them to save me.

"Go!" he shouts, raising the AA12 downhill and holding down the trigger. The weapon thunders as it cycles through shotgun shells at nearly two cartridges per second.

Tsul'Kalu howls as the screaming horde of metal pellets chews through his skin. Flowers of purple blood burst across his body. For a moment, I'm stunned. *Purple blood?* What I once saw as a giant aberration, I now know isn't remotely human.

The way he charges through the gunfire without flinching, without losing his demented smile, chills me more than the Ice Age air.

"I'm sorry," I say to Kuzneski. For not trusting him. For leaving him to die. For the scars on his body. For his sacrifice...regardless of whether or not he intended to betray us. Then I dive beneath the shotgun, slide into the hatch, and fall to the floor below.

The impact knocks the air from my lungs, leaving me a breathless, heaving mess, but it doesn't stop me from looking back up.

The AA12 shotgun clicks empty. Thirty-two cartridges fired into the core of what looks like a man, but is not.

With his dying breath, Future Kuzneski screams, but the sound is muffled when a giant hand wraps around his head.

Holding him up in the air, Tsul'Kalu steps into view above the hole, looking down, still smiling. "Alatisdi tsisdu."

"Everyone in the carts!" I say, using my first real breath to issue the order. Flores yanks on me to follow my own command, but I remain rooted in place, locked onto Tsul'Kalu's eyes.

With a quick squeeze, Future Kuzneski's life comes to an end with a pop. Blood and gore ooze out between the giant's fingers.

My resolve falters and Flores pulls me away. I all but collapse into the cart, propped up by the still living, younger Kuzneski, who looks as disturbed by what he's seen as I am. Perhaps even more so. He now knows what his own death might look like. Especially if Tsul'Kalu finds us again. At close range, the AA12 hit harder than our handguns and the Winchester combined. I'm not sure we'll be able to kill it.

"Go, go, go!" Flores says, and both carts speed away, heading downhill through the tunnel, no destination in mind other than getting the hell away. We're chased by a deafening howl, reverberating through the tunnel.

With distance and time, I collect myself. A minute into our flight, I recover enough to sit up. I lean forward to check on Inola. She's huddled in the front beside my father, who is behind the wheel, and she's held by my younger self in a valiant effort to warm her up.

Her eyes crack open and she whispers. "Thank you."

I acknowledge her with a nod, and say, "'Alatisdi tsisdu.' Do you know what it means?"

She frowns, sags a bit, and then recovers enough strength to say, "Run, rabbit," before falling asleep.

39

After ten minutes of aimless driving through a maze of tunnels, Flores slows the lead cart to a stop, the danger well behind us. Protected by an endless, barren steel tube, I feel relatively safe from immediate danger. But the past, and what lives in it, is far more volatile than I would have guessed.

I suppose whoever was in charge of the Smithsonian Institute's efforts to hide the giants commingling with humanity's past would have guessed, but did any of them know that Tsul'Kalu was a psychopath with purple blood?

Or maybe they did? Maybe someone decided that people weren't ready to hear that monsters were real, particularly ones whose origins are Biblical? But would a scientific organization really hide the truth, even if it wasn't explainable?

Langdon is proof of that. Of course, maybe the Smithsonian is a puppet for a secret cabal or a conspiratorial group? History is full of them. I'm not sure what could be gained by hiding the existence of giants, or Nephilim. I don't know enough about them. At the same time, it could all just be a conspiracy theory. Maybe the giant remains were lost? Maybe the Smithsonian is simply sitting on the finds until they've made sense of them? I feel like there's a novel in there somewhere, but that's a riddle for someone else to sort through. Right now, I need to figure out how to survive a living giant with a hard-on for carnage, and shut down the particle collider.

But not yet, I think.

I'm not thrilled about the idea of jumping further back in time. But we're not prepared for life in the Ice Age. The people of Black Creek are a resourceful lot, and those from earlier generations will be accustomed to adapting to harsh conditions, but surviving in the Ice Age, long term, won't be possible. We need to jump again, but that's where this needs to end. And that can't happen if we're stuck in a maze, hiding from a giant...like rabbits.

"Any idea where we are?" Flores asks, sliding out of the lead cart.

I shake my head. We traveled in a steady downward slope, but we made a lot of turns along the way. All I really know is that we haven't reached the mountain's bottom. "We need to head downhill until the ground levels out. Then I can take a look. If the topography is similar enough, I'll be able to point us in the right direction. But we're going to stop several times to keep our bearings in this maze."

"So you're saying we'll have to go for it," Kuzneski says.

He barely sounds like himself, and his faux positive statement feels wrong. Seeing himself die has left him shaken.

"What?" he says, noting my worried expression. "Ohh, I see what happened. You thought I said, 'go for it," like, 'Yeah! Let's do this!' Like I'm fucking Richard Simmons or some shit. I said gopher it. Like the fuzzy little animal." He pokes his index finger up through his clenched hand, mimicking the small rodent's head popping up and down in the ground. "Gopher, not go for."

He sighs. "This fucking day..." Then he sits back and looks at the empty, curved ceiling.

I share his exasperation. How long has it been since the day began? Seven hours, and thousands of years? I look at my watch. Eight hours, thirteen minutes. We've got a few hours of daylight left...depending on the season. Facing Tsul'Kalu in the dark is not my idea of a fun party. Best if we finish this up, ASAP.

"How is she?" Cassie asks, stepping up beside the unconscious Inola.

My father slips his hand under her coat, holding it against her arm. "Warming up, but..." He motions to her closed eyes. "She'll live, though. She's tough."

"Tough might not be enough," Flores says, and then to me, "ride up front?"

My father nods his approval.

"You're not leaving us?" Owen asks.

"Just switching carts," I tell him. He's still using his body heat to insulate Inola. "Just keep on taking care of her, okay?"

I join Flores and Cassie in the front vehicle, riding shotgun.

"Where to?" Flores asks.

"Down," I say.

"All roads lead to Black Creek," Cassie says, with an attempt at a smile. "Because, you know, Rome hasn't been built yet."

The carts hum downhill. Much of the path is straight, but there are occasional side passages and, when the mountain gets steep, switchbacks. The carts handle the journey down with ease. I'm not sure how they'd fare going back up. Or how much power they have.

Thinking of power, I notice that some tunnels have little to no cabling, while others are thick with the stuff, lining both walls. I direct Flores to follow them, and I find our path downhill is steady. The cabled tunnels are also warmer, suggesting a lot of power is flowing through them.

It's another ten minutes of monotonous tunnel before the decline fades and then goes level. When I spot a ladder up ahead, I tap Flores on the shoulder. "Stop there."

The ladder leads to another hatch, but unlike the first, this one doesn't have a locking mechanism. Instead, it's an actual manhole cover with the letters BC – KY embossed in it. I climb the ladder and put my shoulder into it, shoving the heavy metal up. Once it clears the lip, I push it to the side, embedding it in a wall of white. The snow atop it falls down through the hole—and all over me. Again. My skin bristles at the cold, but I push past my discomfort and scramble up.

You'd think I'd be prepared for anything at this point, but I was really hoping to find an uninteresting view with which to orient myself. Instead, I'm greeted by a fresh scene of horror.

A dozen men and women litter an open clearing, some are face down in the snow. Some are huddled together against the elements. One of them is still standing.

But they are all frozen solid.

And if that wasn't bad enough, they're not alone. A herd of mammoths stands just a hundred feet away. I suspect they were staring down the frozen figures, trying to make sense of them, when I gophered out of the ground and startled them.

The largest of them, the matriarch, takes a step forward, huffing.

"Easy girl," I say, holding out my hands, like anything I say or do will soothe her frayed nerves.

Several of the elephants start stomping on the ground.

Below me, I hear Kuzneski say, "Geez, what the hell is up there?"

When I look down to answer, I'm aware of a smile growing on my face. Of all the things I've experienced since the flux began, these ancient and formerly extinct elephant ancestors are the most amazing. I wouldn't say I was obsessed with dinosaurs and Ice Age creatures as a kid, but I had my fair share of books on the subjects and spent hours turning through those pages. Mostly looking at the pictures, but I developed enough wonder about these creatures to really enjoy seeing them in the flesh. In retrospect, the saber-toothed cat was spectacular as well, but it's hard to appreciate something that would eat you alive if given the chance.

That said, I think the mammoths are about to attempt squashing me. I take a quick look around and immediately recognize the landscape. I'm home.

The house is still there, I'm guessing because of its proximity to the network of tunnels, but it's taken a beating. I'm about to duck back down, when I realize that this house did not belong to me. It belonged to my future self.

That's when I notice the damage.

A side wall has been destroyed, the insides filling with snow drifts. Parts of the outer wall look scorched, and bullet holes riddle the front. A battle was fought here. While I'm not sure whether my future self won that fight, he survived it.

There's nothing for me here.

Either Synergy, the authorities, or I would have taken any weapons I might have had squirreled away. And anything they left behind would have been fair game for the folks in town who don't have much. Anything of value would have been scavenged long ago. As for my personal belongings...I glance down at my father and Owen...

I have everything I need.

From my house, I look left toward Black Creek. I can't see the town from my place in any year, but there's no mistaking the columns of smoke rising into the sky for anything else. Black Creek is still there, and it's still populated.

The matriarch trumpets and stomps her foot. The volume of her blast makes me cringe, not just because it hurts my ears, but because anything within a few miles will have heard the sound.

I hold my breath in the moments that follow, listening to the cold wind, the sound of mammoth lungs breathing, and then the haunting howl of Tsul'Kalu. The call is distant, but it spooks the mammoths as much as it does me. The matriarch reels around and flees, the rest of the pack following on her heels.

They've heard that sound before, I think, watching the terrified creatures charge away. They know what it is. What it means. How long have the giants lived here? How long before man arrived?

Knowing there is no one alive who might possibly have the answers to those questions, I follow the matriarch's lead and retreat.

Back inside, I make no mention of the giant's howl, but it doesn't take an empath to know I've been shaken. When I get back into the cart, Flores gives me a sideways glance. "We good?"

"For now," I say.

We head out again, this time with a general sense of where we should be heading. We make a few turns along the way, and after a short drive, we come to a stop beneath another Black Creek manhole.

Once again, I take the lead, scaling the ladder and shoving away the manhole, groaning as I'm covered in another pile of snow. I scale the ladder and find myself smack dab in the center of town, the courthouse in front of me, the small library behind. I draw my pistol and scan the area.

Aside from smoke rising from the chimneys of the buildings that have them, including the court house, it's a ghost town. But there is evidence of occupation, mostly in the form of footprints.

The question is, whose footprints? What time are they from? And will they be friendly?

"'Bout far enough, I reckon," a man says from behind me. His voice is followed by the click of a rifle's hammer being locked into place. "And in case you're thinking of retreat'n back down yer hole, I've got good enough aim to drop yah, and have no qualms about putting a hole or two in someone who works for Synergy."

The man's threat tells me a few things. First, he knows who I am. And who I work for. He also knows who's responsible for this mess.

Last, and worst, I believe his threat is genuine.

40

I raise my hands, letting the pistol hang limp from my index finger. "I'm not looking for trouble."

"Reckon it found you, then," the man says.

"More than once," I say trying to lighten the mood.

Cassie's voice slips out of the manhole. "What's going on up there?"

"Seems we're not welcome in our own town," I tell her, looking down to find her already scaling the ladder.

"Ain't your town, Synergy," the old man says.

"I'm not with them," I tell him, starting to turn around.

"Don't do it," the man says, and I think I recognize his voice now. Phil Hardy. Owns the only gas station and repair shop in town. Salty old man, but honest...even if he doesn't like you, or who you work for. "I ain't interested in hearing—"

"Mr. Hardy!" Cassie has poked her head above the snowline. Her voice is scolding. "Put that down before you go and shoot the only chance you all have of surviving this mess."

Hardy is silent for a moment, but then says, "You work for 'em, too, Cass."

"You've been kind to me my whole life," Cassie says. "But I won't stand for—"

"You won't stand...? Girl, have you seen what's become of our home? Are you aware of the kind of hell we all've been through? The people you both work for did this. Can you deny it?"

Cassie climbs out of the hole, standing beside me. Her gun is tucked into the small of her back, but I'm not sure she could shoot Hardy, even if he gives her a reason to. I'm not sure I could, either. He's been a fixture in Black Creek since I was a kid.

I turn around and find a hunting rifle leveled at my chest. Hardy is in the second-floor window of the yellow brick courthouse. Despite his thick, camouflaged, winter coat and red trapper hat, he's shivering. But I don't think it has anything to do with the cold, or out of fear for his own life. Like Cassie, he doesn't want to shoot, but that doesn't mean he won't.

"Don't deny it," I say, "but we also didn't know about it, and we're doing what we can to stop it. To set things right."

"You just crawled out of a hole in the ground, armed for a fight, and expect me to believe you're here to help us? I ought to—"

"You ought to put that fool thing away." My father has climbed to the surface behind Cassie and me. When he steps out around us, Hardy is confused and then dumbfounded. "Willy?"

"Back from the dead," my father says with a smile. "Though from my perspective, that never happened."

Hardy slides back inside the courthouse, slamming the window closed behind him.

My father and I glance at each other.

"That a good thing?" I ask.

My father shrugs. "Been a while since he's seen me, I reckon."

"You knew him well?"

"He was one of the Hell's Balls."

"Hell's...balls?"

"High school bowling league team. We thought it was a funny name."

"You *bowled?*"

How did I never know that about my father?

"Before your mother and I..." He smiles. "I was never any good."

The courthouse's front door opens as Hardy charges out, arms open, a smile on his face. The only thing he's armed with is open arms.

He embraces my father, giving him a few manly pats before leaning back and saying, "Lord, it is good to see you again. You've aged a might better than me. You look about as young as you did last I saw you."

"For me, it's 1985," my father says.

"Not just you," Hardy says, his eyes darting around the town. "We got folks from all over history. Was chaotic at first. Some ruffians from the 1800s stirred up trouble. A few people died in the ruckus, but things have calmed down since we made sense of all this."

"You made sense of this?" I ask, sounding more doubtful than intended.

"We had help," he says. "But before you meet him, I need to be sure you all are on the side of angels."

"Buddy," Kuzneski says, as he climbs from the manhole. "We *are* the fucking angels."

"You work for them, too," Hardy says, his anger returning, "and you ain't even a local."

"Is that supposed to be a bad thing, because—"

I put a hand on Kuzneski's shoulder. I don't think he realizes how fiercely loyal and how easily offended long time residents of Black Creek can be when their home is insulted.

Snow crunches behind us and Hardy takes a step. "Who all else do you have hidden away down there?"

As we separate and turn to face the newcomer, I'm half expecting to find Flores, rifle aimed at Hardy's head, ready to end the discussion with the threat of violence. Which would be a very bad thing. While I can't see anyone in the courthouse windows, I have no doubt we're being watched by more than a few folks with guns—and the know-how to put them to use.

Instead, it's Owen, dragging himself up into the snow. My father reaches down and lifts him up, holding him.

"Mr. Hardy, you look old," Owen says.

Hardy smiles, looking back and forth between me and Owen.

"I'm trying to keep my family alive," I say. "Same as most people in town, I'd guess."

Hardy gives a slow nod. "As hellish as this all's been, it's been a godsend for a few folks, yourself included it would seem."

"Is Cassie here?" Owen asks, eyes darting around the ghost town. "You know, *my* Cassie? Young Cassie."

"Watch it," Cassie says, getting a smile out of my younger self.

"Reckon she's around here somewhere," he says, confirming her presence. "Anyone else in that hole?"

"A man from the future," I say. "A good man. And a Cherokee woman in need of a hot fire and something warm to drink." I could leave it at that, but I opt for full disclosure. "Synergy has a number of folks held captive on top of Adel. Men and women from different ages. They're safe, for now, but—"

"Ain't none of us safe," Hardy says. "And don't you go thinking it for a second, or you're liable to wind up like some of the others in town."

You have no idea, I think, but I keep it to myself. Old Hardy is spooked enough as it is. If he knew there was an army of heavily armed drones, Ice Age predators, and what might very well be a Nephilim demi-god stalking the mountain, he probably would have put a bullet in me the moment I stuck my head up out of the snow-laden street.

He looks over at my father and Owen. "Ain't it something?" Then he puts his fingers to his lips and lets out a shrill whistle.

Behind him, the courthouse doors open. A ragtag group of temporal survivors from various time periods steps out. While some still sport their ancient clothing, most are clad in modern winter gear and shoes, no doubt taken from the sporting goods store at the end of the street.

A woman I don't recognize steps past Hardy, holding out a black winter jacket. "Thank you," I say, slipping into the fleece-lined sleeves, zipping up, and hugging myself.

I turn at the sound of more opening doors, and I find people emerging from most of the buildings lining the streets, coming to take a look at the newcomers, perhaps looking for loved ones from their present, or past.

"Owen!" the voice is instantly recognizable, and it all but breaks my heart. Young Cassie breaks away from her mother's hand and sprints through the snow.

Owen squirms out of my father's arms and meets her halfway. I'm caught off guard by the affection they share, wrapping their arms around each other. This is what I passed up on, all those years, bitter at the world for taking my father, afraid to love anyone again.

Adult Cassie and I share a smile, and I take her hand. I'm done missing out. Done not risking my heart and the potential pain that vulnerability creates.

When Owen and Young Cassie separate, he whispers quickly and then points to me and Adult Cassie. The girl's eyes go wide. When she spots our interlinked hands, she looks pleased. Then she approaches.

"Hey," Adult Cassie says, looking down at her younger self. "This is weird, right?"

"Totally," the younger Cassie says.

Adult Cassie crouches and reaches out, embracing her child form. "It's good to see you again."

The younger Cassie giggles. "My voice got deeper." She pulls back, inspecting her adult body. "And I got boobs!" While the rest of us have a laugh, she turns to her mother, who's approaching more cautiously with a large number of people. I know some of them, but most are remnants of times past, including several Cherokee who have been accepted into the town. Hundreds of people fill the snow-clogged street. Black Creek is alive and well, its population swelled, but how long can they survive?

Probably until Tsul'Kalu figures out they're here...

"Mom!" Young Cassie waves her mother over and then points to her older self. "Look! It's me!"

There's a moment of confusion as Mrs. Dearborn looks at her grown daughter. It fades when their eyes meet. Adult Cassie embraces her mother, calm and casual. "Hey, mom."

Unlike me, Cassie would have seen her mother, maybe even this morning. Mrs. Dearborn, on the other hand, is shaken. "You're...so old."

Cassie chuckles. "About the same age as you, old lady." Then she looks around. "Dad here?"

Mrs. Dearborn frowns. "He was out of town while we were shopping. It's just us."

"I'm...sorry," Cassie says, her face sinking with the realization that unlike my father, her father will not be resurrected.

"You'll never be without family," my father says, gently touching her arm. He and Mrs. Dearborn aren't close friends—that kind of thing wouldn't have been appropriate in their day—but our families attended events together and had the occasional game night at Cassie's and my insistence. I also believe she and my mother were good friends before I was born.

Before any more reunions can take place, we need to move indoors, regroup, and then get on our way. While I want another flux to take us out of this frozen hell, we need to be prepared to stop the super-collider when that happens.

"Are you in charge?" I ask Hardy.

"Thank the good Lord, no," Hardy says.

"Look out," a voice says, emerging through the ring of people forming around us.

Hardy points toward the voice. "That'd be him now."

I turn toward the slowly parting crowd. "Let me through. C'mon y'all. Hurry up and—"

The crowd separates, revealing Levi, dressed for winter, a shotgun over his shoulder. His jaw drops open when he sees me and Adult Cassie. Then he looks to the sky, mouths, "Thank you, Jesus," and says, "Father Abraham in a bathrobe, is it good to see y'all!"

41

Gathered around the courthouse's large fireplace, which has been decorative for more than a hundred years, but was functional before that, I start to feel warm. Inola has regained consciousness. She's sipping on, and very much enjoying, some Swiss Miss hot cocoa. Not only is the chocolate drink new to her, but she is mesmerized by the little sweet marshmallows.

Once Levi vouched for us, and our identities were revealed as being mostly Black Creek locals—not including Kuzneski or Flores—the over-crowded town returned to their individual buildings, just trying to stay warm, while Levi, their fearless leader, worked on a plan.

As soon as our group was whittled down to the three McCoys, the three Dearborns, Flores, Kuzneski, Inola, and Hardy, Levi reveal-ed his true colors, asking—begging—to know if we had a plan. He all but melted with relief when I filled him in on Synergy, the particle accelerator, the power station, and our plans to shut it down. He wasn't exactly thrilled about being stuck in the past, or maybe he was just afraid to tell generations of Black Creek residents they'd never return home.

"Had a feeling you were faking it," Hardy says to Levi, when I'm done explaining the plan.

"Faking what?" I ask.

"The confidence. The answers. The boy isn't a real leader."

"Ain't gotta convince me," Levi says, then nods at me. "I've just been trying to act like him."

I'm flattered, but he's wrong. "Isn't a leader in all of history who didn't fake it, at first. And in this mess, no one knows what's happening. Near as I can tell, you've done a fine job keeping people calm, organized, and alive."

"Wasn't all me," Levi says.

"Modesty is another good quality in a leader," I say with a smile. "But...how did this happen? No offense, but you are just a kid, and no amount of acting can change that."

He shrugs. "After me and Cassie got split up, I headed for town, figuring I might be able to find help. When I got here, things were..."

"A right mess," Hardy says. "Lots of fighting. Factions between time periods were forming. Tribalism was setting in. Didn't help that we had actual tribal people among us, neither." He turns to Inola. "No offense."

She just keeps sipping her cocoa, happy with the sweetness and the warmth.

"When I arrived in town, I broke up a fight between someone from the 1920s and someone from the 1980s."

Hardy chuckles. "He gave them a right awful lecture about what it meant to be a resident of Black Creek in any time. Said we was united through the generations. That most of us were kin. That the land was in our blood. Dumbest shit I ever heard, but I'll be damned if it didn't work."

"After that," Levi says, "I told them what we thought was happening. Wasn't really answers. Just theories. But I suppose it was enough. People started asking me what to do, and I started telling 'em."

"You did good," I tell him. "Maybe you can run for mayor."

"Well, I sure as shit ain't working for you all."

After the group has a good laugh at Synergy's expense, a heavy quiet falls over us. I take a moment to take it all in. Owen and Young Cassie are seated by the fire, throwing pine cones into the blaze, only half paying attention to us. They're mostly whispering to each other, picking right up where they left off the day before. Mrs. Dearborn sits nearby, watching them, smiling at their closeness. My father sits beside Inola, who's wrapped up in a blanket, clutching her mug, all signs of hypothermia fading. He's not exactly doting on her. She's a strong woman, and wouldn't have it. But he hasn't left her side, and near as I can tell, she's okay, if not happy, with that.

Kuzneski stands at the back of the room, arms crossed, his frown perpetual. Seeing himself die has shaken him to the core. I understand how he's feeling, but I admit he's got it worse. While my future version killed himself using a poison pill, Kuzneski saw his future self's head crushed in the fist of a giant.

Flores stands by the meeting room's tall windows, hands clutched behind his back, at ease, but vigilant. He's keeping watch as well as he can, staring out at the white coated town, the forest, and Adel...

It's Flores who breaks the silence. "Losing the light."

The sun creeps toward the horizon. With all the snow, it's still pretty bright and will remain so if there's a full moon, but the temperature is going to drop. And no one wants to be outside in the dark with a bloodthirsty god of the hunt.

"Dad," I say, "I want you to stay put." He's about to argue. I don't give him the chance. "People here need protecting, too." I glance toward Owen, little Cassie, and her mother. "I might be your son, but what we're about to do...well, it's what I do best. And having you with me, honestly, I'd be too distracted about the possibility of losing you again."

My father's argument deflates. "So long as you come back."

"That's always part of the plan," I tell him.

But not always guaranteed.

"Flores, Kuzneski..." Cassie takes my hand and squeezes, forcing me to say the name I'd rather leave out. "...Cassie, and I will head for the power station."

"I'd like to come, too," Levi says. "Finish what we started together."

"And I'm staying here," Kuzneski says. "I'm just...I'm done."

There's not even a trace of Kuzneski's good humor in his voice.

"Being in town doesn't mean there won't be a fight," I say.

He nods at that. "But the odds are better. I'd rather be one among thousands, than one among five who, I'm sorry to say, have kind of a big target on their asses. Langdon's not going to take our disappearance sitting down."

Several faces sour at his pessimism. I wish I could say he's not right, but Langdon's response to the elder Kuzneski's death and our escape is probably not going to be gentle. Everything he has to lose is safe at Synergy. The rest of us, especially if we're threatening whatever his endgame might be, are more than expendable. And he's already proven he's willing to kill people who get in his way.

Inola hands her mug to my father and slips out from under the blanket warming her. Despite everything she's been through, her resolve might be the strongest of all of us. "I will join you."

"Great," Kuzneski says, throwing his hands up. "Now I look like a massive puss." Having lifted the burden of risking his life in the woods, his humor is returning.

"You can't," my father says. "Not after what you've—"

His argument is quashed by a glance from Inola.

My father raises his hands. "Never mind."

"Five is enough," Flores says.

He's right about that. The more people we have with us, the bigger our footprint. Most special ops, including any good guerilla campaign, values stealth, smarts, and surprise over brute force numbers. If a mission can be completed without firing a shot, that's a win.

Then again, future me brought a six-man team against Synergy and all but one of them is dead. I suppose the mistake that version of myself made was not knowing about the power station. Soft targets are always preferable to hardened ones. Seems Langdon managed to keep that secret for seven straight years.

"You trust all of them?" Flores asks, but what he's really asking is if he can trust them with his life.

I look from Cassie, to Levi, to Inola. "Well, they're not operators, but they'll have our backs."

"Who's this guy, anyway?" Levi asks, pointing at Flores.

"He's from 2026," I say. "Was trying to stop all this before it happened."

"Only we didn't know exactly what would happen," Flores adds. "Just that it would be bad."

"We?" Levi asks.

"Had a team," Flores says, and then he turns to face us. He points to me. "His team." He nods at Cassie. "And hers, if you're going by who called most of the shots."

"You all have future yous?" Levi's smile fades when he sees no one else sharing his sense of wonder. Then he figures it out. "You said, '*had* a team...' They're..."

"He's the last of them," I say, "And now he's with us."

Levi lets it go with a nod. "Future, huh? You got flying cars?"

"Food shortages, mostly," Flores says.

"Geez," Kuzneski says. "No shortage of wet blankets in the future, though, huh?"

Hoping to get us back on track and then deployed, I ask, "What's the weapons situation?"

"Shit ton of shotguns, a few ARs, and a boatload of hunting rifles. Pistols and blades. Good number of bow and arrows, too."

"Think people will give up a few?" I ask.

"Will if they know what they're being used for." Hardy grunts as he stands from his chair. "I'll go rustle up what I—"

"Uhh, I really don't want to join Team Wet Blanket, but you know all the guns in town won't do shit against that thing."

Hardy's face twists with confusion, but what Kuzneski says next makes the old timer forget all about it.

Kuzneski steps into the middle of the room, looking out of the mountain-facing windows, where Adel is front and center. "And...that."

A billowing wave of distortion explodes up from the mountaintop, spreading high into the sky and outward at a rapid pace. Despite being several miles away, it's going to reach us in seconds. In awe, I step closer to the window, looking up into the sky. The wave is miles high already and careening toward us.

The mountain blurs, its color shifting from dark gray and white to vibrant green.

This is bigger, I think.

This is going to hurt...

"Everyone get down!" I shout, before diving to the floor.

A moment later, a tidal wave of time and space slams into Black Creek, and through my body.

Despite being relatively accustomed to the aftereffects, there's nothing I can do to prevent myself from being thrown across the floor. Like the occupants of a cruise ship in a storm, we're tossed to the back side of the room and compressed against the wall with a collection of furniture. It hurts, but I'm grateful for the wall, and for not being atop Synergy, where the flux moves vertically.

My stomach sours, but doesn't convulse. Everyone else seems equally accustomed to the physical effects, struggling to recover, but not lost in agony or confusion.

A low, moaning honk sounds from outside.

The hell is that? I wonder.

I push myself up and out of my discomfort and stagger back to the window, where I'm joined by Cassie. Our approach slows when we see the landscape. Aside from Adel, the mountains...

The mountains are *gone*. And the forest...it's vast and lush. Tropical, by the looks of it.

The honk sounds out again, drawing my eyes down to Main Street, which is now layered in two-foot-tall grass and contains a very confused animal.

Cassie takes my hand, squeezing tightly. "Is that...?"

"Yeah," I say. "It's a dinosaur."

42

"That's a...a... Ahh...shit." Levi rubs his head, looking down at the armored behemoth. It's a good eighteen feet long, weighs several tons, and is covered in plates that look like a cross between an armadillo and a snapping turtle. It is simultaneously frightening and adorable. Large spikes protrude from its shoulders, making any bite directed toward its neck a dangerous prospect. The creature's yellow-orange color is fleck-ed with brown, and it blends in with the grass. But it isn't perfect cam-ouflage when seen from above. From a distance, the low lying dinosaur might be invisible.

I'm somewhat staggered by the animal. I've already witnessed the reverse passage of time, machines from the future, a saber-toothed cat, a herd of mammoths, and an inhuman monstrosity. But I'm still not immune to the fact, and abject wonder, that I'm looking at a living, breathing dinosaur. Despite knowing it's real, my brain struggles to adapt. I keep seeing it as an animatronic creature, brought to life by motors. But then it moves in a way no robot could imitate, and the spell is broken. For a moment, I forget our dire situation, and I just smile.

"A nodosaur!" Levi thrusts a victorious finger in the air. "That puts us sometime in the Cretaceous, when Appalachia was its own continent."

Everyone in the now-hot room cranes their heads toward the young man.

"What?" He looks offended by our surprise. "Just because I play football doesn't mean I don't know things. Mr. Jenkins, my biology teacher, was a dinosaur nut. I haven't seen him in town yet, but if he's here, he'll tell you. Dinosaurs in this part of the country weren't a big deal until recently. He'd get excited every time some new discovery was made. And I remember this guy..." He points down at the nodosaur, slowly backing away from the court house, its eyes craned up toward the windows full of watching eyes. "...because they found a mummified one, no assembly required."

"So, the Cretaceous," Kuzneski says, frowning down at the dinosaur. "How far back in time does that put us?"

Levi ponders the question for a moment. "Somewhere between a hundred and forty-six to sixty-six million years. I think."

"Well, call me Chaka and fetch me some stone soup." Kuzneski looks at me. "We're going to spend the rest of our lives playing *Land of the Lost*?"

"If we're lucky," is my sour response. Honestly, dinosaurs or not, I'll take the Cretaceous over the Ice Age. The weather is warm and the food sources plentiful. Dinosaurs might be big and scary, but we've got a whole town to feed and enough guns to get the job done.

"At least we can lose the jackets," Kuzneski says, shedding his. "I suppose perpetual shorts weather won't be too bad."

"Might want to rethink that," Flores says, pointing to the window, where what looks like a mosquito the size of my fist is bouncing against the glass.

"And this is why I'm still not going," Kuzneski says. "Have fun storming the castle, and all that."

"Any transportation in town?" I'm hoping for something fast. Agile enough to manage the rough forest floor, like a couple of ATVs. But what I'm offered is even better.

"Bunch a horses," Hardy says. "I'll fetch 'em for ya soon as that Norman—"

"Nodosaur," Levi says,

"I done named him Norman, after my father-in-law, who was just about as ugly, fat, and in the way as that creature."

"I think he's kind of cute," Young Cassie says, standing by a bewildered and quite pleased Owen.

"Cute, but dangerous," my Cassie says, already protective of her younger self.

"He ain't so bad," Levi says, heading for the door. "Nodosaurs are herbivores. Like cows. He'll bolt at the first sign of trouble."

I listen to Levi's footsteps clomping down the stairs. He exits the door below us, shouting, "Hey! Get out of here." He walks into view, waving his arms at the dinosaur. I raise my handgun and aim it at the creature's head.

"Hey," Owen says, disapproving.

"Just in case it attacks," I tell him, but he glares at me until I lower my aim, not because he's won the battle between selves, but because it will appease him, and I'm a quick draw.

I tense when Levi charges out of the building, roaring and bearing his teeth. The nodosaur tenses, letting out another honk. Its armored tail swishes back and forth, mowing down the tall grass. There are a thousand ways this could go wrong, and most of them end with Levi dead, or Owen angry at me for killing the dinosaur. If I can. Those armor plates look pretty tough.

The nodosaur stomps a foot, dragging it through the rich earth.

Levi freezes in place, no doubt sensing what I am—he's about to be run over by three tons of armored dinosaur.

"Owen," Cassie says, her voice worried.

I start to raise my handgun again, but I don't need to finish. With a barking honk directed at the sky, the nodosaur suddenly stands about a foot taller, spins around, and *gallops* out of town. It wasn't as stocky or slow as it seemed, but as Levi hoped, it was a two-ton chicken. Though I'm sure the town's sudden appearance had already spooked it something fierce.

"See?" Levi says from below, his voice muffled by the glass. "No prob—"

A roar, not too close, but not nearly as far away as I'd like, cuts him short. It's powerful enough to shake the glass and rattle my nerves.

"That wasn't Tsul'Kalu," Inola says.

I shake my head. "There are worse things than Tsul'Kalu in this time." The words feel sour in my mouth. An accidental lie. Dinosaurs, like all Earth's creatures, are animals. They've been extinct for millions of years, and many of them could swallow us whole, but they kill to eat, not for the malicious pleasure of it. And from what I saw, the god of the hunt wouldn't have too much trouble handling the nodosaur.

I turn to Hardy. "The horses?"

With a nod, he hurries out of the room.

I approach my father, who's still standing with Mrs. Dearborn. "Stay here. It's the most secure building in town. Try to keep everyone away from the windows and out of sight. Quiet, too. And put the fires out. The more Black Creek looks like a ghost town, the less attention it will receive from anything, and anyone."

"I'm not in charge of these people," my father says. "What makes you think—"

"Most people in town respect the McCoy name," Levi points out, stepping closer to us. "And I'll tell 'em to listen to you."

"You don't even know me," my father says.

"Didn't know me, neither," Levi says. "But you know what's going on, and if Owen thinks you're the man for the job, then you are."

"I know I'm probably on your shit list right now," Kuzneski says. "But I'll watch over your family while you're gone."

"Aren't many people who could watch themselves die and not be affected," I say.

"What's that say about you?" he asks.

"Nothing good, I suppose."

He flashes a grin. "Means you're a fuckin' badass."

"That was fast," Cassie says, looking out the window. I'm about to ask what she's talking about when I hear a horse whinny.

"I'll go fetch some guns," Levi says, heading out the door.

Everything is coming together quickly, which is good. The sun is a bit higher in the sky now, on account of it being summer again or perhaps late spring—the seasonal indicators might be different in this time. Either way, we still have only hours before dark. Maybe less time before we flux even further back in time. I'm afraid to see just how far back we go. There will come a point when we won't be able to survive.

Kuzneski is right. We're going to play out our very own *Land of the Lost*, and since I fully intend on living my life, and making sure everyone in town does as well, the human race is going to get kick-started a few million years earlier.

"Head on down," I say to Inola and Flores. "I'll be right behind you."

While they head out, I crouch beside Owen and Young Cassie. "I want you to look after her," I tell my younger self. "And no matter what happens, you don't lose sight of what's important."

"What if it's him who needs protecting?" Young Cassie asks with a one-sided grin.

"Good question," Cassie says. She's standing behind me, hands on her hips, wearing the same one-sided smile.

"You'll be there for each other, for the rest of your lives, no matter what," I declare.

Owen and Young Cassie both blush. Mission accomplished, I tussle my own hair exactly how I hate it, and stand up.

"We'll be back soon," I tell my father. "Ish. Maybe tomorrow. If you run into trouble you can't handle, or if anything...weird...happens, just get everyone underground."

When he nods, I give him a hug that I hope won't be our last. Then I head for the door.

As we head down the stairs, Cassie nudges me with her elbow. "For the rest of our lives? What makes you think *I'm* okay with that?"

I shrug. "Pretty slim pickins in town."

"Flores is handsome."

"Pretty sure Flores knows better than to mess with me."

She smiles and takes my hand, holding it until we reach the front door, where five horses are waiting.

"Been a long time since I rode," Cassie says.

"Like riding a bike," I say.

"Been a long time since I did that, too, and bikes don't buck when they get scared."

She's right about that. "A horse is only as skittish as her rider."

She lets go of my hand and gives me a shove. "Now you're just making shit up."

Inola mounts her steed, making it look easy.

"Just do what she does," I say.

With two quick jabs from Inola's heels and a "Tick, tick," from her mouth, the horse sprints off. She directs it in a tight circle, before yanking it to a halt. "Good," she declares at the end of her brief ride.

Flores mounts one of the horses, with a lot less flair than Inola, but still makes it look easy. And when Cassie tries, she finds that it is. Levi arrives before I climb atop my horse. He's got several weapons slung over his shoulder, including two semi-automatic rifles with now illegal bump stocks. I'm not a big fan of everyday people carrying weapons like these, but I'm sure glad to have them now. He hands one to me, and the other to Flores. Cassie gets a pump-action shotgun. Levi keeps a shotgun for himself. He offers a third to Inola, but she shakes her head and pats my father's Winchester already holstered on the horse's side. Seems she's adopted the family weapon, along with my father. Which is fine by me. Not just because I want my father to be happy while in the Cretaceous, but also because the weapon packs a punch.

Levi and I climb on our horses and turn south. Where there used to be tall hills blocking the view, there are now flat fields and forest, revealing a tall mound beyond, which would have been hidden in my time, and which now glistens in the late day sun as an array of solar panels gathering energy.

"Wherever there's injustice," Kuzneski says from the courthouse door.

We watched *The Three Amigos* just a few weeks ago, while pulling a night shift. It was a breach of protocol, but back then I didn't see the harm.

"Wherever there is suffering," he adds. "C'mon, do the salute." Behind him, inside the courthouse, I can see Young Cassie and Owen already doing the *Three Amigos* salute. But there's no way in hell I'm doing it. Instead, I raise a hand and say, "Let's ride."

With a nudge, my horse sets out, and the rest follow. With every hoof thump, my smile fades. I'm leaving Black Creek behind me, and I can't help but think it will be for the last time. *Doesn't matter,* I decide, pushing the horse faster. If this doesn't end, here and now, everyone in town, including the people I hold dearest in the world, will likely die.

So I ride hard toward the distant power station, racing the sun as it plunges toward the horizon.

43

"There it is." Flores is crouched beside a tree, doing an admirable job of ignoring the fact that everything here is totally new. Aside from the breathable air, it's like being on another planet. Other than artists' renderings, no human being in the history of time has ever seen any of this.

Following Flores's pointed finger, I see the solar array. It's vast, covering the slope of a pint-sized mountain that's been preserved by the particle collider's effect. I try to picture it all in my mind. The giant ring stretching from below Adel and reaching all the way here on the far side of town. The network of tunnels below the town, directing power and control, all of it creating a kind of bubble around Black Creek. The bubble sustains most of what's inside the area, carrying it all through time. But the bubble has holes, or at least weak spots, I think, which would account for the disappearance of my truck. The effect on that empty stretch of mountain was enough to carry us back in time, but not quite enough for the vehicle. That's my theory, anyway.

At the base of the mountain is a sturdy looking brick building. It's a boxy, non-descript structure bearing no signage and no warnings. No 'Keep Out' signs either, but I think that's implied by the tall fence covered in razor wire.

"Where are the guards?" Cassie asks.

It's a good question. I don't see any sentries, human or drone. The only thing I can hear is a mass of bird calls, some of them recognizable, the munching of our loosely tied horses enjoying a snack of lush foliage, and the gentle whir of a thousand solar panels slowly rotating to track the sun. Reflected light fills the air with an orange glow that's growing duller by the minute.

A bird chirps to our right, so close it must be on the ground. I start to question the bird's proximity and realize I'm once again mistaking Inola's bird call for the real thing. I whistle a reply, acknowledging that I've heard her, and then I motion for the others to follow.

We creep through the tall trees that are weighed down by leaves the size of men. The canopy is thick and all but blocks out the sun, transporting us from sunset to twilight in just a few steps. The air is fragrant with decay and blooming life. Flowers all around slowly close for the night. Bees the size of my hand buzz away, gathering at hives that must be a nightmare to stumble across.

We find Inola crouching inside a stand of ferns, only visible because she's waving me over. Gathered in the greenery, I have no trouble spotting why the facility is quiet. A large portion of the fence has been torn out of the ground and dragged inside. Several of the solar panels at the bottom of the hill have been destroyed. The remains of several men decorate the walls and the concrete foundation upon which the facility rests.

"Tsul'Kalu," Inola whispers.

"Doesn't change anything," I say. "And if he's gone, he's made our job easier."

Inola doesn't react. Her gaze is unflinching.

"Thoughts?" I ask Flores.

"Find the front door, kick it in, try to find a way to shut it down, and if we can't, we shoot the shit out of anything that looks important."

"That's about as complicated a plan as the Army ever comes up with," I tease, "but it'll work." To the group. "Stay low. Stay quiet. Do not fire unless we're in imminent danger."

When I get nods all around, I take point with Cassie at my back, followed by Levi, Inola, and Flores at the rear, watching our six. How many times did I depend on him like this in the future? How many missions did we run together before our last? How many more will there be in the future?

Just this one, I hope.

In a world with one town of people, there won't be much need for a military strike force, unless the dinosaurs rise up against us...

I crouch-walk out of the thick forest, bathed in orange sunlight. If the Appalachian mountains still existed, we'd already be cast in shadow. With them missing, we have about thirty minutes of direct light remaining, and another thirty after that, before the sky goes dark.

Sweeping my rifle back and forth, I step onto the concrete. I slow when I reach the flattened fencing. The razor wire is coated in blood and little bits of what looks like white flesh. I crouch over the gore and when the others gather around me, I say, "It wasn't Tsul'Kalu who tore down this fence."

"How can you tell?" Levi asks. He's been filled in on the monster's existence, but a lot of details have been left out.

"The blood is red," I say. "Is there anything in this time that could do this..." I point to the remains of a man splashed against the side of the power station wall. "And that?"

He thinks for a moment. "Appalachiosaurus. Related to the T-Rex. Twenty-five feet from snout to tail. Has longer forelimbs, though. Not so..." He does an imitation of a short limbed T-Rex. "Would make short work of any of us. Maybe even the Nephilim."

With that in mind, I say, "Let's do our best to avoid contact."

"I'm afraid that doesn't work for me." Langdon's voice is loud. Way too loud. A drone descends from the sky. "Your betrayal is not completely unexpected."

"My loyalty is to Black Creek," I tell him. "You're going to get all these people killed."

"If that were my intention, they would already be dead. Of course, if that's what it will take to succeed in my mission, I will gladly sacrifice you all, starting with those still in captivity here."

The drone does a slow circle, the camera zeroing in on each of us. Inola takes aim, but I push the Winchester muzzle down and shake my head. As loud as Langdon is being, he's nowhere near as loud as a gunshot. So far, nothing has reacted to his voice, so we might be in the clear.

I motion for the others to follow and strike out again, trying to act like I'm indifferent to the drone's presence.

"I see," Langdon says. "Having absconded with the people for whom you care—thanks to my less than trustworthy help—the rest of my prisoners are expendable? You're turning out to be quite the antihero."

The building's doorway is held open by the remains of a guard, the lower half of his body missing. Why would a predator do this? I wonder. I have no doubt an Appalachiosaurus would eat a person, but why would it eat only half a person? Why would it scatter the other people around? Was the attack territorial? Perhaps blind rage because of the strange building and people suddenly in its territory?

"It's looking for you," Langdon says, gaining my full attention. "It has been stalking the mountain, killing everything it comes across. It's quite impressive, really. Sadly, I believe it has discovered your precious Black Creek. How many people are there? How many survived?" The drone's camera shifts back and forth. "I don't see your family with you. You didn't leave them there, did you?"

I tense, looking back toward Black Creek. How long would it take to reach them?

"Oh, don't worry," Langdon says. "I'm no monster."

"You'll defend them?" I ask, wondering if Langdon might actually send his drone army to defend Black Creek in return for me not pulling the plug. It would be a tempting offer, but it would leave us hurtling through time.

He laughs. "No. Why would I..." I can picture him shaking his head at me, and I really want to twist it off his shoulders. "This one drone is all the resources I will commit to the effort, and I have no intention of battling the creature. I will leave that...to you."

Three flares launch skyward, bright in the sun's fading light. Our position has been revealed to anything within a few miles, including Tsul'Kalu.

"There," Langdon says. "That did the trick."

Knowing he's got drones in the air all over the region, I have little doubt that one is tracking the god of the hunt from a distance, even now. If Langdon says the beast is coming for us, I have no reason to doubt him.

"Whatever you're intending on doing, I suggest you hurry," Langdon says.

I'm frozen for a moment. Is he simply taunting me—confident that we will fail, and that Tsul'Kalu will kill us—or is he simply not worried?

Are we too late?

He's trying to get in my head, I decide. "Let's go!" I run for the open door, leading with my weapon, ready to shoot anything that moves.

The drone paces me, staying just out of reach. "Run, run, run, as quick as you can..."

"Hey," I hear Inola say behind me, and when I turn to look, I find Flores squatted down, his fingers cupped together. Inola leaps up, putting one foot in his hands before being launched upward. Inola sails toward the drone, hatchet in hand.

"Holy shit, she's awesome," Cassie manages to say in the time it takes for Inola to reach the drone.

The hatchet strikes hard and true, shattering one of the four propellers. Unable to compensate for the impact, the drone careens sideways and crashes into the concrete. I'm pretty sure it could lift off again, but Levi reaches it before it can, stomping on it with his boots until it's a ruined mess.

"I really hate that guy," Flores says.

Inola picks herself up off the ground, but freezes halfway up, eyes locked on the dark forest.

"Is he here?" I ask, scanning the shadows. Out in the open like this, Tsul'Kalu would make short work of us. Our only hope is to either be gone when he arrives, or out of reach inside a building built to withstand forces stronger than him.

Inola snaps out of her rigid readiness. "No." she says. "Something else."

"Something else?" Cassie asks.

"A face," Inola says. "White, like you." She points at Levi and me. "But not...not like us."

"Not human," I guess.

She nods. "Not people."

"What color was Appalachiosaurus?" I ask Levi.

The kid shakes his head. "Not even King Solomon, with all of his wisdom, could'a told you what color dinosaurs were."

Remembering the white flesh at the fallen fence, I strike out for the entrance again, reaching it with no more interruptions. Aside from the man at the door, the interior is empty, and clean. The violence was relegated to the exterior, but I don't detect any signs of occupation either. Could everyone have died outside? That seems odd. If there were people still alive here, wouldn't Langdon send them for us? We could have been ambushed while he talked my ear off. Instead, he summoned Tsul'Kalu, who might very well inflict serious damage on the power station during his war against us.

Having a bad feeling about what we're going to find, I rush through the facility, kicking open doors without fear of resistance.

"Shouldn't we slow down?" Cassie asks. "This doesn't seem safe."

"No one's here," I say.

"What makes you say that?" Flores asks as we round the one and only flight of stairs. I kick open the door ahead and step into a large control room lined with consoles. It doesn't take more than a glace to confirm what I feared. The station is shut down, no longer sending power to Synergy. Whatever resources Langdon needed to finish what he's started, he's already got it.

We've been on a wild goose chase this whole time, out of his hair and keeping Tsul'Kalu, the only thing he really saw as a threat to his plans, fully occupied.

"We've been played," Flores says, looking at the information displayed on the screen. "It's still collecting power, storing it in batteries on site, but the relay to the main facility has been shut down."

"If there are batteries here..." Cassie says, and she doesn't need to finish the thought.

"Shee-it," Levi says.

A sharp hiss from Inola silences us. She stands still near the door, ear turned up. She stalks out of the room, Winchester at the ready. We follow her down the hall toward a second-floor window looking out at the forest. She crouches down, motioning for us to do the same.

"I don't see anything," Levi says.

"He's here," she insists, eyes laser focused.

"How can you tell?" Levi asks.

Four panicked horses bolt from the forest, charging over the fallen fence and trapping themselves inside the facility. I'm about to note that one of the horses is missing, when I see it approaching...in the sky.

44

"So…" Levi says. "It can throw horses?"

The horse bucks and twists as it pinwheels through the air. Tsul'Kalu is big, but it's hard to imagine he wields the strength to catapult a horse. Unless it really is some kind of demi-god, demon-spawn whose power is unnatural. In the past, writing such things off—including the Bible, in which such creatures exist—would have been simple. But I've not only seen the monster with my own eyes, I'm actually in the past.

Anything seems possible. Demi-gods, demons, even God himself, who I imagine is either really pissed off at Langdon for screwing with the natural order of things He created, or is having a good laugh at our expense.

"Back!" Flores says, diving away from the windows.

The horse slams into and through the glass, exploding shards into the room. The beast lies still, dead from the impact, its neck bent at a sharp angle.

A deep sing-song voice follows the horse. *"Tsisdu…"*

Rabbit.

Tsul'Kalu is definitely here for us. For me.

Ducked down, hidden from anything out in the forest, Levi says, "So, have y'all tried, I don't know, compelling it with the power of Christ or something?"

Inola's face screws up, not understanding the movie reference. It's possible she's familiar with the Bible, but certainly not *The Exorcist.*

"Half demon," I say. "Not possessed by one. And if a few dozen shotgun shells didn't put it down, I'm not sure what good shouting at it will do."

"Then what's the plan?" Levi asks.

It's a great question to which I have no answer. The power station is shut down and abandoned. Whatever we could have stopped by cutting the power, it's too late for that. Langdon has what he needs to get when he's going. He let us come this far because it kept the giant—and us—out of his hair.

"Stealth. Avoidance. Retreat." Flores looks uncomfortable with the rudimentary plan he's just offered. He's not the type to back down from a fight, but he has no illusions about who will win.

On the surface, it makes sense. If Tsul'Kalu can't find us, he can't kill us. But I suspect he's skilled enough to track us down. Even if we split up, he'll hunt us one by one.

"How did he die?" I ask Inola. "Was he killed?"

She nods. "But I do not know how. It was before my time, and those who bore witness were found dismembered by his tribe."

"There's a whole tribe of these things?" Cassie asks.

"Far in the west," Inola says.

"But it *can* be killed?" I ask.

"Maybe if we put enough rounds in it, we'll get lucky," Flores says, and it's as good a plan as any. But I'm still not convinced it's the right play. We also need to protect the remaining horses. Without them, we'll be walking back and getting nowhere fast.

"How fast is he?" I ask Inola.

"Faster than you," she says.

"Faster than a horse?"

No one likes the sound of that.

"You think we can fight it on the run?" Flores asks.

"Not we," I say.

"Uh-uh," Cassie says. "No way."

"Just long enough to buy you all enough time to reach Black Creek first."

Levi's eyes widen. "You're planning an ambush!"

Flores nods his approval. "Could work. There's enough firepower in town to turn that thing into paste. But what makes you think we can reach the horses? Could be that thing chased them in here to flush us out."

Cassie nods. "It hasn't attacked yet."

"Tsul'Kalu is a patient hunter," Inola says. "If we leave, then we die."

"We need a distraction," I say.

"You want one of us to run around out there so the others can escape?" Levi is aghast, despite me saying no such thing. "I think that's—"

"I'll do it," Flores says.

"You'll die," Inola and Levi say in unison.

"I know what I'm doing," he argues. "Won't be hard to—"

"Guys," I say, "we're in the Cretaceous. With dinosaurs. Something killed the people here. Something tore down that fence. And she—" I motion to Inola, "—saw something out there, watching, that wasn't the giant."

"So...what?" Levi says. "You're like a dinosaur whisperer now?"

"Pretty sure there is one thing predators in any time will respond to," I say.

"Wounded prey," Inola says.

"So, step one, we summon a dinosaur. Step two, we reach the horses while the hunter dukes it out with said dinosaur. Step three, we ride like hell to Black Creek." Cassie looks frazzled, but she's wearing her 'let's do this' face.

"Almost," I say. "You four ride ahead."

"Right," Cassie says, expression souring. "The ambush. And if that doesn't work?"

"Get to Synergy. Stop Langdon."

"Love how you make that sound simple," she says.

"It *is* simple," I say, "Just not easy."

She rolls her eyes.

"*Tsisdu...*" the giant sings again, much louder now. Much closer. At twelve-feet-plus tall, it can nearly look up into the window. I wave everyone to move deeper into the building. We slide along the floor, staying low and quiet.

Outside, the monster chuckles. It can hear us. Probably smell us, too.

"So," Levi says. "How do we simulate wounded prey?"

"Scream," Cassie says. "Real loud."

"Now might be a good time to start." Levi's face has gone pale. He's looking past the dead horse, out the window filled with orange light and thick fingers.

Tsul'Kalu's face slides up into view, his eyes burning with savage delight, his teeth bared in a menacing smile. His dark red hair is covered by the saber-toothed cat's head, its skin hanging behind him as a cloak. When he starts laughing, I scream, not entirely out of fear, but my emotions lend an air of realism to the sound. The others join in, wailing as loud as they can. It's a horrible sound, and in any time it sounds like a dying wail.

Of all the possible responses to our screaming, the giant's is the least expected. Instead of trying to crawl through the window, or mocking us, or attempting to throw something at us, it joins in, screaming into the sky. He's so loud that the sound of his agonized voice drowns out our own, and silences us. When he finishes, his voice echoing into the distance, no doubt heard by the people in Black Creek, he turns back to look at us, smiling.

His grin fades when he notices that I'm the only one left, and I have a rifle pointed at his face.

I pull the trigger, firing off a single round when I'm expecting to unleash a full auto barrage. I forgot that the weapon I'm using is semi-auto, with a bump stock, which operates different from conventional arms. The result is that instead of turning the giant's head into pulp, I put a single round into its cheek.

Before I can adjust how I'm handling the weapon, Tsul'Kalu drops out of sight. *Shit.*

I bolt for the window, taking aim as the giant rounds the building's corner. I put three rapid-fire bullets in his calf before he disappears. Despite spattering the concrete with purple gore, the only sound from Tsul'Kalu is one of pleasure. It's almost orgasmic, and really disturbing.

Leaping down a flight of stairs, I reach the ground floor in seconds, and run for the building's far side. At the window, I raise my weapon, expecting to fire into the giant's back. But I don't see anything, or anyone, until a massive hand shatters through the glass, grasps my clothing, and yanks me outside.

I'm tossed to the ground, rolling to a stop in an open courtyard. There's nowhere to hide. Nowhere to run. Off to the building's side I catch sight of Flores, horse reins in hand. He pauses, looking ready to offer assistance. I give my head a slow shake, and push myself up.

He knows the deal. The mission comes first. Right now, Tsul'Kalu is a stumbling block preventing him from completing the mission that future me tasked him with—stop Langdon, even at the cost of my life. Twice.

The giant turns his head toward the sound of fading horse hooves, but he just chuckles. He is supremely confident in his ability to catch the others, which means I need to delay him for as long as possible.

The question is: *how?*

I scan the wounds I've already inflicted on the thing and find them... missing. Purple blood stains his face and calf, but there are no bullet holes. He heals fast. Stupid fast. That's how he survived Kuzneski's shotgun barrage. So how do I stop something that heals?

Go for the kill shot, I think. With people, that's center mass or a headshot. I'm not confident center mass will do it. I'm not even sure a clean headshot will do it. But putting a bullet in this creature's brain should slow it down.

I face the giant, letting him stare me down. The longer this takes, the better the odds are for the others.

Tsul'Kalu says something in a language I don't understand, but the tone is clear enough. He's taunting me.

"You're pretty fucking ugly, yourself," I say, garnering a look of confusion from the creature. He doesn't understand me, either. But he reads my tone just as easily.

He stands up straight, relaxing as he points at me, and then at himself. Not at his body, but at his clothing. The skins of humans and animals hang from his waist in sheets. The saber-toothed skin blows in the wind rolling out from Adel as the sun sets. Tsul'Kalu has been busy collecting trophies, and he's letting me know that I'm about to be next.

I unleash a stream of bullets, tracing them up from his gut and towards his face.

Again, the monster seems to enjoy the pain, but as the first round punches through his neck, he steps to the side.

He's protecting his head...

He dropped away from the window when I shot him in the face, too.

That's the key, I realize. *Head shot, it is.*

As I eject the magazine and move to slap in my only spare, the giant charges, hands outstretched. That's also the same moment something big roars behind me, the sound mixing with breaking branches and the heavy thump of a newcomer thundering into the ring.

45

I try to formulate a rapid-fire plan to save my ass, but all I can manage is to whisper a string of curses so foul I've never said them aloud before.

In the end, muscle memory and reflexes delay my demise. I dive to the side, avoiding the Nephilim's grasp. Or did I? When I roll back to my feet, the giant thunders past, his hands redirected toward a carnivorous dinosaur that partly resembles T-Rex as I remember it from *Jurassic Park*. The shape of its skull is a little different, and at twenty-five feet in length, it's a might smaller. But what really sets it apart is the coat of iridescent feathers covering most of its body. The shimmering green plume seems to glow in the diminished sunlight.

The dinosaur is beautiful, until it opens its jaws, revealing teeth the length of my hand.

Without a trace of fear, Tsul'Kalu leaps at what I assume is an Appalachiosaurus. Its skin doesn't match what we found by the torn fence, but that doesn't mean it didn't ravage the men stationed here. Whether or not it did, I'm glad it's here now.

The dinosaur might be a killing machine, but I doubt it has Tsul'Kalu's intelligence, or his ability to hold a grudge.

Then again, as good a hunter as the giant might be, he's clearly never fought a dinosaur before. The Appalachio turns its head sideways, catching Tsul'Kalu by the waist. The massive jaws squeeze. Teeth plunge into the hunter's flesh. Bones crack from the pressure.

Tsul'Kalu screams in pain.

Or is it pleasure?

Is he grimacing in agony, or smiling in perverse delight?

The scene unnerves me. As I start to back away, the Appalachio gives Tsul'Kalu a vicious shake. Purple blood sprays, coating the building's wall. Organs slip from his ruined gut, decorating the predator's snout and feet.

But the taste of him must not agree with the dinosaur. It gives him one last shake and tosses him to the side. When it turns toward me, snout oozing purple, I realize that, instead of standing transfixed by the unreal violence, I should have run like hell. Now instead of staring down a demi-god with a hankering for chaos, I'm facing off with an apex predator from the Cretaceous.

I suppose part of me wanted to see if Tsul'Kalu could be defeated, but now that he has, curiosity transforms into a thick syrup of 'ohh shit.' The difference is that I'm pretty sure bullets will do the trick.

But I don't want to kill the Appalachio. It's just doing its job, killing and eating, culling the weak, helping evolve species toward humanity's eventual rise. It doesn't deserve to die by modern weaponry.

So I aim for its leg and squeeze off two rounds.

The bullets punch through the thick skin but lack the energy to exit the other side. The dinosaur's leg flinches up. It scratches at the air, chomps its teeth together in my direction, and then forgets all about the wound.

To a creature accustomed to battling its own kind and herbivores with spikes, horns, and armor plating, the slugs might feel like insect bites. It plants its feet firmly on the ground, leans forward and unleashes a bellow that hurts my ears and smells of rotting flesh. Tendrils of drool warble at me, stretching out and falling to slap the pavement at my feet.

And now...it's time to run.

The Appalachio's roar comes to a sudden stop when I start running. The sound is followed by the thump of large feet, vibrating through the concrete.

The door is just a few feet ahead, but not close enough. I can feel hot breath on my neck. Can feel the shadow of the dinosaur's head wrapping around me.

With a shout, I dive through the doorway, sliding across the smooth flooring while the wall behind me explodes inward. Bricks pummel my body. Dust swirls in the air. And then, the Appalachio roars again. Inside the building, the sound reverberates.

I slap my hands over my ears and turn back to find myself just inches from its open jaws. The teeth clap shut, the sound like the crack of a toppling tree. The dinosaur shoves against the wall, spilling free more bricks and inching closer.

Dust makes my feet slip as I scrabble back, my retreat made pitiful by the best shock and awe campaign the Cretaceous has to offer.

When the dinosaur withdraws, my senses return. I push myself and turn toward the building's far exit. From there it will be a quick run past the ruined fence and into the lush forest, where a creature my size shouldn't have much trouble hiding.

Unless Inola's white-faced mystery creature is there. I know now that the past is far stranger than anyone would have guessed. If creatures like the Nephilim can exist, erased from the fossil record by the Smithsonian, what else might we come across? With hundreds of millions of years at play, the possibilities seem endless. Modern people have only been around for 200,000 years. If the Earth is billions of years old, contrary to what many religious folks in Appalachia believe, that's essentially 0%. It seems entirely likely that in all that time, things beyond our imagining and not recorded by the fossil record, could have come and gone.

Which is what's going to happen to me if I don't get the hell out of here.

Before I can make a break for it, the side wall crashes inward, toppling a sheet of bricks toward me. I stumble back as a massive tail crashes through the space, slamming into desks, chairs, and nearly my head.

The Appalachio isn't just hungry. It's pissed.

While the wall continues to fold inward, I bolt from the room, hoping the dinosaur won't think to peek inside. I slam into the hallway wall, denting it with my shoulder, before sprinting for the far exit. I hit the push bar a little too hard and spill out into sunlight, more orange than I've ever seen before. The staggering beauty of it holds my attention for a breath.

Then the Appalachio roars in frustration.

It knows I'm out, I think, sprinting toward the forest.

When the concrete underfoot shakes nearly hard enough to knock me over, I glance back to find the predator rounding the building's corner. It's far more agile than I would have guessed, making the turn with two quick steps, keeping itself upright with its long tail. The dinosaur hits its stride a moment later and it becomes painfully clear that I'm not going to make it even halfway to the forest.

I have no choice, I decide, readying the rifle.

What comes next plays out in my mind's eye first. I'll stop, spin around, drop to one knee, and then unleash a full-auto barrage into the Appalachio's face. Unloading the magazine's 38 rounds will take just a few seconds, thanks to the bump stock, and it should be more than enough to take the dinosaur down. The question is, will it hit the ground, or land on top of me? Making a mental note to dive out of the way if necessary, I stop hard, spin around, drop to one knee, raise the rifle, and—hold my fire.

I have the dinosaur in my sights.

Killing it would be a simple thing.

But I can't.

Not because I lack the will, or because of a desire to become the first PETA member in the history of time, but because what I'm seeing behind—and above—the Appalachio is mind-numbing.

Tsul'Kalu leaps off the power station's roof, soaring a good hundred feet into the air. His body trails an arc of purple blood, gore, and a dangling tangle of his own entrails.

How is he not dead?

How is he moving at all?

What's most astonishing is that he's holding several cords of his intestines between his outstretched arms.

Frozen in the moment, unsure of who I should be shooting at, I decide to once again hold my fire. I'll need the bullets for whoever wins the continuing battle—one that the dinosaur believes is over. Until the giant lands on its back and slings his insides around the dinosaur's neck.

The moment Tsul'Kalu draws back on the intestines, tightening the cords, and yanking the massive head back, I know who's going to come out on top, and that the forest will do nothing to save me.

So I adjust my aim, pull the rifle forward and let the bump stock unleash its hellish, fully automatic fury. A few rounds hit the dinosaur, but most strike the hunter. Purple flower bursts trace up his chest, but they miss his head as he leans to the side.

Definitely protecting his head, I think.

The barrage loosens the giant's grip, allowing the Appalachio to buck him off. The dinosaur spins around, jaws snapping in rage.

Still holding on to his own insides, which are now hanging from either side of the dinosaur's head, Tsul'Kalu pulls himself off the ground and delivers a solid kick to the dinosaur's chin. Teeth snap together. The Appalachio staggers from the impact, but doesn't slow. It whips around, striking the Nephilim with its massive tail. Like a bat against a ball, the giant launches. But he never lets go of his tether.

Instead of spiraling away, the hunter swings in a wide arc that brings him back around the dinosaur. He takes two running steps upon returning to the ground and then leaps onto the ancient predator's back, resuming his strangle hold. As the dinosaur thrashes and gags, Tsul'Kalu locks his confident and unnerving eyes on mine.

He doesn't say it, but I can imagine his thoughts. *Run, rabbit.*

Despite the carnage and the agony he must feel, the giant is having the time of his life. I turn tail and sprint five steps before I'm confronted by a thousand pound creature, rearing up on its hind legs. I pull my rifle's trigger, but the spent magazine has nothing to give.

And it's a good thing. Had I fired, I would have shot both horse and rider.

"Get on!" Cassie shouts.

I waste no time mounting the horse. "You weren't supposed to—"

"'Thank' and 'you' are the only two words that should be coming out of your mouth," she shouts, spinning the horse around. "Now hold on!"

She gives the horse a solid kick with her heels, but I don't think our ride needs any more inspiration to reach full speed than the nightmare playing out behind us.

I glance over my shoulder as we gallop into the dense and darkening forest. Behind us, the Appalachio falls face first to the ground. Tsul'Kalu rides the creature down, standing on its back, tightening his strangle hold. And then with one last parting glance, he smiles at me.

Despite the wonders of Earth's natural history on display with every flux, I've decided that the past can go right to hell.

We punch through the forest's far side, entering the broad clearing of tall grass in which Black Creek has been deposited. The town is right where we left it, but it has company—a herd of fifty-foot-long behemoths that not even Tsul'Kalu could suffocate with his insides.

Right to fucking hell.

46

The giant dinosaurs resolve as we gallop closer. They're duck-billed, but far larger than I'd ever imagined. Unlike the Appalachio, these behemoths have no feathers. Their thick, wrinkled skin, like that of a rhino, is gray with black smudges—not quite spots, not quite stripes. In the shadows of a thick forest, it would make clever camouflage, not that they need it. I doubt there is much hunting them. At least, I hope there isn't.

Walking on all fours, their weight is dispersed, but the ground shakes beneath the herd like a constant low-grade earthquake.

They're oblivious to the structures in town, scratching themselves against building corners and tasting metal surfaces. They're a rowdy bunch, their deep resounding bellows like fog horns. What I can only assume are the males, bump into each other on occasion, snapping at their neighbors and slapping their long tails. While their grandstanding macho behavior might help them woo the larger females, their indifference to the town's presence means it's taking a beating.

Walls crumble as tails whip back and forth. A few buildings are nearly flattened. I wonder how until I see one male headbutt another in the side, toppling him into a storefront, which folds inward.

Black Creek is under assault, and soon there will be nothing left.

I'm relieved I don't hear gunfire.

Bullets and buckshot might just enrage the beasts. Right now, they're just passing through. No need to start a war. But the duck-bills have clearly demonstrated that living in a traditional town, during the Cretaceous, might be impossible. Like all living things in this time, we might need to become nomadic, capable of moving, running, or fighting at a moment's notice.

Cassie slows the horse as we approach the ruined outskirts of town. It looks like the dinosaurs all but charged down Main Street, funneled by the buildings. I don't see any bodies among the debris. The townspeople no doubt heard and felt the herd's approach. The lack of bodies is a relief, but the assault isn't over yet.

"We shouldn't get any closer," I say, and Cassie brings the horse to a stop. "Don't want to spook them." If the herd becomes a stampede, they'll trample the small town to dust.

"Look!" Cassie says, pointing toward the herd's core.

For a moment, all I can see is long dinosaur legs and swishing tails. Then I see a group of people, five in total, comically small among the behemoths.

"What are they doing?" I ask, as they run through the herd, narrowly avoiding being crushed.

The dinosaurs either don't notice the small creatures among them, or simply don't see them as a threat. They show no reaction to the presence of people, other than indifference.

We watch in silence as the small group reaches the center of the overgrown street, and one by one, they disappear into the ground.

"They're retreating to the tunnels," Cassie says.

"Won't be much of a town to stage an ambush from," I note. "And after seeing these things, I doubt anyone feels safe above ground."

I realize that Synergy's maze of tunnels, and the facility atop the mountain, will likely become our home and the birthplace of humanity on Earth. But will that change the future? With a hundred million years between us and the first ape-like pre-humans, an entire civilization of people could come and go in a self-made apocalypse with barely a millimeter in the geological record as evidence. Modern human civilization didn't begin until six thousand years in my present's past, and we're already nearly on the brink of wiping ourselves out. If we do, we'll have barely put a razor thin line in the timeline of history.

When a second group hurries outside and into the tunnels, I wonder if my father and Owen have already made the trip. Was this my father's idea? Or did Flores take over upon his return...assuming he did return?

I get an answer when a group of six horses breaks away from the backside of town and gallops toward us through the field. Flores is in the lead, followed by Inola and Levi. I'm not thrilled to see my father, with Owen, on the saddle in front of him, following close behind. A horse with no rider brings up the rear—my replacement ride.

"Kuzneski is leading the people underground," Levi says, slowing to a trot and circling us. "They'll wait there until we come back for them."

"You know what those things are?" Cassie asks, pointing to the creatures clumsily destroying our town.

"Big-ass-osaurus." He shrugs. "I ain't no paleontologist. I don't—wait, no, they're Hyps...Hypsibema. Pretty much all we knew about them was that they were big plant eaters. I think Big-ass-osaurus is more descriptive. How do you say 'big ass' in Latin?"

"Magnum asinus," Flores says, coming to a stop. Then he turns to me. "Glad to see you made it."

"Wouldn't have, without some prehistoric help," I say.

"And..." Cassie gives me a sidelong glance.

"A very stubborn..." The sentence trails off when I realize I was about to say girlfriend. On one hand, it's rather presumptuous. This stage of our relationship has just begun. But she's also so much more than a girlfriend...and yet, not my wife. My father and Owen's arrival spares me from having to finish.

When they come to a stop in front of us, I vent my frustration at my father. "You shouldn't be here."

"I know you're an adult, but you're still my son. Didn't sit well with me, letting you face danger without my having your back."

"Dad..." I'm touched by his concern. I've been desperate for it most of my life. But at the moment, it's misplaced. If he had seen what I just had... I motion to Owen. "You have to take him back."

"I'd find a way out, if you left me," Owen says. "We started this together, we'll see it through together."

Bold words from an eleven-year-old. They leave me a bit stymied. "I...don't remember being this..."

"Stubborn," my father says.

"Forthright," Cassie adds, like she remembers this side of me well.

"Stupid," I say.

"Well, maybe you've got a shitty memory, too," Owen says, then turns to my father, and raises an index finger to silence him. "We are lost in time, and dinosaurs are destroying our town. I can damn well say 'shitty.'"

My father smiles despite everything my young self said being true.

"Look," my father says. "The McCoys stick together."

"And you'll be alright if we die together?" I ask. "Because that's something McCoys also historically do."

"Owen," Cassie says, nudging me. "Geez."

"So long as we go down fighting," my father says, revealing his own stubborn streak.

Memories of things that will never come to pass flit through my mind. Whispers at the wake and funeral, hushed stories at school. My father didn't die in the first cave-in, he died because he refused to evacuate. He died trying to rescue people.

"I've been given a second chance at life, right?" my father says. "I'm not going to waste it sitting by, while people I love are in danger."

"It's what got you killed the first time," I say, sliding down from Cassie's horse.

I'm surprised when my father slides down from his, standing eye to eye with me. He puts his hands on my shoulders. "And you don't think that has anything to do with the kind of man you've become? I've seen you risk your life a number of times, and not just for loved ones. Life is precious. You know that better than most, I reckon. I learned it when your mother passed. You remember that old cross-stitch hanging beside the bathroom door?"

I nod. It's still there, made by a mother I never knew.

"Greater love has no one than this..." My father waits for me to finish.

"To lay down one's life for one's friends," I say.

"Or his family," Owen says, looking down at me from his mount. "That last bit isn't in the Good Book, but there's no one as flesh 'n blood as you and me. Cept for all the other folks with doubles in town, I s'pose. But they're not here. So fu—"

"Don't push it, Owen," my father grumbles.

"Point is," Owen says. "Get over it. We're here."

"We're all here," Cassie says. "For better or worse."

That's she's co-opted traditional marriage vows into her contribution doesn't go unnoticed by anyone except for her.

"What?" she asks.

"As much as this moment is tugging at my heart-strings," Levi says, "I reckon we should make like the Hebrews in Egypt and get the fuck out." He turns to my father. "Sorry." Then he points into the distance. "Because, you know, *him.*"

The moment Levi points, my stomach sours. His finger extends in the direction from which Cassie and I have just fled. My father and I mount our horses and turn them around. Standing in a line, we gaze out over the golden field cast in the dull light of a sun below the horizon.

Just outside the distant forest, Tsul'Kalu runs toward us at a confident pace. Everything about him says, *I'm going to catch you, kill you, skin you, and wear you.* Worse, his body appears to have healed. His insides have been stuffed back in place, and aside from the dark purple stains on the skins he's already wearing, there is no evidence that he was injured.

Part of me says to retreat to the tunnel's safety. That would protect us from the hunter, but do nothing to help us with our larger problems. And fighting Tsul'Kalu isn't an option. Our best bet is to outrun him, beat him to Synergy, and make him Langdon's problem—something the old man has been trying to avoid since the beast showed up.

"Sooo," Levi says. "What's the plan?"

I turn to face Adel, her tall peak still bathed in the orange glow of day. "We chase the light." With a solid kick, my horse breaks toward the mountain, and the others follow close behind. It's going to be a hard run over steep terrain overrun with animals from the future to the Cretaceous. I have no illusions about it being safe, or easy, but I seriously doubt that there is anything ahead of us that's worse than what's behind.

47

"Are those rabbits?" Cassie shouts over the stomping of hooves and huffing of hard-working horses.

I see the small animals a moment later, sprinting straight toward us before breaking in either direction. A small birdlike predator breaks from behind a tree, pursuing the fleet-footed hares. It's unprepared for the charging horses, and manages only a shrill cry before being trampled underfoot.

Overhead, a massive flock of modern birds bursts into the dulling sky. There's a variety of species in the mix, somehow sensing that their best chance at survival in this new world is to stick together.

Evolution will be forever changed in this iteration of Earth, there's no doubt about that. While some of the creatures transported through time will become easy prey, or lack the numbers to successfully procreate, others like the rabbits...will survive and possibly thrive. They're well known for adapting to a variety of conditions, eating just about anything, and well, mating 'like bunnies.'

Who knows, maybe this world's advanced species a hundred million years from now will be the descendants of rabbits, rather than apes? They've got a head start.

My horse has been well trained.

It barrels through the woods, avoiding trees and obstacles without any prodding from me, staying on course for Adel. The others are keeping up, following my lead.

We can do this, I think, and then I smell blood.

It's carried on the breeze, from in front of us. The strength of it says there's a lot of blood, which is bad, but there's also something unfamiliar and non-human about it, which is good. The horse whinnies at the scent, but it only takes a nudge to keep it on course.

Inola prods her horse up beside mine. "You smell it?"

"We can't avoid it," I tell her.

She nods. "You know what it is?"

At first, I think she's asking a general question, like what's that smell? But then I realize she's asking if I can identify what kind of creature the blood is from. "It's not human. Do you know what it is?"

As the forest thins ahead, a trumpeting call tears through the air. It's joined by others and a series of angry snorts.

I've seen enough National Geographic specials to identify a pissed off elephant, or in this case, a mammoth. But the snorts are new, and I'm guessing, Cretaceous.

"Mammoths," I say to Inola, and when she gives me a questioning look, I say, "The big hairy elephants." And when that doesn't help, I say, "The big animals with brown hair we saw on the way down."

"But that's not all," she says.

I nod. "That's definitely not all."

My eyes widen as the trees thin further, giving me a striated view of the clearing ahead.

Massive brown bodies thunder across the clearing, thrashing their heads about, swinging and lunging their enormous tusks. Their enemies are a little smaller, but also more agile. The bright yellow dinosaurs have protective hoods, like triceratops, and a rhino-like horn atop their beaked snouts. They move on all fours for the most part, but occasionally rear up on their hind legs, standing taller than the mammoths they're battling.

When we clear the woods, my horse rears up. I'm expecting as much and manage to cling to its back while it whinnies and kicks. My ride settles as the others emerge beside us. I'm not sure if my horse has just gotten over its initial fear, or if it feels there is safety in numbers. The rest of the horses take the battle scene in stride. Whoever owned these steeds before has definitely seen action. The horses stomp their hooves, eager to move, but I don't see a clear path to where we need to go that doesn't take us through the Ice Age and Cretaceous reenactment of the rumble scene from *The Outsiders*.

"Raspberry flavored Daniel in the Lion's Den," Levi exclaims when he takes in the scene. "Mr. Snuffleupagus is killing Big Bird!"

He's right. The mammoths, with their thick, fur-covered hides and long tusks, have killed a handful of the dinosaurs, but they're still out-numbered. Several are wounded. They're going to overheat soon, and one is definitely on death's doorstep. Despite being driven to its knees, the mammoth continues to trumpet defiantly, thrusting its tusks back and forth while a pair of the yellow creatures jab their horns into its side.

Blood coats the ferns and grass.

The sounds of battle rise into the darkening sky.

How long until predators arrive?

How long until Tsul'Kalu catches up?

"Is that our house?" Owen asks, pointing to the ruins of our home. The place has been absolutely flattened. The only thing still recognizable is the large propane tank. For a moment, I feel a flash of hope, but then remember that propane tanks only explode in video games and movies. Unless we can set the foliage around it on fire first...but everything here is damp from rampant humidity.

"Not anymore," my father says.

"Think they'll move if we make enough noise?" Cassie asks.

Even if we all start shooting, the pops aren't going to be any louder than the chaos of over-sized battle. Both sides are lost in a frenzy of confused rage. We might just incite violence toward us.

"I think we need to ride through it," I say. Despite the large number of animals on the battlefield, there are gaps through the action. "And if anything gets in our way, we'll drop it."

"If we have a choice, can we shoot the Big Birds?" Levi asks. "I've always been a Snuffy fan."

If I'm honest, I'm kind of rooting for the mammoths, too. Maybe because they're familiar, and somewhat romanticized by modern culture. They *did* share the Earth with people at one time. There must be some strands of distant kinship.

"If you have a choice," I tell him. Our safety is paramount, and I'm certain that if the herd manages to walk away from this fight, they'll eventually overheat and die anyway. Unless they can shed, which I doubt anyone in my time knows.

I'm about to point out a direction and tell the others to follow when I notice Flores is missing. "Where's Minuteman?" I ask.

"Minute-who?" Levi asks.

"Flores."

He hitches a thumb over his shoulder. "Hung back a bit to watch our backs. He shouted it 'bout halfway through the woods."

I shake my head. I'm torn between appreciation and annoyance. Sticking together is our best chance of mutual survival. But keeping an eye on Tsul'Kalu gives us a tactical advantage.

"Sorry," Levi says. "Thought you heard 'im."

The real problem is that now I don't know if we should wait or go. Any path we leave is going to be trampled. Following us alone, through this mess, might not be possible. I'm not comfortable leaving him behind, but the mission comes first.

Well, it should. But it doesn't.

Damnit, I'm getting soft.

I crane my head around to look for Flores again, and I'm surprised when I spot him. He's just fifty feet away, galloping toward us like his horse is on fire and racing from hell itself.

"Go, go, go!" He shouts, waving a hand at me.

My imagination pictures the giant chasing him through the forest, perhaps gaining, ready to tear torso from legs. But then I see reality, and it's not much better. A panicked herd of duckbills charges through the forest, honking in fear.

They're being chased, I realize, and I shout, "Everyone, go!"

My heels thump against my horse's side and I snap the reigns with a "Hee-ya!" The line of horses breaks toward the rampaging battle ahead.

I try to find a path through it, but then I don't have to.

Flores, whose ride has already reached full speed, plows ahead. He weaves a path that, from behind, looks unflinching. I'm sure he and his horse are absolutely freaking out, but they're making it look easy.

The sea of Snuffys and Big Birds seems to part for us, perhaps intimidated by the sheer mass of the duck-billed herd into which we've been absorbed. I can't see past the front wave of dinosaurs, but there could be up to fifty of them, all a few tons larger than our horses. But we're not small enough to go unnoticed by them. As the herd catches up, they veer around the steeds, careful not to step on the smaller creatures in their midst. With brains the size of walnuts, they might not even realize we're not part of their herd.

One of the duck-bills pulls up alongside me. It lets out a breathy honk with each step, its big orange eyes open wide with fright that has nothing to do with us. That is, until it looks at me. Its long head, twice the size of my horse's, cranes toward me. The creature looks concerned upon seeing the horse, but when its eyes meet mine, they flare even wider. The dinosaur honks and veers away. It careens into its neighbors, and they go down in a heap. The herd spreads out wide to avoid the pile up, entering the violent fray around us.

Prehistoric carnage blooms like a bloody death flower.

While some Big Birds fall under the panicked mass of onrushing duckbills, others ram them head on, or tear at their flesh as they pass. The mammoths are no more forgiving, trumpeting loudly and thrashing with their tusks. Some duckbills are knocked aside, where they collide and cause more chaos. The unlucky ones are skewered and tossed about.

Every inch of the field I will one day call home is absolutely over-flowing with a kind of primal madness, the frayed tension of having been ripped through time finally broken free.

The matriarch mammoth lets out an ear-splitting battle cry before thrusting her tusks up into a duck bill. The dinosaur cries out as it's lifted up and catapulted over the scene, trailing a spray of blood.

Levi, now beside me, cranes his head up to watch the spiraling animal's path. "Holy shi—" A pair of jaws slides out of the forest on the far side of the clearing, catching hold of the duck bill and biting down hard. The poor thing is split into three pieces, the core being swallowed whole, the outer two portions falling to the ground. "—HOLY SHIT!"

I recognize the Appalachio species from our previous encounter. This specimen is even larger, and it's incensed by the madness it has stumbled across. Though it has just eaten a third of a dinosaur, it plunges into the field, snapping at everything that passes, catching and killing a large number of creatures it will never consume.

Ahead, a Big Bird on the warpath has set its sights on Flores. Its large beak snaps open, closing in on his horse's backside. I draw my pistol and fire. My first three shots strike the broad, bony shield atop its head. The rounds cut gashes in the thick skin, but fail to penetrate. The dinosaur flinches, but doesn't alter its course.

"Bad Big Bird!" Levi shouts, firing his own weapon at the beast. To my left, Cassie opens fire. The three of us unleash a torrent of bullets at the enraged creature, and it takes six strikes to divert its attention away from Flores—and directly toward us.

While Levi and Cassie continue to fire, each bullet proving how impossible it's going to be for humanity to survive in the time period, I line up a shot, adjusting for the steady up-and-down of my horse's gallop. I slowly pull the trigger, but I never get to finish.

The familiar crack of the family Winchester snaps through the air behind me. The single round plunges into the creature's eye socket—and the small brain beyond.

The big body goes rigid and topples over just in time for our horses to leap over. I glance back to make sure my father and Owen clear the jump, too, but they're not all I see. Inola follows close behind them, holding the Winchester and looking pleased with her shot.

At the clearing's far side, not far from where we exited the jungle, is a face. It flickers in and out of view as large bodies thrash about in the killing field. In some ways it's almost human. The oval shape of it. The forward-facing black eyes. But there's no nose to speak of, and I can't really tell where its mouth is, if it has one.

This is the mystery observer Inola saw at the power station.

For a moment, I'm sure it's looking back at me. I don't sense the small-minded intellect of a dinosaur in its empty eyes. Instead, I see a calculating creature, undisturbed by the battle, or by death. I see intelligence, and interest, but not hatred. Nor hunger.

A mammoth stumbles between us, as it fends off the Appalachio, trumpeting. The pair are separated by the fleeing herd, giving me a clear view of the forest again.

The face is gone.

Mystery is then replaced by fear.

Rising over the stomping of giant feet, the shrill cries of the wounded, and the roars of the enraged, comes another sound.

Laughter.

The booming chortle rises from the field's far side, several hundred feet to the right of where I saw the face. Tsul'Kalu stands in the dying light, a broad grin on his face, arms raised as though to shout 'Yes!'

Where I see death and pain, he finds only delight.

And then, with a quick shift of his eyes, he finds me.

48

Our uphill journey isn't quite as fast-paced as the sprint across the killing field, but the horses are working just as hard, if not harder. They're huffing and frothing, desperate for a break and for a drink they're not going to get. At least not until we reach the peak, and maybe not even then.

We attack Adel's slope at an angle, following a switchback pattern. It's slower than charging straight up, but the grade would be too steep for the horses in some areas. We're making the best time possible. We'll reach the peak in about twenty minutes—far faster than we could manage on foot, even in the tunnels. Even the golf carts, with their small electric motors, wouldn't be able to tear up the mountainside at our current pace, and I suspect they'd run out of juice long before these tough horses.

When we cross the threshold between the encroaching night and the last rays of light still reaching Adel's side, the sun provides me with a bit of hope. It's filtered by the thick canopy, but the jungle is brighter, easier to navigate, and harder to hide in.

I'm not sure if Tsul'Kalu could overtake us and stage an ambush. He might not be fast or quiet enough to pull it off. And as much as he might want to track us down and kill us—for reasons unknown to me—

my gut says he won't be able to resist joining the fray behind us, at least for a bit. When...*if*...he finds us, I have no doubt he'll be bathed in prehistoric blood.

When the Cherokee dubbed him the 'god of the hunt,' they were being generous, or perhaps they just didn't have words for psychopath and serial killer. Then again, perhaps Tsul'Kalu gave himself the title, installing himself as a deity among men. Hell, actual men have done that since the dawn of civilization, all the way up to the modern world, and people *still* fall for it.

When a buzzing sound fills the air, my body tenses. If a flux wave as big as the last hits us now, we'll be launched off the mountainside. But I sense no onrushing wall of temporal power. Instead, the buzz grows subtly louder until I identify where it's coming from: above.

A drone.

My horse flinches at the flying machine's arrival, but pushes past its fear when I give it a nudge. The drone keeps pace with me, twenty feet above.

"Can't say I'm a fan of what you're attempting," Langdon says from the drone.

"Just trying to stay alive," I reply.

He chuckles. "Oh, you're doing more than that. You don't think I'm aware of what is following you to my doorstep."

Going to bring him a lot further than your doorstep, I think, but I say nothing.

"You know what it is," Cassie says, "don't you?"

"Ms. Dearborn, we discovered his identity together. The Nephilim were—"

"You knew from the start," she says. "That's why you're trying so hard to keep it away. You know what it's capable of. You know how hard it is to kill."

"If it *can* be killed," Langdon says after a beat. "You are right, of course. I'm an intelligent man. I did my research. I knew the risks associated with time travel, including who and what we might encounter along the way. We know it died. But not how. The skeletons uncovered by the Smithsonian showed no signs of advanced aging, or catastrophic injury. But they were all missing their heads. Some were missing limbs, as well."

Langdon's words remind me of how Tsul'Kalu took every bullet fired at him, unless they were aimed at his head. And now he's wearing the saber-toothed skull for protection. That's got to be the key, but will a bullet do the job, or do we actually need to sever his head?

"They?" Levi says. "How many skeletons are there?"

"Dozens," Langdon says. "They've never been as prevalent as mankind...not remotely. That they are still not among us suggests the others migrated somewhere else, someplace remote, unbothered by mankind."

"You think *people* chased the Nephilim off?" Cassie asks. "That the Indians somehow killed Tsul'Kalu?"

Another chuckle. He's enjoying this. Relaxed. Whatever he's here for, he's close to achieving it. The drone's presence suggests that we and Tsul'Kalu are still a threat, but he's feeling confident. "It's more likely that another of his kind did the deed. Or something else, equally nefarious, with a penchant for body parts."

"What do you want?" Inola asks, cutting to the chase. I'm impressed with how well she's adapted to her new reality, full of monsters and technology, both of which must be strange to someone who has no concept of machinery, electricity, or theoretical physics. Then again, Tsul'Kalu is straight out of her life experience, and who knows what other ancient North American knowledge has been passed down by her people.

Langdon goes silent, leaving me to ponder Inola's question. What *does* he want? Why is he talking to us now?

"He's distracting us," Flores says, eyes turned downhill.

I scan the forest below, but see nothing more than trees. There are modern birds and squirrels here, but so far, the dinosaurs have avoided this elevated land, probably because the air is thinner, and their big bodies need all the oxygen they can get.

"I don't see anything," Owen says, twisting around my father to have a look for himself.

"Doesn't mean he's not there," my father says. "If he's really a hunter, we won't know he's there until he fires the first shot."

But Langdon will.

"You know where he is," I say to the drone. "You're watching him right now, aren't you?"

"I'm going to give you a chance to turn back," Langdon says, confirming my suspicion by not addressing it. "Ride east and then back down. The land there is clear of danger."

Except for the giant still hunting us.

"Or return to the tunnels, where you will be..." His voice trails off. "I'm afraid your time is running out."

Is he talking about Tsul'Kalu, or another Flux? I'm about to ask when a bullet rips through the air, and the drone. The flying machine falls silent and drops from the sky, narrowly missing my head.

"Sorry," Levi says, holstering his weapon. "Man's a snake oil salesman. The more we listen to him, the more danger we're in."

Can't say I disagree with him, but it would have been nice to get an answer to my lingering question. Langdon isn't afraid to let us die for his cause, but he's not exactly out to kill us, either. Not yet. I suspect his indifference to our fate will shift if we continue to threaten him. He wasn't just suggesting we lead the giant away, he was threatening to take action if we refused.

I want to offer the others one last chance to back out, but we're well beyond the point of no return. Anyone who takes a different route risks being found by the hunter without the full force of our ragtag unit. Going back means fighting Tsul'Kalu head on, and I'm not confident any of us would survive that. Pushing forward is our only real hope of survival.

Langdon has an army of drones, but I know how to fight and destroy tech better than I do demi-gods. The drones are also guided by an AI, whose tactics can be predicted, or by people, whose skills on the battlefield are outmatched by me and Flores. The odds aren't great, but they're the best we've got.

I push my horse harder and continue upward at a steeper angle. The horse whinnies in protest, but it pounds up the hill. If Langdon chose to confront us now, it means we're close...and so is the giant. It also means there's still time to stop him.

I have my doubts about Black Creek's survival in the Cretaceous, having seen the scope of what our small pocket of now homeless humanity is up against, but I doubt things will get easier a hundred million years further back in time. And before that...before the first single-celled organisms split and evolved into things with eyes, and limbs, and brains... I don't think we could even breathe the air.

I yank back on the reigns when the sound of tank treads reaches my ears. The mini-tanks are waiting for us. The moment we emerge from the tree line, we'll have declared war on Langdon and will be cut down.

"We can't go up there," Cassie says, pointing out what I already know.

"And we can't stay here," Levi adds.

"Thank you for making that clear to me," I say, laying on the sarcasm.

"So we'll do both," my father says.

I'm about to point out the many reasons splitting up is a bad idea, when he continues. "Look around. Ignore the new growth. We're near the peak. Near the tree line created by the mine. That hasn't changed. Focus on the topography. You know where we are."

I scan the area, trying to see what he has already, but I'm either too tired or too distracted to spot anything familiar in the failing light. The sun's rays have raced ahead of us, now bathing the barren peak in its orange glow. Soon it will be gone altogether, and the night will fall. I've never been afraid of the dark, but I'm pretty sure that will change in about, oh, an hour.

"Ugh." Owen shakes his head at me, and points into the forest to my right. "The tunnel thing is over there."

My father confirms his assessment by adding, "Maybe we can find a way in?"

"Next time, just spit it out," I say. "I'm too old for lessons."

"'Cause you fail them." Owen smiles at his verbal jab.

"Wise ass," I say to him.

"Shit for brains," he replies.

Levi thrusts his hand in the air, like a student in class. "I'm just going to point out that we've got hot metal death waiting for us up there, and primal rage carnage racing up behind us. If y'all are done being all samesees, I reckon now might be a good time to pick which kind of horrible demise we prefer. 'Cause in a minute, we ain't gonna have a choice."

"Unless we keep on moving up this mountainside," Flores says, "that demi-god asshole won't have a trail to follow."

And there's the problem. Diverting our course risks delaying or preventing Tsul'Kalu's introduction to Langdon and his killing machines.

A howl rolls up the mountainside.

We're out of time.

"Too much talking," Inola says, hopping down from her horse. "Not enough doing." Then she seals her fate, and maybe ours, by slapping her horse's rump and sending it sprinting uphill.

49

The tumult of hooves charging up the mountainside comingles with the grinding crunch of tank treads rolling over the stony clearing beyond the forest's grasp. The steeds charge fearlessly into battle, even when the first gunshots ring out. Even when the mini-guns unleash laser-focused beams of bullets into their bodies.

The horses scream in pain. Briefly.

I cringe at the sound. I had grown fond of the rides, not because I'm an animal lover in general, but because they were good soldiers. They carried us toward and through danger, facing inhuman fears and pushing past them like no person ever could. Myself included. But like all soldiers, their lives were controlled by people whose agenda requires sacrifice.

As the last of the horses cries out, its body slapping onto the hard stone surface a hundred feet above, I push myself deeper beneath the fallen tree that is my hiding spot.

Breathing slowly, face coated with dirt, cloaked in a blanket of thick ferns, I am invisible. Short of being stepped on, I should be impossible to detect. *Should be.*

We know too little about Tsul'Kalu, and what we do know is steeped in Cherokee and Biblical stories that might not be true.

What I do know is that he is an experienced hunter, a savage killer, and a damn fast healer. I also know he's not immortal—in the sense that he can't be killed—and that he's protective of his head. But are his ears sensitive enough to hear my heartbeat? The gentle ebb and flow of air in my lungs? Can he smell as well as a dog? Can his bare feet sense subtle vibrations in the ground if someone shifts their weight? If the answer to any of those questions is 'yes,' then this will go down as the worst plan of my military and security careers.

Then again, it's not my plan. It's Inola's.

She set it in motion by sending her horse uphill. As soon as I saw it charge away, I understood and instructed the others to do the same. The heavy-hooved horses left an easy to follow trail toward Synergy's awaiting drones—the same trail Tsul'Kalu will have followed all the way up the mountain.

Treading lightly, we veered away from the trail on foot, careful to step only where ferns and other unrecognizable ground growth would conceal our footprints. Now we're hunkered down behind a tangle of fallen trees, waiting silently for the giant to pass us by.

And we don't have to wait long.

I hear Tsul'Kalu before I see him. His oversized lungs huff as he charges up the mountain. At his pace, he'd have caught us near the peak, even if Langdon hadn't tried to stop us. Looking through a curtain of moss hanging from the fallen tree's underside, I see him thunder into view.

He's bathed in the blood of whatever creatures he came across in the field below. It's caked dry in some places. Coagulated clumps dangle in his dark red hair, hanging out from under the saber-toothed head-covering. He looks more beast than man now, and that's what he is. Despite being intelligent, he is driven by instinct alone, and a hatred for mankind, particularly those who have managed to wound and elude him. But he's even more savage than the dinosaurs, driven by vengeance rather than simple survival.

He's evil, I think.

I've fought and killed the enemies of the United States, and while their political, religious, or general world view put them

violently at odds with my country, I wouldn't describe them as 'evil.'
Misguided. Deluded. Taken advantage of. But not evil.

Tsul'Kalu is nothing but, and I can't help but wonder if the story of
his demonic genesis might be true. I can't imagine something like him
evolving. Rampant killing doesn't serve the survival of any species, including people.

The very worst of men are always taken down by the best, memori-
alized as madmen by history and generations to come. There is no
evolutionary benefit to being a psychopath, a serial killer, or a genocidal
leader.

But that doesn't stop them from existing. And from Tsul'Kalu's
perspective, there are no consequences for his actions.

We'll see about that, I think, tensing as his pace slows.

When he stops, I start plotting a strategic retreat. The only chance
some of us have at surviving is if we scatter. How long will it take him to
find everyone? How fast can he move?

Too many damn questions!

He crouches where we stopped before sending the horses to their
fate, pressing his fingers into the earth. He lifts his head and sniffs the air.
Shit, I think, but then I realize the air is thick with the scent of horse blood
flowing on the downhill breeze. I hold still when he does a quick scan of
the area. He's suspicious. It's clear the horses stopped, but he doesn't
know why.

For a moment, I think he's going to scour the surrounding area, but
one of the horses above, still clinging to life, lets out a death throe whinny.

With a grunt, Tsul'Kalu launches himself uphill, charging toward
the summit, where he believes his prey await.

I listen to him go, his breathing now frenzied and rough, his body
crashing through brush and branches. Then, for too long, silence.

Did the drones already leave? Have they not seen him? Or are they
simply attempting to not incite his wrath? The latter wouldn't be a bad
idea, but then this is Tsul'Kalu we're talking about. He probably came out
of the womb with a grudge.

Was that monster really born to a woman? I see an image of a
mother carrying that monster baby to term. Did he tear his way free?

Did she survive the ordeal?

I shake my head free of dark thoughts and rise from hiding. If Tsul'Kalu doesn't engage the drones, we might not have long. But then my fears are put at ease when the giant's battle cry rises from above like a volcanic eruption. The cacophonous shriek of metal crashing into stone announces the beginning of his assault.

When it's followed by the whirring of mini-guns spinning up, I leap from my hiding spot and whisper, "Go! Everyone! Now!"

We trample and hop through the forest like bunnies on the run, focusing only on speed, not giving a fluffy-tailed ass if we leave a trail or make a lot of noise. We fully intend to be out of Tsul'Kalu's reach by the time the battle above us is done playing out. And even with excellent hearing, there is no way he can hear us over the buzzing mini-guns.

Plus, he has bigger problems. He can heal fast, and he seems to revel in pain that would send any other living thing into shock, but mini-guns unleash up to 6000 rounds per minute. That's a hundred rounds per second. And I count at least four different weapons unleashing metal fury. When people are struck by a mini-gun barrage they all but cease to exist. The giant is a lot bigger than the average person, but that just means he's a larger target.

He's also quick, which is probably why the guns are firing in quick spurts rather than just unloading a stream of bullets into an unmoving body. It's hard to believe anything could survive against that kind of modern might, but the weapons of modern war were designed to work against people—not demi-gods.

Aim for his head, I think, and I resist the urge to shout it out. As much as I want Tsul'Kalu cut down, I wouldn't mind if he also managed to diminish Langdon's power in the process.

A fleet of flying drones buzzes past overhead. I duck at the sound, watching two dozen of the things careen toward the battle. Langdon is throwing everything he has at the giant. He's been watching Tsul'Kalu long enough to understand the danger the hunter presents.

Explosions shake the forest.

A deep, resonating roar follows, tracing the border between anguish and orgasm.

And then, quiet.

Levi mumbles, "Buddha's shitty britches."

Did they do it? I wonder. *Is Tsul'Kalu—*

A fresh roar, angry and defiant, rips through the air. It's followed by the shattering of something metal and then more gunfire.

Trees behind us explode as an errant stream of bullets tears through the forest. "Down!" I shout, tackling Cassie to the dirt. A line of wood-shredding rounds cuts through the air above us. Some of the small trees shatter and crack before toppling over.

Below me, Cassie's eyes go wide. "Look out!" She shoves me off and to the side, rolling with me. A tree trunk thumps to the damp ground where we'd been lying.

"Thanks," I say, suddenly aware that she's on top of me, her legs wrapped around my waist. Nothing about it is sexual—until we both notice.

She smiles down at me. "Right back at you." Then she's on her feet and yanking me up.

I spot Owen smiling at me, and I shake my head. He hasn't even hit puberty yet.

I flinch at the sound of a second fusillade of bullets, but this time, they're not randomly spraying the forest. They're unleashing hell, but how long can they keep it up? The drones fired a lot of rounds in the first assault. They're going to run out of ammo eventually.

And when they do, will the giant's focus remain on Synergy, or will he come back for us?

Knowing the question is without answer, I focus on putting us out of his reach. "Anyone see it?"

Shaking heads are the only reply.

"Spread out! Keep looking!"

After a minute of searching, I'm afraid we've missed it, or we were wrong about our location, but then I see it—the hatch through which we rescued Inola and confronted Tsul'Kalu and the saber-toothed cat. The snow is missing, but the hatch is easy to identify, because it's covered in the elder Kuzneski's remains.

It's also closed.

Langdon must have sent someone to shut it behind us.

"Here," I say, rushing toward the hatch. I drop to my knees beside it, looking for a latch or a locking mechanism. But it's just a smooth, metal dome. I dig my fingers into the seam and pull. Two of my nails bend and break from the effort, which ends in my hands snapping up. "We're not getting through here without a brick of C4."

Flores raps on the hatch with his knuckles. "Probably more than that."

"What now?" my father asks.

"Langdon's distracted," Cassie says. "He's throwing everything at the giant. Maybe we can breach the perimeter."

"You're forgetting about the spikey death fence," Levi says.

"And there's no way he's left himself completely undefended," Flores adds.

"Do not forget Tsul'Kalu," Inola says. "If he yet lives, and we expose ourselves to him..."

Despite all this, Cassie is still right. We don't have much of a choice.

"Umm," Owen says, but I barely hear him as I look for a fallen tree small enough for us to carry uphill, throw against the fence, and use as crude siege tower. I flinch when he shouts, "Hey!"

All eyes turn down to my younger self, who is standing in a lumpy drying mass of what used to be a person. My heart breaks for him. This is too much. But he doesn't seem to notice where he is and what he's standing in. His attention is squarely on the hatch. "Listen!"

Despite the distant sounds of continuing battle, a repeating squeak rises up from the hatch. We all take a step back and point our weapons down. When the hatch rises and I see the face staring back at me, I nearly pull the trigger.

It's Langdon.

50

"What is *he* doing here?" Flores asks, aiming his weapon at Langdon just as I start to lower mine.

"It's not me," Langdon says. "I'm not him."

I push Flores's weapon down. "It's my Langdon."

"Why are you here?" Cassie asks. None of us trust him, in part because of who he becomes in the future, but also because his presence here is a little too convenient. The last thing any of us wants is to run away from a killer giant and into a tunnel full of Synergy security guards ready to gun us down. By bringing Tsul'Kalu to Langdon's doorstep, we've officially declared war on him.

"My elder self. He fetched me a few hours ago. Wanted me to watch what was happening. Wanted to gloat. He's quite vindictive."

"I've noticed," I say. "But what does he have against you?"

"I couldn't save her," he says, "or wasn't willing to do what was required to save her."

"All this is really for your wife?" Cassie asks.

As indignant as she sounds, I can't help but wonder how far I would go to save her...or my father. What would I have given to have him back? I've already proven I would risk a temporal paradox, and despite the fact that he's supposed to die tomorrow, I have killed, and would kill again, to keep him alive. But would I risk generations of Black Creek residents and defile all of space and time?

Not a chance.

"They kept me in a security center of sorts," Langdon says. "Where they pilot the drones from and—"

"I've seen it," I tell him.

"When that...thing arrived, they all became very agitated and distracted. I saw you on the security feeds and knew this entrance was nearby."

"You *broke* free?" Levi asks, sounding doubtful.

"I'm not a man of action. Not like any of you. I wasn't bound. Given the state of things when I left, I wouldn't be surprised if they failed to notice I was missing. You have to believe me. I'm here to help. That man...that *me*...has my wife. Not his. And I fail to see how his actions will save her, and not kill us all."

A drone tank, mini-gun still spinning and firing, sails past overhead before crashing into a tree and exploding. After ducking and raising his arm for cover, Levi says, "I'm gonna trust him," and starts climbing down into the tunnel.

When he says, "All clear," from below, I motion for the others to head down. Owen goes first, followed by Cassie. My father and Inola have taken up a kind of perimeter, weapons raised toward the sounds of battle.

"Dad, let's go."

He motions for Inola to move, and she does, descending quickly, followed by Flores who doesn't need to be told twice. My father stands, backing up toward the tunnel entrance.

When he stops short, I say, "You first."

"Can't blame a father for trying."

"It's not your job to protect me," I tell him. "Not anymore."

"Sorry about not being there for you," he says. "If I'd known..."

"You'd have still run in, believing you could help," I tell him. "I was angry at you for it, but I've always been proud of you, too."

"Well," he says, turning toward the hatch, "you're doing a better job than I—"

Trees shatter. Bullets slice through the forest. Tracers arc toward us.

"Get do—" My warning is cut short by a bee sting of pain in my thigh that drops me to the ground.

Marine Raiders are trained to assess the lethality and extent of an injury. The general rule of thumb is pain, and the kind of pain. There are several types of agony that are not lethal—like a bullet through a bone. But when the body is wounded in a way that is catastrophic, it knows. The pain of approaching death can be felt in every cell. I've been lucky enough to never feel it, but I've experienced a large enough number of injuries to know the sting on my leg is most likely a graze. Anything more from a mini-gun's 7.62 caliber bullet would be life threatening, no matter where it hit. Especially during the Cretaceous. I don't even bother looking at it when I push myself up.

When I turn back to the hatch and find my father still standing over it, I shout, "Get down there! Go!"

Then I spot the blood dripping from his slack hands. Time slows.

"Dad..."

He turns to face me, eyes filled with sadness more than pain.

No...

God, please, no.

"I'm sorry," he whispers, twisting as his legs give out, revealing a hole in his chest. I reach for him but I'm too slow. My father falls back, toppling through the hatch. The sound of his dead weight striking the tunnel floor is followed by a moment of stunned silence...and then my eleven-year-old scream.

I leap down the hole, landing beside my father's still body, unaware of the pain the drop caused my knees and my open wound. I roll him onto his back, take stock of the wound, and through already blurring eyes, know there is nothing I—or anyone else—can do.

My father is dead.

Again.

Owen's familiar wail of agony stabs me in the heart. When I look up at the boy standing there, staring at his dead father, I shout, "Get him out of here!"

Having my father die was the worst moment of my life, but I never had to go through the scarring turmoil of seeing his bloody corpse.

Until now.

Cassie leads Owen away, holding him as he weeps into her shoulder.

"God damnit," I say, on my knees, my forehead pressed to my father's. Tears drip from my eyes, rolling over my father's face. "God *damnit.* Why didn't you go down? Why..."

Something in my heart and mind changes. Sadness and despair are walled off with the suddenness of a nuclear blast. When I look up at Langdon, he staggers back, tripping as his heels reach the tunnel's upward curve. I lunge, slamming him against the wall.

"Why!" I scream. "Why did he have to die again? What the fuck are you doing?"

"It's not me," the younger Langdon says, hands raised. "I'm not him!"

I'm oblivious to the quivering fear in his voice. All I can see is the face of the man I hold responsible for my father's death. In the past, I had no one to blame but my own father, for trying to be a hero. Now, all my anger is directed at the man who orchestrated this shit-show, who fucked with my heart by giving me my father back and then took him away again.

A hand on my shoulder acts as a trigger. I spin around, throwing a wild punch. Lucky for me, and for Flores, he's got quick reflexes. My fist sails past his chin as he leans out of range.

"Hey!" Levi shouts at me, redirecting my anger toward him. The moment he sees the look in my eyes, he backs away.

"I know you're beyond pissed," Flores says. "I can't begin to imagine what you're feeling. But right now, you're a soldier with a mission, and that man isn't your enemy. Stow it for later."

I understand what he's telling me. I've heard it before. Hell, I've given similar speeches to men under my command. But this is my father...my *dead* father reborn, returned to me, and now dead again. "Fuck you."

"*Owen,*" Cassie says. It's the tone of her voice that catches my attention. Unlike Levi and Flores, she doesn't sound angry or on edge. She's just sad, full of understanding. I know if I look at her, I'll come apart. But then I hear him. The gentle whimper of a broken child. The last time I dealt with this moment, I was at home, in bed, crying into my pillow, my grandfather rubbing my back. Owen is in a dark tunnel, surrounded by monsters from the past, a madman from the future...and the closest thing he could ever have to a brother or a father—himself.

The hardness clutching my chest cracks when I see Cassie, her face wet with tears. She loved my father, too, and I know she loves me. She knows what this moment means to both of her Owens. My legs shake when I walk to her. I nearly fall over when I go down to one knee.

"Owe," I say, using the nickname I always liked, but no one ever used.

His already bloodshot, red-rimmed eyes peek out from Cassie's chest. I reach out my arms and he spills into them, his deep resonating wail returning. My chest heaves once, then again, and then there is nothing I can do to stop myself from joining him. Despite the difference in pitch, our cry is the same. Our pain is the same.

And our anger is the same.

He leans back and through his tears, says, "There needs to be a reckoning for this."

He sounds like a McCoy.

He sounds like me.

I give him a firm nod. "There will be."

We wipe our tears away in unison, and I can see his own heart hardening along with mine. As much as it hurts to see myself so young and full of rage, I also know it will sustain him until this nightmare journey is over. We can cry again when that happens. Until then, we have a reckoning to see to.

I stand and hold out my arms to Owen. He hops up, allowing me to hold him like a smaller child, his arms around my neck, his legs wrapped around my waist. When I turn to the younger Langdon, his eyes are damp. I glance at Flores, Levi, and Inola, and see the same. These are good people. They don't deserve my anger. I'll save it for the man, and the monster, who do.

"I will stay with him," Inola says. As sad as she looks, I sense that this is nothing new for her. She is accustomed to her people being killed, and is already moving past her grief. "I will protect him, until he can be laid to rest."

"Thank you," I tell her.

She gives a solemn nod.

"Now," I say, turning to the younger Langdon, my fury returning. "Take me to him."

51

The younger Langdon leads us on a winding path through the network of tunnels I didn't know existed until today. While some of this infrastructure might be new, Langdon is familiar enough with it for me to know most of it must have existed in my time. Or he has a really good sense of direction. As head of security, I should have known about all this, but it was kept secret. This Langdon might not yet be the evil, twisted, broken version of himself, but he's not fully trusting of other people, which also makes *him* a bit untrustworthy. Or at least paranoid. I think he's on our side, for now, but if push comes to shove, I don't think I'll be able to count on him.

But all he has to do is take me to his older self. Once he does that, he can sit out what comes next.

We stop at the base of a ladder so shiny and new I'm not sure it's been used much at all.

"What is all this?" Levi asks. "These tunnels?"

"Infrastructure," Langdon says. "For the collider. Power conduits. Stabilizers. Venting. Cooling. They serve a large number of—"

"Uh-huh." Flores is either uninterested or not buying the explanation.

"Particle colliders are...unpredictable." Langdon rubs his forehead, looking a bit nervous, no doubt worrying that we think he and his doppelganger have more in common than he'd like to admit. And he wouldn't be wrong. "When CERN was first activated, many were convinced that it would create a black hole that would swallow the Earth. Some still believe that its activation merged two neighboring dimensions of reality, resulting in the Mandela Effect..." He pauses to look at four sets of confused eyes. "A large number of people remember Nelson Mandela dying while in prison in the 1980s, even though he didn't. People disagree about other seemingly well known facts as well. The color of C-3PO's leg. The number of U.S. states. The name of Jiffy peanut butter."

"It's Jif," Levi says.

"Is it?" Langdon's nervousness fades as he relaxes into the world of the theoretical. "Large portions of the population remember history—including recent history—very differently. It's not impossible that—"

"Get to the point," I say, putting Owen down in preparation for the climb ahead.

"The point is that I was trying to prepare for anything."

"I reckon you failed on that account," Levi says.

"Worse than that." Langdon is heavy with regret. "I think my caution provided my future self with the means to warp space-time. I'm to blame for all of this."

Taking ownership of his mistakes is a big step toward gaining my trust, but he's still got a mountain to climb. My instinct is to say something encouraging, to put him at ease, but my engine is burning on rage. Compassion is somewhere in my rearview mirror.

I point up the ladder. "Where will this take us?"

Langdon blinks out of his malaise. "Storage Shed B. Or, rather, where Storage Shed B once stood."

"It's a warehouse now," Flores adds. "We weren't sure what was in it."

Not knowing what's above is tactically frustrating, but doesn't really matter. We're going up. I can find my way to the main building from there, but will still need Langdon to guide me to himself. The real problem is that once we poke our heads above ground, we'll be visible to security...if they're paying attention. But they've got bigger problems at the moment.

"W-would you like me to stay here, with the boy?" Langdon asks.

Owen takes my hand and squeezes.

A distant part of me appreciates the offer. Danger lies ahead. There's no doubt about that. But we're both the only family we have left. I won't leave him behind, and he wouldn't let me.

Cassie knows that as well as I do, and has no trouble reading our body language. She nudges Langdon with her pistol. "All we need you to do is poke your head up and let us know if the coast is clear."

"Yes," he says, taking hold of the rungs. "Of course."

He climbs up fast, showing no fear of what might lie in wait. That's a good sign...until something somewhere explodes, sending a tremor through the ground.

"It's a flux," Langdon shouts, wrapping his arms around the ladder and clutching his eyes shut. We all do the same, sharing the ladder, anchoring ourselves to the floor, but I'm not sure any of us will have the strength to resist a powerful upwelling of space and time.

At least there is a roof over our heads.

When nothing happens, I realize the truth. "Just an explosion."

"That was one hell of an explosion," Levi says.

"Tsul'Kalu must be getting closer."

"It has a *name?*" Langdon's astonishment is almost comical.

"And it's pissed," I say, motioning for Flores to head up next. "So get the lead out."

Flores hustles up the ladder, forcing Langdon to match his pace. The scientist reaches the top, unlocks the hatch, and grunts as he shoves it up. The sounds of battle slip through the opening. Shouts comingle with gunfire and above it all, laughter.

Tsul'Kalu is still enjoying himself.

Langdon looks back and forth, says, "All clear," and then climbs out.

Flores follows quick on his heels. He's out of the hatch for just a few seconds before looking back down and saying, "Good to go."

While Levi starts up, I crouch beside Owen. "I'll be right behind you."

"I know," he says, trying to sound brave, but he's unable to hide the quiver in his lip. He's burning with emotion, for our father and for the chaos he knows lies ahead.

We should be hurrying, but I don't think we'll get another chance to really connect once we reach the top, and since I can't be sure both of us will make it through what comes next, I decide to say my piece now. "I know what you lost today. I know exactly how you're feeling. It's going to attack you more fiercely than anything we face up there. I want you to fight it, to not give in to it. I want you to rise above it. That's what Dad would want, too."

"Isn't that what you did?" he asks.

"I hid from it. Separated myself from the people who mattered most." I glance at Cassie, who's watching with a mixture of impatience and adoration. "And while I can't get that time back, you have it all ahead of you."

"We'll rise above it together," he says, getting a smile out of me.

"Fucking right we will," I say, and he reciprocates the grin.

"We're going to have to do something about your language," he says, doing a spot-on imitation of our father, and for the first time I really see how much I look and sound like him, then and now. I've lost my father twice now, but he lives on in both of us.

I motion to the ladder and Owen charges up. I follow right behind him with Cassie bringing up the rear. We emerge into a warehouse that is far larger than Storage Shed B used to be. Most of the concrete floor is empty, but a few of the small tank drones armed with mini-guns are parked at charging stations. At the far end, the warehouse doors are wide open, the sounds of battle echoing through the broad space.

I duck down when errant mini-gun fire tears a line of holes through the metal walls twenty feet above us.

"This way!" Langdon says, running for an exit on the building's side.

A pair of nervous Synergy workers step out of a back room, their arms laden with ammunition for the parked drones. They're clearly not thrilled to be there. Even more so when they spot us. "Hey!" the chubbier of the pair shouts, "The hell do you think you're doing here?"

Despite being grunts, both of them wear sidearms. I'm about to raise my weapon and kill both—I'm not willing to risk a gunfight—when they spot Langdon and their body language shifts into submission.

"Sorry, sir," Chubby says, eyes on the floor. "I didn't know you were—"

"Carry on," Langdon says with a dismissive wave. "There's no time for words!" I hadn't pegged Langdon for an actor, but his delivery is perfect. Of course, it's probably easy to act like your meaner self while the lives of several thousand people weigh on your shoulders, not to mention having a giant man-killer on the rampage.

We hurry on our way and leave the two men to their work. Langdon pushes through the exit, looks right, shouts, and dives to the ground. A tank drone careens through the air above him, crashing somewhere in the distance. Flores steps out behind him, scans the area, and yanks the man up by the back of his belt. "Move!"

I step out under the dark purple sky already thick with stars, holding Owen around my waist again, handgun drawn and ready for action. A pair of guards—men I don't know—rush toward us. Flores flinches at their approach, but I stop him with a hushed, "Wait!" The two men spot us and keep on moving. With Tsul'Kalu around, they're not seeing us as a threat. And even if they did, I'm sure Langdon's face would get us where we need to go. But the two men barely give us a second glance as they charge past. And then I see why.

The building where we had been kept earlier has been partially destroyed. The people who'd been held within its brick walls are now emerging and scattering, fleeing the madness. I want to tell them to stop. To go back and keep a roof over their heads, but there are too many running in different directions. The only way I can help them is to stop the next flux.

"Go, go, go," I shout, following Langdon across an open courtyard.

"Look out!" Owen shouts in my ear.

Three drones fly past, just over our heads, zooming toward the raging battle. I follow their trajectory and spot Tsul'Kalu in the distance. He's in motion, never slowing, taking hits and dealing out damage to people and machines alike. How much more can he take? How much more can Synergy?

The giant's eyes flick toward us for a moment, and I think he's overlooked us, but then he double-takes and starts laughing again. The way he's moving, he could be on us in seconds. But instead of charging, he lunges at a man trying to escape, grasping him around the waist and lifting him up. The man's high-pitched scream makes me wince. Then the man is airborne, tossed with enough force to break bones and pop sockets loose. His ragdoll body pinwheels through the air, but he's not dead. His scream rises in volume as he arcs up and falls toward us. Anger burns hot until the man slams into the concrete and slides to a stop at my feet. When I see his scarred face, round glasses, and wispy balding hair, my anger fades. Robles. As horrible as his death was, the torturer deserved worse.

"We need to get inside!" I shout, setting Owen down and shoving him past the body.

"Here!" Langdon says, bending over to unlock a side door with an ocular scanner. The keypad flashes green and the lock snaps open. He wrenches the door open and holds it for us while we file inside the foyer of the central science building.

"Stop!" a guard on the interior shouts, already raising a pistol. Now that we're inside and potentially identified by Langdon's people, I don't hesitate.

My handgun clears its holster before the man finishes raising his weapon. I fire from the hip, striking him hard in the chest. His body armor saves his life, but the round hits like a rhino. The man topples to his back, gasping for air until Flores pistol-whips him into unconsciousness.

"Oww," Owen says, rubbing his ears.

"Sorry," I tell him.

He nods.

"Just stay behind me..." I look up at Cassie, "and you behind him." When she nods, I look back at him. "You see me raise this..." I pat the gun. "You cover your ears."

He covers them now and says, "Got it!"

"Why are you covering—" My question is cut short by two gunshots. I spin around to find Flores has just gunned down a second guard who'd just emerged from behind a corner. Unlike me, he aimed high, the first shot missing, the second catching the man's head. While part of the man is blasted backward, the rest of him careens into a wall before crumpling to the floor.

They definitely know we're here, and like the men outside, Langdon is sending them to their deaths.

"Next right!" the younger Langdon says from behind, guarded by Levi and no longer brave enough to take the lead.

I take the turn and recognize where I am. The security center is just ahead. "Stay with them," I say to Levi and Cassie before pointing at Flores. "With me!"

I charge down the hall, weapon at the ready.

When I kick in the door, the men inside barely notice. In part because they're all wearing VR headsets and headphones, but also because they're controlling the fleet of drones battling Tsul'Kalu. The guard Flores killed must have come from here...and Future Langdon is gone. Rather than interrogate the men, who I'd prefer keep trying to kill the giant, I poke my head out into the hall and wave the others in.

"Try to find him," I say, motioning to the wall of security feeds. We scour the images together, but find nothing. After a minute of searching, I lose my patience, yank the VR headset off the nearest operator, shove my gun between his eyes and say, "Where. Is. He?"

The man's nervous eyes flit around the room, looking for help, but all he finds is more people who look ready to throttle him. Then I realize he's not looking at us, but at the security feeds. He points. "There!" The screen in question shows a solid metal door. Closed.

"You know where that is?" I ask the younger Langdon. He shakes his head. I ask the operator the same question by glaring at him and pressing the gun harder.

"P-penthouse," he says, pointing up. "Top floor."

Penthouse? Top floor? Why the hell would Future Langdon be anywhere near the surface?

Because it's time...

His endgame is nearly here.

"When is it happening?" I ask, and can see in the man's eyes that he knows exactly what I'm talking about, even if he doesn't understand it.

"Ten minutes," he says.

52

The elevator leading up is slow, but thankfully devoid of muzak. As tense as I am, I think hearing a Kid Rock song played with an electronic keyboard would put me over the edge.

"Think that was wise?" Flores asks.

While the question is vague, I know exactly what he's talking about. I allowed the security drone operator to not only live, but to return to his job. I knew it was possible that he would raise the alarm, but he'd been fighting Tsul'Kalu. No matter what we were up to, I could see in his eyes that he recognized the real threat. When I let him go, he pulled the VR mask back into place, wrested control of a tank-drone, and rejoined the assault.

"You shouldn't kill people if you don't have to," Owen says, and I'm proud of him. Despite his anger over our father's death, he hasn't lost his moral compass. Killing isn't always the solution...then again, sometimes it is. Mercy has its place, but so does, on occasion, a bullet. And I've got at least one on reserve for Future Langdon...assuming he resists.

And I expect him to.

I don't blame him for my father's death. Not entirely. Without the flux, my father would have still died shortly after the next sunrise. But he has made pawns of thousands of people's lives, resulting in the untimely demise of many who should have lived long lives, and the displacement of countless more. He needs to answer for this, and to be stopped before it gets worse.

"Mmm," Flores says to Owen. "We'll see."

"Have you been up here?" I ask the younger Langdon. "Do you know what we should expect?"

He shakes his head. "It must be a new addition. I've never lived at the facility. I've never even considered it. A penthouse hardly seems appropriate for a research facility."

"Maybe 'Penthouse' is a codename?" Cassie offers.

Levi's eyes widen with good humor despite the circumstances. "Like maybe it's named after the magazine, and there'll be a bunch of naked—"

Cassie nudges him and tilts her head toward Owen.

"—mole rats," Levi finishes. "Naked mole rats. Nasty creatures."

"We saw a *Penthouse* in second grade," I say.

"I'm still trying to recover from that," Owen says. "Stupid Nicky Mazzola."

"Ugh," Cassie says. "Nicky Mazzola. He's not in town, is he?"

The three of us share a smile and then the elevator jolts to a stop. I push Owen behind me, and raise my weapon toward the opening doors. The hallway on the far side is short, straight, and empty, ending at a metal door with a biometric lock.

"Huh," Flores says. It's not much, but I know what he's thinking. With no guards and a single lock, Future Langdon either has an army of guards protecting him, has absolute faith in the strength of his door, or his endgame is too close to stop. Maybe all three.

"Stay on my six," I tell Owen.

"Yep," he says.

Then we creep forward as a group, stopping in front of the door. It's thick and metal, the kind of thing you'd expect to find on a submarine. In fact, that's how nearly all the doors and hatches we've come across are. It's like this whole place was designed to survive underwater, with each compartment able to be completely sealed off from those that have failed.

A muffled explosion shakes the building. It's followed by dull, automatic gunfire, the kind generated by handheld weapons.

Tsul'Kalu has found a way inside the building, and as strong as the doors might be, they're large enough for the giant to squeeze through. If he's as smart as he is savage, he won't have any trouble navigating the building. But will he come here? Is he even hunting us still?

Questions to answer when Future Langdon is dealt with. I look over the biometric lock and am about to usher the younger Langdon to it when I'm struck by a sudden headache. I clutch my eyes shut and wince.

I'm not alone.

"What the hell is that?" Levi asks. "My head!"

Owen clutches my hand, squeezing hard through the pain.

A woman's voice, shouting in pain, emerges from the door's far side.

"Jacqueline..." the younger Langdon says through clenched teeth.

And then the pain subsides. I feel like my mind has been picked through and scrambled. It takes a moment to regain my senses.

"What was that?" Cassie rubs her head, forcing herself to stand up straight again.

"I—I don't know," the younger Langdon says. "But my wife is on the other side of this door." He hurries toward the lock, but I catch his arm.

"Hold on." I turn to the others. "Everyone good?"

They look like I feel, like they've been through a mental meat grinder, but Cassie, Levi, and Flores all nod. So does Owen. To Flores I say, "Clear front and then sweep left. I'll take the right." To Cassie and Levi, "You're on precious cargo duty."

Cassie puts a hand on Owen's shoulder. "Like paper and glue."

"What sticks to me, sticks to you," he finishes.

Been a while since I heard or even thought about that little routine. I'm impressed Cassie remembers it.

"I ain't saying anything cutesy to you," Levi tells the younger Langdon. "Just stay behind me and don't do nothing stupid."

"Are you even trained to use that?" Langdon motions to Levi's weapon. "Who is he?"

"Prospective hire," I say.

"But I'm kinda glad I didn't sign that liability paperwork yet," Levi jokes.

After releasing some tension with a smile, I release Langdon. "Do it."

While Langdon presses his finger against the print reader, and then leans down to have his iris scanned, Flores and I step up to the door, weapons raised and ready.

The door thunks as it unlocks. It swings open without a sound. I step inside a large, open-concept space and sweep right. There's a kitchenette and a dining area. Very modern. Very expensive. Sconces and floor lighting fill the broad space with a warm, orange glow, sunset held captive.

I sweep back to center and spot the elder Langdon sitting in what looks like a futuristic lounge chair, his humorless gaze locked on me. I can only assume that the woman seated across from him is Jacqueline. Her back is to us.

"Clear," Flores says, and I look left. An open door leads to a decadent bathroom with tile floors, a two-person tub and what looks like it could be a waterfall shower.

He's planning to spend the rest of his life here, I think. *Or was he living here in the future, under the watchful eye of his security forces, protected from future me?*

Flores and I lead the way forward, heading straight toward the elder Langdon, looking over our weapons' sights, sweeping back and forth.

"We're alone. There's no need for that." Future Langdon waggles his hand toward our weapons.

"Hands where I can see them," I say.

He raises his hands. "I'm unarmed." He leans to the side and addresses Cassie. "Would you mind closing the door behind you?"

"Shut-up," I growl, weapon still aimed at his head.

"I'm sorry about your father," Future Langdon says. "Truly. Had you left him here—"

Something in my shifting expression warns him that his next words might be his last. He purses his lips, but still looks unconcerned.

"Are you okay?" the younger Langdon asks, rounding the chair in which his wife sits. Her reply is muffled by a gag in her mouth. Her cheeks are streaked with tears. She is an unwilling accomplice in all this. The younger Langdon peels the gag out of her mouth.

"You're too late," she says. "He's killed us all."

"Maybe," Future Langdon says. "But the view will be grand." He motions toward the ceiling, and I look up for the first time. The view above is all sky. Eight segments of domed glass converge at the pinnacle. It looks thick enough to hold back the ocean. The view of the nearly night-time sky is impressive, though the space's warm lighting blots out much of the sky.

"You need to stop it," I tell Future Langdon.

"Couldn't if I wanted to," he says. "And I don't."

"What's the point? Of any of this? You're screwing with people's lives. Tearing them through time."

"The point," Future Langdon says, *"is* life."

"All we've seen is death," Cassie says.

He waves her off. "A temporary state. Soon, we will all be born again. Our bodies remade."

Is Future Langdon getting spiritual? Does he see himself as some kind of temporal cult leader? He could have done that from the future.

"How far back are you taking us?" Flores asks. "Living here is going to be hard enough. Any further back and we'll—"

"All the way," Future Langdon says. "We're going all the way back to the moment when nothing became everything. We will bathe in the light of creation. Our DNA and all its flaws will be remade by the cosmos itself. All of us will bear witness to—"

"You're insane," Levi says. "He's insane. You can't travel to the beginning of time! You can't..." His voice trails off. Not even he is convinced by his argument. Because here we are, in the Cretaceous.

"What would you do to save those you love?" Langdon asks, looking me in the eyes. "What have you done? To save your friends. To save your father—" He glances at Owen. "And yourself. I am sorry about your father's demise, but if he could be saved—"

"Get to the point," I growl.

"Like you, I would do anything to save the people I love." He looks at Jacqueline. "To save the woman I love." There are genuine tears in his eyes when he looks back at me. "You know what it's like to lose people. You know that pain. But do you know what it's like to watch cancer eat them alive? To be helpless in the face of their suffering? Because I do, and I will not allow that reality to exist. My wife will live, no matter the cost."

"You're going to get us all killed," I say.

"*No matter the cost.*" He leans back in his chair, a measure of calm returning. "And can you think of a better way to die? At the beginning of time, witnessing events mankind has debated since we first contemplated where everything came from?"

There is something romantic about the notion, but what good is dying at the start of everything? These people deserve to live. Deserve to wonder about how the universe began, at the marvel and mystery of it. The notion of creation has always intrigued me, in particular because, despite the schism between religion and science on the subject, there really is no schism at all. At one point, there was nothing, and then for reasons unknown, a force beyond comprehension unleashed all of reality. It's the same story, and it's good enough for me. I really don't need to know the specifics.

But I also recognize we don't have a choice.

I lower my gun.

"What are you doing?" Cassie asks.

"What can we do?" I ask.

"He is right, of course," Future Langdon says. "Had you reached the power station earlier, you might have marooned us in the past. But the batteries are fully charged and the wave is building."

"Even if we survive," the younger Langdon says, "we will be lost in empty space, billions of years before our star is born and the solar system's planets have been formed."

I look back at the solid door. It's not only built like a submarine, but also like a space station. *Holy shit, this whole place was designed to float in the vacuum of space!*

"How long do you think we will last? How much food do you have? How much air?" the younger Langdon is incredulous. He almost looks dangerous, face red, fists clenched. As much as I'd like to see him slug his elder self, it's not going to help.

"How long has it been?" I ask, turning to the others. "Since we left the security center?"

Flores checks the watch on his wrist. The way his eyes widen tells me everything I need to know.

"Tick tock," Future Langdon says, and for the first time I really notice his chair. It's modern, sleek, and padded like something a serious gamer would have, with two stark differences. It's bolted to the floor. And it has a seatbelt.

A klaxon blares outside, the volume of it dulled by the thick walls, but the warning it offers is clear: Get inside. Close the doors. This is it. The trouble with all that—and Future Langdon wouldn't know this, being sequestered in his penthouse—is that Tsul'Kalu is also indoors.

"Hold on to something!" I shout, scooping up Owen and running to the dining area. I climb under the table and note that everything in the room is bolted down. Future Langdon doesn't want to be thrown against the ceiling, but he also doesn't want to be decapitated by a loose chair. The whole space, and everything in it is secure...except for us.

Owen wraps himself around a table leg, clutching it tightly, and I do the same, my arms around him, holding him in place. Cassie and Levi join us at separate table legs, while the younger Langdon and Flores charge into the living room. Flores dives beneath a coffee table. There's not much to hold onto, but he'll only be lifted and dropped a few inches. The younger Langdon scrambles back and forth, unsure of where to go.

"Over here!" I shout at him. He spots the free table leg and sprints toward us just as a loud buzz fills the air. The floor beneath us shakes.

The flux is coming.

The younger Langdon dives for the table, slides across the floor, and wraps his hand around the leg.

Then, someone bangs on the door.

Hard.

He's found us.

It's the last thing I think before time and space erupt from below.

53

I remember being lifted off the floor, and then a sharp pain on the back of my head. After that is a blur of distorted voices. Screams really. I'm in a black tunnel, racing toward a bright light. The screams grow louder. Closer. And then I emerge, back into the light of full consciousness, where Owen has been wrenched out of my arms.

He clutches onto the bolted down table leg as time and space bends up through him. "Owen!" he shouts to me, beckoning me from my stupor. I don't remember hitting my head on the table's underside, but that's clearly what happened.

I grasp his small wrists, locking us together. I don't think I can pull him back under, but I manage to anchor him.

Levi, on the other hand, is having a much harder time helping the younger Langdon. The scientist hangs in the air vertically, one hand clutching Levi's. Both men are straining to resist the flow of time, but it's a losing battle.

The elder Langdon watches us with subtle amusement. He catches my eye, grins, and then points to the ceiling before turning his head upward.

I manage to lean forward a little and glance up. The view is... unbelievable. The nighttime sky slowly shifts as millions of years reverse.

I spot what I think is the big dipper, slowly condensing into a different shape, the stars and galaxies making up its familiar form retreating toward their births. Eventually, the position of the stars will be completely unrecognizable.

And then they'll be gone.

If this works the way Future Langdon planned, we'll end up looking at the endless nothing that existed before time.

A large fist pounds on the door. Tsul'Kalu is trying to force his way in despite the flux. If he manages to break in, we'll be at his mercy, which is non-existent. Even if the flux stops, there won't be much we can do to save ourselves. He's finally got the rabbit trapped in a den.

When I look at the elder Langdon, I see fear in his eyes as he redirects his gaze toward the door. This is the one thing he didn't count on. This is how his plan goes to shit. As much as that pleases me, it does nothing to help me or those I care about. If Tsul'Kalu reaches us, we're all dead, whether or not we're bathed in the light of creation...if that alone isn't enough to melt us into space dust.

The scene above draws my attention. Despite our looming deaths, I can't help but watch the retreating universe. The moon separates into a spiraling field of smaller stones, reducing to dust and then, in a flash of white, it's gone. The sky suddenly gets clearer, the stars brighter, as though we're floating in space.

The atmosphere is gone.

We're now predating life on Earth, slipping ever further back through the genesis of creation.

A distant light grows brighter.

The beginning of all things.

"I'm slipping," Owen shouts.

My attention snaps back to him. Taking a risk, I release his right arm, reach a hand out and catch his belt. Pulling him in snaps sinews in my bicep, but I manage to resist the flux and get him down to the floor, where he wraps his whole body around the table leg.

"You good?" I shout over the buzz of reversing time.

"I am, but he's not." He looks over my shoulder to the younger Langdon.

Levi shouts as the scientist is pulled from his fingertips. He's shoved upward, slammed against the roof and dragged toward the apex, twenty feet above the floor. For a moment, I think he's dead, but then I see him moving. He turns his head, facing upward, his view straight up and out. Best seat in the house...until the flux stops. Then he'll fall to the floor and either be killed or severely injured by the impact.

I check on Cassie, whose grip on the table leg hasn't faltered. "How you doing?" I shout.

"Peachy!" Comes her reply.

"In case we don't make it..." I start, still shouting.

She interrupts with, "I know!"

"You know I broke your Michael Jackson record?"

Owen nudges me. "Hey! Don't tell her that!"

Cassie smiles. "I've always known!"

"Mother Teresa on a pogo stick!" Levi shouts, looking toward the ceiling. "It's coming apart! It's all coming apart!"

Massive chunks of what can only be the Earth itself rises into the air, separating into ever smaller pieces. For a moment, we're lost in a sea of stone, watching the formation of our planet in reverse, gravity pushing instead of pulling.

Continents reduce to boulders and then to dust. When it clears, the universe's stars have gathered in a pocket of the sky, growing brighter as it condenses, and then larger as we race toward it.

Blinding white light forces my eyes away. It's impossible to look at, the heat of it warms my skin, but it doesn't scorch. The light is retreating, pulling back, taking us with it.

We are inside the first moments of the universe.

And then, in a sudden moment of absolute stillness and silence, we're beyond it.

The flux stops, but the particle collider's gentle hum continues.

Gravity ceases to exist. I feel my body lift off the floor. Anything not bolted down rises into the air and floats away, including most of the weapons we dropped when diving for cover. My stomach twists, but it's nothing compared to the discomfort of a flux.

"Astounding," Langdon says, but the voice doesn't come from the man in the chair, it comes from the younger of the two, as he pushes himself away from the ceiling. He spins through the air, awkwardly flailing about until he hits the floor and manages to catch hold of a chair leg. "You've really done it," he says to his elder self, and I can't tell if his shock stems from fright or wonder.

Both, I suppose, because I feel the same way. Despite the circumstances, the staggering beauty of what we've just witnessed is beyond comparison.

So why does the older Langdon not look relieved, or happy? Haven't we passed through the energies of creation he so desperately sought?

I shake my head at my inner monologue. The energy was being pulled away from us, not toward us.

He's waiting for something else.

My eyes widen as I realize he's still strapped in.

"It's not over," I say. "It's not over!"

"How can that be?" the younger Langdon asks. "We have arrived. There is no way back. There is no—"

"Was I really this dull?" Future Langdon asks. "Did I really have so little imagination? Time is flexible. Malleable. But it is also resilient, snapping back into place when tension is released. We are tethered to the present. Your present. And in a moment, we will return to it. All of us. And you will thank me for it." He grins. "You will worship me for it."

"Fat chance," Flores says, starting to emerge from beneath the coffee table that held him in place.

I'm about to warn him it's not over when the younger Langdon screams, gripping his head in pain. It's just like before, but it's only happening to him.

When it stops, his face is placid, almost death-like. But then he pushes off the chair and glides toward the door.

"What's he doing?" the elder Langdon asks, his delusions of Godhood diminishing into primal fear.

"Langdon!" I shout. My instinct is to go tackle him, but I don't want to leave Owen.

Luckily, Flores has the same instincts and none of the familial concerns. He launches from the coffee table, on a collision course.

"Langdon!" I shout again, as Flores misses his mark, passing behind his target.

The younger scientist thumps against the sealed door, which has gone silent, and lowers himself toward the biometric lock. His face is blank. Emotionless. His mind is gone. *Something is controlling him,* I think, but Tsul'Kalu never showed any psychic abilities. If he could just control his prey, escape would have been impossible.

He likes the fight, but what's happening to the younger Langdon... It's not passionate, or violent, or even malevolent. He's moving with the calm grace of whatever intellect is controlling him.

The door's lock *thunks* open. The younger Langdon pushes off, gliding back into the penthouse, blinking in confusion as his mind returns. "What happened?" He looks at the slowly opening door. "What did I do?"

On the plus side, there is no sucking of air. The rest of the facility or at least the compartments outside the penthouse, have remained sealed against the vacuum of nothing. On the downside, the long white fingers that wrap around the door as it slides open are not human.

Nor are they Nephilim.

The digits are slender and tipped with thick, gray nails that could have once been sharp, but appear to have been filed down.

The white head with black eyes slips into view. I have a feeling of, *You!* But I don't speak. I *can't* speak. A strange vibration fills my head. I hear sounds, and then feel equal parts confusion, fear, and interest.

I'm feeling what *it* feels. Or are these thoughts? With no common language, true communication, spoken or otherwise, is impossible. All that's left is emotion—something this creature apparently shares with humanity.

When it steps fully into view, I understand what I'm seeing.

"What is *that?*" the elder Langdon says, aghast. In all his observations, he managed to miss the creature's stealthy advance from the power station to Synergy. It must have slipped inside while Tsul'Kalu waged his war.

"A pre-human, intelligent species," I guess, staring into the big black eyes. The face resembles a Cretaceous carnivore. The shape of its skull. The short, but present snout that all but disappears when viewed straight on. Its eyes face forward, making it a strange amalgam of species. Its body is slender, but powerful. Forelimbs stretch toward the ground, but it doesn't use them for standing, though I suspect it could, if it wanted to move quickly. Then I see something interesting. Its hands have four fingers, one of which is a thumb. The hind legs end in three-toed feet, talons present and sharp. Its pale skin is thick with a patch of almost downy feathers running down its back. The feathers shimmer blue and green when it moves. Whatever this thing is, it evolved from some line of carnivorous dinosaur.

And I suspect it is responsible for killing the men at the power station. But was it self-defense, or an act of unprovoked violence? Even if it was the latter, the appearance of a modern power facility and strange new creatures in its territory might have been provocation enough. Either way, this creature has the potential for savage violence...which makes it more human than anyone would like to admit.

It steps fully into the room, revealing a ten-foot-long tail that snaps back and forth, providing balance for its large body.

"Impossible," Future Langdon says. "The fossil record—"

"Is a load'a bull dookie," Levi says, bravely standing to face the creature. "At least in Appalachia. Most of what was here was chewed up and ground to dust by the Ice Age."

He holds his hand out in a peace offering. "We won't hurt you," he says, and while I know it can't understand his words, maybe it can understand his feelings.

The big black eyes shift from person to person. Its facial expression is hard to read, but relaxing. That is, until it looks at the elder Langdon. A sneer twists its slender lips up, revealing needle-like teeth. I think it senses his fear, and hate, and his unending amounts of hubris.

And then its black eyes widen with surprise. I'm not sure why, until a geyser of red blood sprays from the creature's shoulder, floating away in the zero gravity. I shout in pain in time with the creature, sharing its projected anguish. The flailing creature's tail slaps the floor, pushing it toward the ceiling and revealing the source of its wound.

Tsul'Kalu stands just inside the room, clinging to the open door with one hand. In the other hand, he holds a large knife that looks small in his grasp. His body is covered in blood, both purple and red. His human-skin garments are riddled with bullet holes to the point they're nearly non-existent. The saber-toothed cat cloak has been frayed as well, but not as much. And the thick skull still rests on his head, ever protective.

There's a moment of 'oh, shit' silence as everyone in the penthouse glances from one face to the next.

Then Tsul'Kalu smiles, looks at me, says, "Tsisdu," and begins to laugh. The flesh of who-knows-what dangles from his double rows of teeth.

But his smile fades a moment later when the background hum that's been so constant since the particle collider went active suddenly stops and we're plunged into what feels like a vacuum of sound. The pressure of nothing on my eardrums is intense.

The particle collider has shut down. The God and Devil particles no longer orbit each other. The waves that carried us here, that stretched out time, have been spent.

And the tether of space-time anchoring us to the distant future begins to snap back, straight toward the spark of creation.

54

"This is it!" the elder Langdon shouts, a smile on his face. He's not gloating. Not rubbing in his success. He's looking at his wife, ever confident that his actions will spare her from cancer's grasp.

But his joy is misplaced. Not only is there a good chance we're all going to die in the next few seconds, but even if we survive back to the present, we'll still be in the very deadly company of Tsul'Kalu. Worse, we'll have unleashed a monster into the modern world.

How many people will he tear apart before someone figures out how to kill him?

For now, at least, the giant seems distracted by the view above. The absolute void mesmerizes him.

Then, for the first time, I see fear in his eyes.

A deep, resounding rumble, like the roar of a waterfall rushes through us. I can feel it in my body, in my thoughts. My body feels disassembled at a molecular level, but free of pain. For a moment, I cease to exist as anything other than thought. I cannot feel, hear, or see. There is no light, no darkness, just the mighty roar and...a whooshing wind that sounds—or feels—like words sifting through me like a memory. *Who touched my garments?*

What?

Then I'm sewn back together, atoms linking.

I feel again, a strange tingling with no point of origin.

My senses return with a clap of thunder. I can feel Owen wrapped in my arms, his body living, but still. The roar comes to an abrupt end, and my eyes snap open.

We're engulfed in absolute darkness, both outside and inside. Synergy is without power.

How long until we run out of air? Until we freeze?

White light blooms outside the window, filling the penthouse. In the brief moment I can bear to look, I see Tsul'Kalu on his knees, arms raised, head turned up, mouth open in a silent scream. His body appears to be charred, somehow turned to dust. Dark flakes peel away from his body as the light flares brighter and my eyes are forced shut.

Did the light do that to him? Did it affect anyone else? I open my eyes to look, but the pure white light overwhelms me, sending a quiver through my body.

"Don't look at him!" Owen's small voice barely reaches my ear. Despite being right next to each other, he sounds a mile away.

How could he tell who I was looking at? I wonder. *Did he look, too? Or is he talking about someone else?*

The whooshing words come back to mind. Did I really hear them? *No,* I decide, *I experienced them. But who spoke them, and what the hell does it mean?*

The bright pink glow on the inside of my eyelids fades, and despite Owen's warning, I open my eyes. Above, the view is stars. A lot of them, bunched together and slowly drifting apart. We race away through brilliant flashing clouds that coalesce and ignite into even more stars. The universe is being formed around us. Great spirals of light twinkle to life and spin into the distance, everything rushing away from everything.

A cloud of dust envelops us, sifting past the domed window, forming larger chunks that merge and grow. I recognize the scene, played now in fast-forward rather than reverse. We're watching the Earth's formation, but we can only look up.

I flinch when power is restored, the penthouse's orange glow returning. I'd been able to see, thanks to the sourceless light of creation, and the illumination cast off by forming galaxies, but now I can see more clearly.

I stare at the lowest point on the dome, six feet above the floor. *Why didn't Langdon put in any outward facing windows?* I wonder in frustration. The answer is simple, short of a hot air balloon, a sniper's bullet wouldn't be able to find him in here. Not that any bullet in my time could pierce the thick glass.

I flinch when the white, pre-human thing pulls itself to the window's edge, looking out at what I want to see. Like me, it is dumbfounded and curious.

What are you? I think, and the thing turns around to look at me. Pain wracks my head, along with a sense of welcome and wonder. It almost felt like an invitation.

Owen nudges me. "It wants us to see."

We look into each other's identical eyes.

"The flux is over," he says. "We don't need to hide. And I feel stronger than ever. Don't you?"

I hadn't taken stock of my physical state, but the moment I do, I know something has changed. All the aches, pains, bruises, wounds, and muscle pulls my body has been subjected to over the past day are gone. But that's not all. My body feels...new. I feel young. Stronger than ever.

As does the elder Langdon, still seated, grinning at his wife, who's still hidden from view by the chairback.

He did it... I have no definitive proof, but my doubt slips away. We've been undone and remade whole.

The clang of metal on tile snaps my attention to Tsul'Kalu. He's still locked in his pose of anguish—or is he begging? The blade he used to stab the white pre-human has fallen from his loosened grasp. Blackened fingers crumble, giving way to white bone. His face looks sunken and burned, his flesh desiccated and cracked. Strangely, the saber-toothed head and skin were unaffected by whatever turned him into a husk.

But is he dead?

Has to be, I decide, and I allow curiosity to guide me out from under the table. I hold on to the table edge to keep myself upright in the zero gravity. Owen takes my hand and allows me to guide him out.

"What are you doing?" Cassie asks. As aghast as she sounds, she slides out from hiding.

When I push off with Owen, she joins us. An uncharacteristically silent Levi follows. Flores meets us part way, offering his hand to me as we glide on a collision course with the large creature that has killed men before, and is capable of killing us. But I think it means us no harm...for now. With a tug, he redirects us toward the dome's edge. I catch the wall and cling in place, allowing Owen to hold himself against the sill.

Cassie slides up beside Owen. To my left, Levi, Flores, and then the young Langdon arrive, all of us staring out through the thick window, watching as the world is formed. A string of giant rocks rolls through space, colliding and merging, growing larger and larger, until we're a part of it all, looking out at a crude horizon.

Gravity takes hold, gently at first and then pulling down with a force we're all familiar with. Our feet perch on cabinets and furniture, anything to keep our heads above the glass.

There's an explosion of dust, and then, as the Earth continues to form, the dust in orbit drifts together in a ball. Soon the moon is born, its surface pummeled by a string of smaller asteroids.

The pre-human creature chuffs, and I think it might be a laugh. When I meet his black eyes, I sense no anger. The cold stare I saw out in the forest when we were strange trespassers in his world has been replaced by a rabid fascination.

How evolved is he?

How much more evolved will his kind become?

My questions don't seem all that important compared to what lies outside. So I ignore the twenty-foot long, intelligent, albino dinosaur-man and watch the show.

"What is it?" the elder Langdon asks. "What can you see?"

He's clearly afraid to unbuckle, maybe because there's a bumpy road ahead, or simply because he doesn't *know* what kind of road lies ahead. Then again, maybe he's just afraid of our Cretaceous stowaway.

I flip him the bird and return to the view in time to see the sun's appearance. This far back in time, night was day and day was night. We flicker forward in time, the sun becoming a blur of light, as it moves through the sky.

Mountains rise and fall around us, glowing with magma. Oceans rise, covering the dome for a good ten seconds that represents millions of years, and then fall again. Green springs to life, emerging from the ground in thin sheets before growing tall. Generations of landscape whoosh past, growing, twisting, evolving. It's not hard to see the planet growing and aging like a living thing. A life of its own, carrying infinitesimally small beings on its surface, like bacteria on skin.

The world is recognizable now, and I'm pretty sure we're roaring past the Triassic, Jurassic, and Cretaceous. If the pre-human knows we're passing his stop, he doesn't react. He's lost to the sight, marveling at the creation of the planet our two species called home without ever meeting or knowing the other exists.

When the world goes white and the Appalachians spring up around us, I know the journey is nearly complete.

Future Langdon clutches the arms of his chair.

"Hold on!" I shout, lowering myself to the floor as Adel grows up and around us, sealing us in stone. Even the pre-human follows our lead, dropping down. Nimble fingers clutch onto a chair, while its long prehensile tail snaps out and latches onto a support beam.

Light flashes back into the penthouse when the mountain is carved away, bringing us into the final hundred years of our journey.

And then...nothing.

The blue sky above us is unchanging.

"What happened?" Levi asks. "Are we there? Are we back?"

I push myself up and head for the window, but motion outside provides the answer for me. A crow flies through the sky, unaware that anything strange has happened.

"What do you see?" the elder Langdon asks.

I answer without thinking, "Birds."

"Anything living outside would have died during the vacuum," he says, sounding hopeful. "We've made it!"

Despite his hope, his words strike a chord. *Everything outside would have died in the vacuum of space... Every animal. Every dinosaur. Every person. All of this, for one woman.*

No, I decide, *for a broken man.*

"Now," the elder Langdon says, sounding bold and in charge. "If you'd all get the fuck out of my house, I will allow you to live and enjoy what remains of your lives, having seen the marvel of creation first hand."

Future Langdon holds an AR-15 and looks like he knows how to use it. As we back away from the window, I wonder if I could draw my sidearm fast enough to shoot him. I doubt it, and it looks like some of the others were disarmed during the chaos. Their dropped weapons floated away in zero gravity and could be anywhere now. As I raise my hands and step into the center of the room with the others, the pre-human remains at the window, stretching its long neck to take in the Appalachians in all their summer glory. It's oblivious to the confrontation taking place behind it and has no idea what he is saying.

"Each of you may leave," Future Langdon says. "I have not, and do not, bear any of you ill will."

"You were willing to kill thousands," I tell him. "My *father* among them."

"Regrettable. But that time has passed," he says, slipping his finger around the trigger. "Last chance. You can all walk out that door..." He glances at Tsul'Kalu's ruined body, and then at the pre-human. "...and take your albino pet with you. Please. You are all free to go. Well... everyone except him." Future Langdon raises his weapon, turns it on his younger self, and pulls the trigger.

The bullet punches into young Langdon's gut, slips through the soft organs within, and passes out the far side, spraying a cloud of blood onto the charred giant's face...where it is absorbed.

55

"What did you do?" Jacqueline shouts, vocal for the first time, probably because she suspects what has happened, even though she's still strapped down and unable to turn and look. "Who did you shoot? Elias!"

"Still...here..." The younger Langdon holds his hand over the wound on his front side, but he can't do anything about the exit wound on his back. My instinct is to help him. With proper medical attention, the wound is survivable if the bleeding can be stemmed. But I don't think his older self will allow that to happen. He wants Jacqueline to himself, even if she's a prisoner.

At the same time, I want to leave, not just because Future Langdon could mow us all down, but because I don't like how Tsul'Kalu's body absorbed that blood.

"You should go," the wounded younger Langdon says. "I am not worth your lives."

"Elias..." Jacqueline says through tears, making her elder husband grimace with annoyance, no doubt because he has just saved her life. But she's more concerned about the man who he knows failed to do so.

Future Langdon rotates the rifle from one person to another, flinching when the weapon and his eyes turn toward the pre-human. It's no longer looking out the window. No longer distracted. It's facing him, head lowered, body poised to pounce. When they make eye contact, the creature bares its teeth and hisses.

Sensing Future Langdon is about to shoot, I step between them, arms raised. "Whoa, whoa, whoa." My concern isn't just for the strange beast ripped from the past. If Future Langdon pulls that trigger, I suspect he will not stop until we're all dead.

When he holds his fire, I turn to face the creature. Its bared teeth and furrowed brow instill a deep sense of fear. I manage to say one more, "Whoa," trying to emanate calm.

The creature's black eyes burrow into me. I can feel it in my head.

Is this how its species communicates? Having already seen it control the younger Langdon's mind, I have no doubt. For a moment, I consider trying to have it control the elder Langdon, but if its influence on his actions is not immediate, he might still gun us down.

So I imagine the pre-human leaving with us, calmly, without incident.

Its expression softens. Then it looks toward the door.

"Yes," I say, nodding, despite the fact that both word and gesture are meaningless. Assuming anything with arms and hands understands a pointed finger, I motion to the exit. "Go. Please."

I'm not sure if it understands anything other than how I feel, but it looks at the door, then back to me, and then to Future Langdon. There's a moment of stillness, and I can sense it thinking about what to do. Then, it wisely turns toward the door and starts walking. It moves with surprising grace and silence, its long body slipping through the air like a blade. My eyes are drawn to the red blood on its back, already starting to dry. I trace it back to the creature's shoulder, but the wound is gone. Like us, this thing was healed by whatever it was we encountered at the beginning of everything. Cosmic energy? God? Both? All I really know is that it wasn't nothing, and it wasn't an accident.

'Who touched my garments...'

What the hell does that mean?

"We're leaving," I say, backing up so I'm standing in front of Owen again. Strange that I'm protecting him from a man with a gun, rather than a monster out of the Cretaceous.

"Owen," Cassie says, the tone of her voice saying: *we can't let him get away with this.*

"Leave," the younger Langdon says. When she looks down at him, he flicks his eyes toward Tsul'Kalu. He's noticed what I have—the subtle rise and fall of the hunter's charred chest, the twitch of a pulse on the side of his neck. The beast is in shock, but not dead. And if he comes to, while we're all lingering about...it will be a blood bath.

Cassie understands. As do the others. Without complaint, we follow the pre-human toward the door. It ducks down and maneuvers itself through the hatch without grazing the sides.

I can't begin to figure what we're going to do with the thing. And I can't imagine how strange all of this must be for the creature. Could it have any concept of science and technology?

It did use the younger Langdon to open a biometric lock. So it either understood the tech, or his thoughts on how to use it. Maybe both. More importantly, the creature has shown itself to be intelligent and capable of empathy, wonder, and curiosity. It might not look like homo sapiens, but it is more human than the broken man who tore us through time. The real problem is that if we reveal the pre-human's existence to the world, it will receive none of those attributes in return. It doesn't deserve that fate.

Tsul'Kalu on the other hand...he can go visit his father in hell.

And he can take Future Langdon with him. The elder Langdon escorts us toward the door, weapon trained on my back. That he didn't just kill us reveals the man's strange dichotomy. He's not a blatant murderer. He doesn't want to pull the trigger, but he has no trouble sacrificing the lives of people he can't see.

The generations of Black Creek residents have been dead for a long time. He might view killing them in the vacuum of creation as returning things to the way they were. But that's not accurate. If this is a new dimension of reality, then all of these people have new lives to live. New futures.

And if they are dead...

A cold hand wraps around my heart, the anger kindled by my father's death returning.

Not yet, I think. *His time is coming. Get everyone out.*

I lean to the side and spot the elevator at the end of the short, barren hallway. The doors are a ruined mess, the spot where the car should be is an open void. The pre-human steps into the open space, bracing itself with hands, feet, and tail, fearless over the drop. Then it surprises me by reaching out a hand.

"Tarnation," Levi says, and turns to me. "Ain't no way."

"And here I thought you'd grown a pair," Cassie says.

"Hey," he starts, but whatever argument he was about to make is quashed when she steps around him and reaches out her hand.

The pre-human guides her to the edge. Its tail snakes up out of the hole and wraps around her waist.

"Be gentle," she tells the thing, and then to me. "See you downstairs." She's lifted up and lowered from view.

I grasp Flores's arm, whispering, "Get them downstairs and outside. If shit goes sideways, get them off this mountain and out into the world."

"I'll get it done," he says. "Assuming there is a world out there."

When I see Owen freezing up, just outside the pre-human's reach, I say, "You can do it, Owe. I'll be right behind you."

He gives me a withering look, his strong will drawing the line at intelligent-dinosaur tail rides. Then he waves and takes a step closer, allowing the tail to wrap around him and whisk him away.

When I turn back to face the elder Langdon he snaps the rifle up toward my face. A twitch of the finger is all that separates me from the afterlife. "What do you think you're doing?"

"Offering you one last chance at redemption," I tell him. "Let me take them."

"And all will be forgiven?" He scoffs. "I know you better than that. I know you blame me for your father's death."

"He died in 1985," I say, which is the truth...but also not. Not anymore. He died less than an hour ago. Again. Because of... I force my rising emotions back down, focusing once more on the living. I motion to the younger Langdon, now lying still on the floor, one arm pinned under his body. "Him living or dying won't change anything for you."

"But everything for her." He motions to the chair in which his wife is still held prisoner.

I can hear her, crying.

Behind me, Flores is lifted up and transported down the elevator shaft. The pre-human directs its gaze toward me, waiting. There's a stab of pain in my head, and then an intense feeling of being rushed.

It's telling me to hurry.

Tsul'Kalu is waking up.

But the creature doesn't have the full picture. Doesn't sense the smaller pieces coming together. And neither does Future Langdon.

"You think she's going to choose you because you're the last man standing?" I ask. "Does that sound like the woman you married?"

His face spasms a bit. Driven by a broken mind, he hasn't considered the logic behind any of this. Hasn't given thought to the ramifications of his actions on the people involved, the world or universe at large, or even the woman he's supposed to be saving. "She will be grateful. In time."

My response is subtle—a raised doubtful eyebrow—but it's enough to make him consider his future and not like what he sees. His eyes fill with fury as his finger tightens around the trigger. "She will choose me, because she will have no other choice!"

"Yes," the younger Langdon says, rising up behind his counterpart, as I drop to the floor. "She will!"

He plunges the knife dropped by Tsul'Kalu into his older self's back. The AR-15 unleashes a torrent of bullets, as Future Langdon screams in pain and flails back. The weapon falls from his hand as he drops to the floor. He claws at his back, trying to reach the blade that hasn't killed him yet, but certainly will if he manages to pull it out.

The younger Langdon clings to the wall, blood-soaked and barely standing. I look down the hall toward the confused and somewhat aghast pre-human. "Help him!" I shout, and then I charge back into the penthouse, Langdon's AR-15 in hand.

I round the chair holding Jacqueline. Her face, normally so calm and pleasant, is streaked with mascara tears, and it's twisted with emotion. She looks up at me with sadness and regret. "Oh, Mr. McCoy...

I tried so hard," she says, "to not upset him. To keep him calm. To find his soul. B-but there was nothing left of him. Of my husband."

"Your husband," I unbuckle the belt across her waist. She couldn't reach it because her hands were zip-tied together "...is alive." I pull her to her feet. "And on his way outside."

A raspy breath cuts through the room's air.

"Which is exactly where we need to be." I pull her to her feet and guide her toward the exit. The elder Langdon, knife still in his back, reaches for us as we pass.

"Jacqueline! Please, I—"

A swift kick from his wife silences him. She hurries past, enters the hallway, and screams. She throws herself into me, trying to flee from the pre-human, which she had yet to see.

"He's with us," I tell her.

"No, no, no..."

The poor woman has endured a lot, but she really has no choice here. To linger means facing Tsul'Kalu trapped in the equivalent of a human-sized fishbowl...sans the water. I put her up over my shoulder and carry her to the pre-human. She trembles when it takes her, but she manages to contain her screams as she's lowered from sight.

When I head back to the penthouse a pulse of pain in my head conveys frantic concern.

"Almost done," I say, and then I crouch by Future Langdon. He stops reaching for the blade and looks up at me, eyes imploring. "If you pull that out, you'll die quickly. And as much of an asshole as you are, I'll be rooting for you."

I place the AR-15 on the floor and shove it a few feet away.

He's confused until I turn my attention to Tsul'Kalu. Sheets of charred skin flake away, the flesh underneath slowly moving. A ragged growl builds inside his chest. It's taken a while, but the monster is regenerating. He wasn't welcome at the moment of creation, but he wasn't killed, either.

"No," the elder Langdon says. "You can't."

"How many times did you hear those words in the seven years leading up to this moment?" I ask, standing up.

The question hits home and he starts to cry, but all that regret burns away the moment I step back into the hall and start to close the door.

"I'll kill you!" he screams. "I'll destroy your family tree! I'll make you watch. Don't you da—"

His voice is cut short when the door closes and the lock engages, sealing both monsters inside together.

56

"Are we home?" Cassie asks, once we're back outside the building. "Did we make it?"

It's impossible to tell. The stars look right. The universe is done forming around us. The Synergy facility around us is still from the future, but Future Langdon said he planned for us to return to our time, no doubt to avoid whatever justice awaited him in the future. How many people did he kill to achieve his goal? How many laws did he break, both human and natural?

No man should have that kind of power. I determine to dismantle Synergy piece by piece, or just blow it all up. This tech needs to die with its creator. I glance up at the penthouse dome. The orange glow from within, framed by the night sky, looks hellish. Complete with a devil and a demon.

I'm not sure who's worse. While the Nephilim was a destructive power of pure rage and hate, Langdon coldly manipulated people toward his own selfish desires, granting himself power over death, making himself—for a moment—godlike. On the surface, Tsul'Kalu seems to be the worse of the two, but he's really nothing more than his fabled parentage: a demon. While Future Langdon...his power was tempting. I understood him. I empathized with him. And another, slightly weaker me, might have joined him. If that's not the Devil, I don't know what is.

"Smells like home," Levi says, taking a deep breath. He's right about that. The Appalachians of the past all had distinct, earthy odors, while the air here has a background scent of coal mixed in with the wilderness.

"Stay sharp," Flores warns, drawing his sidearm.

I appreciate that he's still frosty and on mission, despite everything we've seen and survived, but I'm not sure there's anyone—human—left alive to fear. Drones in various states of ruin litter the facility floor. If any are still functional, they've been abandoned by their operators, who either fled their stations when Tsul'Kalu entered the building, or were killed by the monster.

A chime makes me flinch. My cellphone. I'd all but forgotten about it. It's been useless since all this began, sitting silently in my pocket, looking for a network that didn't yet exist.

I draw the phone from my pocket. The battery is almost dead, and I have a text message from UNKNOWN that reads: HELLO?

"We're back," I say, "and already getting drunk dialed." I switch over to the phone app and dial 911. My thumb hovers over the call button, but I don't push it.

"What's wrong?" Levi asks. "Get us a ride out of here."

"I believe that would be a wise course of action," the younger Langdon says. He's laid out on his back while Jacqueline applies pressure to his wounds.

"Please," she says. "Hurry!"

They're right, of course. We need help. But when that help arrives... I glance at the pre-human, who is silently stalking the area around us, inspecting everything, agitated, but interested. Whatever it is, it has the heart of an explorer, its fascination pushing the creature past its fear.

The phone chimes in my hand. A new text. WHO ARE YOU?

My face scrunches up, and I look around. I can't help but feel we're being watched.

A new chime, a new message. WHERE DID YOU COME FROM?

Definitely being watched.

I ignore the messages and hit the call button. Phone to my ear, I wait for the familiar rings...but I hear nothing. The call doesn't connect. I confirm the presence of two network bars and try again.

A faint, high-pitched sound makes me wince. I draw the phone from my ear, looking at the screen, but then I realize the shrill cry didn't come from the device. It came from a set of human lungs, muffled by steel and glass.

Tsul'Kalu is awake.

The glass dome, glowing orange, is suddenly speckled by a spray of dark, ruby liquid. I can't imagine what the giant did to Future Langdon, but it was quick and no doubt permanent. The Devil is dead, killed by the demon he unleashed on the Earth.

Our group takes a collective step back when giant fists pound on the glass. Tsul'Kalu unleashes his fury on the wall, punching and clawing until his purple blood mixes with the elder Langdon's. The dome resists the attack, and for a moment, I relax. Then the giant steps forward, the orange glow like fire around him. With a new kind of fury in his eyes, he stares down at us and then slowly steps away.

Well, I don't like *that*. Tsul'Kalu just transformed from a monster driven by instinct into a killer with cold, calculating eyes.

"Can we leave?" Owen asks, clutching my hand.

"Like now?" Levi asks. "We can get a head start if we—"

"Hiking down Adel in the dark with a wounded man isn't going to go quickly," Flores points out.

"We'll take the tunnels," Levi says. "There have got to be more carts underground. We can take them down to Black Creek faster than any ambulance can make the round trip."

"That might be our only option," Cassie says. She's trying to make a call on her phone, but not having any more luck than I did. "Calls aren't getting through."

"What about those texts?" Flores asks.

I look down at the phone, considering how I might ask the stranger for help. Whoever it is already knows we're here. But do they know we're—

The phone chimes. HELP EN ROUTE. DO NOT SHOOT.

"What is it?" Owen asks, when I flinch at the message.

"Whoever this is," I say, holding up the phone, "they can see *and* hear us."

"That doesn't sound good," Levi says.

"They say help is incoming."

Levi's expression softens. "But that's not bad."

"They're watching from above," Flores says, looking up at the sky. "Listening through the phones. Blocking our calls. Sounds like the government to me. Which could go either way for us, but..." He looks to the pre-human, still distracted by the new world in which it has found itself. "... for it, that's not going to go well."

"We need to hide him," Owen says.

If we want the pre-human to survive, he's right. But I'm not sure if that's the right call. The creature is out of its time, and while it sided with us under extreme circumstances, we have no idea what it's capable of, or what it might do if set free on this world. Like Tsul'Kalu, the pre-human could wreak havoc. But would it?

Only if provoked, I think. It seems reasonable enough, but it did kill those men at the power station...I think. The big question is, how will it handle being the last survivor of its kind, separated from its time by tens of millions of years? That would be enough to break most people. Will this creature be any different, intelligent or not?

"He did right by us," Owen says, no doubt sensing my doubts. "We owe it to him to do the same. It's what Dad would do."

I give him a nod. "We'll do what we can...but there's a good chance they already know he's here."

The sound of a door creaking open draws my attention back to the building from which we escaped. It could be captives who managed to survive, drone operators, or security forces who don't know the fight is over. I raise my weapon toward the steel door as it swings open to reveal darkness.

The lights inside have been destroyed since our exit.

A low, rumbling laugh rolls out of the doorway.

Shit.

"How'd he get out?" Levi asks.

The answer sails out of the door and topples over the concrete. The elder Langdon's torso and head tumble to a stop behind the still living, younger man and his wife. They both shout in fear and attempt to move, but he's in too much pain.

Tsul'Kalu is smarter than I thought, just like the pre-human, who is... where the hell is he? I do a quick scan and don't see the thing anywhere. Tsul'Kalu's laugh provided all the distraction it needed to slip away... which is probably the smartest thing it has done.

"I want you to run." I tell Owen. And then I turn to Cassie. "And you to go with him."

"Owen..." she says.

"Get to the tunnels," I tell her. "Please." I squeeze Owen's hand, but then let go. "You keep her safe, too."

When Tsul'Kalu steps into the well-lit courtyard, I shout at them. "Go!"

She takes Owen's hand and pulls him away. He fights her for a few steps, but then they're both running through the open gate and into the dark woods.

"I totally would have taken him, too" Levi says, and then grins in the face of death, pistol in hand. "Just saying, is all."

"How you want to play this?" Flores asks, stepping between Jacqueline, the wounded Langdon, and the beast.

"Aim for the head," I say. "When you're out of ammo..." I glance down at my boss and his wife, knowing that she won't abandon him, and my next words will seal their fate. "...run. If you can."

Tsul'Kalu steps into the light, naked save for the saber-toothed cat helmet and cloak. While still towering over us, his body has lost some of its mass. His skin appears thin. Rice paper over muscle. But the gleam in his eye is no less ferocious, and Future Langdon's torn apart body is a testament to his remaining strength.

"Alatisdi tsisdu," he says with a grin.

I raise my handgun. "Not this time."

My first shot grazes the side of his forehead, just below the cat helmet. The next several shots strike his forearms as he raises them up in front of his skull and charges. We unload our weapons into him as a group. I'm hoping one of the hard-hitting rounds will slip through the meat of his arms and strike his forehead, the only part of him he's bothering to protect.

Damnit.

Why didn't I put a bullet in this thing's forehead when I had the chance? I want to blame it on shock and distraction. I had just witnessed the universe unmade and remade, not to mention being befriended by an ancient intelligent dinosaur-thing, but I don't think that's it. I wanted it to live long enough for Future Langdon to reap what he'd sown. A bullet was too easy for him, but not nearly enough for Tsul'Kalu.

I was foolish to believe Future Langdon's dome could contain the beast. Even without his body available to unlock the door, how could I know whether or not the giant would escape?

I couldn't. I didn't. And now people might pay the price with their lives.

I put all my anger at Tsul'Kalu, and at Future Langdon, and at myself into each squeeze of the trigger, hoping it will somehow impart each round with more power. But the bullets fail to do the only thing for which they were created.

My gun runs dry first with a click. The giant is just thirty feet out and closing. When Levi and Flores run dry, I shout, "Go! Now!"

The pair bolts in opposite directions. If either had looked back and seen me stationary, they might have hesitated out of loyalty, but there's nothing they could do to change what's about to happen.

I drop the gun's magazine and slap in my only spare, giving me thirteen more tries at the monster's head. I hold my fire, waiting for him to peek. As powerful as he might be, he doesn't have X-ray vision.

When I see his eye, I pull the trigger.

A howl of pain that morphs into delight follows. I struck his eye, blinding him on one side, at least for the moment. His sudden lack of depth perception might give me an advantage, I hope, or throw him off course. It does neither.

He runs straight forward, on a collision course with me, and with Jacqueline. I hold my ground, squeezing off rounds, trying and failing, over and over, to strike his head.

He's just a few steps away when the gun runs dry again. "Sorry," I say to Jacqueline, but my apology is cut short by the loud crack of a rifle.

The bullet strikes Tsul'Kalu in the side of his head, exiting the far side in a spray of gore. The giant spills sideways, topples to the ground and rolls to a stop at my feet. The saber-toothed skullcap has been knocked free and lies several feet away.

I jump back, and against the better judgement of paramedics around the world, I take the younger Langdon by the arms and drag him twenty feet away. He grunts in pain, but doesn't complain.

"Keep the pressure on," I tell Jacqueline, and then I step closer to the giant, inspecting the fresh wound. The purple hole is already shrinking as the skin around it stretches out and grows thinner.

Not dead.

I turn toward the rifle's report and find the weapon protruding from the dark doorway of the now-ruined warehouse through which we entered the facility. I can only see the front end of the weapon, but I recognize it immediately.

A Winchester 1895.

My *father's* Winchester.

"Inola?" I say, but then I take in a sharp breath when my father steps out of the shadows, looking down the weapon's barrel.

"Step back, son," he says. "Looks like it ain't done yet."

Inola follows him out of the dark, armed only with a hatchet.

I'm stunned into inaction. My father, like Tsul'Kalu, lives. But while the giant has always been able to regenerate its body, my father's resurrection from the dead is miraculous. "Dad…" I say, turning toward him, numb to the danger behind me.

"Get down!" he shouts, snapping me out of my emotional cascade.

I duck and turn around to see Tsul'Kalu sit up. My father pulls the trigger again, this time striking and all but destroying his lower jaw. The laugh that comes from the giant this time is gargled through purple blood. But the hunter continues to rise.

"Aim for its forehead!" I shout, backing away until my foot bumps into Jacqueline.

My father takes aim, but holds his fire as several loud thumps sound out above him.

A white blur launches from the warehouse roof.

The pre-human.

It didn't leave. It was just waiting for the right moment to strike. I'm not sure what it would have done if the right moment hadn't arrived. It might have let me and the rest of us die and been on its merry way. But it didn't, and I suppose that says something about its character.

The large, white creature lands in front of the Nephilim, and with what appears to be a fighting technique rather than what you'd expect from a dinosaur, it spins around, striking with its tail. It sweeps the giant off his feet, but Tsul'Kalu rolls backward, regaining his footing. He tries to shout something with his reforming jaw, but only manages to spray blood across the pavement.

The pre-human gives him no time to recover. It moves in, ducking below a punch thrown by the giant, wraps its tail around Tsul'Kalu's waist and hurls him against the main building's wall, which is dented by the bone crushing impact.

Tsul'Kalu slouches, but doesn't fall. The beating has taken the wind and humor out of his sails, but he's not yet defeated, if he *can* be. His body starts to stitch back together as the pre-human closes in, but my father slows the healing process by pumping and firing round after round into the giant's broad torso. Inola adds to the assault by throwing her hatchet with such skill that Tsul'Kalu has to turn his head at the last moment to avoid taking the blade in his forehead. Instead, it punches into the side of his head, where the bullet wound has just healed. It's enough to keep the hunter-god on the defensive while the pre-human launches its attack.

Driven into a mindless fury, Tsul'Kalu charges his adversary. He's already faced a dinosaur and lived, but this specimen has the intellect of a man, if not more, and proves it by ducking Tsul'Kalu's hooked fingers and driving a fist into his gut, and I mean *into* it. The giant's thin skin and recovering body provide little resistance.

While the giant is doubled over, the pre-human grasps the giant with its tail, lifting him off the ground. Then it twists its long neck around while lifting Tsul'Kalu closer.

The giant's eyes go wide and it attempts to scream—truly scream—for the first time. It knows what is about to happen. The pre-human's mouth opens to reveal twin rows of deadly-sharp serrated teeth. Its lipless mouth hid the scale of its bite radius, which is easily big enough to envelope the giant's head...or that of a human being.

The pre-human thrashes while yanking with its tail. It takes some effort, but when the head finally comes free of Tsul'Kalu's body, the giant goes limp. Both pieces are dropped to the concrete, discarded with the same indifference to which the giant subjected his victims.

The pre-human stumbles away, and for a moment I think it's injured. Then I realize, as it spits purple blood from its mouth, that it's just disgusted.

"That, there, is some nasty shit," my father says, stepping up beside me. He gives me a sidelong grin and asks, "You okay?"

Knowing the danger might not yet be over, I contain the raw emotions swirling in my gut and manage to say, "Am now."

"Likewise," he says. "Never better, actually."

I hold my hand out for the rifle, and he gives it to me. I approach Tsul'Kalu's head and roll it over with my foot. The face is a mess, but its one good eye looks up at me, still moving, still conscious, still alive. For a moment, I think it's smiling, but then its forehead turns up in fear when I point the rifle at it.

I smile back and pull the trigger.

The forehead folds inward, softer than I'd have expected. The face snaps rigid. Unmoving.

Dead, at last.

I let it roll to the side, lower the Winchester and turn toward my father. Behind him, Kuzneski emerges from the shadows, followed by Hardy, and an endless stream of Black Creek residents. They survived in the tunnels, sealed inside Synergy's protective shell. I'm relieved to see Young Cassie and her mother among the throng.

"Dad!" Owen shouts, as he sprints back from the dark woods, the adult Cassie close behind. My father scoops him up, hugging him hard. "You're alive!"

"Someone bigger than us saw fit to give me a second chance," my father says, and he smiles at me. "Again."

I join the hug, sharing the moment until Kuzneski says, "Umm, what the fuck was that?"

I turn to see the pre-human's white tail slip away past a segment of ruined fence, disappearing into the dark woods beyond. For a moment, I reckon the emergence of so many people scared it off, but then I hear the heavy beat of helicopter blades.

Pain stabs my head for a moment, followed by a feeling of gratitude ...and then silence. The pre-human is gone.

"Long story," I tell Kuzneski. "But it's not a threat."

The still emerging townspeople make way for a black, unmarked helicopter as it thunders into view overhead. It kicks up a swirling cloud of dust before touching down. As the rotors slow, and the wind settles, two figures climb out of the side door. The first is a short woman I reckon is in her sixties. She's carrying a large, heavy purse and wearing too tight clothing and a sassy expression. The second is a man who walks with authority, but is dressed in jeans and a T-shirt. They're definitely not from the government.

My phone chimes and I glance at the screen.

WE COME IN PEACE.

Is that humor? Are they trying to be funny? I didn't see the man or woman sending a text, but it's clearly from them.

As the helicopter winds down, the pair takes their time looking at the people around them. Eventually, they make their way toward me, looking over Levi, Flores, Kuzneski, Owen, my father, the adult Cassie, and myself.

"Okay," the older woman says, "who stepped in shit? Cause it smells like something nasty died up in here."

I step to the side, revealing Tsul'Kalu's headless body and ruined head.

"Ahh, touché, something nasty *did* die up in here."

I smile despite myself. The old lady, at least, is funny. Her eyes travel from Tsul'Kalu's remains to the wounded Langdon and Jacqueline. Her eyes widen. "Oh, my." She rushes over, sliding her large purse off her shoulder and digging inside. "Through and through?" she asks, looking back at me.

When I give her a nod, she digs into her purse and pulls out what looks like a first-aid kit. "We'll get you patched up." I flinch when she opens the kit and withdraws a syringe, but she doesn't inject him with anything, she simply squirts the dark contents over the wound and waits for it to spread out, sealing it tight. Then she flips him over and repeats the process. "It's a temporary fix. He's going to need surgery, but he's not going to bleed out."

While all this takes place, her counterpart doesn't do much more than look at each and every face around him. He's on edge. Or is he distracted? Then he blinks and seems to see me for the first time. He smiles. "Looks like you've got a few thousand people with no records I can find, a facility that didn't exist until a short while ago, and..." He looks around standing on his toes. "Am I wrong, or was there a dinosaur here a minute ago?"

"I'll answer your questions when you answer mine," I say.

He pauses, and then says, "How about we trade? You answer a question, I answer a question. I'll start. Who are you?"

"Owen McCoy."

"I mean, *all* of you."

"The residents of Black Creek, Kentucky," I tell him, and then I decide to hold nothing back. "Circa 2019, 1985, 1945, 1921, 18—"

"Time travel... Huh," he says, unfazed. "That'd explain it."

"It would?"

"Well, some of it," he says. "Except the Black Creek bit...since there is no Black Creek, Kentucky and never has been. It's nutso. Obviously. But nutso is kind of my business these days. Annnd you haven't disagreed."

"And you are...?"

He holds out his hand for me to shake. When I take it, he says, "Dan Delgado." He motions to the woman. "This is my associate, Winifred Finch. We're in a unique position to help you all, but I'm going to need a little honesty in return. You've been forthcoming so far, and I appreciate that. You've clearly been through something..."

"Nutso," I say.

He snaps his fingers and points at me. "Exactly. But I have more than a few concerns in regard to who you are, why you're here, where you came from, and who, or what, you might have brought with you."

Delgado is a stranger, but he's got a way about him that says he's a good guy, and honest. That he's here instead of the government means he's got resources. If we've returned to a future where Black Creek and all its residents never existed, I'm not sure how he can help us...but we'll clearly need someone's help. "If you can help all these people, I can do honest."

"Good," he says, casual and calm. He points at Tsul'Kalu's body. "Let's start with what the hell that is."

"Would you believe a half-demon, half-human giant referenced in the Bible and worshiped as the god of the hunt by the Cherokee?"

"Some of whom are still with you," he says, looking at Inola, as she reunites with her people. "And yeah, you're talking about Nephilim. Sucks that they're real. But he looks pretty dead, so let's talk about that dinosaur..."

When I say, "It's not exactly a dinosaur," he tenses. It's the answer he was expecting, but not the one he was hoping for. "I've been calling it a pre-human, but you know what it is, don't you? Wait, you're not from the Smithsonian, are you?"

"The Smith...what? No. And yes," he says. "I know what it is. We call them the Others."

EPILOGUE

Six Months Later

"Pass the peas?" Young Cassie asks, and before anyone can move, Owen has snatched up the bowl from across the table. The move isn't exactly polite, but she grins her thanks and accepts the bowl in a way that makes their fingers touch for a moment.

Everyone else at the table, including the pair's grown selves, have a good smile at the burgeoning romance. They've been inseparable since the events that transplanted multiple generations of Black Creek to a world that had never heard of it...until now.

Thanks to Delgado and his resources, which I still don't entirely understand, Black Creek has been built up in what was an empty valley in this world. Not only did they rebuild the town in record time and pave roads connecting us to the world, but they also recreated its history, both in the construction and on the Internet. The town has its own website, a Wikipedia page, and a few Yelp listings for the spattering of local dives.

There have been some changes. Houses have been upgraded and neighborhoods created to support the population growth. I no longer live at the mountain's base. Instead, I reside in what is registered as a yoga retreat center atop Adel, concealing the facility that still exists under

the earth. Delgado has shown no interest in resurrecting Future Langdon's technology, but he's not yet ready to destroy it, mostly because it
would be difficult to conceal. And that's the strangest thing about him.
All of this has been done under the radar, without the U.S. government's
involvement or knowledge. Delgado is like a one-man black op with an
unlimited budget and reach. Every single Black Creek resident has a
social security number, birth certificate, medical history, and even a few
criminal records, though nothing more glaring than traffic violations.
Some, like me, have our military records back. For those of us who lived
in the modern world, he's done his best to return what we had, and then
some.

We've had a few confused locals from nearby towns pass through,
all of them dumbfounded by how they'd never heard of Black Creek.
Other than that, the world hasn't really noticed our arrival. Helps that
even in this time, people aren't paying much attention to the struggles of
Appalachia and the good people who live here, though I wish things
could be different.

Delgado had to get creative for folks from the distant past. Language
and cultural barriers have made progress slow, but with Inola's help,
even the Cherokee have become grafted into our odd new town. While
many of the people work on the Black Creek construction projects, just
as many have gone to work for Delgado, including Kuzneski and Flores,
who is visiting for the weekend after spending a few months at Delgado's
facility in Dulce, New Mexico, the epicenter of his own world-changing
story.

He explained it to me once. UFOs. Cryptoterrestrials. Grays. Nano-
tech. Some guy named Lindo. Honestly, it sounded like a load of crap. If
not for our own unbelievable experiences, I think I would have commit-
ted him to a loony bin. I've yet to visit Dulce, but once Black Creek is
squared away, I'll make the trip.

Despite his honesty, I think Delgado is still holding something back.
Something to do with the pre-human, which he believes is either one of,
or the ancestor of, his cryptoterrestrials—an ancient civilization that
predated humanity, but didn't quite survive beyond our arrival...not in
their original form anyway. I'm fuzzy on the details, but maybe there will

come a time when I can join his crusade. For now, I am content to sit around a dining room table with my family and friends, sharing a meal inside my new home—Future Langdon's penthouse—the only portion of Synergy's top side to survive the renovations. And the only place on Earth where you can break bread in a dining room that was present at the dawn of creation.

Despite all that happened here, and what had to be cleaned out of it...the place feels like it's been charged with positive energy. The air feels fresher, like at the beach, or after a thunderstorm in spring, even though it's now winter outside.

"Y'all better save some of that for me," Levi says, leaning over the table to snatch the peas from Young Cassie's hands.

"Hey!" Owen says, coming to her defense. "You're always hogging the peas, Uncle Levi."

"That's 'cause you two are pea vultures." He scoops two big spoonfuls upon his mashed potatoes and then passes the peas along to Mrs. Dearborn, who accepts them with a smile before dishing them out to everyone on her end of the table—my father, Inola, and Flores.

Inola lived with her people for several months, helping them assimilate into the new world. She had her struggles, too, but my father was often by her side, even as he tried to catch up with the modern technology that Owen and Young Cassie had no trouble grasping. A month ago, Inola moved in with my father and Owen, living in a much larger, much nicer version of our old house, built right where it used to be.

Our Langdon and Jacqueline live in town. She works in the library while he teaches science. Neither will be allowed to return to Synergy, but they're also not prisoners. They've chosen to stay and live a quiet, small life together. They're often seen strolling the streets, hand in hand. To this date, there is no sign of cancer or illness in Jacqueline...or anyone else in town. The elder Langdon got the happy ending he wanted...just not for himself.

I take a moment to enjoy the sound of hushed conversations, clinking silverware, and shuffling chairs no longer bolted to the floor. It sounds like home. Like family. It's something I never believed I would have.

Cassie must sense the moment, because she reaches over from beside me, takes my hand, and squeezes. "This is nice," she whispers to me.

"Can't imagine anything better," I reply.

"In the end, it was kind of a blessing," she says. "Don't you think?"

On the surface, the obvious answer is no. People died. Some horribly. Families were torn from their homes, from their very times, and faced with the unthinkable threat of being shot, eaten, crushed, or obliterated at the moment of creation. But from what I've heard, most people in town had hard lives before, had already lost their families, had struggled to make a living, were being forced from their land, or had thought they would never have a future. The broken, poor, and destitute were plucked from the Earth and brought here, and there isn't a single person in Black Creek that doesn't want to be here.

I don't remember much of the sermon given at my father's funeral, but I do recall the pastor speaking about how we're refined by the struggles of life. That hard things happen so that a greater good can emerge, so that those who live through it, can be closer to God on the other side. 'You can't push yourself back to the surface,' he'd said, 'until you reach the bottom.'

I remember thinking it was bullshit at the time. I had a few choice words for God, too. But all the years spent without my father made me the man I am now, the man who came back to Black Creek, who worked at Synergy, and who was in a unique position to save thousands of people, with a lot of help. And now, here I am, seated across the table from my once-again-living father.

Can't say I believe all this was the work of some supernatural being, but I do see the pattern in it, like a thumbprint. My father has been hard at work, proselytizing me whenever he gets the chance, but I don't know...

Feeling content, I cut into my steak, stab it with my fork and—

The ding of a knife against glass stops me in my tracks. My mouth is now salivating at the smell of fresh-cut meat smothered in mushrooms and onions, but I realize my mistake.

My father wants to say grace.

But that's not what he does. Instead, he holds up his glass and says, "To my son. Never has a father been prouder of his boy."

"Cause there's two of us," Owen says, getting a laugh. Then to me, he says, "But he's talking about *you*."

Whatever this is, Owen's in on it.

"There's not one of us that isn't here on account of your actions. Without you, we'd have been lost out in space with all them sorry dinosaurs and mammoths and whatnots. It's been some time since all that, but I wanted to thank you properly."

He reaches down below the table and lifts out a wrapped gift that I can already see is a framed image. He hands it to Owen, who passes it on to me, grinning wide.

"It's not much, but I reckon you'll like it. Just a little something for the house, and—"

"Opening," I say with a smile, digging my hand inside the paper. I tear it away and mentally stagger for a moment, looking down at the revealed image. "I don't understand. Nothing from the old world made it. How did..."

"I helped your mom make the first," Mrs. Dearborn says. "Wasn't hard to recreate."

I lift the cross-stitch out and hold it up for all to see.

Inola reads it aloud, "Greater love has no one than this: to lay down one's life for one's friends." She smiles. "Fitting for a McCoy."

All three McCoy men seated at the table blush to a degree. Before I lower the cross-stitch down, I notice writing on the back.

Mark 5:30

My forehead scrunches up. That's not the right verse. The quote on the front is from John 15:13. I look up at my father, who's wearing his know-it-all, mansplaining grin.

"What's this?" I ask, turning the frame around so the others can see the back.

"A Bible verse," Levi says, like I'm a dope.

"I know, but which one?"

My father clears his throat and says, "At once Jesus realized that—"

"Really?" I say. "You're going to bring him into it now?" While I'm more open than before when it comes to the subject of God—what we experienced was beyond science—I was hoping for a relaxing night free of religious debate.

"No time like the present," Cassie says with a grin. "Or the future. Whatever this is."

She's in on this, too?

Like everyone else sitting around this table, save for Flores, she's been going to the new church on Sundays. From what I've heard, the services are standing room only, and more than a few debates have sprung up as believers separated by decades have doctrinal disagreements.

"Jesus realized," my father continues, "that power had gone out from him. He turned around in the crowd and asked..." My father looks to Owen, who is beaming about his part in all this.

In his small voice, shaking with excitement, he says, "Who touched my garments?"

A hundred different pre-packaged religious arguments flit through my mind as neurons fire, looking for the right one. But I'm dumbfounded when the words sink in. I stare at the smiles around the room. Only Flores seems flustered.

"Are you fucking serious?" he asks, and no one scolds him. The gravity of this moment calls for a good four-letter word, if not more than one. He turns to my father. "You heard that, too?"

My father nods. "We *all* heard it, but not all of us understood it." He turns to me. "And now you do." He gives me a wink and then takes me off the hook with, "Rub-a-dub-dub, thanks for the grub. Amen. Let's eat!"

The remainder of the meal is pleasant, but I'm left with a weight on my shoulders. While the others enjoy some mint chocolate-chip ice cream with hot fudge and pineapple—Owen's request and my old favorite—I slip outside for a breath of cold air.

I look up at the sky, holding my arms against the cold. The stars are bright, the Milky Way in full view, but they look dull compared to what I saw during that last flux. The memory of those events is still clear, as is the deep voice that seemed to move through me as I was broken down and reassembled.

"It sure is something," my father says, stepping up beside me. I'm pretty sure he's not talking about the stars.

"Yep," I say, not giving him an inch.

"I'm not gonna pressure you. You'll come to terms with what you experienced in your own time. In the meantime, I just wanted to thank you. For doing right by my memory in my absence."

He's nervous. Rambling. "What are you really here to say?"

He smiles. "Not going to let your old man beat around the bush, huh?"

"You aren't so old," I tell him.

"Life sure has thrown us a screwball..." He exhales, watching his breath rise into the nighttime air. "And I reckon what I'm gonna ask you is par for the course at this point."

"Shoot," I tell him.

"Well, I was wondering... Well, I was hoping you'd be my best man."

"Are you serious?" I say, voice booming. If not for the smile on my face, he might have taken my outburst as anger. "Holy shit. When?"

My father chuckles. "Well, I'm not exactly fond of living in sin. Inola and I aren't sleeping in the same room...and she's not a patient woman. So..."

"Soon, then?"

"Very."

"Who's livin' in sin?" Owen asks. He's standing behind us, holding a bowl of ice cream out to me.

"You know it's below freezing out here," I say.

He shrugs. "It's our favorite."

I take the ice cream and look back up at the stars. I stand there with my impossible family, admiring the cosmos.

"So...." my father says.

"Of course," I give him a sidelong smile and take a bite of the ice cream. The flavor transports me through time to memories that are far fresher for Owen.

Then I wince as a sharp pain slams into my forehead.

"What is it?" my father asks, an edge in his voice.

"Should I get the others?" Owen asks, worried. "Should I fetch the guns?"

When the pain clears, I give my head a shake, smile, and put all their fears to rest.

"Brain freeze."

While the pair has a good laugh at my expense, I do my best to laugh along while eyeing the dark forest around us. But it's a challenge, because I've just lied to the two of them for the first time. It's faint, but I'm struck by deep feelings of anger, sadness, and confusion, none of it belonging to me. The pre-human...the cryptoterrestrial...has explored our world, and doesn't like what it's found.

I try to emote a welcoming message for it to receive. Despite Delgado's experience, I still consider the ancient creature an ally. But its presence fades, and I realize it had come only to say goodbye.

I linger by the door after Owen and my father enter my home. I look out at the dark once more as wind swirls snow across the open mountaintop. "Stay out of trouble," I whisper, and then I step inside to rejoin my family.

AUTHOR'S NOTE

If you're a long-time reader, you're probably thinking, "Will there be a book merging *The Others* and *Flux*?!" The answer is, "I'm not sure." As always, it depends on sales. Honestly, I hadn't planned on featuring the pre-human cryptoterrestrial until I reached the Cretaceous and had an "oooooh" moment, where I realized I had inadvertently set up the overlap. Once I realized it was possible, I couldn't resist.

If you're a new reader, you're now thinking, "What is *The Others*?! Who the heck was Dan Delgado? What in tarnation is going on, y'all?!" Good news: I have a better answer for you than I did for the long-time readers! *The Others* is a novel that came out about a year ago, featuring Delgado and Winnie. Their search for a missing little girl leads them down a rabbit hole of Mormon cults, corporate espionage, and alien abductions. If you enjoyed *Flux*, you'll love *The Others*!

Now, if you enjoyed *Flux* (or *The Others*) and would like to see them continue and/or merge, the best thing you can do is post reviews on your favorite online vendor or on Goodreads. Every review helps a ton, and I read every single one (even the bad ones).

As always, thank you very much for coming along for the ride, and I hope you enjoyed the books. I wouldn't be here without the support of my awesome readers!

—Jeremy Robinson

ACKNOWLEDGMENTS

Thanks to Kane Gilmour for the awesome edits, as always, and to the best proofreaders an author could hope for, Roger Brodeur, Lyn Askew, Dee Haddrill, Elizabeth Cooper, Dan Delgado, Kyle Mohr, Sharon Ruffy, Becki Laurent, Kelly Tyler, and Julie Carter. Thanks Hilaree, Aquila, Solomon, and Norah, my very own tribe spanning generations. Love you guys.

ABOUT THE AUTHOR

Jeremy Robinson is the international bestselling author of over sixty novels and novellas, including *Apocalypse Machine, Island 731*, and *SecondWorld*, as well as the Jack Sigler thriller series and *Project Nemesis*, the highest selling, original (non-licensed) kaiju novel of all time. He's known for mixing elements of science, history and mythology, which has earned him the #1 spot in Science Fiction and Action-Adventure, and secured him as the top creature feature author. Many of his novels have been adapted into comic books, optioned for film and TV, and translated into thirteen languages. He lives in New Hampshire with his wife and three children.

Visit him at www.bewareofmonsters.com.

Made in the USA
San Bernardino, CA
28 December 2019

62413954R00229